dig yourself

Also by Mikki Goffin

WASTED

dig yourself

Mikki Goffin

Weidenfeld & Nicolson
LONDON

First published in Great Britain in 2003 by Weidenfeld & Nicolson.

A CIP catalogue record for this book is available from the British Library.

ISBN 0 297 82948 3

Typeset by Deltatype Ltd, Birkenhead, Merseyside

Printed by Clays Ltd, St Ives plc

Weidenfeld & Nicolson

The Orion Publishing Group Ltd
Orion House
5 Upper Saint Martin's Lane
London, WC2H 9EA

For Jeremy Lee – a very special person

Acknowledgements

Cheers to Jeremy Lee, Rosemary Scoular, Sophie Laurimore, Michele Hutchison, Alice Chasey, My Old Man and Richard Munro.

Contents

Prologue

Old Millennium

Mark, a scene from somewhere in the middle of nowhere, May 1998

> 'Women may be able to fake orgasms. But men can fake whole relationships.'
>
> **Jimmy Schubert, US comedian**

In the very early hours of the last day of May 1998 Mark found himself stoned and oblivious on the back seat of a fume-filled car surrounded by dope-smoking strangers and trying to focus on a plastic figurine of Homer Simpson dangling from the rear-view mirror. It had been a typically decadent night, as unmemorable as all such events ultimately and invariably were, but in any case his mind was on other things. He was thinking about a recent event, the terrible memory of what had happened one week before, almost to the hour. The final showdown, the big bust-up.

He was holding the stub of a joint between his fingers, but it had gone out some minutes ago. He absently pulled on the roach, soggy and limp with spit, and reached up awkwardly to flick the dead joint out of the tiny gap at the top of the window. He was crammed up against the door on the left side of the car and something was digging into his leg but he couldn't move. He was vaguely aware that a girl was half-sitting on his lap, leaning forward between the two front seats with her back to him and her skirt pushed up around her hips, one skinny arm draped lazily around the shaded figure sitting in the driver's seat. She was drinking from a bottle of Budweiser and Mark had his right hand down the front of her knickers, although he had no recollection of putting it there. He tried to make out the other people in the car, sluggishly searching his database of friends and acquaintances in a vain attempt to establish how he got there, and which if any of the five others in the car was one of those friends or acquaintances. He certainly didn't know the girl on his lap, but was not as alarmed as perhaps he should have been when he belatedly discovered where his right hand had found refuge. Nor did he move it. He closed his eyes and tried to remember. He had been recalling last week so vividly, and yet he did not have a clue where he was just one hour ago, and how he ended up where he was now.

Back to Claire. His room, in bed, five past midnight.

They had been back from the pub by half-eleven, leaving Tamworth and Jonesey to their usual Friday night club–kebab–cab–puke–pass-out ritual. Claire had been uncharacteristically brazen that night – a combination of one too many Smirnoff Mules and the novelty of having the flat all to themselves unleashed an unusually fiery and wanton side of her character. A side of her Mark wished she might have tried unleashing a bit more often. She asked Mark to make her a cup of tea, but when he returned to the sitting room from the kitchen with the brews and the Hobnobs, Claire was naked, lolling on the sofa with her arms stretched above her head, pouting like a porn star. Her clothes were scattered on the floor and she playfully flung one last item, a red lacy G-string, at a gobsmacked Mark. She said: 'Bollocks to tea. Come here and fuck me.'

Two swear words in one statement. A record for sweet, clean-talking, clean-living, Claire. As for the content of the statement, that was utterly unprecedented.

Thinking about her, how she had been that night and how she was throughout their relationship, an unfamiliar and deeply powerful emotion swelled up inside Mark. He could admit to himself now that he was missing her more than he could bear; even those things he had always found infuriating about her. The way she said 'actually' all the time; her taste in music (Billy Joel, Marvin Gaye, Whitney Houston, Celine Dion, Sade, Aretha *bloody* Franklin); those weird, mercurial mood swings; the endless hours in the bathroom; her erratic reactions to innocuous but honest comments Mark might make; similarly hostile reactions to tactfully dishonest comments Mark might make. The interminable shopping escapades. Her needlessly lengthy and frivolous telephone calls to girlfriends who bitched about anyone and everyone just for fun, especially him. Picking at her food whenever they went out to eat. Her nagging intolerance of some of his most compulsive and inexorable habits: chain-smoking, binge-drinking, nose-picking, navel-gazing, breast-obsessing, bollock-scratching, wind-breaking. And of course, her mother. One thing he knew he certainly wouldn't miss. Her *bloody* mother. Dear God, the ache inside him was alleviated by that sole consolation: *I will never have to see or speak to that bloody woman ever again.*

Physically, of course, Claire was practically perfect. Mark rarely settled for anything less, and although he would be the first to confess that he himself had never been particularly remarkable to look at, he had always possessed the elusive and unerring ability to enchant all qualities of the opposite sex with ease. It was a mystery, but it probably had something to do with his unique gift of the gab, virtually guaranteed to charm the pants off even the most aloof and forbiddingly attractive female. Well, it had worked with Claire, at least.

Come here and fuck me, she had said to him. Not a request, a demand. He liked those kinds of demands. *Those* kinds of demands he could willingly deal with. And Claire hardly ever used the 'f' word. She rarely got much ruder than 'bugger', 'damn' and 'shit'. It wasn't her style; she was far too distinguished. Mark thought about that slutty look, the jaunty little tits and slender legs splayed with irresistible carelessness, the pert, sinuous body inviting him, begging him, *ordering him*, to ravish her. There was no hesitation, once he had recovered from the momentary disbelief.

And so the tea was left to go cold on the sideboard, the biscuits ignored, the late-night light-entertainment programme on the television forgotten. Mark had finally picked up her light, tense body, carrying her to his room to conclude the unusually athletic and adventurous act behind the privacy of a closed door, on his bed, concluding with a loud, strangulated moan while Claire's fingernails drew blood from his shoulders. That was a first as well; scars he would happily parade, like the livid knife wound he had received following an initially light-hearted drunken tussle with an Arsenal fan outside an Ilford pub when he was eighteen. A dozen stitches and an impressive four-inch scar across his collarbone for an entire lifetime. Fingernail scratches down his back. Like those of the men from those weird African tribes who were compelled by ancient tradition to prove their worth by piercing their most sensitive parts with red-hot spears, his were all manly scars. Proof of his heroism and prowess.

He hadn't lasted as long as he would have liked, but the booze made him quick and Claire's spontaneous and unexpectedly ravenous approach overheated his ardency. Afterwards, just gone midnight, Radio One quietly churning out a chillout session of ambient sounds in the background, the pleasantly pungent reek of raw sex in their nostrils as their laboured breathing returned to normal. Mark's buttock in the wet patch and he didn't care, barely even noticed. Claire whispered something and he grunted in reply, feeling his eyeballs roll to the back of his head, his heart perceptibly slowing its rhythm. The welcome oblivion of sleep gradually injecting its tranquillising chemicals into his brain, bit by bit by dreamy bit, the dimmer switch in his mind turning a fraction at a time.

'Mark . . .'

Her arms tightening around him, her lips against his ear. She kept repeating his name, but Mark could not respond, dream sequences already arranging themselves into subliminal flashes, muscles melting into the mattress, brain relaxing into sludge.

'Mark?'

But then, five little words. Just softly, quietly.

And Mark heard these five little words as clear and loud as the searing screech of a Monday-morning alarm call through a killer hangover. They penetrated his consciousness, bringing him round like a cold slap in the face. The words intercepted his trance-like state within a second. A further three or four seconds and the groggy lump of his brain processed them, extracted meaning from them.

'I've come off the Pill.'

And then all at once, every limb suddenly rigid with fear, every nerve ending alive, eyes reflexively flickering open to stare fixedly at the blank wall opposite. Five small words that had the power to seize him, plunge him into a spiralling free fall of cataclysmic terror, speeding up his heart rate to an adrenalin-fuelled hammering. Like jumping from an aeroplane without a parachute.

In hindsight, Mark could admit his initial reaction had perhaps been a bit over the top. If only he had been given a bit of *warning*. Women, they have so much untold power over men. And such awesome power. They can enfeeble and emasculate with words alone. They make such strange and irrational demands, and for no apparent reason they can go from demure and adorable to tempestuous and terrifying in a matter of seconds.

He shifted slightly but couldn't get comfortable, and the girl on his lap arched her back and rubbed herself against his knee with a sigh. Her hair was long and loose and dirty blonde and Mark was close enough to smell the sweetness of shampoo on it even through the smoke. His hand foraged in the springiness of her pubic hair, the soft fabric of her knickers fretting against his knuckles as he desperately tried to think of her name. What was it she had said to him? They had definitely exchanged a few words, and Mark felt certain that she had told him her name and where she lived, and may even have laughed politely at a crap and unfunny comment he had made. He wouldn't put his hand down any old bird's knickers, not without finding out some pertinent details first, not before establishing *some* sort of rapport. If not a name, at least an idea of age. Under eighteen and over forty would usually be a bit of a no-no, even in the sorry state he was in. Judging only from how she was dressed and the feel of her body, Mark safely assumed that she was well within the acceptable age range, probably early twenties. What *was* it she said to him? Lucy or Lisa or Laura. Definitely an 'L' name. He started to remember small moments, mixing them up with the Claire Issue, which was still looming in the forefront of his mind.

Shitty nightclub in Romford; drum 'n' bass at ear-splitting volume and plumped-up cleavage bursting out all over the shop, pubescent girls done up like ballsy women and salacious men prowling the premises, marinated in Hugo Boss. Wired guy with shaggy hair offering him a tab. Tipping it back, down the hatch with a swig of bottled water. Crushed at the bar for far too long, just to surrender a ten-pound note in exorbitant exchange for two pints of tepid, diluted lager, and a Vodka Red Bull with too much ice. Ecstasy kicking in like quicksilver before he saw to the bottom of the glass and the lights began warping, flashing technicolour strobes through and beyond his dilated pupils. The heat of a thousand animated bodies steaming perspiration through Mark's clothes, saturating him in minutes. Not caring, going with it, dragged onto the dance floor by some mouthy bird with huge hoop earrings and a perm.

'Did you hear me, Mark?'

Claire was back inside his head. 'Did you hear what I said?' Her voice was as loud and clear as if she were beside him again, he could almost feel the heat of her breath against his ear.

Why hadn't he reacted in a normal, adult way? Why couldn't he have said something other than:

'Well, what do you want me to do about it?'

By now he was awake, and painfully conscious of the fact that he was awake.

'Oh, Mark . . . can we . . . I mean, I think we should . . . you know, *talk* . . .'

Who was that in the passenger seat? Whoever it was must have had very long legs because the seat was pushed right back and Mark was forced to contort all five-foot-ten-and-a-half-inches of his frame into the tiny space like a folded deckchair. His lack of leg room meant that much of his lower body had gone numb, particularly the small portion of his lap on which the girl was now squirming. She had her back to him still as she tilted her face and eased forward to receive a kiss from the bloke in the driver seat, and while they smooched away, her hand reached behind her and moved slowly up Mark's inner thigh, pausing for a moment at his groin. Mark respectfully noted that the slobbering bloke in the driver seat was about twice his size and that the situation was in potential danger of turning into a bit of a low-key group-sex session. He didn't feel any urges whatsoever, even with at least two of his fingers now fully engaged inside the squirming girl's knickers and her bony buttocks grinding with considerable ardency. He wondered if he should remove his hand and get out of the car, but he had a feeling that he was miles from home in the middle of God knows where and besides which, he was unable to move. The effects of the Ecstasy had dwindled away, and by this stage the dope had zombified him almost completely. He was functioning solely on autopilot, and fading fast. He heard a zipper go and looked down to discover his fly undone, and the girl's hand groping away inside with presumptuous intent. Not wanting to appear rude (or – Heaven forbid! – ungrateful), he loosened his belt for easier access. There were two more people on the back seat, and one of them, another girl, awkwardly straddled the other one (probably a bloke although Mark couldn't tell for sure), and they necked each other and shared a smoke and made some whispering noises.

Lisa or Lucy or Laura meantime had successfully unearthed Mark's cock after a blind, one-handed tussle with his lower garments. He was quite gratified and most surprised to observe that it was well on the way to becoming a not entirely unimpressive erection. He silently congratulated himself on his extraordinary virility and as she expertly manipulated it to its full turgid glory in a few swift strokes, he tipped his head back and closed his eyes, just letting her get on with whatever it was she wanted to do. She was still otherwise preoccupied with French-kissing the driver, and his great tattooed hands were all over her, ambling brutishly from hair to shoulder to breast to thigh, over clothes, beneath clothes, every readily available inch of her. The other couple were now screwing, and quite enthusiastically too, and the girl kept hitting her head on the roof of the car as she gyrated up and down, up and down. Yes, safe to assume the other anonymous figure on the back seat was definitely a geezer. Mark was vaguely perturbed. How the hell did he get into this situation? How should he get out of it? Did he want to?

'Of course we can talk,' he had said, wanting to do nothing but sleep and forget about those five little words. 'Off you go.'

Claire let out a humourless little laugh of exasperation, and he felt her hand on his shoulder, gently at first and then gripping tight. 'No, Mark . . . we need to communicate . . . *properly.* I mean, like, a proper *conversation.* Don't you think?'

'Claire, please, I'm tired . . .'

'Don't you have anything to say?'

'What about?'

'I've stopped taking the Pill. Isn't that a good place to start?'

'Not really.'

'Look at me.'

He had turned on his side and looked at her. She was doing that clever thing with her eyes; a kind of reverse Medusa Effect. Instead of turning men to stone, some women have this knack of turning men to mush just by looking at them in a certain way. It's practically infallible, and no man is immune. Just before and just after sex is a time when men are most susceptible, and when the woman is most likely to take advantage of this mentally vulnerable state. Mark's eyes adeptly dodged Claire's without being too obviously evasive.

'I love you,' she said, timing it just right.

'Yeah, yeah. Love you, too.'

Sincerity: another of his weaknesses. Even when he really, *truly* meant something, he still managed to make it sound like a lie, or at the very least a slight bending of the truth. Claire ignored the lack of conviction this time, glossing over it with a firm, tight-lipped kiss on the mouth and a dopey, delirious grin, which stirred up a sense of foreboding deep within Mark's already troubled psyche. He knew better than to be fooled by her apparent mellowness.

'And I've been thinking . . .' she had begun, unpromisingly, tracing her finger down his chest, over his abdomen, circling a glitter-glazed nail around his belly button.

'. . . Now we've been together for . . . quite a long time . . . I mean, *happy* together, actually. What I'm saying is . . . we've really got something good going on here, haven't we?'

This was, without doubt, an introduction to a potentially very unpleasant scenario, and Mark was quick to act on his instincts. 'I need a drink. D'you want one?' Suddenly he discovered the energy to spring his body out of bed and clamber clumsily into a discarded pair of boxer shorts, but his attempt to divert the subject had been neither subtle nor successful.

'Fuck's sake, Mark' Claire snapped. 'You've got real problems, you know that?'

'What? What have I done now?' The innocent look was played with aplomb; wide eyes and bewildered expression, hands raised to the heavens: *absolve me from blame, I am but a man.*

'It's what you haven't done, Mark. Can't you see?'

Mark couldn't see, and he didn't want to see. He wished she'd just give it a rest. Unlike the other girls he had been involved with, Claire was older than him – not much, only three years, but still enough to make a difference. At least it had certainly made a difference to Claire. Once she had got beyond her relatively buoyant early-to-mid-twenties, the ticking of her biological clock had all of a sudden turned into more of an ominous clanging, and that clanging seemed to get ever nearer, ever louder with every passing month. She had soon lost interest in the once-favoured debauched weekends and dusk-till-dawn clubbing and en masse drinking sessions, instead happily settling for nights in with videos and 'healthy eating' cookbooks, yoga on a Wednesday evening and her Female Fiction Readers' Club every other Friday between work and a wine bar.

Mark wasn't ready for a more temperate and adult routine; he needed the consistent company of mates, reassuring reminders of his youth. The habitual lifestyle patterns that were his *raison d'être* – those regular and often regrettable things he was loath to change, the very epicentre of his own precious universe. His culture. His Life.

Claire had tried to explain, patiently at first, using the simplest and most direct terms she could, so her confounded boyfriend might understand.

'You always try to change the subject,' she said. 'What am I to think? I want us to move in together, Mark. Just you and me, nobody else. You know? I want to be able to walk around naked, to leave the bathroom door open, to make love in every room whenever the urge takes us. Perfect privacy. I want us to be a proper couple, living together in a place of our own. I want . . .' she hesitated, tucked some hair behind her ear, studied him intently with those wide almond eyes, intoxicating cobalt blue, smudged at the lashes with kohl and mascara. With a heavy sigh, she went on, 'I don't know, I suppose I just need something more permanent, you know? For starters, I'd like . . . a bit more commitment from you . . . just a small indication to prove that you're serious about me, about *us.* That you *really* want me. Is it too much to ask? Come on, Mark, is it so unreasonable?'

Jittery with nerves, Mark had lit up a cigarette at this point. He knew already, all too well, how arguments like this invariably ended up.

This was what Mark was about to do now, while he was remembering, as the girl on his lap shifted forward and the bloke at the wheel adjusted his seat and moved around, trying to avoid impaling himself on the gear stick. Mark always kept an emergency fag in his top pocket or behind his ear, and an impromptu romp in a car parked God knows where with some people he didn't know seemed to be a good call for lighting up. He placed the filter between his dry lips and realised his lighter was in the back pocket of his jeans and, given his current position, there were likely to be some major logistical problems retrieving it. He kept the unlit fag in the corner of his mouth and pondered his circumstances. The bloke in the driver's seat was now getting his dick energetically suctioned by Lisa or Lucy or Laura, and he was muttering and grunting some vague words of rapturous encouragement as her head bobbed up and down with an almost comical pornographic vigour.

Mark felt a cloying sense of revulsion, but still he didn't make a move. He considered an escape plan, just in case . . . A little bit of pressure applied to the door with the force of his shoulder, and just a gentle pull of the handle on his left-hand side, and he should (theoretically) go tumbling out onto the ground.

'You know I want you,' he had told Claire, inhaling deeply. 'You know I'm serious about you.' He knelt on the edge of the bed and bent to kiss her shoulder, still slightly tanned from their recent holiday in Malaga. 'I've never been more serious about anyone.'

She studied him for a moment, then she pulled away from him with a petulant noise, whipping the covers from her naked body. She knew all the favoured tactics Mark employed at emotionally awkward moments, how he would often dissemble and bluff and beguile and deceive, often only mildly or even unintentionally, just for an easy life. She was unconvinced by even the most apparently sincere of loving gazes, even when Mark was trying hard enough to convince even himself. She retrieved one of his unwashed, crumpled work shirts from the carpet where it had been discarded the night before and pulled it on, buttoning it in the middle. She tossed her head towards him defiantly, wavy strands of her dark brown hair falling into her eyes, while Mark smoked bashfully and stared down at his bare feet, trying not to yawn.

'Why don't you try proving it for once then?' she challenged him.

'Sometimes, I can't help feeling that . . . oh, it's hard to explain. It's as if your heart's not in it. Like I'm just something you do in your spare time.'

'Jesus, Claire, that's a bit harsh.'

'Harsh? I haven't even started yet, actually.'

Mark collapsed onto his belly and stuffed his face into the pillow with a groan.

'Why do you have to be so evasive?' Claire persisted, moving closer to him and plucking the cigarette from his fingers. 'Have you not heard of communication? What's the point of having a relationship if we don't ever *communicate* with each other? I mean, we might as well just meet up every now and then and fuck and go home without saying a word to each other.'

She was using the 'f' word a lot that night. Mark turned his head and ventured his conciliatory smile, taking the risk that it might look mocking and menacing rather than mollifying as intended.

'And don't bloody look at me with that gormless smile. This is serious.'

Claire had always found it hard to maintain maximum seriousness with Mark: just a single glance at any given moment could have her creased up with laughter, and then she would be angry at herself for letting his infuriating insouciance get the better of her. Not this time, though: her face was set into a solemn frown and no amount of impish banter and facetious facial distortions from Mark would make her back down. She took two puffs from the cigarette and hunted for an ashtray, or something that would suffice as an ashtray. 'This is a disgusting habit, too,' she nagged, making do with a half-empty jar of salsa chip-dip, which had been breeding bacteria beneath Mark's bed since the previous weekend. 'You're such a bad influence on me. I hadn't smoked for ages when I met you, and now I sometimes just . . .'

'Can't help yourself?'

Claire eyed Mark appraisingly as if she couldn't decide whether to kill him or kiss him. She pursued a different line of harassment instead, suddenly pushing herself up from the bed and waving her arms around dramatically. 'Look at the state of this place!' she exclaimed. 'How can you live like this?'

She bent down and scooped up an armful of clothes and threw them into the corner of the room, then proceeded to collect together all the old cups, saucers, cutlery and plates that had been congealing their various stains in well-concealed nooks. Mark wondered where she got all that energy: not just the energy to goad him and put him down and wind him up, but the energy actively to rearrange his life at such inopportune moments. Those very moments when he was feeling closest to her. His eyelids were starting to feel heavy again and all he wanted to do was smoke one more fag and drift off to sleep, with Claire perfectly naked and mercifully silent in his arms. Just this once.

'Jesus *Christ*! You're so bloody lazy!' Claire huffed, blustering about, picking up crisp bags, beer cans, empty fag packets, old rail tickets, crusted socks recently used as emergency wank rags, pages ripped out of magazines, chocolate wrappers, dirty and clean boxer shorts jumbled together, banana skins, packaging for various gadgets, damp towels, McDonald's cartons and paper bags, polystyrene cups with chewed straws stuck through translucent plastic covers, biros without lids, lids without biros, pizza boxes, CDs without cases, cases without CDs, torn envelopes without letters, scrunched letters without envelopes, empty wine bottles, sachets of Alka Seltzer, newspapers from days or possibly weeks before.

'Claire, please darlin', I'll clean it up in the morning, alright? Why do you have to get like this *now*? I'm knackered . . .'

She ignored him, as he was half expecting. 'Such a slob! Shameless!' she went on, throwing all the rubbish into a waste-paper basket that was already overflowing. 'So much rubbish! I'll have to get a bin liner from the kitchen . . .'

'No, don't bother,' Mark sighed, rolling himself up in the quilt. 'We don't have any.'

'Well, what do you use then?'

'Oh God, I don't know. Plastic bags? Whatever.'

'How *do* you live like this, Marky?' Claire asked, pausing her energetic clean-up operation after unwittingly discovering a collection of irredeemably malodorous smalls, piled up in a cohesive bundle beneath a desk scattered with defunct detritus. She put her hand over her mouth and turned away in disgust, shaking her head.

'Really, you need a woman's touch, you know that?'

'Maybe I do, but right now I just want some peace and quiet.'

'There's no point just sweeping things under the carpet, you know,' she said. 'I mean, I can't even *see* your carpet, for crying out loud.'

'I like it this way. It's just how I am.'

'Well may I suggest you change, just a little bit? A pig wouldn't even live in this mess!'

'This pig would.'

'We'll have to see about that.'

Mark had not picked up on the implicit threat. 'Jesus. Give it a rest.

Come to bed for God's sake, woman,' he mumbled. If he had turned to see the expression on his beloved's face at that point, he might have chosen his words a little more carefully.

Mark tried to get a look outside the car, but the window was steamed up and it was too dark to see anything more than the silhouetted outlines of a few trees. He caught the bright white swell of headlights of passing cars in the rear-view mirror, and just beyond the windscreen he could make out two or three other parked cars in front, although he was unable to see if anyone was inside them. He tested the door to his left, but it didn't give when he pulled the handle and he couldn't find the lock. He tried to open the window but was unable to get enough leverage for anything more than a two-inch gap at the top.

Lisa or Lucy or Laura seemed to be getting plenty of leverage, however. She had her backside pointed towards Mark's crotch and her mouth still firmly attached to the driver's dick. Despite his misgivings, at this juncture Mark was beginning to feel the hungry, imperative pull of sexual desire invade his otherwise impassive state of mind. Considering she was working with one hand behind her while simultaneously giving pleasure at the other end, Lisa or Lucy or Laura was doing a pretty good job. The other couple were giving an Oscar performance now, really putting some welly into it, thrashing about wildly and crying out in unison, as if they were determined to out-climax each other. The girl opened up the front of her dress and the bloke mashed feverishly at her breasts, squashing them roughly as if testing the ripeness of hard fruit.

Mark wondered how he would describe this episode. Erotic? No, not quite. It was more humorous than erotic, really. Like a grainy home video on Television X, a bunch of pissed-up would-be porn stars of questionable to mediocre attractiveness letting it all hang out in a car. The type of scene he wouldn't even recall for future masturbatory purposes, as the lewdness and absurdity of the situation by far exceeded the eroticism. Although, maybe, if he couldn't think of anything else . . . exchange the two geezers for two more birds maybe . . . that could work . . . that certainly had potential . . .

Lisa or Lucy or Laura was gyrating about and before Mark (now fully engorged and ready for action) could suggest to her, 'Hey, take a seat,' she tugged aside her gusset and eased herself onto Mark's hard-on, shaking her hair back as she pushed down with a little whimper and a shudder.

Mark was at once torn between repulsion and exhilaration. After a second or so of confused panic, he went with the latter. *Sod it*, he thought, *you're only young once.* Take what you can whenever it's offered. Better to regret something you have done than something you haven't, etc. He grabbed the girl's hips and felt the tensile muscle of her buttocks beneath his hands, appreciating the unexpected intimacy while simultaneously feeling appalled at himself. God, what was it she had said? Lisa or Lucy or Laura? Think, Mark, *think*. *Try* to remember. She might be one of those girls who gets arsey if the bloke they've just shagged can't remember her name. Perhaps, he mused, he wouldn't have to talk to her afterwards. Still, always best to be on the safe side. Safe side? Mark's heart leapt as a thought entered his mind: maybe she's a prostitute. She had that disconcertingly casual, come-on-then-let's-just-get-on-with-it kind of manner. But no, she couldn't be. Prostitutes don't do it without condoms. Mark relaxed. It's all OK. She was just a horny bird, and probably too pissed to know better. Hey ho. What the hell.

Impaled at both ends, Lisa or Lucy or Laura quickly established an agreeable rhythm, and Mark moved his hands up inside her top, marvelling at the smooth supple warmth of her skin, gliding his fingers across a tight stomach, then holding each side of her slim waist as she undulated back and forth. He was stuck some place between delirious enjoyment and catatonic horror. His ambivalence excited him and petrified him.

The other couple had stopped now. The girl glanced towards Mark, the features of her face fleetingly illuminated by the lights of a car behind. For a terrible moment, Mark recognised Claire's sulky smile, Claire's luminous eyes, the auburn hair falling in wavy wisps down over her ears, across her flushed cheeks. It was definitely a Claire-esque expression: a kind of *darling, I could kill you in my thighs* look, tempered by an unmistakable and fairly anomalous *don't touch what you can't afford.* But it was only for a brief moment. This girl was not as pretty as Claire, a little too rough around the edges. And Claire would never have sex in the back of an overcrowded car. Especially not with these kind of people. It was just not her scene: too common, too tawdry. The girl's forehead was shiny with perspiration and her breathing was shallow and rapid. Mark blinked and shook his head, feeling his vision distort and fuzz, like being on the verge of a bad trip. Without saying anything, the girl leaned towards Mark and produced a lighter, sparking up the fag that was still dangling from the corner of his mouth. Then, before he could even inhale, she plucked it away and smoked it herself, batting an impertinent little wink at him before offering a puff to her breathless companion, who was busy zipping himself up. Mark noticed something gold-coloured glinting around the girl's neck, and he fixed his eyes onto it, trying to focus.

'Do you know what, I've had it up to here with your attitude,' Claire had berated him. 'You just don't listen. You haven't grown up. Your mum was right about you all along.'

'What the fuck?'

'And stop fucking swearing! You always swear and it pisses me off something chronic. It's not like it makes your sentences sound any more meaningful or important. Or interesting, for that matter.'

'Hold on. My *mum*? Please, please. Explain. What the fuck has this got to do with my mum?'

She let out a long sigh. 'Oh, never *mind.*' She flumped back huffily onto the bed beside him and pulled at his shoulder, forcing him to face her. 'Listen, I would really like us to live together, but I think it's fairly obvious we'd probably end up killing each other.'

Mark pondered this, playing with the buttons on the shirt Claire was wearing. She allowed him to slip the shirt from her shoulders and nuzzle her breasts. She smelt of moisturiser and the scent of his aftershave overpowered her lighter perfume. After licking her right nipple and letting his mind go blank, he said, 'Not necessarily. But I don't think it's a very good idea.'

Another bad choice of words. He felt the sharp end of a bony elbow dig into his chest.

'Why not?' she demanded. 'We practically live together anyway. All you need to do is . . . get your act together a bit. You know?'

'Claire, you just said yourself that we'd end up killing each other. I'm merely agreeing with you.'

Mark was beginning to feel the unmistakable simmering of hostility emanating from his soon-to-be-ex-girlfriend at this stage. She took a deep inhalation of breath before launching into the next impassioned diatribe. 'I didn't *want* you to agree with me!' she exclaimed. 'God, Mark! You can be so stupid sometimes! I do want us to move in together, of *course* I do. Permanently. Properly. I want it more than anything.' The anger gave way to tears, which of course are always so much harder for a vexed and perplexed boyfriend to deal with, and she turned away from him, presenting him with a naked, reproachful back and an opportunity to prove he wasn't really such a hopeless case after all.

Mark was truly flummoxed. Another unforgivable faux pas escaped from his lips before he had the chance to stop himself. 'Well, you can't move in here, love. This is a boys-only zone. And I don't fancy moving into your gaff with your parents and sisters around.' He had hoped this admittedly imprudent statement might lighten the mood, but Claire was very sensitive to the fact that she was still living with her parents. At twenty-seven years old and the eldest of four relatively headstrong and independent girls, it was not something she was proud of. However, it had enabled her to save up a tidy little sum for a deposit on a house of her own. The trouble was, she wanted to buy herself a respectable family home, not just some funky little studio apartment where she could live in free and easy solitude.

Oh no. Not Claire. She was a woman for whom family was of the utmost importance, above all other things. She wanted kids, a cat, a car, Ikea catalogues, pedal bins, ironing-board covers, tablecloths, napkin rings, coordinating cushions and curtains, candelabras, tasselled lampshades, a pebble-dashed drive, routine, domesticity. The full works. And Mark was the man she wanted to share it all with.

Mark, rarely able to think beyond next weekend, wanted none of that. But sometimes, as he was rapidly beginning to realise, merely by being *with* someone, you can be cunningly deluded into thinking that what you really want isn't actually important any more. You start to come around to their way of thinking, even if you have to be dragged there kicking and screaming. Your thoughts are no longer your own. You become, in effect, a *unit*. At first it's subtle things. Pausing outside jewellers and allowing yourself to be dazzled by the diamond rings, never quite close enough to look at the prices. Browsing in Habitat and using vague, evaluative phrases such as 'hmm, that's rather nice', cooing over nothing more earth-shatteringly interesting than a ceramic mug set or a glass chopping board. You know you're done for when you start making earnest purchases of said items. If, after a certain length of time, you still get on reasonably well and want to sleep together more often than you want to throttle each other, love warps itself into the sinister guise of full-on commitment. Some relationships work because you stay together despite any differences you might have, and each day, month, year that passes is tallied against your desire to break free and play the field. After maybe a year, or two, or three, so much has happened and so much time has been invested in that one relationship that it becomes almost unthinkable to bring it to an end. You may still want to do things to jeopardise it, you may even act on those desires, but ultimately you don't really want to terminate it just because it's so much damn *effort*.

'You really think I'd want to move in *here*?' Claire spat disdainfully. 'With you and the Wanky Brothers in the bachelor pad from Hell? Do me a favour Mark. I'm not that crazy about you.'

'Well, I'm happy here.'

She hesitated, looking around unappreciatively at the poster-smothered walls and the other 'hundred-per-cent heterosexual geezer' paraphernalia. Mark liked to surround himself with such tangible reassurances of his unquestionable heterosexuality. The nubile two-dimensional female forms mounted on eye-boggling life-sized posters were spread out indiscriminately on all sides of his bed, the secret stash of porn with its welded and well-thumbed pages kept schtum in an old shoe box behind his wardrobe, while discarded issues of *Viz* and *Maxim* flung about with gay abandon (make that *straight* abandon) across the floor contained the countless simple secrets of the collective male consciousness. Being one of the boys necessarily means continually reminding yourself what's worth living for, acknowledging the fine line between lechery and misogyny and devotedly keeping up with the trends, while maintaining the outward impression that it all comes naturally and effortlessly. Mark was, without doubt, one of the boys. Naturally. Effortlessly.

'But . . . but you'd be *happier* with *me*,' Claire ventured eventually, softening her tone. 'Just think about it, Marky. With our salaries we could get somewhere really lovely. One of those new homes in Hornchurch, maybe. Or even Billericay. We wouldn't have to buy at first, not if you don't want to. Renting would be okay. Just so long as we're together, right?'

Mark was thinking *shut up, shut up, shut up*. He mumbled, 'Yeah, maybe. One day.'

Claire sat up and crossed her legs and pulled her hair into a ponytail. 'How about next weekend then?'

'Uh?'

'Next weekend,' she repeated, brightly. Mark was thrown once again by the sudden inexplicable lightening of her mood. 'House-hunting,' she added, rubbing her hand between his shoulder blades, like a master stroking a faithful old dog. 'We'll take my car, yours is too unreliable.'

Surely the entrapment process was supposed to be subtler than this? Mark checked off the list, carefully considering an appropriately evasive plan of action: (1) contraception abandoned, (2) state of room criticised, (3) the phrase, 'You need a woman's touch', (4) even worse, 'Your mum was right about you all along', (5) talk of house-hunting and settling down. Something was dawning on him: Claire was slowly but surely turning into a *mum*. And the last thing Mark wanted to be was a *dad*. He needed a 'get out of jail for free' card. And fast. Before it was too late.

Mark realised he was already quite close to coming, although the threat of imminent ejaculation receded every now and then as his mind kept unpredictably mulling over less sexy preoccupations. He had been focusing on the other girl's necklace for so long that his eyes had glazed over. Meanwhile, the girl who was riding him appeared to be steadily approaching the apex of her excitement and her movements were getting faster with every stroke. The girl with the necklace bent forward again and, to Mark's astonishment, grabbed the back of his head and forcefully pulled his face towards hers, kissing him full and deep on the mouth. As their tongues entwined, Mark drifted back into willing compliance, letting the vague sensations just wash over him.

He had dreamed of situations like this. For years he had conjured up fantastical possibilities, while keeping the fantasy well and truly within the 'nice as a wank scenario, but will never bloody happen for real' domain. Which is, of course, where most fantasies belong, and where they should stay. He was slightly disappointed that he wasn't feeling the immense surge of unrestrained voracious lust that he would normally derive from vividly imagining such a prurient situation while indulging in a little light hand relief. Somehow the actual physical experience, as *rara avis* as it was, didn't quite have the exquisitely erotic edge that the tantalising *idea* of group sex had seemed to promise during those feverish *ménage à une* imaginings.

Getting it on with two different girls at the same time, in an anonymous overcrowded car at some twilight-zone location in space and time . . . this, surely, was the stuff of dreams. But that was just the problem. He might as well have been dreaming, as the cumulative effects of sleep deprivation, mental exhaustion and the waning chemicals in his bloodstream had rendered him a prone subject, an automaton. If he hadn't been pinned down at the groin, he could have just floated off, up and away, through the car roof and into the sky. Nothing felt real. It was as if he was experiencing it vicariously via some kind of virtual reality. The rhythmic movements of Girl One's arse; the sticky graze of Girl Two's lips on his neck; a hand from nowhere brushing his knee; the feel of coarse, long hair through his fingers; the grizzled noises emanating from the driver. None of it was *real.*

He squeezed his eyes shut and then opened them again and looked down. Girl Two's necklace was one of those personalised pendants you could get from Argos and other cheap jewellery outlets. The name, carved in a fancy script font on a thin gold chain, was 'Lisa'. Mark wondered why some girls wore their names around their necks, but then he supposed he should feel grateful for it. Those things must save loads of blokes from those awkward spells of amnesia; that terrible, *er, what was your name again?* moment. This did present a slight problem, though. If Girl Two was called Lisa, then what was the name of the girl riding him? It was *definitely* an 'L' name.

But did it really matter any more?

'Lisa,' he whispered, not meaning to say it aloud. He absently fingered the pendant and then moved his hand down over her exposed breast, still only vaguely aware of his actions. She responded by kissing him again, then pushed up his T-shirt and nestled her face into his chest, breathing in his body odour as if she was getting high on it. Mark was slightly taken aback. He tentatively lifted his free arm a fraction and lowered his head to give his armpit a surreptitious sniff. All he could smell was smoke and marijuana and fetid body heat, with a slight vestigial hint of perfume.

Then, before he knew it, it was all over. The girl on his lap bucked once, twice and with the final downward thrust, Mark emitted an involuntary grunt as he experienced a familiar, quick pulsation. But it was hardly the powerful, Herculean ejaculation he would have expected – more like a briefly pleasurable trickle, altogether somewhat disappointing in its force, effect and quantity. With frightening synchronicity, the driver clutched at a handful of the girl's hair and made a weird gurgling sound, like a baby with chronic wind. Mark's dick instantly went soft and flopped out as the girl wriggled off his lap, now entirely preoccupied with the driver's orgasmic deluge. Sounds like a pretty hefty one, Mark mused grimly, desperately trying to blank out the unpleasant noises coming from both parties. He rearranged himself, zipping up his trousers and checking for stains. Then, just as suddenly as it had started, the session ended – a packet of tissues was passed around calmly, along with a bottle of tepid mineral water, some Polo mints and a communal Silk Cut cigarette. It all became absurdly respectable. Within minutes, everyone was slumped back, smoking or sleeping or skinning up, and the driver started up the engine, turned the car around and began driving down a near-deserted dual carriageway that Mark didn't recognise.

'Where do you live, Mark?' the driver asked, yawning and running a hand through his hair. He turned the volume up on the car radio and tapped out a rhythm on the steering wheel to an Underworld tune, which blared out tinnily from the cheap speakers behind Mark's head.

Mark racked his brain. 'Er ... Redbridge Road?'

Was that right? Was that where he lived? Then he thought: *How does he know my name? How the fuck does he know my name?* He turned to look at the two girls. Lisa was applying pale-pink lipstick and the other girl was rubbing cocaine into her gums, pointedly ignoring him as she squirmed about uncomfortably, adjusting skewed knicker elastic through the rucked material of her skirt. The bloke on the other side had fallen asleep, slouched against the door with his cheek pressed to the window and his mouth hanging open. The figure in the passenger seat, who had hitherto been silent and inert was vomiting into a plastic bag.

'Alright mate, I'll drop you off first, OK?' The driver skidded noisily at a roundabout and took a sharp right, narrowly avoiding a set of traffic cones at the edge of the road. The music thudded on until Mark felt like his brain was going to split. He was overcome by the desire to sleep, and his head rocked to the side with the relaxing motion of the car. Under normal circumstances, he would probably not have felt so calm about being driven at breakneck speed down a motorway by a burly bloke who was under the influence of God knows how many kinds of stimulant drug and extra spaced out from the naturally soporific effects of fellatio. He rested his head on the girl's shoulder and she shoved him away impatiently and asked him for a cigarette. He mumbled that he didn't have any more left, although he wasn't sure if this was true. She appeared displeased, but silently handed him a compact mirror with a negligible scattering of greyish cocaine on it, smeared across the surface by wet fingers.

'It's good,' she said, flicking her hair out of her eyes and uncrossing her legs.

Mark wanted to say *What's your name? Where am I? Who are all these people? How did I get here?* But somehow the moment just wasn't right. He took the mirror and half-heartedly swirled his fingertip in the filthy particles, not really knowing what to do with it.

'Makes you horny,' she added, somewhat pointlessly, edging slightly nearer so Mark could smell the semen on her breath.

'No shit,' he said blandly, running his fingertip over his gums gently at first, and then hard, with a toothbrush motion.

'We should do this again some time,' she murmured, with a little laugh in her voice, which Mark perceived as irony. He said nothing. Massive Attack now blared from the radio, and the driver boosted the volume up still further, the noise resounding relentlessly in Mark's ears.

His last conversation with Claire replayed itself in his head as the cocaine numbed his lips, and he turned it round and round, trying to make it seem less dreadful than it had been.

'I don't want to live with you yet. I'm not ready for any of that. Why do you always have to bring this subject up when you know how I feel about it?'

'What are you saying? You just want me part-time, not full-time?'

'If you want to put it like that, then yes. For now, part-time works best for us I think. It doesn't mean I don't –'

He had been cut short when he realised she was getting dressed. 'What are you doing?'

'Getting dressed.'

'Yeah, I can see that, but why?'

'I don't think we should see each other again.'

'What? What the hell are you on about now?'

Her gaze was cold-blue, adamantine. 'I'm leaving now, and I don't want to see you again,' she said. Her voice cracked and she cleared her throat and continued, louder and stronger, but now avoiding his perplexed expression. 'Look, I'm breaking up with you, alright? Is that so hard for your stupid male ego to handle?'

It was as if they were speaking different languages. Mark was floundering with a vocabulary of one or two confounded English phrases, while Claire jabbered at him in fluent Venusian. Everything was going right over his head. '*What?*'

'You and me. It's over. Understand?'

'No, I *don't* understand. Have I missed something? A minute ago you were talking about us living together, now you want us to split up? Over what?'

'You know.' Her voice remained hard, but Mark could see the aqueous glisten of tears in her eyes in the semi-darkness as she retrieved her bag from the floor. 'You know what.' She fumbled for a tissue and blew her nose.

As a last-ditch attempt, Mark had tried the pleading/needing approach. 'C'mon Claire. Don't be like this. We need each other.

We're good together. I . . . love you. Really. I do. I don't want us to fight over something like this. It's just stupid.'

The wet eyes stared back at him, for a brief moment looking vulnerable and hopeful.

Mark had held out his arms, wholly expecting her to collapse into them and weep herself into another sexual frenzy, as she had eventually done every other time they went through this tiresome conversation. Mark didn't even see it as an argument – merely that Claire had one point of view, and he had another. That's what relationships *should* be about, right? Tolerance of one another's conflicting viewpoints. No reason for it to blow up into a full-on barney.

Wrong.

'Fuck you,' she said.

She had only whispered it, barely audibly, but Mark heard it loud and clear. What he should have said in response, maybe, was: *Alright, come back to bed, we will talk about this tomorrow, I promise.* With hindsight, he knew, he *should* have agreed with her. Placated her. Made some guarantees. Offered her some semblance of sensitivity. A calm and considered response was appropriate. But he was tired, fed up and vaguely aggravated. So instead he sighed and said:

'Yeah. Fuck you too.'

Claire threw something at Mark, shouted a final obscenity and bustled out of the room, leaving a fragrant waft of Obsession and an almost palpable feeling of animosity in her wake. Mark looked down to see a single earring shining in his lap. With a sinking feeling, he realised it was not one of Claire's earrings. It was too cheap-looking, too ornamental and large. He put his head in his hands and called himself a stupid fucking arsehole. Then he called himself a total and utter shit-for-brains prick. He had discovered, the hard way, the true and far-reaching implications of infidelity. Once you have done the dirty on someone, even just a drunken one-off, even when they claim to have forgiven you, it's never ever forgotten. It festers. The memory of it lingers – it diminishes in time, but it doesn't go away completely. It dents the trust, and that damage is only superficially repairable. The deceit always left a trace, especially when the victim of the infidelity was someone as hypersensitive and highly strung as Claire. Mark had been unfaithful to her once and once only during the first year of their relationship, which was quite miraculous given his past track record. Even more miraculously, he had told Claire about it. Confessed everything.

And, as anticipated, she had screamed, slapped, insulted, rebuffed, ignored a fortnight of phone calls and, finally, forgiven him. Mark never wanted to go through that again. So, many months later, some time in early March 1998, after an extremely unwise but practically unavoidable one-night stand with a buxom and forthright college student called Mandy, Mark had decided it was probably best not to tell this time. It had been a necessarily brief encounter, of course, but from what Mark could remember, Mandy had possessed all the things that Claire didn't: a wantonly sluttish appetite for meaningless and messy sex (great), enormous zeppelin tits (OK for a change), formidable thighs (all the more to grab hold of), and a virtuoso talent for oral sex the likes of which Mark had never before encountered. Which was nice.

The sex itself was far from disappointing, but the protracted sense of shame and self-loathing that followed was what made the whole experience so utterly awful. Mark was deeply dismayed with himself, but not so full of guilt and suicidal urges that he felt compelled to inform his insanely jealous girlfriend of his latest misdemeanour. Like any rational male, he had no desire to wake up one morning and find his testicles in the fridge. The cheeky incident was therefore kept secret, known only to himself and Mandy, and to his closest comrades Jonesey and Tamworth, who had heard most of the whole debacle through the paper-thin walls. True to some unspoken inter-male confidentiality clause, they would take this sordid secret to their graves without breathing a word to a single soul. Besides which, they didn't much like Claire, passing her off as a bit 'clingy and hysterical', which to them was not quite compensated for by the fact that she was 'easy on the eyes'.

Mark's left foot was tingling with pins and needles, and when he tried to move it the sensation became even more pronounced, almost painful. He handed the mirror back to the girl. The coke was having no effect on him, other than making him feel as if someone had punched him in the mouth. Numb foot, numb mouth, numb brain. The driver slowed and then accelerated suddenly, and Mark was jolted back violently in his seat. The girl laughed and squeezed his knee. 'You should've been warned about Gary's driving,' she said. 'He's gonna get someone killed at this rate.'

'Oh great. That's good to know,' Mark muttered, not feeling disposed to return her smile.

'Hey,' she whispered, her hand creeping up his leg towards his crotch. 'At least we'll all die on a high.'

There was a gruff chuckle from the front, not unlike that of a brainless cartoon sidekick. 'You're a fuckin' poet, sweetheart,' the driver remarked, looking over his shoulder with a cretinous grin and inadvertently swerving the car steeply from one side of the road to the other with a squeal of tyres. After a fleeting moment of panic and a couple of choice four-letter words, he regained control of the steering wheel and increased velocity again. The overworked engine protested with a loud growl, and Mark began to wonder in some earnest if he'd ever make it home alive.

The scenery whipped into a shadowy blur outside the window. Lisa asked the driver to open a window and he obliged. The cool draught sharpened Mark's dulled senses, and he soon became acutely aware of a desire to piss.

'You've been very quiet all night,' the girl said, putting the mirror back into her handbag and batting her eyelashes at him. 'What are you thinking about?' She kissed him briskly on the corner of his mouth, and he licked at the bitter saltiness of her taste without thinking.

'Nothing,' he said, which was not too far from the truth. Then, almost against his will, he asked her, 'Could I have your number?'

She laughed out loud again, and Mark sensed something ominous and cruel lay behind the laughter. He took this to mean she had no intention of giving him her number, and a small part of him started worrying, suddenly but not altogether irrationally, about venereal disease and, with equal dread, about the conviction of his earlier performance. Why *wouldn't* she want to give him her number? Is she that much of a slapper or was he so disappointing as a fleeting sexual encounter that she wouldn't want to take it further?

'Got a pen, Lisa?' the girl asked her friend. Her voice was the gravelly, bored Essexual drawl Mark was so familiar with; reassuringly unaffected and unrefined, with lazy fricatives and guttural vowels.

'Nah. Eyeliner alwight?' Lisa offered, fishing into a cosmetic bag.

'That'll do, cheers.'

So, unexpectedly and despite his best efforts, Mark had lost the woman he loved. He let her go, and he hadn't tried calling her back or attempting an explanation. Partly because there wasn't one (he doubted she would accept 'Sorry love, it was just a moment of weakness, that's all'), and partly because at that moment, he was feeling almost as pissed off with her as she was with him. However, he had ignored his misgivings and phoned her the next day, leaving a feebly contrite message with her mother, who had been particularly frosty with him. That is to say, even more so than usual.

He had found it difficult to get on with Claire's mother, the indomitable Mrs Penelope Mortimer, ever since the early days of the relationship, when Mark had mistaken mother for daughter over the phone and let slip a puerile comment about a French maid's outfit and a pair of fluffy handcuffs. Another example of how embarrassment may well fade over time, but a mother never forgets. And how a Jewish mother rarely forgives, especially when it comes to the leading astray of an adored daughter by a 'dirty young boy from the wrong part of town'.

All subsequent attempts to ingratiate himself into Claire's close-knit family either failed or backfired badly. The only family member with whom he had any kind of affinity was poor old Terry Mortimer, the put-upon patriarch, who doted unerringly on his wife and daughters for reasons Mark could only assume stemmed from latent insanity and masochism. But Terry knew his place and rarely offered Mark more than a raised eyebrow and a sympathetic grimace in times of trouble. He knew it was best to keep quiet, and Mark couldn't blame him. Spinelessness was preferable to death by hen-pecking, after all.

Despite the apologetic message, Claire had not returned his call and he had too much pride and not enough patience to continue pestering her with further calls. The idea of sending flowers had crossed his mind for a split second, but he concluded that this would be a corny and naff gesture, not to mention a waste of thirty quid that would be much better spent on a round or two down the pub. If you can't forget about your troubles and sorrows, drown them in cheap ale with your mates.

And so Mark had endured a whole week without her, without even speaking to her. It was only now, in this surreal situation, that it dawned on him how much he wanted her back. Here he was, in the back seat of a maniac's car, fixedly staring once again at the plastic figurine of Homer Simpson dangling from the rear-view mirror, trying in vain to establish some kind of connection with a random girl who had just had sex with him. Maybe Mrs Mortimer had been right about him all along. Maybe he really wasn't good enough for her baby. He really was just a dirty young boy from the wrong part of town.

'Here y'go,' the girl said, tearing the corner out of a nightclub flier and scrawling the last digits of her phone number with the blunt, smudgy nub of a brown eyeliner.

'Prob'ly best not to call me at 'ome unless you wanna get the Spanish treatment off me folks. Mobile's on most of the time, or text me, or leave a message, whatever. I'm working down the gym most days anyway.'

Mark tried to decipher the words and numbers on the scrap of paper, but couldn't make out anything in the darkness. He looked at her and asked, 'You work in a gym?'

'Yeah, that new one in Brentwood. Right posh. Know it?'

'What are you then, a . . . gym instructor?' Mark's imagination scampered friskily into overdrive. Surely there were few sexier occupations a girl could have than a gym instructor?

'Yeah, on Mondays and Wednesdays. Lifeguard at the pool other days.'

'Lifeguard' was most definitely one of the few. '*Really?*' he breathed heavily, sounding far more impressed than he had intended to. Then he cleared his throat and muttered casually, 'Well, that sounds like a . . . nice job to have.' His mind was at once filled with images of stretched spandex, figure-hugging lycra, thong leotards, *Baywatch* and legwarmers. He had had a thing about legwarmers ever since *Fame*. As a young bug-eyed boy he would sit transfixed in front of the telly as the kids from *Fame* pranced about for all they were worth in their bad seventies clobber. Legwarmers did something for him even then. It was their total unashamed lack of proper functionality – like a long woolly sock without a foot. They seemed perfectly pointless and yet they were sexy by virtue of their pointlessness. Kind of like crotchless pants.

The girl shrugged. 'Yeah, it's OK. I'm saving up to go to uni next year.'

Mark took this on board and worded his next question with some difficulty. 'How . . . er . . . old are you?'

She smiled and fiddled with a strand of her hair over her shoulder, playing the coy little girl role with surprising conviction, especially in light of the sordid acts she had carried out just a few minutes ago. 'Twenty today,' she confessed. 'How about you?'

Mark was thinking that they should perhaps have had this conversation *before* they had sex, but played along nevertheless. 'Twenty-four.'

Her eyes widened. 'Bit young for me,' she whispered, the precocious young voice of worldly experience.

'Well. Happy birthday,' Mark said, choosing to ignore the deliberate condescension.

'You already said that. You lot sang me "Happy Birthday" when we were leaving the club.'

'Did we?' Mark had no recollection. 'Well, happy birthday again.'

She glanced at her watch. 'It ain't any more.'

'What?'

'It stopped bein' my birthday two hours ago.'

'Oh.' Mark felt compelled to continue some kind of conversation but had now run out of things to say, so he just folded the scrap of paper and put it in his pocket, knowing he'd probably forget about it and it would end up in the washing machine.

'What do you do then?' she asked him.

'Me? Well . . .' He considered lying, but was unable spontaneously to invent anything impressive enough to justify the lie. 'I'm a . . . trainee estate agent. Er, sales negotiator. Er . . .'

The admission escaped nanoseconds ahead of his brain. Only then did he think of what he could have said, *should* have said (stuntman, lawyer, actor, archaeologist, pilot, rock star), rather than venturing the bald truth. Estate agent, sales negotiator, it all boiled down to the same thing in the end, whatever fancy language you dressed it up in.

'Oh,' the girl nodded slowly. 'Right.' She looked at him as if he'd just told her that he liked to eat his own faeces. 'Is that . . . fun?'

Mark spotted a glimmer of a chance to redeem himself. 'Nah, it's well boring most of the time, but . . . the money's good and it's only to tide me over before I start on my proper career.' He was well aware that he was talking out of his arse, but the girl was so far gone on coke and dope that he hoped she wouldn't notice his blundering improvisation.

'Really?' she said, sounding utterly uninterested.

'Yeah, reckon I'll be on thirty grand by next year, the rate I'm going.'

'Really?' she said, suitably sceptical but slightly less uninterested.

Mark put his arm around her and she didn't shrug him off, but nor did she appear to relish the embrace. Mark was strangely drawn to her aloofness, and the shameless masochist in him rose to the surface. 'I like you,' he slobbered, the last of his self-consciousness having finally slipped away. It was the slurred, imploring endearment of a man so far gone on tiredness and bad drugs that all dignity had diminished.

'Yeah, whatever,' she responded indifferently, lighting a half-smoked cigarette salvaged from the floor, jangling a multitude of metal bracelets down her right arm. Then she raised her voice and asked the driver. 'Where the fuck are we now, Gaz?'

The driver made eye contact with her in the rear-view mirror and

Mark noticed with some alarm that his pupils were like saucers: huge, glassy black circles against bloodshot white. He had the unsettling appearance of a madman on a homicidal rampage. 'Just comin' up to Redbridge station,' he replied.

'Oh, yeah, just drop me off here, that's great,' Mark managed to stutter, snapping back to reality for a moment.

'What, here?' The massive pupils glanced over at him but the car didn't slow down.

'Yes, really, here is just great.' Mark wondered if he was the only person in the car who was shitting bricks. He could not wait to get out of the car and face whatever unearthly monstrosities outer Essex might have in store for him at two o'clock on an eerie Sunday morning. Anything would have been preferable to staying in that speeding car with a whizzing imbecile behind the wheel.

The car screeched to a sudden standstill, throwing everyone forward as it did ninety to nought in a matter of seconds. Mark hit his head on the front passenger seat, but pretended to not be terrified out of his wits.

'That's some driving technique you've got, Gaz,' he finally managed to say, forcing a chuckle.

Gaz grunted incoherently and Mark wondered if he should say something else to him, just out of politeness: *cheers mate, see y'all later*, maybe? The girl leaned across him and opened the door wordlessly, almost as if she was dismissing him.

'Well,' Mark sighed deeply, considering what concise little farewell speech might be appropriate in such a situation. 'It's been emotional.'

'Tell Jonesey he owes me fifty quid,' Gaz said, staring straight ahead and turning off the ignition. The chassis seemed to sigh and collapse with relief beneath them.

'Jonesey?'

'Yeah. For the pills. Don't forget to remind him, the shifty Welsh cunt that he is. He's got my new number.'

Mark was beginning to remember who 'Gaz' was now. Jonesey's regular drug dealer and 'mate', although 'mate' would imply friendship whereas – given their frequent exchanges of insults and the odd punch-up – there was no love lost between the pair of them.

'Sure,' Mark mumbled. 'I'll get him to call you.' He turned to the girl. 'See you then.'

She dragged on the cigarette and didn't look at him. 'Yeah.'

'OK. Yeah. Thanks for the . . . lift. Bye everyone.' He rolled out of the car and his legs gave way beneath him and he tumbled onto the kerb. Finding his face pressed against cold concrete and limbs inertly splayed across the pavement, he was tempted merely to stay there and fall asleep.

The girl leaned out and dropped her fag end into the drain, inches from his head. 'Call me,' she said as the car started up again, slamming the door just in time as it thundered off into the distance, spewing out billows of thick grey fog behind it.

Call me. It was more of a demand than a request.

He listened out for the last, angry fart of the engine as it revved to the max, and blearily watched the rear lights slip away into the darkness. He slowly got to his feet, clinging to a convenient lamp post for support, his head swimming with deranged and disjointed cycles of disorienting thought. He felt in his pocket for the scrap of paper and unfolded it, squinting at the eyeliner scribble under the sickly yellow luminescence of the street light:

LOUISE
0181 487 6642
mobile 07931 745241

Louise! Of course, *Louise.* He remembered now. He had known all along that it was *definitely* an 'L' name. He thought he could be onto a winner with this one; all pining over Claire now momentarily sidelined. He smiled to himself and tucked her number back in his pocket with a self-satisfied smile, and then he was overwhelmed by a surge of nausea rising from his gut to his chest and he turned around and threw up into the gutter with an almost artistically fluid movement.

New Millennium

Mark, a scene from elsewhere, 22 January 2000

The world was supposed to have ended three weeks ago. At the very least, there had been the promise of something amazing, something historical and cataclysmic. A monumental happening. But still it turned. Nothing really changes from one moment to the next, from one year to the next. Things just move on. A different age, a brand new epoch, but still the same old ways. People die, people are born. Gangs form and splinter. Couples get together, relationships fall apart. Cycles of decay and rejuvenation.

Twenty-one days after non-Armageddon, Mark was slumped in the corner of his former (now reinstated) local, bored out of his skull, surrounded on all sides by the drone of the usual loquacious regulars. The Barley Mow is equidistant from the railway station and Mark's family home, plonked on the edge of an ugly industrial estate and overshadowing the soggy, flat expanse of Rivington Hill Park. Dismal and dusty and teeming with perennially pissed divorcees, geriatric gents and elderly widows, the pub is a meeting place for the stalwarts of the community, ancient eccentrics who smoke and cough and rattle right up until closing time. Wedged between a derelict house and a kebab bar misleadingly called 'Merry Munchers' (now rapidly going out of business thanks to the recent invasion of a McDonald's around the corner), the Barley Mow has established a well-founded local reputation as a good old traditional English pub. Staid rather than stuffy, it is a patriotic museum of a pub where all the indigenous fossils merrily gather and blather and dither and blither on a daily basis until exhaustion or inebriation finally winds their dialogue down to sporadic snores, belches, dribbles and grunts.

Rivington Hill is perhaps best described as a mildly miasmic microcosm situated on the periphery of a metropolis. An afterthought of a town with few, if any, redeeming features, save the low house prices and a modern and politically correct (if not entirely harmonious) multicultural mix. Merry Munchers and McDonald's are considered the more salubrious of its fine dining outlets. Indeed, they are the only restaurants within a two-mile radius, unless you consider the somewhat unfortunately-named 'Seaman's Feast', a fish-and-chip take-away situated on the other side of the railway bridge, which has been run by the same family of toothless but cheerful Romanian refugees for as long as Mark can remember. But as far as gastronomical cuisine goes, the average local resident would rarely think to question the nutritional authority of the famous golden arches or to resist the stench of an unidentifiable carcass as it does its nightly spin on the stick. Other establishments include a cramped grocery and general provisions store, a funeral parlour, a tyre and spare-parts outlet, a permanently shut hardware store, an off-licence, a Post Office/stationery shop, a hair salon, a florist, a petrol station and a grotty newsagent's. This scant, eclectic strip of tumbledown businesses is the sum total of Rivington Hill's amenities. Similarly, the Barley Mow is the only 'proper' pub for almost a mile, its only competition being the Royal British Legion hall situated on the other side of town, which had its heyday in the eighties when ballroom dancing, bingo, cabaret and Friday-night raffles were all the rage. And times have changed quite dramatically since then.

Mark is discussing topical issues with Thurston. Or rather, Thurston is subjecting Mark, and indeed anyone else who may be listening, to a series of random and meandering conjectures, assertions and postulations, at some length. Thurston is eighty-three, an inveterate employer of often amusing malapropisms, with a shock of white hair flattened by a tweed cap, a comedic beard that looks too big and unkempt to be real and a penchant for brown corduroy, Golden Virginia and gassy ale. He wears a poppy on his lapel all year round because 'it's important to remember the brave who died when the world is so full of shits who just carry on livin'.'

He calls Mark his 'venereal friend', when he isn't calling him 'sonny me lad' or simply 'son'. Mark doesn't know why he keeps ending up in there surrounded by his late grandfather's erstwhile gang. It seems to him that ever since he moved back in with his parents and, more specifically, since Caroline left, he has been spending more and more time in this dull yet strangely comforting environment – blending into the background, blotting out the noise, stocking up on the cheap beer in between leaving work and going home, or sometimes sneaking in at weekends before heading into the city. The boredom factor used to overwhelm him, but now he has perfected the art of 'switching off', having discovered that elusive and mystical plane far beyond the monotony of the here and now. He has even started reading – proper books with solid text throughout and no pictures – an unthinkable transition from the book-spurning, comic-browsing Mark of the previous century. And so he often sits there for hours and either reads or pretends to read, while his mind wanders freely, often going blank or shutting down completely.

A short attention span is a distinct disability when you are a resident of Rivington Hill: a tiny, provincial town for the underclass on the London/Essex borders, forgotten by time, with nothing to occupy restless young hearts and minds short of aimless criminal activity and/or alcoholic oblivion. Even Mark's newly disciplined attention span is being tested to the limit: he has been reading the same page of his book for the past hour without absorbing a single word. He inherited a pile of books from Caroline. She got rid of most of her belongings before she left, and for some reason she chose to bestow her entire book collection upon Mark, her most long-standing and, arguably, most illiterate and cerebrally challenged friend. Most of them had gone straight into a bin bag for Oxfam – dozens of so-called 'holiday reads', girlish romance-themed novels with pastel-splashed covers and tenuous plot summaries suggested by the title and given away completely by the blurb on the back – but Mark kept the few that he knew he wouldn't be embarrassed to be seen reading. Martin Amis, Will Self, Irvine Welsh, Roger Hargreaves – and certain other authors, mostly male, whose vocabularies exceeded his by about a thousand words.

Despite being initially engrossed in it, he has experienced various problems with this current book – a turgid tome with a labyrinthine plot and long sentences crammed with obscure words and a weird obsession with bananas, of all things. He feels cheated and a little annoyed that there isn't even a little bit of gratuitous sex thrown in to give his work-battered brain a rest from having to think all the time, or just to spice up the relentlessly clever stuff. However, Mark is very impatient and he's only got as far as page ten, with about seven hundred and fifty pages still left to go. Caroline assured him that it was one of the best books she had ever read, so he's resolved to persevere with it at least to the end of the first chapter. Given the banana obsession, Mark muses, there's bound to be something a bit spicy in there somewhere, surely. And if it's about war, there must be some serious violence and macabre detail as well.

Every now and then, pricking his easily diverted concentration, Mark will pick up the odd snatch of dialogue from the burbling huddle of characters around him. Thurston might lean over towards Twiggy and Fats, his two assumed 'war buddies', firing off weak puns or conspiratorial asides that nobody else is supposed to or would want to understand, or else he will turn awkwardly in his seat to ask Mark's opinion on something and Mark will just look up from his book and smile, nod, shrug, raise his eyebrows expressively; whatever simple reaction he might deem appropriate. Mark still plays a peripheral part in the old folks' social discourse, but rarely contributes his own thoughts into the forum. He has only been alive for twenty-six years after all, not even a third as long as the sage and aged Thurston. And Thurston is always ready to remind Mark of his seniority, frequently holding it up as a statement of supremacy, of immunity to contradiction and criticism, just in case Mark should dare to feel at liberty to cheek him – 'Sonny, respect yer elders. I've bin round a lot longer than you and your lot, so watch yer lip, yer hear me?' Mark has therefore learned to keep his opinions mostly to himself, knowing that he would otherwise risk sparking off a heated and tiresome debate with him on one side and everyone else on the other, quick to batter down even the most well-structured and seemingly rational of arguments he could possibly hope to offer in support of his case.

Thurston is in an unusually buoyant mood today – or at least, he was at midday when he first arrived, throwing off his mangy old coat and rubbing his hands together with a throaty chortle at the prospect of another afternoon of alcoholic oblivion in the company of his friends. ('Friends' meaning those people who have become his friends by default, simply because they too are regulars, they too live locally and have nowhere else to go and nothing better to do with the finite expanse of time that shrinks before them.) The conversation has natural peaks and troughs with occasional prolonged silences, but Thurston as ever has been providing much of the material, giving his typically outspoken soapbox routine on one issue to the next with the help of digressions, misinformed or malformed opinions and a selective short-term memory.

In his own way, Mark is fond of all of the aged regulars, just as they are fond of him; and despite having nothing in common with anybody there, he perversely enjoys feeling like a part of the furniture, a sounding board for the Geriatric Generation. He himself is the sole representative of the Degenerate Generation, and the gap between these two diametrically opposed generations is vast beyond mere years. Mark has given up defending his contemporaries and openly taking pride in his youth and the 'load of cobblers' culture that goes with it. He just listens, taking little or nothing in. Although he gets incessantly talked at and reprimanded, he frequents the pub for the strange sense of tranquillity and calm it instils in him – a chance to clear out his brain, to forget about the real, fully charged, highly stressed world of demands and demons that whips on regardless outside those four mildewed, magnolia walls. The Barley Mow is almost like a rest home, with its unmistakable ambience of mustiness, dustiness, oldness, reminiscence and rumination. From the heavy, hypnotic swing of the grandfather clock's pendulum to the copperplate bust of Winston Churchill on the bar to the pencil-sketched pictures of the local area through the ages scattered over the walls, from 1850 to 1975; everything about the place is there for the benefit of the old, a perfect time capsule to make them feel welcome and comfortable and *necessary.* A *special* rest home that gives its clientele a final chance to relive old times with the invaluable aid of affordable ethanolic fuel, in an environment where they are safe, protected from the younger generation and all the maligned gadgetry and nonsense that goes with it. A place where memories are dredged up, discussed at length, temporarily forgotten and then remembered and discussed all over again some days, hours or minutes later. Where beliefs and values really and truly matter, regardless of their logic and their source of reference. Merely *expressing* them renders them worthy, tenable – not just another spurious fragment from a disjointed stream of consciousness, a concertinaed carriage from the wreckage of a crashed train of thought.

Len, the erstwhile and locally revered landlord of the Barley Mow, is a wily, lively octogenarian with all his own teeth, three ex-wives and a decrepit but volatile Alsatian called Betsy (in respectful memory of wife number three). In the sixty years he has run the pub he has taken millions in pensioners' beer money and knowingly sired four children, all of whom have blessed him with between three and five grandchildren, although since the death of his third wife he rarely sees or hears from any of them. He has lost count of how many great-grandchildren have descended from his original four offspring and so at Christmas time he sends good wishes to all the various names and addresses in his little black book, from Adams to Zebowitz, stuffing each envelope with a crisp fiver, an invitation to the traditional Barley Mow Boxing Day bash and a standard greeting card scrawled inside with the universal greeting 'God bless you all, whoever you are'.

Len understands the needs of his regulars, and he knows he doesn't have to do anything much to keep them coming back. His only requirements are to pull the occasional pint, employ a youngish barmaid (between thirty-five and forty-five is ideal) with a nice smile, good banter and a great pair of jugs, keep a plentiful stock of pork scratchings and cheese rolls and always, *always* agree with people. This isn't hard, because Len has no real opinions about anything. He puts his longevity down to a combination of malt whisky ('a measure a day keeps the grave at bay'), an absence of backbone that is perceived by his friends as an endearingly laissez-faire and carefree attitude ('just let the missus go ahead and nag at you, it's a lot easier that way') and, more recently, the discovery of Viagra. Now sex is one thing Len does have an opinion on. Wife number four is half his age at forty-two and ever since they were married, in the summer of ninety-eight, Len has not been able to wipe the grin off his face. The new Mrs Len has willingly assumed most of her husband's former duties around the pub, as he tends to be preoccupied with more important things these days, such as passing out in front of *Antiques Roadshow* or lame evening family quiz shows and sitcoms, or imbibing successive pints of bitter until a similarly dormant state has overpowered him. His body might be obsolescent, but he's sure as hell resolved to get the most out of what he's still got. Viagra is his new best friend and even Mrs Len has problems keeping up with him, especially after working a whole day behind the bar, pulling pints and lugging barrels and humouring the regulars.

Conversely, despite various long-term and regular abuses, Mark knows his body is still very much in its prime, but he hasn't been getting too much out of it lately. The official reconciliation with Claire on New Year's Eve was certainly pleasurable, but ever since he has been wondering if it was really worth it; if it was really *wise.* ('Wise' and 'sensible' have only just been accepted into his vocabulary: a sure sign of approaching maturity.) Four weeks back on track and the routine has set in again already, the 'girlfriend versus mates' debate is a contentious issue once more, the old habits are still there, differences of opinion threatening to cause a crack or drive a wedge.

Thurston takes a long, rattling breath. 'So, where's that lovely young lady of yours this evenin'?' He leans towards Mark, having just concluded a long-winded monologue about the Third Reich and, with equal passion, the exorbitant price of local cab fares. 'You not takin' 'er out somewhere nice tonight?' Drool creeps from the side of his mouth into his crusted, crumb-flecked beard.

Mark nods wearily. 'Yeah, well, I'm meeting her in about an hour,' he says, stifling another yawn. 'We're going to the cinema, I think. If there's anything worth seeing.'

Thurston's leathery face cracks to a lascivious grimace as he nudges Mark, firing off a suggestive wink to the rest of the assembled oldies. 'Cinema, eh?' he croaks, 'Still, don't s'pose you'll get to see too much of the film though, son? Will yer, eh?'

Mark manages a gritted smile and turns back to his book, the words swimming on the page in a black fuzzy blur. Claire had expressed more than a passing interest in a gratingly predictable boy-meets-girl-and-everything-turns-out-so-damn-perfect movie; the new Meg Ryan/Tom Hanks combo romance or some equivalent mawkish mush. In any event, Mark had been emphatically disinclined. His primeval preference had always been for the all-out blood-and-spunk-splattered action thrillers; the type of movie that makes you feel reconciled to having a safe and boring life while giving you a sensational two hours of blissful escapism. The type of movie most men feel obliged to favour over all others in order to prove their machismo and preserve their much-vaunted superiority and potential, (if never truly actualised,) heroism. The guy gets the girl and the glory but has to maim and kill and deftly avoid his own untimely death before he's in with a chance.

If only it was that simple in real life. If only it was that interesting. And inevitable.

'Lovely girl, that one,' Thurston mutters, half to himself. 'Carol, innit?'

'What?'

'Your girl. 'Er name's Carol, innit. Or is it Karen?' He shifts slightly in his seat, a rasping fart escaping from his backside that he either doesn't notice or isn't in the least bit embarrassed about.

'Claire,' Mark says, moving his chair further away and feeling the embarrassment for him.

'Eh?' Thurston is almost completely deaf in one ear, unlike his friend Clifford 'Fats' Bunting, whose various escapades in the Marines left him with no hearing whatsoever, a slight limp and a recurring skin complaint.

'Her name is Claire,' Mark enunciates patiently. 'My girlfriend. She's called *Claire.*'

'Claire,' Thurston echoes blandly, repeating it a couple of times under his breath as if learning a foreign word. A strange look flashes into his eyes. 'No, that ain't it,' he says. 'Carol. I'm sure it's Carol.'

Mark drops his book. 'No, Thurston. You're thinking of Caroline. Please try to understand,' he sighs. 'As I have explained to you about a hundred times now, *Caroline* is a mate of mine, she's my *friend.* My friend who happens to be a *girl.* Remember? The one who went away a few weeks back? Quite short and . . . er, kind of plump, with long brown hair? You used to say if you were fifty years younger . . . '

Mark uses his hands to indicate Caroline's approximate height and width and hair length, but Thurston's look is blank, his grey eyes glazed. Mark tries a slightly different tactic. 'You know, the one I hung out with all the time when I was little. Caroline Shaw! Little Caro! Come on, you *must* remember her! She was almost like my sister, for Christ's sake! We were in here all the time when we were kids. She used to beat you and grandad at darts.'

A dawning recognition suddenly lights up the old man's face. 'Worcester sauce!' he exclaims triumphantly.

Mark is fast reaching the end of his tether. 'What the . . . ?'

'Worcester-sauce-flavour crisps,' Thurston says cryptically, folding his hands together and smiling to himself. 'They was 'er favourite.'

Mark begins to understand, although he can't quite see the immediate connection. He thinks there are many more memorable things about Caroline than her preferred flavour of crisp. 'Yeah, well, that's right Thurs,' he says. 'Anyway, whatever, that's Caroline. Now, *Claire* . . . she's my *girlfriend,* yeah? We've been together on and off since ninety-seven, and as I told you just the other day, we're saving up for a place together. That's why I've moved back with my folks for a bit. Caroline has *gone away* now. Remember? Claire is the one I am meeting in . . .' – he steals another quick look at his watch – '. . . fifty-eight minutes. And counting.'

Thurston takes a swig of Guinness. The foam clings to his wiry moustache, and some of it spills down his brown-and-green checked pullover to join an eclectic collection of other stains, some of them dating back to the early seventies. 'Caroline gone?' he says, after a moment's silence.

'Yes. She left a few weeks ago.' Feeling the last of his patience ebbing away, Mark picks up his book, determined to battle on to the end of the current chapter before leaving to meet Claire.

'Where's she gone to, then?' Thurston scratches his beard, pulling at the coarse wisps like a philosopher deep in thought about his next ground-breaking theorem. ''Oliday, is it, or what?'

After encountering another unfamiliar word, Mark's eyes dart listlessly around the room for something else to focus on other than Thurston's unpleasant leer. 'Kind of, I suppose. Er, well, no actually, come to think of it. Not really.' He shrugs, tries to smile. 'She won't be coming back anyway. Not for a long time.'

He is surprised and a little dismayed to find that he has difficulty recalling an exact image of Caroline's face. He can accurately envisage the unique indigo-blue eyes, the shape of her nose, the lips, the hair, but not all at the same time, not so he is able to form a complete and distinct picture of her in his mind's eye. He has known her for twenty years and became almost as familiar with her face as he is with his own, but a separation of just a few weeks and a few thousand miles has somehow eroded or blurred the Caroline photo-library archive of his memory, leaving him with the various bits and pieces to glue together, like an Identikit. He resolves to refresh his bank of mental images by consulting his old photo collection when he gets home. Bring it all flooding back again with some snapshots of the past. He rarely looks at his photographs, confined as they are to a shoe box and an old biscuit tin under his bed, destined to be referred to only in his rarer moments of sentimentality.

Lately these spells of sentimentality have not been so rare. The emotions he feels are strange, ambivalent. Looking at photographs of a bygone era can instil such deep pangs of intractable unhappiness and poignancy, even when the happiest of times have been captured and freeze-framed for all eternity. It's a happiness that can never be felt again; exquisite and unique to that isolated moment in time. That's what makes it feel so utterly sad.

Although Caroline has always maintained that she can recall their first encounter as children right down to the very last detail, Mark is unable to remember the first time he ever saw Caroline. At least, he certainly can't remember it with the same degree of clarity and acuity. One minute Caroline wasn't there, and the next minute, there seemed to be no escaping her. She encroached on his family life until she became a normal and regular part of it. His mother adored her from the start. She was always a hit with the oldies ('Oh isn't she just a *total* sweetheart? So polite!'), and he lost count of how many times he had been told by well-meaning relatives that he 'could do worse'.

But while Mark can't remember the first time he saw her, he

remembers very clearly first *noticing* her. It is possible to know somebody for years and still never really notice them. It takes some kind of instant revelation to notice someone, to notice the *real person*. Often, the longer you know someone superficially, the less likely you are ever to discover who they really are, simply because you deduce far too much, or far too little, from the surfaces, and assume that that is all there is to know. With a bit of extra digging, a bit of effort, you will find that another human being is more than a distinguishable face and a body and a fuzzy, half-revealed personality.

It was during a nature walk at school, a bracing October morning. Mark casts his mind back: a slightly unhinged Scottish teacher with a penchant for fungi; a minor rebellion; a priceless moment of enlightenment occurring somewhere amid the humdrum – suddenly, and for no apparent reason, seeing Caroline through new eyes, almost as if a veil had been lifted. Twelve years ago Caroline had stopped being the annoying, scruffy little kid with a crush on him. Something elusive startled him; made him finally take notice. He had consciously recognised something in Caroline that day, that instant, by which he felt slightly intimidated and overawed. She had said something, he couldn't even recall what it was exactly, but it had been enough to make him look at her and when he did he found himself unable to tear his eyes away. Unlike all the other times when he had granted her no more than a cursory glance, his eyes remained fixed on her. There was something intangible and wholly indefinable about her, beyond the straggly hair and shabby clothes, behind those big china-doll eyes. Whatever it was, it threw a whole new light onto the strange, awkward, tenacious little girl who had literally crashed her way into his life a few years before. It was a flattering light. It transformed her. It transfixed him.

He remembers that from that day on he always felt a little bit emotionally vulnerable with Caroline around; an overwhelming temptation to be entirely himself in her company. There was a subtle warmth and genuineness about her that he found unsettlingly attractive, although this had been fairly easy for him to ignore when there was never any sexual chemistry on his part to compound the attraction. Caroline's appeal was different, it was an elusive and indescribable thing that brought out the softer side of his own character, and obviously that was not a desirable thing for a boy like him to expose. He trusted her and they shared a strange closeness and mutual understanding that transcended pride and gender, but nevertheless he didn't ever want to *appear* vulnerable. Not to her, not to anyone. He liked to keep his defences up, play the hard man. That was what he was all about. That's what he had always been about.

Thurston snaps Mark out of his reflective nostalgia. 'Why's that, then?' he asks.

'Hmm? What?'

Thurston furrows his eyebrows; two unruly clumps that straggle towards the bridge of his nose in a formidable V. 'Why ain't she comin' back?'

Mark feels an uncontrollable surge of irritability rise up inside him, and attempts to wash it away with a few mouthfuls of watery dry cider. 'She's . . . off exploring,' he tells him, with a vague, offhand gesture. 'Gone to live in Australia for a while. Landed there from Singapore last week, I think,' he explains, remembering the brief postcard he received from Caroline a few days before. It was hastily and sloppily written, full of clipped and perfunctory phrases and a muted, tepid kind of excitement, as if he had been the last on her list of postcard recipients. Almost as if she had written it out of obligation, as an afterthought. 'It's something she's always talked about doing, and . . .' Mark's voice drops an octave and he looks down at his feet. 'And . . . well, she's finally gone for it, y'know.' He shrugs, glances back up at Thurston's inquisitive expression, then quickly drains the remainder of his pint, avoiding further eye contact.

Thurston chuckles humourlessly. 'Absence makes the heart . . .' he begins, leaving the cliché dangling like a hanged man. He picks up on Mark's sudden sombreness, and pats him on the knee with a wry grin, a misjudged attempt at empathy. 'Missin' 'er, are yer, son?'

Mark grimaces. 'Don't be soft.'

The grin broadens into a full *idiot-savant* beam, the badly fitting and discoloured dentures clacking loosely in his head as his jaw becomes animated with grim amusement. 'Heh, heh. Bad luck, son. Still, there's this Clara girl . . .'

Mark snaps. 'Fuck's sake! It's *Claire.* C-L-A-I-R-E. *Claire.*'

Thurston dismisses Mark's slipped expletive, which is uncharacteristic of him as he usually considers swear words an unforgiveable sin unless they are a compulsory part of the sentence. For example, when discussing pop music ('What the fuck is that all about then, eh?'), inflation ('Might as well surrender me whole fuckin' pension for the price of a ruddy newspaper and a packet o' baccy these days'), young people ('fuckin' fuckers'), crime rates (ditto), war experiences ('the best and worst fuckin' days of me 'ole bleedin' life, I tell yer'), etc.

The old man sighs deeply. 'Well, never mind,' he says at length, staring at a lone moth forlornly circling the dim light bulb above his head. 'Eh? Chin up, sonny. Nice-lookin' lad like you will never go lonely for long.' He rubs his bulbous nose with the back of his hand and coughs some phlegm into a grubby hanky produced from his sleeve. His nose was shining with a slightly pink hue at first, but over the course of the afternoon it progressively deepened through every shade of red, now resembling a radioactive tomato. 'Hey, tell you what. Here you go.' He strains forward in his chair and presses a fifty-pence coin into Mark's hand. 'How's about you go and put a song on the old jukebox. Liven the place up a bit.' He slumps back and flings one flannel-trousered leg over the other, satisfied that he has fulfilled a significant avuncular duty with this random gesture. The red protuberance in the middle of his face glows.

Mark is quiet for a while, staring alternately at the glinting coin in his palm and the mischievous glint in Thurston's wily black pupils. 'Er . . . great idea Thurs,' he says slowly, reciprocating the twisted smile. 'There's just one slight problem. This pub does not have a jukebox, and in all the years you've been coming here it has *never* had one. The landlord is practically prehistoric and most of his customers are at least sixty. Half the people in here are deaf as posts.' He nods towards Fats as an immediate example. Fats is being loudly berated by another man's crazed wife about something or other, but he has his hearing aid switched off and appears to be in a beatific trance.

'And even those who aren't deaf have no concept of music after Vera Lynn's lot,' Mark finishes, with a sideways glance at Dennis 'Twiggy' Twigg, who is notorious for bursting into tearful wartime song soon after downing his second or third pint, 'White Cliffs of Dover' and 'We'll Meet Again' being his particular favourites.

Thurston blinks rapidly. 'Oh.' His hand moves up to finger his beard again, and he distractedly combs out various flakes and fluff particles, which drift away on the dusty air with the other moulted motes. 'Well, maybe I'll suggest it to old Len,' he says eventually. 'We could do with summink in 'ere, I reckon. A telly, maybe. Never liked them things much meself, but still . . . ' He taps his pipe sharply on the table, and the sound wakes up Baby Stan, who is, as far as Mark is concerned, the oldest person in the entire world. He is called Baby Stan as a long-standing 'joke' which, like the man himself, simply refuses to die.

Baby Stan is sitting directly opposite Mark, sandwiched unobtrusively – almost invisibly in fact – between the burlesque Fats and the diminutive but no less conspicuous Twiggy. His head is rocked to one side on a floppily fleshy stem of a neck, his droopy face a weathered map of folds and wrinkles and liver spots. Baby Stan sleeps nearly all the time, seated in the same dilapidated chair by the inglenook fireplace, day after day. Now and then he will wake up and have a bit of his beer and a bleary blink around at his surroundings (*Am I dead yet?*), but he is known to make a single pint last eight hours. Now that he is temporarily back in the land of the living, he gives the assembled congregation his gummy grin (*Hey everyone, I'm back! I'm still here you know, I'm still alive!*) before shakily reaching out a wrinkled, veiny hand towards the half-empty pint glass on the table in front of him. After taking a noisy slurp of the tepid beer, he resumes his habitual slouch and seconds later he is sound asleep again, saggy and inert.

Meanwhile, Thurston is smoking his pipe quietly, his cracked greyish lips sucking at the stem and puffing out streams of acrid smoke in Mark's direction. Mark yawns widely and checks his mobile phone for missed calls and text messages. This is a compulsion of his and a particularly repetitive one when he is bored.

Nothing.

He silently fumes and curses his mates for being so selfish and negligent. 'Phone me, you arseholes,' he hisses under his breath. He concentrates on sending out a psychic emergency message:

'Mark to mates, this is Mark calling any mate. SOS. Am feeling like shit, am stuck in shitty pub and weird senile old man is talking at me nonstop. Save me now with one phone call. Please. Over and out.'

'Course, you youngsters take it all for granted these days,' Thurston muses, taking the pipe out of his mouth and pointing it at Mark accusingly. 'Oh yes.'

Mark regards him quizzically. Across the table, Twiggy puts his arm around Mrs Fats – a nervous, jumpy woman with a wispy, shrewish face – and starts softly crooning: 'There'll be bluebirds over . . . '

Thurston continues, clambering up on his soapbox again to deliver a specialised and well-rehearsed rhetoric.

'I tell you, my venereal friend, you lot really don't know what you got till it's gone. It's all handed to you for nothin' an' you never has to lift a finger. My Lily, God rest her soul, she wouldn't stand for any of this technological business. All we had in our house was this little battery wireless an' a 'lectric fire in the sittin' room. No washing machine. No, she did it all by hand, my Lily, an' wrung it all out on a mangle afterwards. And never complained once. Tch! You lot have it so easy, it makes me blood boil when I hear some of the words that comes out yer mouths, and the behaviour I see from even the little 'uns. Cheeky blighters, they've bin dragged up, most of 'em. Dragged up by their parents, then drugged up by their good-fer-nothin' friends. They expect somethin' for nothin', the lot of 'em. Such a shame. It breaks me bloody 'eart, really it does.'

He shakes his head and uncrosses his legs; the voluminous beard set wagging with each impassioned assertion. Mark is overcome by a sudden, powerful waft of must that emanates from Thurston's clothing.

'My Lily never wanted kids,' Thurston goes on. 'An' these days you wonder why anyone does. Now it's all computer games and fancy videos and teenage sex and ecstatic drugs and them bloody mobile things and God knows what else.' A cloud of smoke pours out of his mouth with a disdainful hissing sound. 'Ruined,' he concludes sadly. 'They've bin bloody ruined, they 'ave.'

Mark forces himself to take a renewed interest in the book. Thurston has only just passed the boundary between sobriety and total intoxication (there is never any 'tiddly' or 'merry' stage between these two extremes for Thurston), and is becoming increasingly spirited. Ignoring him will take great effort, but Mark does his best, flicking forward a few pages until he stumbles across an attractive word or phrase, preferably sexual or violent or rousing in some way.

'An' yer can't even trust the ruddy supermarket these days,' Thurston goes on, slightly off tangent but still following the same approximate theme ('How things have changed for the worse since I were a lad'). He thumps the arm of his chair and a billow of dust flies up, floating hazily around his fisted hand. 'Y'don't know what it is you is eatin' half the time, what with these genitally modified vegetables an' all. Y'know, I blames them politics people. Them government types, shifty sorts, let me tell you. Don't trust 'em. No. No. Shifty bloody bastards, the lot of them.'

He folds his substantial arms defiantly across his chest, breathing heavily from the exertion of his zealous outburst. Thurston is notorious for getting wound up easily. Having been disappointed with what followed from an apparently promising sentence ('They bent over, unaware, the saucy darlings, of the fatal strips of white cotton knickers thus displayed, the undercurves of baby-fat little buttocks a blow to the Genital Brain, however pixilated . . .'*), Mark tries to imagine what a 'genitally modified' vegetable might look like.

*

* Thomas Pynchon, *Gravity's Rainbow* (p. 13).

Gina, probably the most chatted-up and hard-done-by barmaid in all of England, or at least in Essex, comes around to collect the empties. At forty she is the second youngest person there, and she gives Mark a strange look as she stoops to stack the glasses and change the ashtrays. The look says: *What the hell are you doing in a place like this?* Mark merely checks the time, wondering why it has taken an hour for ten minutes to pass.

Thurston is still merrily gassing away. 'Course, I'm tryin' to grow me own spuds now,' he rambles on, packing his pipe with more tobacco, 'jus' like what your grandfather did for all them years. At least when you've grown 'em yourself yer know for sure they ain't bin tampered with. 'E loved that allotment 'e did, your old grandpa. Grew all sorts of veg. Fruit too. Strawbs, blackberries, even rhubarb if I remember right. 'E'd spend hours in that place, do you remember? When you was a nipper, 'e'd give you and yer little friend a basket each to collect up all the strawberries in summer, and you ate so many you'd make yersels sick.' He chortles gruffly and touches Mark's shoulder. 'You were a right scally you were, m'lad.'

Mark watches as Thurston's nose turns purple right in front of his very eyes.

'Oi, 'old up Gina love!' Thurston cuts short his dawdle down memory lane, and necks the last dregs of his Guinness before waving the pint glass in the air. 'One more empty over 'ere m'darlin'.' He jerks his head in a vigorous 'come hither' gesture, his grin taking on a smutty twist. The tip of a yellowing tongue emerges fleetingly from the corner of his salivating mouth and his left eye begins to wink with such alarming ribaldry it seems to take on a life of its own. Gina peers wearily over at him, a staggered tower of stacked glasses gripped in each fulsome arm. 'I'll give you empty, you dirty old bugger.'

Thurston is delighted at this repartee; the serpentine tongue flickers and the eye goes into overdrive. 'I only wish you would, my darling. I only wish you bloody well would. Reckon I could do with an emptying, eh? Eh?' He nudges Mark, hoping for a bit of back-up, a bit of fellow male assent. Mark, as openly chauvinistic as the next man, merely offers Gina a look of sympathy and embarrassment. Like any seasoned barmaid, Gina is hard as nails, and well accustomed to dealing with such situations in a polite and direct fashion. She takes the glass from Thurston with a curt 'Thank you,' and when his arthritic paw gropes out at her she pats him away calmly and says, 'Thurston my love, your pacemaker would pack up before I'd even got you down to your incontinence pants.'

The eye ceases winking and the tongue retracts as the expression crumples to one of umbrage and defiance. 'I'll 'ave you know I'm in full control of me bodily functions,' Thurston objects. 'Nothin' wrong with me old ticker or me bladder, thanking you missy. I can keep up with the best of 'em, me! Sometimes need a fork-lift truck to get me up an' runnin' but after that there'll be no stoppin' me . . . heh! Heheheheh!' He dissolves into a brief chuckling fit until he is overcome by persistent coughs and emphysema. Then, red-faced and watery-eyed, he wheezes into his hanky again, while Gina shakes her head and disappears behind the bar with a penitent glance to the heavens.

Over recent weeks, Mark has learned that there is in fact no such thing as a 'typical' old person. Every hour he spends in that crumbling museum of a pub, even when the minutes drag by like an endless history lesson, provides him with a strangely enlightening glimpse into another world, an insight into a psychosocial sphere so far removed from his own that it has become an almost irresistible alternative. There is something fantastically comforting about it. After years of being popular, gregarious, socially revered among friends, Mark is beginning to feel a strong desire for a more sedate and leisurely life. He would never admit this to Tamworth or Jonesey or any of his other mates (in fact he is still yet to admit it even to himself), but he finds it hard to keep up. It's fast becoming a chore. A bore even.

The constant work-related, social, family and relationship pressures he encounters on a day-to-day basis have become such a universally accepted part of life that they are not even perceived as sources of stress. The tacit competitiveness that exists between even the closest of mates; earning just about enough money to keep you just this side of broke; taking the stick for mistakes and accepting more and more responsibility in a job that ties you down and wears you out and represents nothing more to you than a necessary means to an end. Learning to accept defeat. Knowing when to give up. Retaining pride. Maximising masculinity. Keeping ambitions realistic. Accepting that realism will nearly always be disappointing. Always drinking whatever is put in front of you. And fast. Never turning down the offer of casual sex. Never cheating on your girlfriend. Making sure she doesn't find out when you do. Dealing with all the emotional stuff without talking about it to anyone, ever. Joining in where appropriate. Knowing where to draw the line. Thinking about the future tomorrow. Buy now, pay later. Self-preservation. Self-abuse. Keeping up appearances. Playing down emotions. Individuality. Group mentality.

Mark is tired. Mark wants to retire. Mark wants to *be* old so he can have a reason to feel and act so old. To while away the odd weekend pottering about the home like his parents do, briefly feigning interest in long-adjourned DIY projects, watering plants, admiring the overgrown garden and making statements relating to the lawnmower and the length of the grass, writing letters to his MP and watching telly from the comfort of his bed. The lure of the ordinary, the trappings of established adulthood. Surely this was his next objective?

Wasn't it?

After all the tension and cross-purposes and bickering in their relationship, hadn't he promised Claire, hadn't he *assured* her that he was going to grow up and give her what she needed? That he'd move back in with his parents so he could save up some money, so they could finally buy a flat together, a place of their own? He'd said it, he remembered saying it: *you and me, together, in our own place.* Hadn't that promise signified the first nail in the coffin of his carefree youth, regardless of whether or not he lived up to it?

'Why so bleedin' miserable, son? You're a young man with his whole life still in front of 'im,' Thurston had once told him, his tone full of envy and the formidable threat of admonition. Lacking a book or any other suitable distraction at the time, Mark had actually listened to this particular lecture. 'Make the most of it while you got it, 'cos let me tell you, it will pass you by before you know it.' He had gone on to recall a number of 'amusing' and 'exemplary' anecdotes from his past, rounding off with one of his favourite expressions: 'They don't make people like they did back in them days, that's for sure.'

Whatever Thurston meant by that, Mark is inclined to agree. He can't see himself sixty years from now pissing his twilight years away and dreaming of the eighties, the nineties, and this, the New Millennium in all its overhyped glory: of how things were *when he were a lad.* He can't see himself like that because it's already starting to happen. He has recently found himself reflecting, reminiscing and regretting, much more than looking forward to the future.

Often it will take something trivial and seemingly insignificant to trigger a vivid and specific memory, a private and precious revisiting of the past. Sometimes the memories represent a certain isolated moment in time, a feeling relived, a sentiment, a sensation, an atmosphere. School crazes, the first feeling of belonging, five-a-side football in the rain, Rubik's Cube, New Romantics, fighting at the school gate over a red-haired girl called Molly Broom, sticker and card swaps in the playground, his first West Ham match, his first West Ham victory, stories before home time, *Saturday Superstore*, comics, penny sweets, sticker albums, the day his tree house was destroyed by a storm, passing fads, failing exams, scratching names into a wooden desk with the point of a compass, defacing school books, chickenpox and chicken soup in a caravan in Dublin, old routines, the smell of childhood Christmases, the death of his first pet, candles on a birthday cake made by his mother, defacing brick walls with a declaration of love (or what felt like love at the time), inane television programmes, stealing his brother's pornography, his first cigarette, his first CD, his first taste of beer, acid house and raves, just say no, saying yes, his old gang's aimless visits to the park with bottles of Thunderbird or White Lightning. Hanging out. Stupid parties. Spin the bottle. The last day of school. The day he passed his driving test. Spaced-out fumblings on back seats and benches. His eighteenth, a stripper and a near-fatal incident on the Central Line. He remembers a beach in Newquay with Caroline. A beach in Malaga with Claire. Holidays in the sun with the lads and those pointless competitions, with an arbitrary score system and league table. Ibiza hard house, Amsterdam smokescreen, non-stop insomnia in Costa del Sol. Communicating before mobile phones and email existed. The Tube. *The Word*. Happy Mondays. Trippy weekends. His first interview. The songs that encapsulate memories; powerful flashbacks with theme tunes. His grandfather's funeral ('Jerusalem'). Princess Diana's funeral ('Candle in the Wind'). The Millennium Dome ('Things Can Only Get Better'). A beach in Benidorm with . . .

He recollects these things, even the most recent ones, almost as if someone else had lived his life for him and he was nothing more than a compelled onlooker privy to every intricate moment and emotion of another, fugitive existence. He is New Mark looking back on Old Mark, and the two are as separate and distinct as Thurston the shambolic old man looking back on Thurston the war hero. One is inextricably linked to the other but they can never be considered one and the same person. The fragmented memories weave themselves together from a distant, dreamlike perspective that becomes ever more distant with the passage of time, and these intertwine to make up his personal movie reel: *The Story of Mark Crozier's Remembered Life (such as it is) from circa 1980 onwards.*

Twenty years. Where had they all gone? What had he done? Seemingly unconnected, shadowy images flowing and merging together, a half-blurred series of photographs slowly forming in a tray of rippling developer fluid in a dark room. When he remembers, something is tugging him on the inside, electric synapses connecting his heart to his brain: a light switch clicked on in the recesses of his mind that sheds light only onto certain isolated details, keeping the rest in darkness. He is nothing more than the sum of all the parts of what he has experienced, whether he can remember or not. He feels a sense of bitter-sweet fondness and sympathy for Old Mark. The sense of superiority or simple suffering that comes with hindsight can never be underestimated. The power of 'if only'.

Reminiscence is regret versus celebration, and the degree to which one outstrips the other is a sure indication of how successful your life has been.

Funny things, memories.

'*And Jimmy will go to sleeeeeep ... in his own little room again ...*' Twiggy is still lost in music, his beady eyes closed and his small hands held aloft as he yodels away in solo, impervious to the sober indifference of his friends. Mark knows all the old songs by now but never joins in. It isn't his place to join in, even if he wanted to. Besides, he does not, he *cannot*, have a clue what great, convoluted, painful, tragic, epic memories these people are trying to relate to him. His own memories are just so simple, recent, rudimentary, small-scale. Silly in their deep personal importance and significance. But they are his *life*. They are what he is.

Somebody begins tinkling lackadaisically on the antiquated mahogany piano at the far end of the pub, and before too long a friend joins in for a hearty rendition of a Chas 'n' Dave number. Old Len, drunk and red-faced on his usual bar stool, provides a clumsy, clunky accompaniment by jangling a couple of metal spoons against his leg, while his dumpy little wife polishes glasses behind the bar and tries not to look as exhausted as she feels. Residual Christmas decorations are still draped over the top of the bar and a few still dangle feebly from the ceiling – thin, moribund ropes of gold and silver tinsel, mirror balls and flimsy metallic streamers. They now look lacklustre and faintly ridiculous.

Thurston's eyes are beginning to droop. Mark also feels overcome by lethargy now. The potent and pervasive tranquillising effect of the Barley Mow has finally taken its toll on his brain. His muscles keep relaxing and jumping as he battles against sleep. Fats approaches the table with the next round of drinks and a few people perk up noticeably, one or two eagerly making a grab for their usual beverage before Fats has even had a chance to put the tray on the table.

Thurston too becomes temporarily alert, and has a hearty gulp from his fourth pint of Guinness before he collapses back, sighing with satisfaction.

'Australia, eh?' Thurston mumbles after a short pause, gazing towards the frosted window at the gathering darkness outside. 'Other side of the world, is that.'

Mark has got as far as page fifteen of his book now, and it's still bananas and random verse. He closes it and puts it down on the table with a groan of defeat. 'What are you talking about *now*?' he asks Thurston.

Thurston looks wearily back at Mark, remembering all too clearly what he was like at that age. Impulsive, reckless, arrogant, foolish. All those things and more. Supercilious, cocksure, attention-seeking, hopeless, hopeful, needful, *lustful*. All noise and unimportance. Just starting out with a head full of nothing. Dreams of heroism.

But he had been killing men at that age. He had lived each day as if it was his last, because on each and every day that he woke up to a new blood-red dawn his very existence was both a celebrated bonus and a lamented curse. Life on a knife-edge in a hellish dugout with his friends dropping like flies around him, knowing it could be him next. Sometimes wishing it would be him next.

'Look, it's snowin' now,' he says eventually, half to himself, turning his craggy face back towards the window. The sky is velvet-black and cloudless. Powdery white flakes drift by, and the street light on the pavement opposite flickers on and off intermittently. Twiggy finishes his song, wipes away a stray tear and knocks back his lager shandy in one go. Thurston yawns and starts whistling tunelessly through his teeth, drumming his fingers on the arm of his chair. 'Must be about time for you to go and meet your girl,' he says, not moving his eyes from the window.

'Er, yeah . . . I suppose it is,' Mark replies, without stirring in his seat.

'Be seein' yer again soon son, I s'pose.'

'Yeah. No doubt. Laters, yeah?'

A final glance at his watch confirms that more than half an hour has passed without Mark even noticing. He too has become a victim of the time warp. Claire is used to Mark being late. He keeps everyone waiting. He always has.

After summoning up some drive and shaking himself into full

consciousness, he pulls his coat on and checks his pockets for wallet, keys, phone, bus pass.

'Don't forget yer book,' Thurston says, pointing at it. 'That's a good one, that is.'

Mark is taken aback. 'You've read it?'

'Years ago, sonny.'

'Well . . . I've kind of . . . given up on it. You can have it.'

Thurston laughs and shakes his head. 'That's the trouble with you lot. You give up on everything without even trying. You're all so bloody soft.'

'Well, you read it again if you like it so much,' Mark retorts bluntly. 'I don't have the time. Go on. Take it.'

Thurston is too tired and drunk to argue. 'Me old eyes won't be able to see that small print no more. Still . . . could get someone else to read it to me I s'pose.'

'Yeah, you do that.' Mark nods and waves politely at all the other just-conscious oldies, most of whom feel energetic enough to acknowledge his departure with a slow blink and a reptilian smile. As he walks towards the door, Thurston calls after him, 'You be givin' that Carol one from me won't you, sonny?'

Outside, the dim yellow street light hums low and sputters out completely. Bracing himself against the wind, Mark scurries outside into the arctic darkness. The pub door slams shut behind him, sealing off the familiar, strong waft of warm beer and tobacco. His breath frosts crystalline white in front of his face. He digs his hands into his pockets and presses forward, not bothering to look back or to give a final wave goodbye over his shoulder.

Memories 1981–1999: Caroline

1

Sexless in Essex

'You do not even think of your own past as quite real; you dress it up, you gild it or blacken it, censor it, tinker with it . . . fictionalise it, in a word, and put it away on a shelf – your book, your romanced autobiography. We are all in flight from the real reality. That is a basic definition of *Homo sapiens*.'

John Fowles, *The French Lieutenant's Woman*

The only real problem with childhood is that it's essentially all over in a flash and you can't possibly know at the time that who you are and who you will become hinge almost entirely on those precious, innocent, ephemeral years. Whether you are nurtured and cared for by adoring parents or hurled in the deep end of life's sink-or-swim cesspool from the outset, childhood provides the very foundation of your adult existence. It forms you, moulds you, every level of personal experience during that first decade or so ultimately deciding if you are going to be a wimp or a winner, a fighter or a bystander, a sheep or a shepherd, a misfit or a conformist, a taker or a provider. Whether you get your own way or get walked all over.

I remember very few childhood days with quite as much clarity as the day I met the Crozier family. It is my earliest and most cherished memory. On my way to the airport on the second day of a new millennium, I experience a protracted attack of nostalgia, and when I start to look back on my old life, that is still the predominant memory, the one I keep coming back to. Or the one that keeps coming back to me.

Even with all that occurred after that turning point, the events of that day remain vivid and detailed to the extent that even now, almost twenty years later, I am able to relive it moment by moment. So the delineation of my life must, necessarily, begin from that point. The Day in my Past that changed my whole Future. The Day I met the Croziers.

I met Mark long before I had been able to make considered judgements about who and what I was, where I wanted to go and what I had to do in order to get there. Timing – that's another important thing. The timing has to be spot on. Infinite possibilities present themselves every single day of our lives, each one of them splitting and dissipating a million times with every chosen course of action, every decision taken, each and every minutia of daily existence: cause and effect, thought and behaviour, deed and misdeed. Everything spirals from everything else; one thing leads to another. Yoko Ono apparently once said that the odds of not meeting in this life are so great that every meeting is like a miracle, and 'it's a wonder that we don't make love to every single person we meet.' An extreme notion perhaps, but certainly not an unpleasant idea to ponder upon – if the world happened to be populated exclusively with attractive and lovable people. But let's face facts: it's not.

There's another, slightly less radical theory. Apparently, for every single one of us glorious, independent individuals, there's a potential market of at least – at *least* – twenty thousand ideal partners somewhere out there in the big wide world. Twenty thousand perfect matches! Isn't that incredible?

How many of us would be quite happy with just one? How many of us would be more than content with a semi-ideal; a 'consolation prize' in fact? If there are twenty thousand ideals, there must be getting on for a million or more *pretty crap, but will have to do I suppose* partnership possibilities. So while we're settling for one of them, the common-or-garden, bog-standard, warts-and-all partner, we are letting not one, not two, but *twenty thousand* perfect little fishies slip through our net. Like catching an oyster and throwing away the pearl.

But anyway, me and Mark. There's a saga. A love story with a twist, you could say. An anti-romance, perhaps? I don't know. Even that sounds too romantic. All of the elusive knock-kneed, gut-churning, starry-eyed stuff is supposed to start yanking at your heartstrings right from the first moment you meet; a sense of spontaneously *knowing*: this is the one. *I have found The One.* (That is, one out of a possible twenty thousand, but that doesn't sound very romantic in all conscience.) But it's not enough just to find The One. There has to be a connection, way above and beyond sexual attraction and mutual tolerance and compatibility. Love without balance is nothing. Love with *effortless* balance – if you've got that, you've cracked it. It's real, it's for ever, it's as damn near perfect as you're going to get. That's what 'it' is.

But I fell in love with the wrong person. Right from the start, I didn't stand a chance. It's an outrageous cliché I know, but in reality, when you are at the wrong end of unrequited love (which *is* the wrong end?), there is nothing commonplace about it at all. And by love, I don't just mean that rapid, uncontrollable flush you get in that Special Someone's presence; that somersaulting lurch in the stomach, that unfettered fluttering, the surge of hormones, the ache for touch, the all-consuming dementia and brain-invading obsession. At the start though (and we're going way back here), I must confess I was afflicted with all those symptoms. I just tried to ignore them.

People think that when your best friend is of the opposite sex there is (naturally! of course!) always the possibility of the old 'sex thing' getting in the way. But when that person has been your best friend all your life, and you are quite blatantly mismatched on so many levels and bicker like brother and sister, the *When Harry met Sally* dynamics are probably not so viable. Probably not even an issue. Instead people wonder how you remain friends at all. Familiarity breeds contempt.

Whereas I am a little bit plain and plump, well stacked, compactly packed and basically pretty much unremarkable all round, Mark is in a whole different league. Again, a grotesque cliché: Little Miss Frump falls for Mr Cool. Mark has – or rather, he has cultivated – a quirky, asymmetric, rough kind of handsomeness that often leaves susceptible females frantically panting and pouting in his presence without even realising it. He likes to think his mates are in awe of him, to the extent that he has totally lost sight of what he actually wants for himself. He acts out his life like it's one big meaningless game of one-upmanship derived directly from the pages of *Loaded*, doing everything for the amusement and admiration of others, and consequently the enhancement of his own inordinate ego. A cheeky gobshite on the surface and yet, in my own humble opinion, something quite elusively spectacular and adorable underneath it all. A little brain-dead, a touch cold-hearted, very shallow, confusingly likeable, my best friend ever in the whole wide world, that's Mark.

He wasn't always like this, though. In fact, that isn't the real him at all. Not the Mark I can see even when I want to punch him, scream at him, smother him. For the first ten years at least, he did unremittingly display that same brash and brazen attitude that is typical of little boys who will nonetheless somehow, eventually, grow up to become sensible, responsible (and even sensitive) men. The attitude reaches its peak at about thirteen or fourteen, and is really just a preliminary purging of excess machismo, a theoretically transient stage in male development while they battle with testosterone overload with onanistic overkill. Mark's mind is still firmly entrenched in this attitude. I suppose it's one that's difficult to shake off, because blokes get so comfortable with it, like a pair of old slippers. They just can't help themselves. It's just too easy. Tiny teenage minds trapped within hulking great men's bodies. For all eternity.

We had always got on though, Mark and me, ever since we were little kids. At least, we did once he got over his natural disdain and distaste for me. His initial aversion and his callous indifference to my affections slowly gave way to a much more amenable mutual understanding. We used to tear chunks out of each other and hurl insults and make each other cry just like any ordinary schoolfriends would (well, he would make *me* cry anyway), but we didn't need to tell each other how we really felt. We had affection for each other, and while his was as grudging as mine was rampant, it was as true a friendship as a boy and girl could realistically hope for. Even when we were declaring our hatred and contempt for each other in the playground and on the estate, even when we ignored each other for days on end over the usual trivial issues that vex the minds of temperamental children.

I discovered I had a certain easy, asexual rapport with blokes as I got older: 'honorary geezer' Mark used to call me, presumably meaning it as some kind of compliment. Tragically, however, all the men I got involved with on a level above and beyond friendship never seemed particularly to like me. Why not? Well, I had my own theories, until I finally woke up and realised reality doesn't have to keep turning around and laughing in your face unless you keep letting it.

My last proper boyfriend (if both 'proper' and 'boyfriend' are used in their loosest possible sense) was a Phil Collins fan called Stuart with a big flashy car and an ego to match. He was the wrong man for me for so many reasons I don't know where to begin.

How about this for starters? He called his penis Colin. I kid you not.

We met during my final year at university and established a routine that lasted nine months – a surprisingly long time, considering I had become insanely bored before the end of our first month together; before he'd even moved into my student house with me. And this is how it went: I would return home from an afternoon shift or a particularly taxing day of lectures – knackered, invariably pissed off and grouchy, in need of a hefty drink and a bubble bath – to find him slouched on the sofa with both hands down his pants, watching

Emmerdale or *Tomorrow's World* (he had a thing about northern accents and futuristic gadgetry).

Things reached breaking point when I came home a couple of hours early one day to find him slouched on the sofa watching *Countdown* with someone else's hands down his pants. I'd like to say tantrums were thrown, furniture and crockery hurled, bones broken, aptly named appendages severed, but the truth is, I really couldn't have cared less. In fact, I found myself feeling relieved – even *grateful* towards the 'other woman'. I was unable to summon up very much ill feeling towards either of them. After all, who could blame the poor man? He was only a slave to the arbitrary cravings of the diminutive but demanding Colin, and, I must concede, she *was* thinner than me. How could I possibly assume that my existence should stand in the way of what is only natural between two compatible human beings?

So it's probably fair to say my last foray into the world of love and romance ended a little inimically. Even so, I wouldn't say I have a history of disastrous relationships. Not quite. More like a disheartening succession of totally crap boyfriends. And then, after university, those fragmented 'wilderness years' during my early twenties, I inevitably reached that agonising stage where I felt like I could have been – *should* have been – going somewhere, and aiming for something worthwhile. But, rapidly losing heart and hope, I did precious little to change the grating monotony of my lifestyle or boost my depleting *joie de vivre.* The plodding treadmill of life started to catch up with me, and the damn scenery was not changing and it sure as hell wasn't getting any better.

I didn't have much of a start in life, to be fair.

I was raised on a typically squalid council estate just outside the worst part of the East End of London, eldest daughter of a hopeless, pissed-off alcoholic mother and an emotionally and geographically distant, overweight, unemployed anonymous whose paternity is and shall remain questionable at best. I was called (but never officially christened) Caroline Elizabeth because my mum thought it sounded posh – two polysyllabic names would surely increase my chances of one day becoming a somebody, rather than remaining a nobody. Well, that was her distorted reasoning. But then, my brother is called Kevin, and my sisters are called Teri, Sharon and Jolene, so I actually think I was quite fortunate as far as names go. My mum's reasoning must have distorted itself back to some kind of realistic normality. Kev, being the eldest of my mother's brood, decided it was his responsibility to set an example to the rest of us – so from age nine his life revolved around petty crimes that soon escalated into pretty bloody serious and even life-threatening ones.

The boredom threshold for the kids on our estate was pretty low. Summers were worst. Kids aged between eight and eighteen would hot-wire cars and crash around without a single thought for anyone or anything – all they knew was that they were bored out of their skulls, frustrated and resentful because their parents didn't give them the attention or care they craved, and because they felt unjustly deprived of all the things most people outside the estate had: homely homes with room to breathe, shiny cars with sunroofs and power steering, holidays abroad, new clothes, the toys that were advertised on television, things, things, so many *things*. And don't try telling any kid that money can't buy you love. Money gets you *things*, and those *things* make you happy, and if you don't feel happy you don't feel loved. A child's perspective is simple, but so easily disrupted when emotions are thrown out of balance by a lack of *things*, whether this lack is real or imagined. It is impossible for them to see beyond their own tiny microcosm. It is impossible for a child ever to think of itself as truly fortunate, because there will always be someone else with more, or better *things*. As a group, deprived of these *things*, we were a child psychologist's worst nightmare come true.

And there were so bloody *many* of us.

The equally bored and frustrated adults, crammed together in their assigned council boxes like battery hens, listlessly reproduced over and over again on an aleatoric mix-and-match basis, simply because there was nothing better to do. Because, for some mystical sociological reason, neither contraception nor abstinence was ever an option for them. Most of the time, they didn't even have a relationship. It was procreation for recreation: with every randomly fertilised ovum the imminent birth of another Rivington Hill Estate baby was often accepted with ho-hum compliance and vague unease on the mother's part, and with a temporary surrendering or a one-way ticket to a faraway destination (prison, perhaps) on the father's part. The novelty, such as it was, wore off in an instant, and yet still the babies came, on and on and on. Better to be a parent than nothing at all, I suppose.

And so there were loads of us; screaming, imbecilic, uncontrollable, sad little kids who ultimately grew up to be carbon copies of those pathetic cases that spawned us. The cycle went on: we were the kind of people (scum, leeches, *parasites*) that the diligent taxpayer rightly complains about, the millstone around the neck of society, the endless drain on England's parsimonious budget. We stood no chance in the big bad world of consumerism where wealth and breeding and prestige spoke louder about an individual than anything we could control.

Mum had given birth to Kev when she was just a few weeks short of her sixteenth birthday; then she was housed by the council and, following two or three further doomed and transitory relationships, I was born just over a year later. All I really know about my father is that he is now serving the last five years of a mandatory thirteen-year sentence in Wormwood Scrubs for several acts of arson and armed robbery and the odd attempted murder. My mum doesn't even have a photograph of him, all she could tell me (indeed, all she has seen fit to tell me) is that he was 'a large fella' called Brian, who had a metal plate in his head and preferred mayonnaise on his chips to ketchup. These tenuous insights don't give me much to go on of course, but perhaps I should be grateful for small mercies. In any event, although I did have occasional pangs of curiosity for a time, I suppose it is best that the details of my father's true identity are kept under wraps.

My genetics have cruelly rendered me mediocre and unremarkable, physically at least. I have my mother's rich chestnut-brown hair, but the similarities end there. I have a broad, heart-shaped face with a faint smattering of freckles and prominent, dimpled cheeks that blush at the slightest provocation or mildest exertion. The best I can say about my appearance is that I have 'unreleased potential' – at least, that is what I was once told by a pathologically patronising orange-faced sales adviser at the Clinique counter during my first and last visit to Selfridges' cosmetics and perfumery department.

While my mum's eyes are hazel-brown, small and close-set, mine are wide and clear, a kind of weird violet colour and positioned far apart, the distance between them and their unusual colour lending me an almost oriental look (some less charitable people might say 'fish-like'). But despite having been cursed with substantial myopia, I like my eyes. There is nothing shifty about them at all, which is why I'm convinced I couldn't have inherited them from my father either, whoever and wherever he may be. I can't lie with my eyes; they are too innocent-looking, too big and expressive. Very feminine eyes – *bewitching* is how my mum describes them. (She sometimes tells me I am her most beautiful creation, but only when she is severely under the influence.)

I have to admit that all this is a misleadingly pleasant description of my appearance. My proportions are in fact a little imbalanced, too irregular to be considered pretty in the archetypal sense; even when I lose some excess weight (of which I have been cursed with abundant supplies), there is still something not quite right about my build and my bearing and the overall balance of my facial features. Kev once described me as 'squashed and stretched in all the wrong places', and I suppose there's more accuracy in that description than I'm comfortable with.

For several years, right up until just before Teri, the youngest, was born, the five of us lived in the worst block on the estate. It was ostentatiously called 'Arcadian House'; a huge lump of ugly concrete split into a hundred-odd poky little back-to-back top-to-tail shitholes, inhabitable and inhabited only by the most desperate charity cases. The entire ground floor was totally ruined by unchecked and persistent vandalism; nearly all the windows were smashed in and boarded up, and it was so disgusting even the squatters couldn't stand it. The area around it was used by all as a rubbish tip, and vast numbers of local kids would often use the building as target practice for their dog-shit missiles, and also held competitions to see who could break the highest window. We were on the seventh floor, so we were just about safe from most of the hurled boulders. The more accomplished and equally prolific rogues of the estate – the joyriders, the thieves and the muggers – tended to pose more of a threat.

I have no idea how or why, but in spite of everything I managed to do well at school. Maybe this was another rogue feature of my mysterious genetic composition; a quirky aberration that skipped a generation or suddenly appeared as if by magic to compensate for a historic succession of no-brainers. Us lot have been pissing against the wind and into the gene pool for decades, but sometimes even the most catastrophic DNA combinations can beat the odds. I suppose, as a rule, everyone has got to have *something* good about them, regardless of their genealogy and their upbringing. So, ignoring my many physical and character flaws for now, I suppose I was fortunate inasmuch as I was born bright and ambitious, with a stubborn determination to succeed and to achieve against the odds. While all the other kids bunked off in gangs to spend their days vandalising property and joyriding and hanging around outside railway stations and corner shops, I rarely took so much as a day off sick.

Perhaps after seeing the comparative palaces in which my mainly middle-class grammar-school friends lived with their seemingly perfect families, I came to view my estate as something less than satisfactory and normal: something a bit horrible and shameful. Something substandard and ugly. Certainly somewhere I didn't have to stay and make do with. Poverty and deprivation are only relative concepts, of course, but maybe it was a sense of gross injustice about the way the world was, even on this small scale, maybe it was my outraged childish jealousy and rancour that kick-started something in me, something that told me: *but you can do better than this, you can break free, it doesn't have to be like this for ever.* And any one of us angry, unhappy little liabilities could theoretically have broken free, become functional citizens with nice houses and good jobs and flashy cars and branded clothes. We could have been one step nearer to the lauded celebrity lifestyle we read about in the magazines and newspapers. We could have become *important.* But we told ourselves that we didn't care. It wasn't worth the effort of scratching out that microscopic, remote opportunity, hoping against hope, when we saw how insultingly easily that same opportunity came to so many others, just for being born into the right kind of family. Those kids who lived in the same borough and yet a million miles away, those kids from families that were like the families in daytime soap operas. Perfect. Precious. Protected.

The 'easy' option, to stay where we were and to do nothing except hate it and stick with it, was paradoxically the toughest of all. But the vast majority would just get on with it, skipping school, stealing, fornicating; playing the various survival games of the impoverished, passed down over generations, whatever illicit tactics that may have entailed. Not out of choice so much as necessity. It was a case of merely surviving, *existing*, scraping by, rather than living, having a life.

Surviving poverty takes guts, even if you end up merely resigning yourself to it. Perhaps that should be: *especially* if you end up resigning yourself to it. When you are a kid it is worse because it quickly produces an inferiority complex, a destructive world view based on deep-rooted self-doubt and animosity, boredom, empty bravado and laziness, each one of these negative aspects perpetuating and exacerbating the others. Breaking free of it takes something much more special; a little bit of luck, vision, hope and mental fortitude. I was lucky. I had more than most. But I don't think I would ever have come to realise it had I not taken the seemingly foolhardy action of acrobatically dismounting my brother's bike outside Mark's house that fateful day. It was the summer of 1981. I was five years old.

In so many ways, meeting Mark and being accepted into the Crozier family both saved and doomed me. Considering all the possible alternatives, the way things ultimately turned out and how they could have turned out, I would like to think of them as my unlikely personal saviours.

2

Precious Things

'I believe that the experience of childhood is irretrievable. All that remains, for any of us, is a headful of brilliant frozen moments, already dangerously distorted by the wisdoms of maturity.'

Penelope Lively, *Oleander, Jacaranda*

I suppose you could say that memories provide a video archive of personal experiences, the definitive life record that can be recalled at will. They represent everything that you are, what you have become and even what you could have been.

But of course, memories are, by definition, only an *interpretation* of events – your own interpretation, from your own limited perspective. Imagine if you could go back in time and relive, frame by frame, the significant moments of your life – those all-important events, exchanges, encounters – and view the experiences in a more interactive and pragmatic way. A special kind of introspective retrospection: all those memorable times revisited, recreated, logged and stored, played back, analysed. Imagine if you could actually break it down into chronological instalments, downloading each episode exactly as it happened, watching it as if on a big cinema screen with the wisdom and detachment of hindsight, like an ongoing soap opera or epic film that is compelling and important to you and only you. You could attach a caption or a pithy theme tune to each scene, pause and rewind to scrutinise the finer details, label every episode with a place and time and subtitle, think about how you might handle certain situations differently if you were given the chance to do it all over again. You will be in control this time around: the producer, the director and the leading, eponymous role in the star-studded story of your own life! The funny moments, the sad moments: would you laugh, would you cry all over again? Would you have chosen different co-stars? Would you have harsh words with the scriptwriter? The casting director? How much would you edit? Would you categorise it as a romance? A tear-jerker? A saga? A luminary drama? A comedy? A black comedy, perhaps? An action thriller? A horror? Something more surreal? An allegory? Or a boring waste of time filled with one aimless, meaningless pursuit after another?

Like remembered fragments of a weird or abstruse dream, these archived memories will supply the ultimate review of your life so far, filling in the manifold gaps and disambiguating where limited memory fails. You can begin at last to realise how every decision and action and every indecision and inaction ultimately affected the rest of your life, and you may even be able to clarify where you went wrong by identifying the catalyst cock-up for all other consequent cock-ups.

My remembered life: how different is it from my actual life? Even with the dubious clarity of hindsight, I hold out little hope of ever being able to answer this question adequately. Sitting on a Heathrow-bound train with Robbie Williams on my Walkman, I try to place it all in chronological order, running through all my precious memories, this time without illusions and tears and only the slightest regret and wistfulness.

I became aware from an early age of what was, to me at least, a slightly bizarre phenomenon. I first noticed it in Rivington Hill, the sub-standard suburb in which I spent the first eighteen years of my life, and had initially thought it was just a local thing, peculiar only to Rivington Hill – which was, after all, peculiar in many other ways too. But then I also noticed it during my limited nationwide childhood travels, from Liverpool (visiting my crotchety, nicotine-raddled grandmother at her cramped, tat-filled two up, two down terrace in Bootle) to Newquay (Mark's grandparents' gorgeous, rose-bedecked Cornish cottage) and more localised Essex escapades. The phenomenon (although I suppose strictly speaking it's not so much a phenomenon as a mere observation) is this: no matter how small, provincial and peripheral a residential area is to a main commercial town centre, you can virtually *guarantee* that there will be at least one hair salon – usually with an exquisitely shameless name such as 'Hair Looms' or 'Aristocuts' or 'Beyond the Fringe' – and also, almost always, a less jocularly titled funeral parlour. This may seem like a commonplace and uninspiring thing and hardly a curiosity of great wonder, but nevertheless it deeply puzzled and perplexed me for some years – at least until I discovered that there are much more interesting things to puzzle and perplex myself over.

But still, why a hair salon *and* a funeral parlour? Why not just provide a chemist (for home hair-dye kits and death-delaying drugs)?

Surely this would be more useful to a wider range of people from all walks of life – won't there always be a demand for prescriptions, emergency contraception, decongestants, slimming products, deodorants and all that? And yet, even if the town consists of just two shops and nothing more, it is highly likely that one will offer 'Cut Price Cuts' and the other will offer 'coffins, cremations and compassionate service'.

If nothing else can be said of Rivington Hill, then, it was at least good enough to bestow its inhabitants with somewhere to get their hair styled and, just next door, beneath a more discreet and weathered black-and-white sign, somewhere to help them with the ceremonious despatching of a loved one to the 'other side'. While very few of the children who grew up in Rivington Hill considered the undertaker's lot to be especially covetable, most of the little girls either wanted to be a nurse or a hairdresser when they grew up. At least, this was their ambition up until the age of ten, at which point they would quickly become too preoccupied with impending puberty to bother thinking about anyone's hair and health except their own. The little boys, rarely holding aspirations beyond the realistically attainable, mostly wanted to be the errant partners of hairdressers or nurses. At least these humblest of childhood dreams were often realised.

Imaginatively enough, the funeral parlour was called 'Rivington Hill Funeral Directors' (subtitle: 'providing an efficient and affordable service to the dearly departed since 1902'). From the age of three, after my first attack of head lice, I was quite a regular at the busy hands and clippers of one of the gum-chewing peroxide clones at the hair salon. But it wasn't until some years later that I got to see what Rivington Hill Funeral Directors looked like from the inside. Until then, it remained an arcane and mystical building, and every time I passed it, I would press my face to the window to try to catch a tantalising glimpse of what lurked inside, past the shabby front door with its incongruous tinkling bell and solemnly shuttered blinds. Before I was granted a fleeting peek beyond the conspiratorial veil of a gauzy curtain, however, my mother would grab me by the arm and pull me away, leaving a steamy imprint of my nose and lips on the glass along with the grubby whorls of my fingertips.

As soon as I learned to talk, every adult I encountered tried in vain to teach me to stop talking. And as soon as I learned to form words into questions, there really was no stopping me. I asked questions about anything and everything, mostly just for the sake of it, sometimes purely to annoy, seldom caring too much about the answer because even the most illustrative and direct answer would invariably lead to another question.

'What's a funnel directors do, Mummy?' I asked my mother over breakfast on the morning of the day I would meet the Croziers. It was the last day of my first-ever year at school. I was almost six years old and my reading and investigative skills were rapidly overtaking other more basic abilities, such as being able to feed myself properly. I clumsily shovelled a runny spoonful of Ready Brek from my bowl straight down my green-and-white gingham-checked school dress, just managing to catch a tiny morsel in my mouth as the spoon made its wobbly trajectory towards my face. I looked inquisitively up at my mother through a straggled fringe, but she was busy mixing up baby food for ten-month-old Sharon and didn't look at me when she answered.

She didn't bother to correct my mispronunciation. 'It's for when you snuff it,' she intoned, leaning over the table to grab a bottle of milk, and absently dropping ash from her third cigarette of the morning into my Ready-Brek sludge. She was twenty-three and had just found out she was expecting her fourth baby. I remember knowing this before it had been officially confirmed because although I was young and innocent, I was also pretty shrewd and precocious – irritatingly so. I had seen the tell-tale blue box in the bathroom ('a yes or no result within five minutes!'); I had silently noted that her mood swings had become even worse than usual over the last few weeks; and, crucially, Kev, Shaz and I had recently been introduced to 'Mummy's new friend', a plumber called Johnny from Basildon who had a hairy back and made our bathroom smell bad.

All these factors counted as solid circumstantial evidence of another *in utero* Shaw family member, potentially if not actually. But perhaps most significant of all, my mum had used the communal seventh-floor payphone that weekend to call my grandmother in Liverpool (with whom she shared a grudgingly close but mutually suspicious and tense relationship), and she had cried out loud with real tears while using phrases such as '. . . just can't cope with another one' and '. . . but I've only known him for two months'. I had been listening in to the conversation, as nosy and curious children so often do, clinging on to our front door, peeping my head surreptitiously into the grey, echoing corridor where my mum stood with her back to me, a receiver pressed to her ear and a soggy tissue clamped to her eyes. Children don't like to see their mothers cry – it makes them seem vulnerable, weak, fragile. And the last thing you want in a place like Rivington Hill is a vulnerable mother. Watching her, I felt tears well up in my own eyes, a nasty, squirming sensation in my stomach, an acute sense of mortification that my own mother could cry so openly when she hadn't even hurt herself.

I never usually cried – I liked to hold things in. It made me feel stronger, superior to all the other estate kids who were my age and cried like pathetic babies if they slipped over and grazed their knees on rough concrete or got punched and kicked by their older siblings. Kevin liked to kick me, but I kicked him back harder. I disliked my brother with a passion. I didn't want another one. And I certainly didn't want another sister – I already had one of those, too, and all she did was make endless noise and mess.

'Snuff what, Mummy?' I cocked my head to one side and tried to look angelic, hoping not to exacerbate her mood further with my usual repertoire of tiresome questions – she was never at her best in the mornings, and I had a habit of bringing out the worst in her whatever time of day it was. My 'angelic look' attempt was a long shot – I had cereal plastered all around my mouth and splattered down my dress, and my hair hadn't been brushed or washed (or deloused) for days. Mum didn't even venture a look at me, anyway – she was balancing Shaz on her knee while trying to ignore Kev flicking stale cornflakes at her from the other end of the room, using his Action Man as a catapult and making vigorous if unrealistic machine-gun noises with each projectile.

I tried a different approach. 'Am I going to have another sister?' I chirruped, having just decided that the 'sister' option was the lesser of two evils (another Kev would be insufferable; another Shaz might be just about manageable, at a push). This question at least made her glance towards me.

'What?' she snapped, still distracted with spooning warmed semolina into her younger daughter's various orifices – down an ear, up a nostril, into and promptly straight out of a bawling mouth. Shaz wilfully refused to eat anything unless it had an obscenely high sugar content, minimal nutritional value and lots of artificial colours and flavours. Inedible objects retrieved from a filthy floor were often sucked or gnawed, but other than that, she was one hell of a picky eater.

'What gave you that stupid bloody idea?'

As this latest interrogation had obviously made her angry, I shrugged meekly and went back to my previous questions. 'What's a funnel directors for and what's snuff it mean?'

Mum threw the pink plastic spoon down on to the table with a sigh and shifted Shaz on to her other knee. She fixed me with an especially steely look until I was unable to return the glare. I bowed my head so that my chin touched my chest, despondently sticking my fingers into my cereal bowl.

'You always have to ask me questions, Caroline,' she said wearily. 'So many bloody questions, all the time.'

I was the only one of her offspring who she frequently referred to in a deliberately polysyllabic way, as if my full name had somehow become a curse, an impediment. All the others were granted punchy sobriquets, pet names: Kev, Shaz, Jo, Tel (Teresa automatically became 'Teri' within hours after her birth, and then simply 'Tel' not long after that), and mum referred to them by these affectionate abbreviations no matter how annoyed she was with them. At first I thought it was because I was special. 'Caroline' had an air of inscrutable nobility about it. It was a good name – you had to use lots of different sounds to say it. I liked it that way. But my mum often said it as if it was an insult.

'Sorry . . .' I muttered, swirling my hand about in the Ready Brek residue.

'Don't play with it, eat it,' she scolded, reaching over and slapping me on the wrist.

'Don't wanna.'

'Don't argue with Mummy, I'm not in the mood.' She finished her cigarette, grinding the stub into a tea-ringed saucer while struggling to keep a fidgety Shaz clutched on her lap. 'Right then,' Mum said, giving up her struggle and letting Shaz slither to the floor, where she soon consoled herself with a discarded cork from a wine bottle which, unlike the maligned semolina, was willingly placed straight from the unhoovered standard-issue council carpet into her mouth. Her three tiny teeth chomped down on it eagerly while she made ominous bubbling noises from the other end. Mum stood up and pulled her dressing gown tightly around her skinny body. 'Kev, put those cornflakes back in the box and get your bag. Caroline, can you . . . oh, shit . . . oh, for God's sake, look at the *state* of you! That dress was clean on today!'

She looked at me in dismay – buttons missing from my oversized, threadbare cardigan, brownish slop dribbled down the front of my school dress, odd socks (one black and ankle length, one white and knee length), plimsolls with holes (my only pair of shoes), matted hair and filthy face. She surveyed me for a long time, weighing up the best course of action. Eventually, she said, 'Go and get your other school dress out of the laundry bag.'

'Oh, but *Mummy* . . .'

'Look, I know it's too big and covered with pen but it's probably a better bet than that one. Take it off now. You're a bloody disgrace. Sometimes I wonder why I bother.'

'Bother with what?' I asked, dropping my cardigan to the floor and pulling the sullied dress over my head to reveal Kev's coveted Spiderman pants. Our grandmother had bought a novelty 'superheroes' briefs set from Woolworths for Kev's seventh birthday. The other two in the set were Batman and Superman, but the Spiderman pants were my favourite of the lot. Each pair had a special 'willy pouch' feature, which I found highly amusing as I had seen Kev's willy and it certainly wasn't big enough to warrant a pouch.

'Why are you wearing your brother's underpants?' Mum demanded, hands on hips now, something about her hesitant tone suggesting she didn't really want to know the answer.

I shrugged, twanging at the elastic. I liked the saggy bit at the front. Sometimes I wished that I had been born a boy. I didn't care much for the girlie pink-and-white frilly things with bows and rosebuds that I was supposed to wear. 'Couldn't find anything else.' I said. 'All dirty.'

Kev ceased his cornflake fusillade to decapitate my favourite (that is, my *only*) doll, hurling the crayon-defaced head at me with a disgruntled grunt.

'Anyway,' I said, 'I don't have to go to school just because *you* say so.'

'Really? Is that really what you think?' she challenged me, stepping closer, her intense brown eyes blazing beneath her heavy eyebrows.

I stamped my foot obstinately. 'I'm not going! And that's it!'

For a split second I thought she was going to hit me, but instead she turned away, muttered, 'Fine. Have it your way,' and bent down to pick Shaz up from the floor. Shaz was still trying to ingest the cork, but had also been taking an unhealthy interest in a nearby ashtray, overflowing with butts, ash, fluff and other miscellaneous detritus. Mum plonked Shaz in her pushchair and, despite a good deal of wriggling and clamorous objections on my recalcitrant baby sister's part, eventually managed to buckle her in, tightening the straps around her tiny, straining shoulders. Shaz screamed blue murder until her face went crimson.

'Hey, that's not fair!' Kev piped up, pulling his unironed shirt out of his regulation green shorts and grinding a scattered collection of cornflakes into the carpet with the heel of his shoe. 'If she's not going, I'm not going!'

'Shut your hole, Kev,' Mum snapped. 'Now listen, I'm going to have a shower and get dressed. If you two aren't ready for school in five minutes I'll fuckin' put the pair of you up for adoption.' And with that, she exited the room in a lingering waft of greasy hair, fatigue and cigarette smoke, slamming the door behind her. Kev and I blinked at each other, momentarily dumbstruck. Shaz's noise quietened down to a miserable snivel, but then she started up again, even louder. Still dressed only in mismatched socks, worn-out plimsolls and boys' pants, I walked over to her pushchair and tried to mollify her by rocking it backwards and forwards. It made absolutely no difference, and still she squawked at the top of her lungs, on and on, like a pressure cooker primed to explode. The sound went straight through me. It riled me that something so small and so pampered could make so much angry noise, so persistently – and for no obvious reason, either. I wished I was still a baby. Sometimes I got an overwhelming urge to pinch Shaz really hard, somewhere particularly soft and sensitive on her chubby pink body. Give her something *real* to cry about.

'Take them off,' Kev said finally, slamming his Action Man down and scowling at me. 'They ain't yours.'

'I'm keeping them on all day, and I'm gonna wee in them, too.'

'You ugly fat smelly bitch!' Kev exclaimed furiously, using the same standard insult he always used for anyone – male or female, fat or thin – who happened to be getting on his nerves. 'Give them back!'

'Too late. Finders keepers.'

He stomped towards me and lashed out, hitting me just below the ribs. I was slightly winded, but managed to kick him pretty hard where I knew it hurt most, and he doubled over in pain and sank to his knees. 'I hate you!' he cried, clutching at his groin.

I took advantage of his weakened state while I had the opportunity and stabbed the toe of my left plimsoll into the small of his back, exclaiming, 'Kiss my butt!' As derogatory remarks go, this was my personal favourite. I used it frequently and indiscriminately, not really knowing exactly *why* it was offensive, but well aware that it sounded pretty damn nasty and always had the desired effect. It's what the bad guys said to the cops in American movies, and most people seemed appropriately shocked and displeased when I used it against them, albeit screeched out in a five-year-old Essex-girl accent rather than a gun-toting drawl. I was yet to pluck up enough courage to say it to my crabby old schoolteacher, Miss Wibberley – but it was only a matter of time. We had a mutual dislike and mistrust of each other that had been brewing ever since my very first day at Willow Lane Primary the previous September. She wore scary glasses that made her eyes look like an alien's. And she had really big nostrils. Really, *unnaturally* big nostrils. And they flared out – billowed – when she got angry, which was nearly all the time. I *longed* to tell Miss Wibberley to kiss my butt. (Not that I'd want her horrible, snaky lips anywhere near my peachies; just for the perverse pleasure I'd get in seeing those capacious nostrils in full flaring mode and those alien eyes bulge out with impotent fury.)

Kev got to his feet and punched me in the face, then grabbed my arm and gave me a Chinese burn, maliciously twisting the tender flesh above my wrist until it turned bright red. I yelped in pain, wildly yanking at fistfuls of his hair and scratching his face, but he pulled me to the floor and overpowered me, landing a rapid succession of random slaps and punches over my head and upper body. Eventually, my flailing fist caught him in the eye and he rolled away and searched the floor for a suitable missile to hurl at me. He made do with an old hardback copy of *Grimm's Fairy Tales*, which caught me on the back of the head with a considerable 'clunk' sound. I seized my breakfast bowl from the table behind me and sent it flying Frisbee-style in the direction of my brother's head. Milky slop flew onto the walls and spattered the carpet as the little plastic bowl went spinning in the air, finally rebounding off Kev's sneering face before hitting the floor. Kev's once-white shirt was now decorated in a similar style to my school dress, and I watched in excited horror as his expression became twisted with a renewed surge of animosity.

'Mum's gonna kill you!' he whooped, lunging at me again.

I don't know the exact point at which Mum walked in on our fight, but Kev had straddled and immobilised my upper body and was pelting me repeatedly with Lego bricks of various sizes when I heard her voice from above.

'Get off your sister NOW, KEVIN!'

His head whipped around and at once his look of blazing hatred transformed into one of wounded inculpability and little-boy-lost sullenness. 'But muu-uummee, she started –'

'Fuckin' NOW, Kev!'

He scrambled to his feet while I stayed sprawled upon the carpet, exaggerating the extent of my injuries with whimpers and moans. Mum was standing at the doorway in her bathrobe with a greyish towel wrapped around her head like a turban and a very displeased look on her face.

'Get up, Caroline.'

'He hit me, Mummy, it hurts . . .'

'Get up.'

'But Muu-uummmeee . . .'

'Get the FUCK up, NOW!'

I got up, suddenly feeling self-conscious about my semi-nakedness and ashamed that I had let Kev's bullying get the better of me. It was a common situation, in which I had to look like the innocent party while at the same time not permitting Kev the upper hand. Mum's shouting competed with the wavering caterwaul of Shaz's wailing, so the room became filled with highly charged and voluminous expletives as my brother and I received a furious tongue-lashing.

'She wouldn't take my Spiderman pants off,' Kev whined, once mum had paused for breath. 'She said she was going to wee in them.'

Mum responded to Kev's defence argument by giving him a short, sharp clip around the ear and a gruff 'Shut it.' Kev was rendered silent and fought against tears while I smirked at him, delighting in his discomfort and doing my utmost to make it worse. Mum saw my smirk and slapped me harder, striking the back of my head just where *Grimm's Fairy Tales* had already caused a slight bump. 'And you can wipe that bloody look off your face,' she barked.

Jutting out my wobbling lower lip and feeling the onset of a snot avalanche, I looked down at my feet so nobody could see the spontaneous tears well and overspill in my eyes.

'Kev, tuck your shirt back in and get your lunchbox from the kitchen.'

Kev obeyed, not forgetting to give me a hostile glare as he tramped past. '*She* started it,' he muttered, still trying in vain to win Mum over. Mum ignored him and turned to me. I felt like running to the corner of the room and curling up into a little ball, magicking myself away to my special faraway fantasy land where there was no school, no horrible teachers, no disgusting brothers and sisters, no grouchy mummies. A place where all the sweets and toys were free and my dolls could speak to me. A place where I would be allowed to wear boys' pants every day if I wanted to.

But it was no time for fantasy land. My mother's temper was a facet of my reality that I sometimes couldn't even hope to avoid or escape. She grabbed my shoulder and bellowed, 'I've just about had it up to here with you, Caroline.'

'Ow! Up to where, Mummy?'

'Shut up! For Christ's sake just SHUT UP, will you?' Still holding my shoulder in a vice-like grip, she marched me to the bathroom, still steamy and sickly-sweet smelling from her shower. She rubbed a rough, damp flannel over my face and, pointedly ignoring my snivelling protests, found an old nit comb in the cabinet and tried, unsuccessfully, to tug it through my hair. 'God! You're such a bloody mess,' she huffed, irritably snapping the metal teeth through my disaster of split ends. 'Why can't you at least try to look like a good little girl? Even if you can't act like one.'

'That hurts, Mummy . . .'

'Look at me,' she said, pulling me towards her and staring into my face. Her eyes were still darkly flashing with rage. 'Do I look as if I care?'

'I don't want you to comb my hair . . .' I whimpered. 'I like it how it is . . .'

'So you want to go to school looking like a scarecrow?'

I didn't, of course, but I nodded defiantly anyway, squeaking the sole of my plimsoll across the tacky linoleum floor and not moving my eyes away from my rubber duck, which was sitting on the bath rack a few feet away, atop a blue sponge.

'Fine,' she said. ('Fine' was one of her most overused words, but she would draw out the 'f' because she really wanted to say 'fuck'.) 'I'll get your other school dress. Don't you dare move.' She plonked me on the edge of the bath, put the nit comb back in the cabinet, and hurried next door to her bedroom. The entire flat seemed to reverberate when she banged the door behind her this time. I stayed sitting there, looking around our dismal bathroom. The bath was very small, very stained and avocado-green. When I swung my legs, the back of my feet made a hollow, drumming sound against the side. If I were to topple backwards, I would crack my head on the wall tiles behind me, with their grubby grouting and chipped borders. The toilet was an off-white colour and had a turquoise pedestal mat at the base and a fluffy seat cover in conspicuously uncoordinating peach. A novelty toilet roll holder knitted by my granny sat proudly on top of the cistern, but it would be some years before I realised just how tasteless, pointless and grotesque this was. The sink did match the bath, at least, except it wasn't quite so stained and one of the mildewed taps was bronze-coloured instead of chrome. The plug was attached by a rusty chain, and old soap smears in pink and cream skid-marked the enamel surface. I leaned over, turned the cold tap and watched the water sputter out. I thought about brushing my teeth, but even if I had stood on the edge of the bath and stretched up I still wouldn't have been able to reach the bathroom cabinet, where the toothpaste was usually stored. My eyes roamed towards the wicker bin. Mum's pregnancy-test box was still in there, as was the white stick with its two terrible pink eyes.

I jumped down and clambered on top of the closed toilet seat. By standing on tiptoe and craning my neck I could just about see out of the small square of the bathroom window above, although there was never very much to look at beyond the semi-translucent glass. It had a pull-down blind, covered with a thick layer of dust, and the top section had a piece of cardboard tacked to the frame and the lower pane by several ripped lengths of brown masking tape. It was impossible to open the window more than a couple of inches because the hinges were jammed. On this day I did manage to glimpse something out of the window, though. At the top of the old oak tree on the other side of the road, two magpies circled each other before settling together on the highest branch. It made me remember the rhyme Miss Wibberley had taught us in class the week before: 'One for sorrow, two for joy, three for a girl, four for a boy . . .' I sang it to myself under my breath and wondered what it meant. Somehow it seemed even more ridiculous and meaningless than rhymes such as 'Little Boy Blue' and 'Hickory Dickory Dock'.

'Get down from there and put this on.'

Mum hurled my school dress to the floor, interrupting my tuneless rhyme. She had thrown on some old clothes, obviously in haste (pale-blue jogging pants with scuffed flat-soled evening shoes, and a dirty white vest with no bra underneath), and her hair tumbled in messy wet tendrils around her shoulders.

'Magpies, Mummy,' I said, pointing at the window. 'Two for joy.'

She made a strange noise and rolled her mascara-clogged eyes. 'Do me a favour!'

'No, *really* . . .' I insisted, still standing on the toilet seat with my back to her and making desultory butterfly shapes with my hands for no apparent reason. 'We were taught that at school so it must be true. One for sorrow, two for joy, three for a girl, four . . .'

'Did they also teach you that little girls who disobey their mothers will be locked in their rooms all day with nothing to eat?' She stepped in front of the cracked mirror on the left wall (it had been put up a little too high in order to conceal a particularly unsightly and stubborn damp stain, so even my mum, at five foot six, had to wear high heels in order to get a good head-and-shoulders view of herself), and pondered her reflection sombrely for a few moments. She applied a layer of dark-red lipstick, which only made her look even more washed out. She sighed and pushed her hair away from her face, then changed her mind and let it hang back down. I hopped down to the floor and put the grubby green-and-white uniform over my head, slipping my skinny arms through the roomy cap sleeves and smoothing the checked polyester down over my knees, where the hem should have ended. Instead the length fell to just a few inches above my ankles, and the stitching at the hem was coming away, frayed and tattered. The dress was obscenely creased, more than a little malodorous and stained with random red and black ink, mostly on the narrow white collar. Still, my mother had been right – it was a better bet than my other dress, probably. Just about.

'Mummy . . . ?'

'What?'

'Are you still going to put us up for adoption?'

'Don't be stupid. Do up your buttons and smarten yourself up.'

'If you are, can you make sure I go somewhere different from Kev? I really hate him.'

'Whatever.'

'Please, Mummy, I don't want another brother.'

She shot me a stern look. 'We can't always get what we want,' she muttered, drawing me towards her and yanking my hair into a stubby, messy little ponytail, securing it roughly with green elastic. The rings on her fingers kept knocking the bruise on the back of my head, but I didn't say anything. 'There,' she said. 'That will have to do.'

She regarded me with narrowed eyes. 'You know, you could be such a beautiful little girl, Caroline,' she murmured in a wistful tone, patting the top of my head and offering me a momentary smile of sad affection. Even at that young age I knew that this would be as close to a compliment as I was likely to get from her.

Kev called out from the lounge: 'Hurry *up* for God's sake, I've been ready for *ages*.'

Mum's smile swiftly disappeared as she took my hand and marched me out of the bathroom and back into the littered lounge.

'Shit! *Shit!*' she hissed, 'It's already nine, I'm going to get yet another whinging fuckin' letter from your crappy bloody school at this rate. Thank God it's your last day, I've had enough of going through this shit every bloody morning.' She blustered about, gathering up various items from the floor and searching for a relatively hygienic dummy to plug up Shaz's (still screeching) mouth. 'Fuck 'em, that lot should try living with you three little brats just for one day, see how well *they* cope with it.' She unearthed a suitable dummy from beneath a sizeable mound of assorted Mothercare paraphernalia, dipped the rubber teat in a jar of clear honey then bunged it forcibly in Shaz's mouth. The silence was instantaneous. Nothing was guaranteed to pacify my little sister more than a honey-soaked dummy.

'Miss Wibberley has twenty-one children to look after at school,' I piped up. 'And most of them are even worse than me!' Then, upon seeing Mum's stony expression, I added, 'But she's old and mean and not nearly as pretty as you, Mummy.'

'Nice try. Open the front door, Kev,' Mum replied tersely, retrieving my cardigan from the floor and throwing it at me. 'Caroline, help me with the pushchair down the stairs will you, love?' Every now and then I would be granted a small expression of fondness – 'sweetie', 'love', sometimes even 'darling', and the novelty of the endearment would shock me into automatic obedience.

As was the usual ritual, we struggled out of the front door, the cumbersome and antiquated buggy rattling about awkwardly as its wheels became stuck and unstuck, creaking off every which way like a wayward shopping trolley. My mother always acted as if she had no patience left at all, but manoeuvring that accursed child-filled contraption for distances of up to five miles every day would be a test of anyone's endurance. Plus of course she had seven flights of steps to negotiate every time she wanted to leave the flat. Arcadian House did have a lift, but even when it worked, it was heady with the stench of a public urinal, and it wouldn't be uncommon to find used needles and certain other unsavoury detritus scattered about with carefree abandon by some of our more antisocial neighbours.

Somebody once got fatally stabbed in that stinky, sinister lift back in December 1973, just a few months before Mum first moved in to the flat. And thus began the Legend of the Arcadian Ghost, the anguished, restless spirit of this poor unfortunate soul who haunted the lift day and night, eternally pissed off that he had lost his life over nothing more than a twenty-quid debt and an unintentionally fruitful fumble with the bumptious wife of a deranged skinhead. The stair option was therefore the best option, indeed the only option for the faint-hearted or those remotely concerned with self-preservation. I have always had a morbid fear of lifts, and there is little doubt that the Arcadian lift, that clunking metal death trap with its vengeful, ghoulish inhabitant, is the one and only source of this profound phobia.

During the brisk ten-minute walk to school, Mum resolutely wheeled Shaz through the uneven pavements of broken glass and splattered dog mess, looking straight ahead and quickening her step at every corner, so Kev and I had to trot alongside to keep up with her.

'Hey! Ellie!' The loud, shrill voice of a breathless man cried out behind us, and Mum slowed slightly without stopping or looking around. 'Hold up there, love! Me an' the little 'un can't keep up with your lot!'

The voice was, unmistakably, that of Big Gay Gordon, a very amiable and mild-mannered middle-aged man who lived in one of the flats above us. He was dressed crazy-casual as usual (orange flip-flops, purple shorts, a knitted tank top offset by a short-sleeved Hawaiian-style shirt, with the whole ensemble topped off by a beige sun hat), dragging his daughter Amber along by the hand. She smiled at me shyly as they approached, twisting one of her beaded plaits around her fingers. Amber was in my class at school. I liked her because she had better toys than me (most of them being still in one piece at least) and a bedroom all of her own, she never spoke very much and she didn't mind when I bossed her about. In short, The Perfect Friend.

'Gawd almighty Ellie, what do you put in your cereal, love? Whatever it is, I need some!' Gordon, a chronic asthmatic and year-round hayfever sufferer with a hole in his heart and only one fully functioning lung, puffed and wheezed painfully into an inhaler. Mum stopped for a few seconds while he tried to get his breath back. 'Still, lovely weather,' he panted eventually, somewhat extraneously, raising his bloodshot eyes to the crystalline blue sky.

Mum sighed and shook her head then pushed onwards, saying, 'We're late as usual,' as if it were an excuse to move on ahead without the need for further pleasantries. Gordon was bent over in exhaustion with his hands clutching his knees and his head bowed, still gasping for air. Kev and me were supposed to call him 'Uncle Gordon', but I had heard mum call him Big Gay Gordon in private to her fellow chain-smoking, estate-lurking friends and I also knew she didn't want me to know that she called him that. Childhood ammunition comes in many forms.

'Maybe we should wait for Big Gay Gordon,' I said, tugging at Mum's jogging pants, wearying of her long, brisk strides. 'I want to walk with Amber, Mummy.'

'Don't call Uncle Gordon that,' she said, with a shifty sideways glance. 'It's not nice.'

'But you –'

'Just . . . keep it buttoned, young lady, all right?' She upped tempo again, and muttered over her shoulder, 'Walk with 'em if you want, it makes no difference to me. But you was supposed to be at school twenty minutes ago so you're only gonna be wastin' even more time.'

This didn't bother me in the slightest and so I lagged behind, watching Mum's busy rear end vanish around the next corner with Kev practically cantering now to keep pace with her, his tatty shoelaces trailing behind him.

'Now then! *There's* a little lady not to be messed with,' Gordon grinned, almost admiringly, once he and Amber had caught up with me.

I took his free hand in mine and said, 'Don't worry about her, Uncle Gordon. She's having another baby.'

He seemed to relapse into another asthma attack at hearing this. 'You're pullin' me chain, Miss Caroline!' he cried, clutching dramatically at his chest as if the news was a shocking revelation. I didn't think it was shocking at all. Just a bit annoying, really. My mum was a woman and women had babies; it was a perfectly normal and natural state of affairs. Grass was green, sky was blue, mums kept having babies until they got too old to have any more. I was aware that a man of some description was often necessary somewhere along the line, but obviously I was yet to discover the grisly details of their involvement in the whole process. I smiled up at Gordon's big red face and giggled. I liked the way he called me 'Miss Caroline' – it made me feel like one of the delicately girlish, well-to-do characters out of *Huckleberry Finn*.

'It's true,' I said smugly, proud of my elementary detective work.

'Well,' he exhaled noisily, running the back of his hand across his shiny forehead, 'I have to say, your mum's one helluva woman.'

The three of us dawdled along, hand in hand, only breaking the chain when we encountered a narrow stretch of pavement or an inconsiderately erected lamp post or bollard. There was something really special about my friend Amber. Every now and then I'd look over at her and feel a deep pang of affection and awe: those gorgeous fuzzy plaits down her back, the wonderful whiteness of her teeth, the fullness of her lips, the broad, blunt shape of her nose. Amber was exotic and diffident and breathtakingly beautiful. And Amber was special because she had *two* parents. *And* both her parents were daddies. Gordon had been living with a gaunt and fashionably dishevelled freelance photographer called Patrick ever since Amber was a tiny baby. As far as I could tell, Amber didn't have a mummy. But even that fact alone wasn't why Amber was so special. Gordon and Patrick were both white and Amber was black. Not just tanned or brown or cocoa-black, like the Husseins and the Shaheeds and the Bensons and the Dhaliwals. Amber was ebony black. Shoe-shine black. ('As black as the night!' my grandmother would say.) With fabulous Afro hair tamed into hundreds of trailing braids. Even though I had a tendency to be intrusively nosy and outrageously rude, I had never dared ask how it came to pass that two white, funny-looking men had managed to produce a striking, dark-skinned girl. Never mind the biology of the thing. Gordon had apparently once been married to someone from a faraway country I had never heard of, but for reasons shrouded in secrecy (to me at least), it 'hadn't quite worked out', and I was unable to glean further details of Amber's heritage. But I openly envied Amber's alternative family. It must have been cool to have two daddies. Especially such caring, silly, funny daddies. Gordon and Patrick both doted on her and, for an estate kid, she was pretty spoiled. For a start, she had three brand-new dolls and one of them was a Barbie. I had just one very old and ugly doll that I had named 'Patsy' and, thanks to Kev, she was now headless. I suppose I did have another doll, but that was nothing more than a cloth beanbag with sewn-on eyes, a toggle button for a nose and orange wool glued on for hair.

'Hey look, you two! A magpie!' Gordon exclaimed suddenly, releasing my hand and pointing ahead. 'I can't remember if that's supposed to be lucky or not.'

We watched the bird hop audaciously in front of us and peck at something on the pavement before flapping out of sight.

'It's one for sorrow,' I noted despondently, turning my head to watch it disappear over a distant roof. I desperately scanned the sky to seek out its airborne mate, but only spied a couple of wood pigeons on a nearby fence and a cluster of starlings and sparrows twittering on a bird table in a front garden as we passed by.

'Is that right? Well, we'll just have to look out for another one then.' Gordon squeezed my hand reassuringly and started whistling the theme tune to a kid's programme that I recognised but couldn't quite place. Mum had only recently acquired a television set, thanks to an ominous favour she was owed by someone from the third floor who worked in 'removals'. It was black and white and the picture flickered and fuzzed and most of the controls were missing or didn't work properly, but it was just about better than nothing and had quickly become the main (or only) source of communal entertainment in our flat. I had spent the last few weeks familiarising myself with all the best shows, which naturally provided me with another interminable topic of conversation at school. I was unable to say with any certainty what colours Big Bird and the Cookie Monster were, but then that didn't really matter – it was all so exciting and *educational.* And, as much as I hated school, learning new things never failed to excite me. Whether it was Miss Wibberley standing at the blackboard trying in vain to instil the relatively tedious principles of basic addition, subtraction and multiplication, or Oscar the Grouch in his trash can telling us how useful the letters 'F' and 'O' are. *Sesame Street* was just the best, but mum said it gave her a headache.

'Magpies are the thieving birds, aren't they?' Gordon mused, half to himself. Amber and I stared at him vacantly. 'Yes. They like to take trinkets,' he went on. 'They're attracted to bright, sparkly things. If they see something they like, they will nick it. They like to fill their nests with them, you see. Not unlike some of the characters around here, I might add.'

'Oh,' I said, thinking Gordon had probably gone a little bit mad.

I fell into uncharacteristic silence until we finally arrived at the school gate a few minutes later. By that time I had assured myself that I wouldn't be breaking any rules if I added the one 'rogue' magpie to the two I had previously sighted, effectively sacrificing my joy to avoid sorrow. This, I concluded with irrefutable logic, meant that Mum's next baby would most definitely be a girl.

I remember racing across the school playground that afternoon, out of the gates, swinging my plastic lunchbox by its yellow handle, with Amber and Katie (another estate mate, from another block) scampering along beside me. It was the end of July but the day was overcast and unpleasantly sticky and the sun had been struggling since early morning to penetrate stubborn layers of thick cloud. The typically British summer weather did not affect my euphoric mood, however. One year at Willow Lane Primary had convinced me that school was essentially nothing more than a child's prison, a sinister building filled with stern grown-ups called teachers who got cross if you didn't behave right or learn the stuff they told you to remember. After three long terms broken up by two short holidays with two even shorter half-term breaks in between, we had finally been awarded a 'Get out of jail free' card. For six whole weeks!

'Race you to that tree!' I screeched, once the lollipop lady had helped us across the main road, making sure I was a good distance ahead.

'Not fair!' Katie whined, trying to catch me up and tripping over her own feet in her haste. Katie got nits even more often than I did and she was even clumsier than I was – and that's saying something. I looked behind me just in time to see her go flying across the pavement and, as she crash-landed hard onto the rough concrete, I ran smack into the tree, knocking my shoulder and the side of my head, the impact propelling me backwards with a great and sudden force. I lost my balance and fell on my backside with a bump, and my lunchbox went hurtling behind me and clattered onto the road. Amber stopped and stood over us and did not laugh at the sight of her two friends helplessly dazed and sprawled, which is what I would probably have done if I had been her. In fact, she looked as if she was about to cry.

Katie picked herself up quickly and brushed herself off, smiling through her tears. I felt like a cartoon character who had just been struck with a heavy object, and could almost literally see the stars whirling around my head. I hoped I wouldn't get one of those big, instantly protruding bumps, like the calamitous cartoon characters always got when they collided headlong into something – poor old Tom, Sylvester, Elmer Fudd, Daffy Duck, Wile E. Coyote and their lot. I still bore the various minor wounds from my squabble with Kev earlier that day – a crimson scar here, a yellow bruise there. If I was a cartoon character I would be called Caz the Klutz. Or Blunder Girl! Me and Amber would have made a great cartoon double act; she would be the wise one, I would be the one getting us into trouble all the time. Like Laurel and Hardy.

'You OK, Caro?' Amber asked, after I had failed to get up after a few moments. She retrieved my battered old lunchbox and handed it to me, anxiously glancing at my head for signs of obvious damage.

'Bit dizzy,' I muttered, struggling to my feet and clutching my sore shoulder. 'You OK, Katie?'

Katie was so funny and sweet. She could have had a show all of her own. She was like Mr Magoo and Scooby Doo rolled together. Her eyesight had been really bad ever since she was born, but she refused to wear her glasses unless it was absolutely necessary, because she hated them. They were, admittedly, very ugly glasses, with thick translucent blue frames, and sometimes she had to have a plaster stuck over one of the lenses, for reasons I could only guess and didn't want to ask about for fear of upsetting her. The plasters made her look even funnier, and the boys would laugh and laugh and she would cry and run away to hide in the toilets. Once she got so upset and angry she threw her glasses to the ground and stamped on them, and wouldn't stop stamping and hollering until Miss Wibberley physically restrained her. I hoped that I would never need glasses, because I knew that my mum, like Katie's mum, would only be able to afford those horrible NHS ones, and wearing those would ruin my chances of ever being taken seriously. I had enough trouble as it was, having been cursed with two left feet and a tendency towards habitual haplessness.

'I'm OK.' Katie tried to focus on me, but her eyes were rolling all over the place. Katie went cross-eyed whenever she was excited or scared. Sometimes she even went cross-eyed for no apparent reason. It was often difficult to work out whether or not she was actually looking at you. I couldn't help smiling at her as she hobbled towards me, biting her lip through her pain. Katie looked like she was probably a bit of a wimp and a crybaby, but she was a tough cookie underneath her awkward, gangly, bespectacled exterior. I was very fond of her, and felt a bit sorry for her, too. Even at that young age, the prettiest always got away with more, and poor Katie was not, alas, a pretty girl.

'You're bleeding,' Amber said, pointing at Katie's cut knees.

'Oh well,' she shrugged, looking down and letting out a little sigh. 'Anyone got a tissue?' The blood was trickling into the tops of her white socks, and there were pieces of grit embedded in the palms of her hands.

'I've got my old hanky,' Amber offered, holding out the limp rag. It used to be her 'security hanky', and she would scrunch it up in her fist and suck her thumb, twirling her hair dozily with her other hand. It was her way of relaxing, of feeling safe and content. Nowadays she rarely sucked her thumb though, and the hanky was used mainly for leaking noses and mopping up the bloodied knees of oafish friends. (Amber never hurt herself, she was far too sensible and agile for that.)

'Thanks.' Katie dabbed at the cuts, which weren't so bad after all, and we continued walking homeward, more slowly now, like shambling old women. Amber went in the middle and put her arms around our shoulders, helping the pair of us limp along. My head and shoulder were still hurting, and I was feeling a little disoriented and dizzy, but I talked and talked endlessly about nothing in particular, in an unconvincing attempt to disguise my delicate state and stop myself from sobbing.

We arrived at the estate with only a few further diversions on the way: another little trip from Katie on a loose paving stone, and my insistence that we cross the road to stroke a timid-looking tabby cat. Katie lived in one of the modern blocks on the estate: one of three practically brand-new, low-rise, redbrick buildings with flower-filled balconies and clean staircases. Compared to Arcadian House, it was positively luxurious. Amber and I stood and watched as Katie hobbled through the front entrance and waved at us before going up the stairs to her first floor flat, where no doubt her mum would be waiting with a vat of warmed Alphabetti Spaghetti and a rack of slightly stale, thinly sliced white toast: the standard post-school teatime snack, often complemented with a jug of tepid Kia-Ora and a digestive biscuit.

'Are you going on holiday?' Amber asked, taking my arm as we continued past the rows of sixties terraces and maisonettes towards the main central pentangle of council-flat blocks.

'I don't know,' I said, kicking a stone at a burnt-out car. It spun off the blackened bonnet and back onto the pavement by my feet and I kicked it again, harder. 'Mummy said we might go to Liverpool and stay at my granny's house.' I watched the stone roll away down the gutter and disappear into a drain with a final little skitter.

'Oh.' She was silent for a while, and looked down at her feet as she scuffled along. 'Daddy and Patrick said we might go to Hastings,' she said eventually. 'Just for a week or something.'

'Where's that?'

She shrugged. 'They said it's like Southend except better. There's a beach there and stuff. Even donkey rides too. We're going in Patrick's car, but we have to wait until Daddy's hay fever gets better. He's sneezing all the time and his eyes go puffy and red like he's been crying.'

A thought occurred to me. 'Can I use your bike while you're away?'

'What's wrong with your bike?'

'It's not really mine. Mummy told Kev he should share it with me but he hits me if he catches me riding it.'

'Your brother's mean.'

'I know. He's had the stabilisers removed as well now, because he knows I can't ride a bike without stabilisers.'

'He's mean,' Amber reiterated, fingering her plaits. She glanced over at me. 'Hey, shall we take my bike to the park later? It won't be properly dark for ages so Daddy won't mind.'

'Daddy won't mind what?' Gordon's voice boomed behind us. We jumped in fright and turned around. Gordon grabbed us by the shoulders and pulled us towards him.

'I've been looking all over for you two cheeky little scamps,' he scolded, although there was very little anger in his voice. I had never known Gordon to get angry, not *properly* mad, like Mummy sometimes did. The nearest he came to it was vaguely miffed. 'I thought you said you were going to wait at the school gate for me to pick you up.'

'Sorry Daddy . . .'

'It's OK, Uncle Gordon,' I piped up, quick to defend my friend (who was incapable of defending herself). 'Me and Amber and Katie are big enough to walk home by ourselves now, it's not far. The lollipop lady helps us across the main road and we know not to speak to strange men unless we know them.'

He gave me a curious look. 'What happened to your head?'

I gingerly put my hand up to the side of my head. There was a tender bump just above my right eye and I winced when my fingers touched it. 'Oh,' I said, feeling small and silly. 'I ran into a tree.'

'Did you, now?'

'Yeah . . . it's nothing, really . . . it doesn't hurt or anything.'

He shook his head and ruffled my hair. 'What are we going to do with you, young lady? Go home and clean yourself up, it's a wonder you don't drive your poor mother sick with worry.' Turning to Amber, he said, 'Come on, you, tea's ready soon. Bangers and mash, your favourite. Say goodbye to Caroline.'

Amber sighed and pouted, but dutifully reached up to grip Gordon's outstretched hand, giving me an apologetic stare through her long, feathery lashes. 'See you,' she mumbled.

'What about our bike ride?' I protested.

'Not today, love,' Gordon said. 'Maybe tomorrow.'

'But . . . but . . .'

'Sorry, love.'

'Yeah, sorry Caro. Maybe tomorrow.' They turned, both of them offering me the same humble little smile over their shoulders as they walked towards the entrance of Arcadian. This strange way they both had of smiling – a deliberately appeasing but indubitably sincere and sweet smile – was the only outward hint that Gordon and Amber might possibly, by some amazing and freakish twist of nature, be related to each other. They did share certain mannerisms, but the similarities were so subtle as to be barely perceptible. They trudged up the steps and pushed the heavy front door, which slowly swung shut with its usual heavy creak and click once they had disappeared inside.

I didn't want to follow them inside; I didn't want to go home. There was something depressingly unhomely about home, dismal Arcadian with its ugly rainbow of graffiti-sprayed gibberish and expletives all over the internal and external walls. There was nothing comforting about the home comforts that awaited me up there in the cheerless little place on the seventh floor of that menacing grey tower block. A dirty little box of a kitchen with a noisy and bereft fridge breeding mould and an oven that was black with accumulated grime; tacky cabinets with no doors and stacked-up tins of unpalatable gunk. A room called a lounge or a 'living' room where the television sat on its flimsy cardboard pedestal spewing out its daily anaesthetic. The single bedroom with old pine bunk beds (Kev top, me bottom) and no curtains at the draughty window, original flock wallpaper that peeled in broad, curling strips along the damp brown walls. The nocturnal, wild-eyed couple in the flat next door who beat each other up, their screams and body blows amplified through the paper-thin walls from midnight till morning. Such things were commonplace in our block. Fights and sirens, drug raids, incontinent drunkards hanging off the stairwells after kicking-out time, irate husbands locked out by their wives for spending all day and every penny of their benefits down at the pub, closed doors kicked in, open doors slammed from their hinges, children abused and neglected, vandals and opportunists loitering around every corner. It was not a place for the faint-hearted.

After serving us up a quick, simple supper and putting Shaz to bed, my mum would start getting weird with a bottle of stuff called brandy or gin that smelt like paintbrush cleaner. This was a ritual, every day. Weekends and holidays were worst because she had to look after all of us all day long and couldn't deal with it, so she would often start getting weird with the brandy or gin as soon as she woke up, she said it was 'her way of getting through the day'. I told myself I didn't mind, that I loved her no matter what, and I knew she loved me back despite some of the things she did and said, or more to the point the things she failed to do and say. I just wished she would stop having babies.

Mum only had a limited amount of love and care to give out, and the more offspring she brought into the world, into *our* little world, the more thinly this limited maternal devotion had to be spread. But every time she met a new man she thought it was a new chance for real love, and having his baby was her simple way of proving that, of earning his respect. She couldn't see that she had it all the wrong way around. Even at the tender age of five, I had learned well from my mum's mistakes, and I was steadfastly resolved: I was never, ever going to love or even kiss a man and no man was ever going to persuade me to have his babies, that was for definite. I was pretty sure that Mum *did* love her kids, even me, but we must have been a constant reminder of the mistakes, of the bad men. Every one of them had turned out to be unsuitable and unsavoury, and it wasn't really my mum's fault, and it wasn't from lack of trying on her part. I misbehaved just for attention of course, like all children do, because even a slapped bottom or temporary food deprivation or a screamed admonition was better than a wall of apathy. *Anything* was better than nothing, surely.

There was a distant rumble from above and the sky suddenly spiralled and seethed into a clamouring arc of blackness, smothering all traces of fading light. The storm that had been threatening all day was finally starting up.

An idea came to me as lightning flashed in a livid, shocking strobe across the sky. I'd go on a bike ride on my own. All by myself. And I was going to take Kev's bike, even without the stabilisers, even in this weather, and ride it all around the estate without falling off once. Yes. That's what I was going to do.

They would all be up there now, Kev probably watching *Crackerjack*, Shaz making noises and smells in her high chair. Meanwhile Mum would be bashing pans and cans and spoons about in the kitchen, taking the drink slowly one sip at a time at first and then gulping it down later on until practically the whole bottle was gone. I used to ask her if I could try some but she said it was special lemonade for mummies only and I'd have to make do with milk or squash. Then I would catch a whiff of it on her breath and be glad I hadn't drunk any. The smell made me gag, made my eyes water. She would drink most of it after we'd all gone to bed, and sometimes in the middle of the night I would feel too scared to get up to go to the toilet just in case she heard me and made me sit on her bed in the dark while she talked to me in a strange voice about things I didn't understand. I knew she was still my mummy but it was like looking into the eyes of a possessed stranger, some kind of a monster, when she was like that. Most of the time it would knock her out though, and she would oversleep in the morning so we'd have to go to school without breakfast, and with our uniforms inside out and back to front, labels sticking out and jam smeared everywhere. Those mornings she would be very grumpy and wouldn't say a word to us unless it was to tell us off.

The rain started coming down, initially just the odd stinging wet strand that caught the end of my nose or the back of my neck with a cold tingle. Then, with the next crack of thunder, the raindrops got fatter and harder until finally the slate sky split wide open and the faintly metallic smell of precipitation filled the air. I loved that smell. I loved thunderstorms. And even though after a moment or two it was pouring down on me, plastering my hair to my cheeks and sticking the thin synthetic fabric of my dress to my cold, prickly skin in widening wet patches, I was still determined to go on a bike ride. Just to the other end of the estate and back. Or maybe as far as Bluestone Rise, where all the council houses were much nicer and the road curved around at the top and I could race back down the hill at great speed without even pedalling. I'd be OK. It was still too early for the weirdos, they weren't usually hanging about until long after my bedtime. It was quite dark already because of the storm, but I wasn't afraid of the dark anyway. There wasn't much I was afraid of. I tilted my head backwards to taste the rain on my tongue, letting it drench my face. I felt like a wilting flower that was finally being watered. The torrential downpour, the menacing fury of the storm and the sudden inky blackness of the sky instilled a peculiar sense of passionate excitement in me.

As the rain continued hammering down, I wondered what it might feel like to be struck by lightning: would it hurt or would I make a funny noise and jump up in the air with white fuzzy sparks all around, like in the cartoons when they messed around with electric sockets? Would I die with a silly look on my face, my mouth in a permanent 'O' of surprise? Miss Wibberley had warned me that if you were wet in a thunderstorm you would die instantly in a frazzle if you got struck by lightning, so you should remember to wear rubber wellies and stand under a tree and hope the storm passes. If the tree you are standing under gets hit, you are very unlucky because that's your lot. She then hastily reassured us that the chances of getting hit by lightning were about the same as seeing a dodo in a poncho riding a scooter, so we needn't worry. Miss Wibberley came out with some silly things sometimes. I often wondered if she was quite right in the head.

The thunder rolled on and I stayed standing outside Arcadian with my face turned upwards, enjoying the deluge and not really worried about getting struck by lightning. This was the first evening of my first summer holiday and I had every intention of getting saturated, and if the lightning was going to hit me, it might as well give me its best shot. After a couple of minutes, I braced myself and went inside to get the bike.

Kev kept his bike in a communal storage cupboard on the ground floor of Arcadian, and nobody stored anything in there that was worth nicking: Kev's ancient old Raleigh Junior bike was quite safe among the accumulated junk. It had been passed down as a gift from my mum's friend for Kev's fifth birthday, and she had purchased the bike second-hand for her own son before I was even born, indeed before I was so much as a glint in Big Brian's shifty eye. It was therefore very old indeed, practically obsolete really, but Kev wasn't allowed a shiny new one until he was eight, and that wouldn't be for ages. It used to be blue, but the metallic paint had nearly all chipped away to brown rust and it made a clanking noise every time the wheels turned. I scrabbled around inside the cupboard, clawing through cobwebs and tripping over dilapidated prams, broken cribs, three-legged chairs, cardboard boxes filled with assorted bric-a-brac, the odd obsolete ironing board, upright vacuum cleaner and sewing machine, plastic bags of musty-smelling books, tins of old paint.

The bike was in its usual place, propped up in the corner, only marginally less rickety and defunct than the rest of the collection of bicycles and tricycles and plastic kiddies' pushcarts. Not without some effort, I wrenched the bike out of its resting place and wheeled it back outside, tentatively testing the bell and the brakes. The bell made a strained and rather pathetic tinkling sound when I pushed the lever with my thumb and the brakes squeaked painfully, but it was nevertheless roadworthy – just about. At first, I didn't feel brave enough actually to get on the bike, so I just pushed it about, up and down the road outside Arcadian. I had once tried riding a bike without stabilisers and ended up with all manner of minor injuries. Kev fancied himself as a bit of a cycling expert and he could even do tricks now, like riding with one wheel and spinning about and flying off slopes. He sometimes fell off, but he rarely caused any severe damage, much to my annoyance.

The rain eased slightly and I splashed the bike through the puddles, soaking my socks as I stamped about, kicking up dirty water and squelching through the whisked-up mud in my squidgy plimsolls. Just when I thought I couldn't possibly get any wetter, a car came whizzing past, sloshing through a deep puddle by the kerb and sending up an enormous spray like a tidal wave that completely covered me in mud and rain. I was delighted. After the car had passed, I left the bike against some railings, ran over to the deep puddle and jumped straight into the middle of it. It was so deep it came halfway up my shins. I kicked about for a bit, and looked across at the three tower blocks, with Arcadian in the middle, the tallest and ugliest. Rain was supposed to make everything look even more depressing, but because this part of the estate was so awful anyway, the thunderstorm had enhanced it in a weird way; bestowed it with a soft-focus, almost Dickensian quality. I could hear muffled shouts and the screeching and honking of cars in the main road behind the park; the resonant gurgle of water through the gutters.

I waddled back towards the bike and made a first attempt to straddle the saddle. It was positioned about three inches too high, and even on tiptoe I couldn't quite touch the ground when I sat down on it properly, buttocks splayed out behind me at some weird, back-bending angle. Just getting on the thing was a bit of a hazardous venture for me, but using the railings as support and keeping the bike tilted to one side at a forty-five-degree angle, with one foot flat on the ground, I eventually built up enough confidence to push myself off. I tried once, and failed. I gritted my teeth and gripped the handlebars until my knuckles whitened, and tried again, and failed. I kept trying, toppling over onto the railings or clattering to the wet ground every time, until finally, at about the tenth attempt, I managed to secure the pedals and push down with my feet, keeping a wobbly but nevertheless just about upright position.

I maintained some approximation of balance, and cycled a distance of about ten meandering metres before realising I had two choices: increase speed and thus risk a spectacular and exhilarating death, or hit the squeaky brakes, come to an abrupt halt and inevitably topple over yet again. Of course, the latter option was rejected without too much consideration. Now I was more or less stable even *without stabilisers*, I was determined to make the most of my moment of glory, and if it meant grievously damaging myself, then that was just a risk I'd have to take. And so my heart leapt with trepidation as my confidence grew and, with a few further wobbles and near-crashes, my fear gave way to joyous excitement.

I felt like I was going about a hundred miles an hour as the wind whipped through my wet hair, icy against my cheeks. I hollered out loud with delight, skidding through puddles, weaving between trees, benches and pillars, past rows and rows of maisonettes and swerving from pavement to road and back again with little thought for my safety. I was approaching Bluestone Rise, with its nursery school and library and tiny parish church, and the dozens of lovely new terrace houses that disappeared up the hill and round the corner into a cul-de-sac. The grotty part of the estate was now several hundred yards behind me, and as I entered Bluestone Rise the road began inclining steadily, and I had to pedal harder to keep up momentum. When I was about halfway up, I began to feel frightened because I knew there was no turning back and I was still wobbling quite perilously. The front part of the saddle was so pointy and hard that I couldn't find a comfortable position, Kev could ride a bike without sitting on the saddle at all. Sometimes he rode it without touching the handlebars. He didn't seem to have a care for the rules of cycling proficiency. But then, neither did the bike itself.

I fidgeted on the saddle and twisted the handles in my tight fists, concentrating on getting to the top of the road, focused on the little steeple of the parish church in the near distance, just visible beyond the crescent at the top of the slope. After some effort, I huffed my way to the top and the bike started making strained creaking noises, and with every revolution of the wheels some component of the knackered contraption seemed to groan in agony beneath me. If I had been a little older and wiser, if I had been blessed with any common sense, I would have attempted to dismount there and then, however much minor physical damage this might have caused. But I was five-nearly-six, feisty and furious, my eyes were fixed straight ahead, and there was no way I was giving up when I'd already got so far. Another minute or so and I would make it to the church, then (assuming the frame didn't suddenly collapse beneath me) I would be able to turn the bike around and freewheel it back down again. I had it all planned: I would stick my legs out and close my eyes, keeping the handlebars firmly gripped as I plummeted back down the hill against the wind. That was what all the big girls and boys did, and I could do it too. I was *going* to do it, just to prove I could.

In winter Bluestone Rise was the ultimate sledge-ride venue; the slope was just steep enough to maintain a respectable velocity, but the road evened out a little towards the bottom so there was time to slow down before hitting the busy road below at full pelt. With the first snowfall, excited families from all over Rivington Hill would come here carrying new sledges of all shapes, sizes and colours, and spend hours trudging up and then whizzing down with their scarves flapping behind them. Up and down, up and down, all day long. Often the children got bored before the parents did.

'Sledge' was top of my Christmas list that year, and I had already written my letter to Santa so he would have plenty of time to get me the exact one I wanted. Barbie had been relegated to third place on my wish list (after Etch-a-Sketch) – I was a girl with priorities, and I always had Amber's Barbie to play with, anyway. Last time it snowed we had tried to use a plastic bag as a cheap alternative to a proper sledge, but it ripped before we'd even got halfway down, and it certainly wasn't very aerodynamic or expeditious – just a bit embarrassing. Amber had let me have a go on hers, but it just wasn't the same as having your own. Kev had asked for a sledge two years in a row, but he still hadn't got one. I said it was because Santa only got nice toys for nice kids, and he said that would probably explain why Santa never usually got me anything at all.

I slowed down as I approached the church, awkwardly clambered off the bike and turned around to survey the wonderful view. This was my favourite part of the town, and this was the nicest aspect: the top of Bluestone Rise, just outside St Luke's, looking down over the roofs of the little houses below. From here, far to the left, I could see the row of little local shops, the Barley Mow pub, the British Legion where all the dads hung out, and a little further away, my school. Over a mile away to the other side, just visible in the distance, was the main shopping precinct, the car park for the Sainsburys and KwikSave supermarkets, and the leisure centre. And I was there, at the top of the hill, looking down on it all, standing in the sticky summer drizzle holding on to a rusted old cycle. I suddenly felt an inexplicable rush of pure happiness and exhilaration. I was invincible. I could do anything.

To an audience of one soggy cat and a nearby cluster of fluffed pigeons, I was going to prove myself. I turned to face the church and bowed my head respectfully, muttering a little prayer under my breath, because I didn't know much but I did know that praying was what people should do if they were about to embark on a dangerous exploit. Then I looked at the cat and said, 'Wish me luck,' before getting back on the bike. The cat, sensing imminent calamity, streaked across the road into a front garden, disappearing over the fence. My feet touched the pedals, pushing down again a little gingerly at first. The bike tipped forward and my fingers were poised and ready over the brakes, prepared for the rapid declivitous plummet. Then, before I knew it, the steep gradient sent the wheels into a turbo spin and picked up an immediate speed that I wasn't quite prepared for. My excitement changed to apoplectic terror as I realised that Bluestone Rise was not nearly so long a road on the way down as it appeared to be on the way up. In a matter of seconds, I was already halfway to the bottom and the bike was out of control and I was not happy any more. The brakes! The brakes! In my confusion and blind panic, I turned the handlebars to the left and swerved sharply, accidentally sounding the bell as I squeezed down on the brakes with all my strength.

I heard something fall off the back of the bike with a clatter, but I wasn't sure what it was. At that exact moment, the front wheel hit the kerb, the brakes squeakily executed their delayed effect, too late, and I went hurtling over the handlebars in a graceless somersault. With an audible and hefty impact, I cracked my head on the edge of the kerb and landed with my full weight on my right arm.

Of course I had known pain before, more times than I cared to remember. But the pain that ripped through my body after it fell hard onto the rain-drenched pavement was unlike any pain I had previously experienced. When I tried to move, a scream escaped from my mouth, an agonised scream that rang in my ears, piercing through the ominous, muffled sound of my own frenetic heartbeat. As real as the pain was, it was only secondary to my fear – it was beginning to dawn on me that I had hurt myself quite considerably and, even worse, I was out there on my own.

Given my situation, I had no other choice but to rely on the kindness of strangers. And in a place like Rivington Hill, this is wishful thinking stretched to its very limits. I let out another cry, but by this time I was only semi-conscious and it wasn't as powerful as my first scream. My head was pounding with pain and my vision was strange and blurry, like trying to wake up from a bad dream. When I gingerly explored around the inside of my mouth with my tongue, checking all my teeth were still there, I tasted blood, unmistakeably sharp on the inside of my cheek. On the other side of the road, a spiky-haired woman wearing an apron and a pair of rubber gloves opened her front door and peered out curiously, presumably concerned that one of her own children had had an accident – or perhaps she was just morbidly curious about all the noise. She noticed me and I noticed her notice me, but then she slammed the front door shut again, concern quashed and curiosity sated. I heard a couple more doors open somewhere behind me, and hoped with all my heart that somebody would be kind enough to peel me off the pavement and tend to my various injuries. But those doors were closed again, once I had been assessed as neither a close relation nor a potential fatality.

I wondered how people could be so cruel and unfeeling. I was small and defenceless and grievously wounded, lying there in abject and obvious agony beside a battered bike in the middle of a respectable residential road, and nobody could be bothered to help me. I also wondered, hysterically, through my fading consciousness, if I'd have to have my arm amputated. I was lying across it in an extremely awkward position and when I lowered my head (just a fraction, for fear of dislodging the salvageable parts of my brain) I could see my fingers, bunched and blue, the tips just visible beneath my prone body.

I tried crying out again, but this time it was nothing more than a squeak. I closed my eyes, hoping that I would pass out completely and so become impervious to the pain. Through my clenched eyelids, a sudden reddish flare of light indicated that a car had turned into the road, its headlights wavering and brightening as it approached nearer. Judging by the low, purring sound of the engine, it was slowing down, and I squeezed my eyes more tightly shut and prayed that it was a nice person who would help me. It wasn't.

Through the eyelashes of one half-opened eye, I saw it swish past, splashing up puddles and then parking way up at the other end of the road. The driver got out, locked the car door and walked up his front path calmly as if I didn't exist. As if he hadn't seen me, when I *knew* he must have done. I was beginning to lose my faith in human nature – not that I had much of that to begin with. I started whimpering, unable to sustain a sound of sufficient volume or pitch to attract anybody's attention. I must have been lying there for five or ten minutes at least, with every minute feeling like an hour, but finally, I heard a woman's voice somewhere above my head. I knew immediately, instinctively, that it was the voice of someone who was going to help me. I tried lifting my head to see where the voice was coming from, but every part of me felt paralysed. So I merely whimpered again, slightly louder so the woman could be in no doubt that I needed urgent assistance. A pair of feet in well-worn towelling slippers appeared before my eyes. The lady was standing in the road and shouting out something to someone else. It sounded like, 'Billy, get a blanket,' but by this stage my hearing was also getting fuzzy and her voice was like a distant echo. Above the slippers, I saw the hem of a dark-blue velour skirt, and then the lady crouched down in front of me, just on the edge of the road by the kerb. I was unable to see her face, but she had long brown hair, a lighter shade than mine and longer, and streaked with a few silvery strands. It swung over her shoulders as she bent towards me, so close that I felt the ends whisper against my cheek.

'Oh you poor, poor, precious little thing,' she crooned, 'which parts of you hurt?'

My voice, usually a wearying and garrulous jumble of badly pronounced words, was nothing more than a feeble mumble. 'Every part,' I told her, truthfully.

'Don't you worry, we'll get you a blanket and take you to the hospital.'

The dreaded 'h' word penetrated my grogginess. 'No!' I managed to cry out. 'Not the hospital!'

Despite my vocal protests, I did know that hospital would probably be necessary. But the mere thought of going to hospital was too horrible to contemplate. All those unsmiling faces! The caterwaulings of unimaginable pain and horror echoing around the bare walls! Those malicious metal instruments! The sharp glint of needles under striplights before they were shoved into flesh! Doctors and nurses in blood-splattered uniforms racing around like headless chickens, trying to save lives. And the smell, the *smell*, Dettol soap and placenta and cold gravy and floor polish.

I did not want to go to hospital.

I was convinced that my head had broken wide open like an egg and the yolk of my brain was spilling out onto the pavement, oozing between the cracks of the paving slabs. Maybe I would die. I wondered what would be better: dying, or surviving but having no brain and stitches around my head for ever, like Frankenstein's monster. The lady touched my cheek tenderly, and the back of her hand felt soft and warm against my clammy skin. 'The hospital will make you better again. They did for my Marky when he broke his ankle. He even got a lollipop at the end for being so brave!'

'I don't want to die!' I exclaimed.

The lady laughed. 'You're not going to die, silly girl,' she said. 'You've just had a little accident. I'm sure your mummy must have told you not to go racing down that hill on a bike by yourself. In this awful weather, too. Do you live around here?'

I felt sick and dizzy, stuck somewhere in between wanting to throw up and wanting to faint. 'Yes.' I closed my eyes again, blotting out the swimming blur of colours and movement. 'But my mummy doesn't really care.'

The lady was not at all pleased to hear this. 'Don't be silly, of course she cares. She's probably worried sick about you.'

I thought about what Gordon had said to me earlier: *it's a wonder you don't drive your poor mother sick with worry*. Or drive her to drink, maybe. Surely I wasn't to blame for that? I knew I could be naughty, sometimes even quite deliberately naughty, but I wasn't *that* bad. Not as bad as, say, Douglas Frampton and Jeffrey Zamani and Michael Blundell who were in my class and drove Miss Wibberley up the wall much more than I did, and much more often. Some of the girls were no better. Paula and Candice Haslam were twins and even though they were only seven months older than me, they stole cigarettes from their mum and smoked them with the fourth years behind the big bins at break time. That was *real* naughtiness, surely. It was certainly way beyond mere cheekiness.

'So where do you live then?' the lady persisted.

'Arc . . . Arcadian House. With my mum and my brother who is horrible and my baby sister Sharon.'

'Oh. That's the very big block in the middle of the estate, isn't it?'

For reasons I couldn't quite understand, I felt ashamed. 'Yes,' I mumbled.

'Well.' The lady appeared to be stuck for words. She looked around and noticed the bicycle. 'Oh, your bike! I'll just pop that inside and my husband will take a look at it for you.' She straightened up and I heard the squeaky clank of steel and creaky clunk of wheel as she moved the bicycle away. Another shooting pain ricocheted through my head, and when the lady reappeared she pressed a tissue against my forehead. When she took it away to inspect it, the tissue was soaked with blood.

'Is it very bad?' I asked tremulously.

She folded the tissue and reapplied a clean corner, dabbing carefully. 'No, you might need a couple of stitches, that's all.'

My heart started pounding. 'I need to be *sewn up*?' I spluttered, thinking with a sudden start that maybe my nightmarish Frankenstein's monster premonition wasn't such a fanciful idea after all. The sight of blood wasn't what scared me; it was imagining the extent of my injuries – and my imagination had a tendency to run riot. I checked the lady's expression for signs of terror or repulsion, but she didn't seem to be too affected. Maybe it *was* just a little cut, but then – just as feasibly, to my mind – it could be much, much worse and I might be disfigured for life.

'Don't look so scared, you'll be right as rain in no time,' the lady assured me.

Right as *rain*? What a peculiar expression, I thought. Rather than ask her what it meant, I said, 'My arm really hurts. I think I might have broken it.'

'Maybe it's best if we . . . wait a minute.' She hurried away and I heard some muffled voices. A moment later she was back again, and said, 'My son has phoned for an ambulance. They'll be here in five minutes.'

In fact, they were there in fifteen minutes, and my bewildered little body was laid on a stretcher and whisked away to the hospital. The lady (who, in the interim, had introduced herself as Beverley and promised to stay with me) held my hand throughout, for which I was eternally grateful. The swirling blue lights and the bustle and noise and the weird clinical people in fluorescent jackets telling me to try not to move was enough to terrify me out of my wits. After a blurred, tearful episode in the A&E waiting room, I vaguely remember lying flat on my back staring up at a too-bright cylindrical light while a man in a white coat bent over me, flashed a torch in my eyes and patched up my head. He then, to my horror, tried bending my arm out at the elbow, and when it cracked loudly and I (naturally) screamed out in pain and horror, he simply said, 'Whoops, you got yourself a little fracture there young lady, by the feel of it.' By this time, I was ranting and raving like a loon, but the lady – kind, lovely Bev of whom I knew nothing more than a name – soothed me by plying me liberally with liquid refreshments and kind words.

Of course, this particular fragment of my cherished memory is a little unreliable, not to mention clouded by delirium and distress and the effects of the painkillers. When the hospital had done their best to repair me, and once I had calmed down and become coherent again, Bev said, 'What's your telephone number? I have to phone your poor mother to let her know what's happened . . .'

'We don't have a phone,' I said, closely inspecting the curious sling in which my right arm was now cradled, and feeling a deep flush of pride that I had been brave enough to see the ordeal through. I had been given a bright red lollipop to prove it, too.

'But . . . surely there's some way I can contact her?'

I sucked contemplatively on the sugary orb and stared down at my plimsolls, still soggy and filthy. 'No.'

Bev opened her handbag and fished around for something. 'Do you know,' she said, 'I told you my name but I still don't know yours.'

I slurped on the lollipop and told her.

'Caroline what?'

'Caroline Elizabeth.'

'Surname?'

'Shaw. That's my mum's surname, I don't have a dad really. My mum is going to have another baby soon, and then there'll be . . .' I counted aloud on the fingers of my good hand, '. . . five of us.'

'And you live in Arcadian House?'

I nodded. 'Seventh floor. Flat number fifty-nine. Five-nine. It used to say it on the door but the numbers fell off.'

Bev raised her eyebrows. 'I see. Well, I can either take you straight home now, or . . .' She pulled her purse out of her bag and excavated a ten-pence coin. 'I could get my husband to pick us up and you can come back and have dinner at my house. If you'd like to.'

I thought about it for all of one second. 'Can I come back to yours please, Beverley?'

She smiled and squeezed my left hand in hers. 'Of course you can. If you're sure your mum won't mind. Come on, Caroline Elizabeth Shaw, let's call my taxi service and go home to get some food into you. You're thin as a rake, child.'

Bev's husband was called Sean, and he had a car that always broke down and a job that worked him too hard and paid him too little. Bev told me this while we waited for him to pick us up from the hospital reception. He had apparently had a look at my bike – or rather, Kev's bike – and managed to mend most of the superficial damage. I was very grateful to hear this, although slightly doubtful that it was the whole truth.

'He's quite a handyman, bless him,' Bev said. 'He can be grouchy and bossy and unbearable, but . . . I suppose I can be, too, sometimes.'

I peered at her suspiciously. I couldn't imagine Bev ever being any of those things. She was the nicest adult I'd ever met. I asked her, 'Do you have children?' – even though I knew she had at least one son because I remembered her mentioning him.

Her smile broadened. 'Two boys. William – Billy – he's my oldest, and Marky, he's my baby.'

'You have a baby?'

'Well, a seven-year-old baby.'

I frowned at the strange contradiction. 'Does he go to Willow Lane?'

'Yes. He's probably the year above you. Mr Scully's class?'

Mr Scully was going to be my new teacher after the summer holiday, and he was a funny, globulous little man with a nasal voice and a ponytail. He was slightly odd, but preferable to Miss Wibberley by a long chalk.

'He's going into Mrs McLeod's class after the summer. She seems like a nice woman.'

Mrs McLeod had once told me off for throwing an apple core into a hedge, but apart from possessing what seemed to be an obligatory quirkiness, evident in some form or other among all the Willow Lane teachers, I quite liked her.

'Yes,' I said, 'but she has a funny loud voice.'

Bev laughed. She seemed to be fairly amused by me, no matter what I did or said.

'Oh, I do like you, Caroline,' she said simply.

This was very heartening for me to hear, especially from an adult who seemed to be relatively sane. I put on my most polite voice. 'Thank you Beverley. I like you, too. You've been very kind to me.'

'Please, call me Bev,' she said.

I glowed with pleasure and pride. 'My granny calls me Carrie. But you can call me Caz or Caro,' I said. 'Or anything you like, really.'

Again she laughed; a lovely, light, lilting laugh that warmed me to her even more.

After we had shared one more weak tea from the vending machine, Sean picked us up in a dark-blue Ford Escort. He was indeed a little bit grouchy and the car was indeed a little bit old and unreliable. It stopped and stalled and spluttered several times on the way back to the house, and Sean lost his temper and bashed the steering wheel with his fists and used the 'f' word a lot.

'Calm down, love, we're nearly there now,' Bev whispered, touching his alarmingly large bicep with her comparatively tiny hand. The flash of her wedding ring caught my eye, and I wondered if it was a real diamond.

'This fucking car, I've had it up to here with it,' Sean cursed, accidentally blasting the horn as he assaulted the dashboard, making me jump. I was sitting in the back seat, registering Sean's expression in the rear-view mirror and feeling increasingly nervous. By now my lollipop was nothing more than a thin, soggy white stick with a tiny sliver of shiny red at the top. I cracked it with my teeth, and decided to keep quiet. Bev's husband did not seem like the type of man who appreciated idle chit-chat.

'It's done us well, though, darling,' Bev was saying. 'We've had it since before Billy was born, after all.'

'It's scrap, that's all it's good for now,' Sean grunted, finally managing to start the engine again after several failed attempts. 'Fucking thing.'

'Please, love, easy on the swearing.'

'Fuck that, I've had a shitty day.'

'Well, what about poor old Caz, then?' Bev said, turning in her seat and winking at me. I wished she hadn't drawn attention to me. I just smiled and shrugged and kicked my feet out against the front seat, admiring the plasters on my knees and the numerous cuts and grazes down my shins. 'Poor little thing has been in the wars. Split head, fractured arm, grazed knees and elbows . . . took quite a tumble, didn't you love?'

'It's not so bad,' I said. 'The doctor told me I only need to keep it in the sling for a few days, and it doesn't hurt much any more.'

This was sort of true; it was more of a dull ache now. Sean looked at me properly for the first time, and didn't smile. Instead he turned to Bev and muttered, 'Another one of your strays, Beverley.'

I didn't know what he meant by this, but it didn't sound very friendly. I sank down into the seat, trying to make myself smaller, less intrusive.

'You collect charity cases, love,' he went on, 'you fuckin' collect 'em. You seem to forget we're not far from being charity cases ourselves.'

This man was in a really foul mood. Bev didn't contradict him, she just stared out of the window, but I noticed her jaw tighten and she took some deep breaths before saying anything. When she did, her tone was one of forced jollity. 'I'll make us all a lovely dinner tonight, how about that? Yes? Darling?'

'Hmph.' Sean turned the car and I pressed my nose against the window as we sped past the park, and then past Arcadian House. I wanted to point and say, *I live there, just on the other side, about halfway up*, but I stopped myself.

Sean pulled up to the side of the road and Bev lifted me out of the car. I was perfectly capable of walking, but I enjoyed being fussed over, so I let her carry me through up the front path, which was flanked by scented clusters of colourful flowers and leafy plants and shrubs. Despite being tiny, the front garden was packed with more foliage and blooms than I had ever seen before: pastel sprays of candytuft, bright sunbursts of freesia and peonies, fragrant carpets of love-in-a-mist, larkspur and thyme, copious tendrils of ivy and jasmine twining up the trellis on the outside wall. It was a delight for the senses, every shade of every colour and every shape of leaf and petal. I felt like Dorothy after the hurricane, stepping out of her black-and-white world into the breathtaking Technicolor of Oz. There was a hanging basket outside the front entrance porch that overflowed with tiny pink flowers. Bev accidentally knocked my head against it as she carried me through the door, but it didn't hurt. I was still feeling a little overawed by the whole experience, but soaking up every single sensation and stimulus as if I had entered some strange alien planet.

'What's the time?' I asked her as she laid me down on a huge squashy sofa in a lounge that smelt not unpleasantly of dogs and burnt toast and pot-pourri.

'It's not even six o'clock yet,' she said. 'Now, I'm afraid as you'll notice we have a bit of an . . . extended family. This house is just overcrowded with people, and animals, and junk, and . . . God, all sorts. Excuse the mess. I would say it's not always this bad, but I'd be lying.'

Excuse the *mess*? I felt like I was in paradise, sprawled there on a sumptuously comfy old sofa in a house that already almost felt like home, even after just a few seconds of being there. If she wanted 'mess' she should have seen where I lived – this was pristine in comparison.

I looked around in wonder at my new surroundings, taking it all in. In the corner on a low, polished wooden shelf unit was a television set, bigger than ours, and probably a colour one – but it was switched off so I couldn't be sure. On top of the telly there was a crystal vase of artificial lilies and a framed wedding photograph. To the right, there was a large mahogany display cabinet filled with glasses and goblets and tumblers and various items of memorabilia – a ceramic thimble collection, half a dozen small animal ornaments, a couple of fairly unattractive trinkets, several fine china tea cups and a commemorative plate in the centre. On a shelf underneath was another wedding photo, but black and white and larger than the other one, framed in brass. The walls were covered with plain eggshell-blue wallpaper, and the rear window was edged with heavily embroidered curtains, in cream and pale gold. To me it seemed like pure luxury.

'Do you want a drink, Caro?' Bev asked.

'Yes, please.'

'Lemonade?'

It just kept getting better.

'Oh, yes *please*!'

I felt like I had entered a parallel universe, an alternative existence that made my own seem even more bleak and unappealing in comparison. Despite my insistence that she wouldn't even have noticed my disappearance, Bev sent Sean around to inform my mum that I had had a little accident but was safe and would be escorted home later. He returned from his errand some minutes later and I heard him tell Bev that the television was on loud and all the lights were on, but nobody came to the door so he had just shouted the message through the letterbox. Bev said, 'Oh well, I don't suppose there's much more we can do.'

Over the next few hours, I met more people and pets than I thought could ever possibly fit into a little terraced house. Norman (three-legged golden retriever); Percy (another dog, a border-collie cross with all legs intact but only one eye); Sheldon and Beaker (cockatiels, the latter of which suffered from Tourette's); five cats, one of whom was definitely called John although I couldn't be sure of accurately recalling any of the other names; two adult rabbits and five babies; a fox cub called Pongo; an elderly human gentleman called Ned who was Bev's father; Billy (Crozier number-one son); a tank full of unnamed tropical fish; a balding guinea pig; an outside aviary of vociferous parakeets; and last but not least, 'baby' Mark (Crozier number-two son).

Over a dinner of pepperoni pizza and more lemonade, while Beaker the cockatiel persistently jabbered obscenities from his cage and Norman the lopsided dog snuffled inquisitively at my crotch, the elder members of the Crozier family chatted to me in an open, friendly way, as if they'd known me for years. Mark and Billy, on the other hand, mostly ignored me, but despite being slightly in awe of Billy (he was more than twice my age and broodingly attractive, as older boys so often appeared to be, purely by virtue of their seniority) I didn't really pay much attention to them, either. I was fascinated by Grandad Ned (they all called him Grandad, even Bev). The pair of us hit it off immediately, and he regaled me with stories about old times and seemed only too happy to answer my many questions. He told me he had come to live with his younger daughter and her family after his 'darling' Nancy had departed this world in the winter of seventy-nine, and he subsequently sold their marital home in Tilbury ('Too many memories, enough to drive a grievin' old man round the bend').

'And they haven't been able to get rid of me ever since,' he added, grinning over at his sombre-looking son-in-law.

'Yeah, not for lack of tryin', neither,' Sean mumbled, nudging his elder son in the ribs. 'Gotta get our hands on that inheritance, eh son?' Billy grimaced and got down from the table without asking, and without thanking his mother for a dinner that was, as far as I was concerned, the most delicious I had ever tasted.

Ned shook his head. 'Ha! They'd be lucky, I haven't got a bean!' he chuckled, leaning closer towards me with a waggle of his big white eyebrows. 'Do you think I'd live here in this madhouse if I didn't have to?'

'Nobody's forcin' you, Grandad,' Sean said.

I finished my pizza slices in silence and Bev kept refilling my glass with lemonade. It was slightly flat, but much nicer than the cheap, additive-packed orange squash I was accustomed to at home.

'Thank you very much for dinner, it was yummy,' I said, swallowing the last of it.

'Well, I'll be blowed!' Ned exclaimed. 'Such lovely manners for a poor little orphan in the storm!'

'Oh no,' I hastily corrected him, 'I'm not an orphan. I live near here with my mummy and my brother Kevin and my sister Sharon who is a baby.'

I noticed Bev and Ned exchange looks, and I straightened up in the chair and went on, almost like a recital, 'My mummy taught me that I should say please and thank you and sorry because it costs nothing and it makes people think better of you.'

Three sets of eyebrows shot up in unison. Sean stopped chewing and looked up from his newspaper in astonishment.

'Well, your mummy's taught you well,' Bev said, after a short pause. 'And you should be getting back to her soon, young lady.'

'Oh, it's OK, she'll be on the floor by now,' I said. 'She drinks a lot of special lemonade, you see. Not like this lemonade though, hers smells funny and tastes horrid. It makes her tired. She might not even have noticed I'm not there actually.'

There was a very long silence.

It was broken by Mark. 'Oi, pass the ketchup, Mum,' he said.

Finally, with my right arm in a sling, five stitches in my head, fresh scabs patching both my knees and tatty fabric Elastoplasts dangling from my various wounds, I reluctantly left the hospitable warmth of the Crozier house, escorted back home in the darkness by Grandad Ned. He helped me put the bike back inside the dingy storage cupboard and assured me that the damage was hardly noticeable – which was a lie, but nevertheless a lie that I appreciated. It was more than could be said for my own sore and battered body, at any rate. Once I had waved him goodbye and hobbled awkwardly up the seven flights of damp, piss-spattered stone steps to the flat (scary lift still out of order), I found the front door left ajar and my mum sprawled across the lounge carpet, face down, listening to 'Jolene' by Dolly Parton on the record player.

It was half past ten. She had drained the best part of an entire bottle of brandy and was slipping in and out of consciousness.

I considered the scene for a few moments, listening to the rasping sounds of her breathing and the familiar wail of police sirens in the streets outside. 'I hurt myself today, Mummy,' I said eventually, stooping to pick up the empty brandy bottle from the floor and depositing it on the table with the cluttered assortment of crusted dinner plates.

She moved her head and groaned, a web of tawny hair covering her face.

'Mummy, I hurt myself,' I repeated, jutting my plastered arm outwards like a broken wing. 'But it was OK 'cos a kind lady took me to the hospital and let me eat dinner at her house afterwards with her family. And she has lots of animals in her house and in her garden and she let me hold her rabbits and feed her baby fox. She found it by a roadside and somebody had run over it in their car and just left it there but she's looking after it now until it gets better. It mostly eats cat food, but the lady has five cats anyway so they all have to share.' I paused for breath, knowing from experience that she probably wasn't hearing a word of what I was saying, but still intent on relating the evening's experience, purely for my own benefit; running through the awesome events in my mind with avid delight: The Day I Met the Croziers. Or even better: The Day the Croziers Adopted Me. It was worth all the pain, it was worth the aching arm, the bloodied knees, the concussion, the wrecked bicycle. It was the family I had always wanted, the family I would never have. A Family. A *Real* Family. A mummy and daddy who loved each other so much that they lived together, in the same house. Together. Probably for ever. And oh, those magical wedding photos! They were black and white but so beautiful! Like a fairy tale come true! So long ago, so many years, and still going strong. Still together, even now in the times when colour photographs exist. It was unbelievable! To think I could be part of such a wonderful and miraculous thing; an *extended* family. Three generations, all happy together. A loving home.

You're welcome back any time, the lady had said. Beverley Crozier, that was the lady's name. I repeated it over and over under my breath. *Call me Bev*, she had said. And: *We've really enjoyed having you with us tonight. You will come again, won't you?*

'Oh, and Mummy, they said I could go back there whenever I wanted. They were really nice to me. The grandad has pieces of shell in his leg from the war. Did you know they dropped shells in the war? Shells! But they still hurt lots of people. They even killed some people. He says it sometimes makes him walk funny and makes his knee go all weird so he can't bend it. That's maybe why he uses a walking stick. He likes gardening and he knows all the names of all the plants in all the world. He told me that there's a flower shrub called Carolina Allspice. And a type of white rose called the Queen Caroline. Or something. Did you name me after a rose, Mummy? His name is Ned.

He is very old and he has lots of medals that he won for bravery and for not dying. His wife died though and I feel sad for him because they had been married for hundreds of years so he must miss her an awful lot. Also, Mummy, there is a boy called Mark who I think is in Kev's year at school but he didn't say much to me. His brother Billy is thirteen next year and I'm going to marry him when I grow up!'

I was now totally convinced that my mum wasn't paying any attention whatsoever, hence this last, absurd announcement – the infinitesimal possibility of which nevertheless gave me a frisson of excitement when I said it out loud. There was just so much more to say, I was quite literally bursting with news, yearning to spill it all out to someone, to anyone. With my mother it was falling on deaf ears, but I wanted her to take notice, I *needed* her to care, just this once. I stood over her and prodded her shoulder. 'Mummy?'

She made an ominous growling sound, and even from a distance I could smell the alcohol on her. All of a sudden it was as if the whole room had become saturated with the stench of spirits; a stench that I would come to associate with my mother more than any other smell, as it overpowered the flat's usual bland blend of cheap fags, imitation perfume, economy cooking, musty clothes and curdling milk. There was an air freshener on standby in every room, but their effects were self-defeating and short-lived. Spraying a concentrated mist of 'pine forest' or 'magnolia and orange blossom' in an area redolent with a whole host of stubborn smells can only result in a brief coughing fit and a full-on nostril assault as the fight between flora and fungi renders the air temporarily unbreathable. But *this* smell, this brandy breath, had the edge: it was the reek of futile escape, of failure, of despair. As festering fragrances go, it was the most deeply suggestive and by far the most terrible. It wasn't the first time I had seen my mother drunk, but on this occasion it really bothered me; it *enraged* me. I prodded her harder, then seized both shoulders and gave her a shake.

'Mu-mmeee! Wake up! I want to tell you about what happened to me today!'

'Hrrrmmphh.'

'*Please . . .*'

Both her clouded eyes opened slowly and peered at me as if at a stranger. 'Jolene,' she whispered. 'How about Jolene?'

'What?'

'Hmm . . . Jolene is a nice name,' she murmured dreamily, as the final chorus of the song strained from the one functioning speaker in the corner of the room, balanced precariously on top of a badly assembled bookshelf amongst a scattered chaos of baby toys, worthless ornaments and photo frames. This bookshelf, unlike every other item of furniture we had accumulated and arranged in our makeshift home, had not been begged, borrowed or stolen. Along with the archaic record player it housed, and a collection of appalling records (Dolly Parton being among the best), it was a spurious 'gift' from Shaz's father – presumably to compensate for his absence from every single stage of his daughter's life, with the probable exception of her conception.

'Who is Jolene?' I asked, the answer dawning on me as soon as I had asked it. 'I was right!' I babbled at once, standing up straight and clapping my hands together. 'I *am* going to have a sister! I knew it!'

Mum smiled weakly. When you are a council-estate mum, the simmering sense of apprehensive pleasure and excitement that is traditionally supposed to arise from the expectation of a 'new arrival' diminishes markedly with each successive pregnancy. This is because so many council-estate mums, bless their plucky little hearts, are doubly cursed: their trusting natures are such that they are let down by men time and time again, while they are also inexplicably more fecund and receptive than any other breed of woman on earth. This catholic, laissez-faire approach to family planning stems not from religion or even from slackness, but from mere resignation and a self-flagellating, indefatigable optimism: *if this one knocks me up, maybe (just maybe!) he'll stick around and I'll finally have myself a proper family . . . and if not, hey, I'll deal with it alone just like I always have.*

They want a perfect family of their own, and they will try and try and try again until their egos and their wombs are battered and bruised to buggery in the quest to get that elusive match just right. But invariably they will end up with something a million miles away from their idealistic girlhood dreams: squalor where there should be splendour, poverty where there was supposed to be plenty, profound loneliness where they naively expected lifelong partnership. Hoping to give birth to a brood of decorous angels who will bestow them with oodles of much-craved unconditional love, they will more often produce a proliferation of obnoxious, ungrateful brats who have inherited all the very worst genes of the absent losers who fathered them.

When she found out she was pregnant with Kev, my impatient, gutsy, fifteen-year-old mother had apparently ripped off her school tie and whooped with delight; then quick as a flash she moved out of her own home of Liverpool and asked Kev's dad (her first, her one true love) to marry her, after applying for a council flat near his own home town of Chigwell in Essex. One emphatically declined proposal, one traumatic birth, one ill-advised relocation to the arsehole end of the country where she didn't know anyone, hundreds of dirty nappies and sleepless nights and countless shattered illusions later, the discovery of my conception some time later was met with a slightly more cynical, 'Oh, fuck.' Kev's dad emigrated post-haste shortly after Kev was born, breaking his under-age lover's fragile heart and thereby prefiguring a lifetime of drudgery and inevitable disappointment. While my mum was still nursing her broken heart and trying to conceal her stretchmarks and post-natal exhaustion, my father blundered on to the scene and took advantage of her vulnerability. A young, disillusioned, single mum – an easy target, a foregone conclusion. I never did want to know the details of how I came into existence, and little wonder.

And so it was. This was the day-to-day stuff that made up our lives. The more our dreams elude us, the more we must detach ourselves from the bleakness of what we have inadvertently allowed to become our reality. While some people are handed a ready-made reality on a silver platter, with a virtual guarantee of a glittering future, others have to carve out their own from whatever they can salvage. Everything hinges on the uncontrollable, on random allocation, on individual nascent blessings and curses.

The song ended and the needle on the record scratched to a halt. Looking down at my feet, I bashfully confessed, 'I'm afraid I crashed Kev's bike . . .'

I chose my moment carefully, knowing that I was unlikely to receive a scolding or indeed any form of acknowledgement, but able to feel virtuous for being so honest and owning up. My mum rolled on to her back, pushed her hair out of her eyes and gazed at the stippled ceiling, yellowed by the humming fluorescence of the strip light and the nicotine of a hundred thousand cigarettes.

I couldn't quite make out what she said before she passed out cold, but to me it sounded like, 'Oh shit what the fuck am I doing?'

I gazed at her for a while before turning the light off. With my good arm, I cleared away most of the dinner plates from the table, poured myself a glass of orange squash, covered my supine mother with a dirty sheet and quietly went to bed, thinking all the while that Caroline was a much nicer name than Jolene.

After such initial excitement the summer holiday rapidly lost its appeal. There were still no seaside plans – in fact the only time my mum took me out was to the park and the supermarket. Amber and Katie had already gone away (to Hastings and the Isle of Wight respectively), so there wasn't even anyone to play with, and my injuries rendered me pretty much out of action and therefore indescribably bored.

It was just over a week after my accident that I chose to accept Bev's generous and rather rash open invitation, and returned to the house at 28 Bluestone Rise. I knocked tentatively on the door with the hand of my good arm. The flowers in the front garden were still a blaze of colour, but somehow they didn't seem as vividly bright and vibrant as that fateful, unforgettable evening when I had been carried up the little path through the entrance porch, my senses both heightened and warped by delirium and confusion. I waited a moment and then knocked again, hoping it hadn't all just been a dream.

I was waiting on the doorstep for a long time before anyone opened the door. As diminutive as I was, I felt particularly tiny when I averted my eyes to gaze up at the formidable hulk of Sean Crozier, who was wearing a plastic Union Jack bowler hat and – to my utmost surprise – a pink ballerina tutu over his faded, paint-splashed jeans. His feet were bare and dirty and he was eating a hot dog, the mustard and ketchup smeared around his lips and a couple of days' shadowy beard growth giving him a shifty, indolent look. He was silent at first, merely staring down at me quite intensely, and for a brief, panicked moment I thought about running away.

'Oh, hello, you,' he said eventually, his face breaking into a smile of recognition at last. 'The stray has returned, I see.' He took a big bite from his hot dog and winked at me. A globule of ketchup slopped down onto his T-shirt, creating a glutinous crimson streak in between two other patchy stains, probably beer. I smiled back bashfully, wondering what to say but grateful that he knew who I was, at least.

Sean turned his head and yelled, 'Bev, your little friend has just turned up! That kid from last Friday!'

There was a shout from an upstairs room, but I was unable to make it out. Sean turned back to me. 'Don't you know it's the wedding today?'

I was nonplussed. 'Wedding?'

'You're missin' it,' he said. 'Charles and Di. They're gettin' married. Right now. On the box.'

'Oh.' I wondered why anyone would want to get married on a box.

Then I tried to think who Charles and Di were. The names definitely rang a bell somewhere. Were they a local couple? No way – there was certainly nobody called 'Charles' residing in Rivington Hill. One or two Charlies maybe, but that was about as good as it got. Sean noticed my confused expression and said, 'Come on, take a look around, why d'you think everyone's got flags up at the windows, eh?'

I stood down from the doorstep, feeling a little intimidated by him. He carried on talking, leaning against the front door with his plastic bowler hat tilted over his eyes. 'Course, Bev has already put in her order for God knows 'ow many of them bloody ugly commemorative mug things. And tea towels. Plates, pens, wine glasses, you name it. Everyone and his newsagent is cashin' in on this malarkey. It's bad taste, if you ask me. It'll be bloody loo seats and bog paper next with their smiley royal faces plastered all over, you just wait an' see.' He was talking to himself really, because I wasn't following a single word. But when I looked across at the other houses on the street, there was indeed a Union Jack flag hanging up at just about every window. One house even had a huge banner of Charles and Di's engagement picture flapping away in the breeze outside their bedroom window. When I saw that, it finally clicked.

'Oh, the *Royal* wedding!' I exclaimed. 'Prince Charles and Lady Diana!'

Sean swallowed a last mouthful of hot dog and regarded the strange little urchin on his doorstep with some amusement. 'I don't dress up like this every day, you know.'

I was relieved to hear this, because he did look very silly and I didn't know him well enough to tell him so.

'Who is it?' Bev asked, as she ran down the stairs into the entrance hall and came to the door at last, wiping her hands on her apron. 'Oh!' Her face lit up when she saw me, much to my relief – I hadn't been entirely confident of the kind of reception that I might have received. 'Hello, you!' She turned irritably to her husband. 'You could have let her in, Sean. *Honestly!* You'd leave the Queen herself standing out on the doorstep, you would.'

Sean shrugged and ambled back into the front room, and Bev opened the door wider, ushering me inside with a wave of her hand. 'I'm so sorry about him,' she said. 'He's been drinking, the great oaf.'

I blinked at her, not knowing what to say. There was a short, slightly uncomfortable silence.

'Well. Anyway. How are you? Better now I hope?' Bev finally ventured.

'Yes thank you, Beverley. I can write again now. Although not very neatly.' I waved my right arm and waggled my fingers to prove everything was now more or less in full working order.

'Good. I'm glad to see you've made a very speedy recovery. Now! Here we are! Come through, come through.' She turned around and opened the door into the front room. I was shocked and daunted to see not one, not two, not even three or four, but *five* males in the room. I counted them: Sean (one), Billy (two), Mark (three), and two others (four and five), both of them Sean's age, slouched beside him on the couch with their feet hoisted up on the coffee table and cans of beer gripped in their hands. Grandad Ned was nowhere to be seen. I hoped he hadn't died of old age. And where were all the animals? I couldn't even hear a defiant 'bugger off' from Beaker the cockatiel, or the excitable panting of a disabled canine.

'Everyone, this is Caroline,' Bev announced, putting her arm around my shoulders. 'Mark, Billy, you remember her from last week. The little girl who had the bike accident?'

Neither Mark nor Billy offered me anything more than an uninterested glance. The two strange men on the couch with Sean tipped their beer cans at me in lazy acknowledgement. I suddenly felt very small and scared. And very overwhelmed. Sean took pity on me and pulled up a saggy old pouffe, giving it a solid thump with his fist, as if to check it was still serviceable. 'Come on love, come an' sit over 'ere with us. Bev will get you a drink and we can all watch this silly palaver on the telly,' he offered.

I hesitated, but Bev gave me a little nudge and said, 'Don't be shy, love. You sit with the boys and I'll bring in the crisps and cola.'

'And more beer!' one of the men called out, waving his can in the air and rounding off his request with a lengthy, rumbling burp. I thought he looked like a grizzly bear, all belly and beard and beady button eyes. No, not a grizzly bear, actually. He was Bluto out of *Popeye*. He even had the same voice. All that was missing was the hat, really. This Bluto was all flab and facial hair. I edged towards the proffered pouffe, still unsure. A Union Jack flag was draped over the back of the couch. There was a Monopoly board on the floor, with its various bits and pieces strewn all over. The men began talking to each other in strange, low voices and guffawing with short bursts of gruff laughter, as if resuming a previous discussion. Not wanting to interrupt or draw attention to myself, I sat down quietly and turned towards the television set. The apparition, in full colour in front of my eyes, took my breath away. Almost without meaning to, I said out loud, 'Oh doesn't she look *beautiful*...'

The men stopped talking and laughing. Even Billy and Mark turned around to look at me. I burned with embarrassment, but Sean quickly came to the rescue. 'She sure does, young lady, and we was just wondering what she's doin' marryin' that jug-eared cretin!'

They laughed again, loud and uproarious.

'Guess what?' Sean said, leaning forward and tapping me on the shoulder gently. But I couldn't take my eyes off the screen, I was mesmerised. Princess Diana was walking along a red carpeted aisle, the elaborate ivory train of her gown sweeping along behind her in a rippling arc. It was magnificent. I had never seen anything like it before. I hadn't even thought a dress like that was *possible*, not in my wildest dreams. Sean pointed and hiccuped, apparently quite unmoved or at least unimpressed by the spectacle. 'That dress she's wearin',' he said, 'that bloody great meringue of a dress, that's worth twice as much as this bloody house, you know!' He took a sip of beer and licked his lips. 'Twice as much, at least.'

I wasn't sure what to say to this. 'But . . . but it's such a *lovely* dress,' I stammered.

Sean made a choking sound. 'Damn right it's a lovely dress. Twice as lovely as the house I'm livin' in, apparently! Jesus Christ! It's enough to make a grown man weep, it is. Workin' every hour God sends to pay off the sodding mortgage, I am, and it's a bit of a slap in the face when your whole salary amounts to half a yard of posh bloody wedding dress.'

I felt confused. 'It *is* very . . . big,' I offered, hoping this obvious observation might somehow mollify him. 'And very long.'

'Yes, that's right,' Sean said, lighting up a cigarette. He looked back at the screen and didn't blink for a while. 'It's very big and very long.'

One of his friends began chortling again, but Sean didn't join in this time. He threw his head back to down the last of his beer, then crushed the can, lobbed it towards the wicker basket, and missed. Appreciating the opportunity to make myself useful and perhaps score a few brownie points, I got up, retrieved the can from the floor and put it in the bin, where there was already a considerable pile of other empty cans.

'Blimey, you got her well trained,' Bluto remarked to Sean. 'I could do with a kid like that round my place. My lot are fuckin' useless, if you'll pardon the French.'

I didn't like his tone but smiled at him anyway. Sean said, 'Yeah, cheers love, you're a diamond,' and I thought I might burst with gratitude at this simple and only semi-sincere remark.

'Dad, I'm *bored*,' Billy moaned, projecting his gloom as is a thirteen-year-old boy's wont. He lay on his back across the carpet in front of the television with his hands behind his head and sighed dramatically. 'Who gives a shit about this anyway? They're all just boring snobby bastards with too much money.'

'Oi, watch yer fuckin' language, son,' Bluto scolded, wagging a podgy finger at him.

'Yeah, you ain't too old for a spankin', you know,' said the other man, who had a beard as well, but also a bald pointy scalp, giving him the somewhat amusing appearance of having his head on upside down.

'Get lost,' Billy said, smiling and flicking them the V.

'Hey, steady on boys, there is a lady present,' Sean said. 'Best behaviour please.'

It took me a while to work out that he was referring to me. I'd never been called a lady before, not without the prefix 'young', which doesn't have quite the same effect somehow.

Mark piped up, disdainfully, 'She's not a lady. Nobody asked her anyway.'

'That's enough, Mark.' Sean raised a finger and an eyebrow and Mark scowled.

'Well, it's true,' he grumbled.

I felt the need to put the record straight, even if just to prevent Mark from resenting me any more than he probably already did. 'It is true,' I said. 'I'm not a lady.'

Sean looked taken aback. 'Well, never mind. It's not appropriate language, anyway.'

'You what?' Upside-Down Head Man goggled at him incredulously. 'What's all this about "appropriate language" all of a sudden, Crozzie? Since when did you give a fuck?'

'Never mind.' Sean smoothed down his tutu and the pink netting sprang up again, jutting from his lap in a ridiculous erectile frill. 'Come on, let's get with the spirit of things, eh?' He called out to his wife. 'Come on love, we're gaspin' for more beer in 'ere.'

'Alright, alright, I'm coming.' Bev dutifully appeared with a tray of crisps, peanuts, three cans of Coke and three cans of beer. I wondered why somebody as lovely and headstrong as Bev would let anybody boss her around the way Sean did. I liked Sean, but there was something overtly male and brusque about him. 'Here we go,' Bev said, putting the tray on the table once three pairs of oversized male feet had been temporarily removed.

I desperately wanted the company of another female, and so was relieved when Bev finally sat down in an armchair in the corner with an exhausted sigh. The stench of potent testosterone and socks and beer burps was becoming overbearing. 'Don't you think Lady Diana looks so pretty in that dress?' I asked Bev.

'Oh, don't start all that again,' Billy whined. 'Of course she looks good, they've spent millions on this bloody wedding.'

'Billy, if you've got nothing nice to say, why don't you go over to Tom's. I hear he's got that new computer game you were talking about,' Bev said.

Billy's brow unknitted itself, and his expression became animated. 'Really? The Amiga one?' he said, his pre-pubescent voice squeaking with excitement. I was amazed at how quickly and easily his moods changed. In the true fickle style of the young child, I decided I didn't want to marry him after all. He was far too surly and intimidating.

'Yes. And you can stay the night over there as well if it's alright with Mary. It will give me one less mouth to feed, at least.'

I thought this could be a subtle dig at me. I hadn't intended on staying very long, and certainly didn't expect dinner. After all, I had turned up uninvited. I even thought peanuts and Coke was going a little overboard on the hospitality.

Billy left promptly without a goodbye, slamming the front door so hard that one of the picture frames in the hall fell off the wall. The rest of us watched the rest of the wedding with only a few more comments passed between us, and many more burps, including an unexpectedly stentorian one from me. I began to feel more at ease after that, and quite happily sat there drinking my Coke and sharing a packet of crisps with Mark, even though he still refused to reciprocate my smile or even to meet my eye.

After about half an hour or so, I began to fidget and wondered how much longer the wedding coverage would go on for. After all, for any interested but ultimately detached outsider, the novelty of a wedding wears off remarkably quickly, no matter how amazing the bridal gown or how extravagant the ceremony or how passionate the love between the bride and groom appears to be. I also wondered if I might be outstaying my welcome. But I felt so at home there, in spite of the strange men and the mild hostility of Bev's offspring. This was nothing in comparison to the all-out loathing and antagonism I received from

Kev on a daily basis, the laconic scoldings of my mum and the incessant wailing of Sharon.

And the Crozier family house was so *nice* – it had two levels, an upstairs and a downstairs, like a proper home, and the rooms were cosy but not poky. The fridge was full, the kitchen smelt of warm baked bread and washing-up liquid, the bathroom was clean and the carpet was nice and springy with hardly any stains. Mark and Billy each had their own room, decorated to their tastes, and their wardrobes were full of all the clothes they could ever want. I was aware of a feeling, deep inside me, that was tantamount to jealousy but yet not quite jealousy. All I could ever want was within these four walls: a real family, a real home, a real sense of identity and belonging. And security. So why didn't Mark and Billy seem happy and content? Didn't they *know* how lucky they were?

After the balcony kiss, and once the excitable cheering crowds had finally disbanded, the event was finally over. I thought to myself: what next? Do they have a party? Would they get to live in a palace all of their own now? Does Diana get to keep that dress? If so, when would she wear it again? Maybe she might give it to Oxfam, and that way someone else could feel like a princess for a day, and all the starving babies in Africa would benefit as well.

Bev interrupted my ruminations. 'Well, what a lovely ceremony,' she said. 'Let's hope they are very happy together.' She stood up and stretched. 'Sean love, will you give me a hand with the barbie?'

I looked up curiously. 'What are you doing with Barbie?'

The men chortled.

'Grillin' her and then stickin' her between two bread rolls,' Upside-Down Head Man said, holding his not inconsiderable stomach as he rocked with laughter.

'Don't be cruel, Barry,' Bev said. She turned to me and said, 'How about you help me instead then, Caro? The state Sean's in, I doubt he'll be much good anyway.'

'I'm perfucktly sober,' Sean objected.

I was still horrified about the whole Barbie thing. 'Help you with what?' I asked frantically.

'The barbecue. Ned's out there now burning something or other, you can smell it from here! We've got burgers and sausages and chicken wings . . . whatever you like. Veggie burgers for me, of course. Sean has already attacked most of the hot dogs, but there's still plenty to go round.' Bev held out her hand and pulled me up. 'I take it you will be staying for lunch?'

'Er . . .'

'Go on, love, Bev needs another woman to talk at. You'll be doin' us all a favour,' Sean said, winking at her. 'Mine's a beefburger with extra chilli sauce and pickle, please. And don't bloody burn it, neither. I like to still see pink on it.' He belched and changed channels on the television, but was dismayed to find almost exactly the same thing on the other side.

'Sean love, it's a barbie,' Bev said. 'You can't make a decision between rare, medium rare and well done. You'll have your burger black and crispy, like it or lump it. Now come on, Caro, let's get the meat out of the freezer and make some tea.' We wandered into the kitchen and Bev put the kettle on and told me to go outside into the garden and say hello to Grandad Ned. I wandered out of the back door into the sunshine and found him standing on the patio brandishing a pair of tongs, while an unknown child of about two years old sat in a sandpit by the shed wearing a nappy and a sunhat. Grandad Ned was turning slabs of cremated meat on a crackling barbecue, and humming a song to himself.

'Hello, Grandad Ned,' I said, squinting up at him.

He studied my face for a while, not registering who I was at first. 'Oh! Little Carol!' he exclaimed, when he finally recognised me. 'The soldier has come back from the wars!'

'It's Carol*ine*, not Carol. And my arm is nearly all mended now. Well . . . I can just about bend it, anyway. See?'

'So it is. Now, would Carol*ine* care for a burger?' He pointed with his tongs at the flambéed patties on the grill. 'They're cooked to perfection.'

I was doubtful. They looked a bit shrivelled and sad to me.

'Bev is making some tea, I think,' I said, not wanting to seem rude or ungrateful. 'Do you want some?'

'Ooh, lovely.'

'What's that baby doing there?' I asked, peering over at the pink-faced, pop-eyed little child in the sandpit, who was now banging a plastic blue spade against an upturned bucket and gurgling happily.

Ned looked over his shoulder and frowned. 'Do you know, I can't remember. You'll have to ask Beverley. She seems to inherit various little cute things all over the place. I can't keep up with her.'

'That's Eddie,' Bev called out from the kitchen. 'I'm looking after him for somebody. He's a lovely baby.'

I regarded him for some time. 'He's quite ugly,' I commented, unable to find anything lovely about him at all.

'Hmm, better ugly and well behaved than pretty and a pain,' Bev said, coming out into the garden with an armful of various sundries. 'Here you go, have one of these choc ices before they melt.'

I gratefully unwrapped one and bit the corner out of it. 'You missed the wedding, Grandad Ned,' she said. 'Lady Diana and Prince Charles.'

'Nah, not interested in all that, duckie. Had to keep an eye on junior out here and had some more bulbs to plant, anyway.'

'Bulbs?' I thought this was most peculiar. 'In the . . . soil?'

'Oh yes, they'll grow up lovely they will, by next spring them pots will be burstin' out with the most beautiful flowers, mark my words. Pinks and yellows, all sorts. You wait and see.'

I glanced over dubiously at the three large terracotta pots. 'Hmm. That's not for ages though.'

He laughed. 'You youngsters, you're so impatient!'

'Hey, guess what, I'm six next week!' I announced, suddenly remembering.

'Are you really?'

'Yes. On Tuesday.'

'You havin' a party are you?'

I shrugged and looked down at the patio, kicking a piece of charcoal. 'Don't think so,' I said. 'Mummy said she might take me out for a meal, though.'

'Oh, that'll be nice.'

'Yeah. McDonald's, probably.'

'Well. That should be . . . fun. McDonald's, eh? Getting any nice presents?'

'I want a Barbie, or a sledge. Barbie for birthday, sledge for Christmas. That's all I want. And a Care Bear. The blue one with the cloud on his tummy. Not a Tiny Tears doll, though, they're silly. My friend Amber got one of those and it's just like all the others except you give her water and then it comes out of her eyes and in her knickers, but only if you shake her about a bit. Oh, and one of those things that you can do pictures on. I want one of them, and a fashion wheel too. And some felt-tip pens, in every colour. And some more Famous Five books. And a Lego set. One that's better than my brother's.'

'Oh, yes. I see.' Ned obviously wasn't exactly au fait with little girls' wish lists, so he didn't interrogate further. He flipped the burgers, sat back in a stripy deckchair and turned his face towards the sun. 'Lovely weather,' he sighed. 'You'll have to come out with us lot when we go down to the seaside, last weekend in August. Bev and Sean have got a little caravan right near the beach, you see. Clacton. They bought it when they were first married, back in the sixties when all that silly love and peace nonsense was going on. That was their first home, that caravan. Her mother an' me nearly had a fit when we saw it. They painted it yellow and orange. Can you believe it? Yellow and orange, by God! Sight for sore eyes, let me tell you.'

I nearly choked on the last mouthful of my choc ice. '*Really?*' I couldn't imagine Bev and Sean living in a yellow-and-orange caravan.

'It's a beautiful caravan, Dad.' Bev corrected him sternly, saving what was left of the burgers from the grill and shoving them inside some floury baps with a noisy squirt of mustard. 'You and mum only hated it because it didn't agree with your stupid bourgeois ideals and standards.'

Ned cast me a bemused look, and I responded with a confused one.

'Whatever you say, love.' Ned humoured her, sensing, rightly, that this was the advisable thing to do.

'All my most cherished memories are of when I lived in that caravan,' Bev went on dreamily, arranging the burgers on a large platter and ripping open a pack of frozen sausages. 'They were the best times.' She placed the sausages on the grill and they hissed loudly. She poked and turned them distractedly with a spatula. 'We had no money, just a caravan and each other. It was wonderful.'

I looked at Ned and he tapped his wrinkled forehead and mouthed the word 'crazy'.

'But still, that was a long time ago,' Bev concluded, snapping out of her nostalgic mood and smiling forlornly. 'Dad, make yourself useful and take these burgers in to the boys. And those beers on the side over there, too, if you can manage it.'

Ned pushed himself out of the chair with a groan and obliged in a slow and shambling fashion, mumbling something under his breath about why couldn't they come out and get it themselves, the lazy buggers.

I was going to interrogate Bev about the holiday and the caravan, but then Mark came out into the garden complaining of being bored, loudly and angrily, as if it was someone's fault. Bev looked a little exasperated and, to my acute embarrassment, suggested he might want to play spinball on the lawn with me. Mark made a disgusted noise and glared at me accusingly. ‘Oh bloody hell, are you *still* here?’ he demanded.

3

Remarkable Mushroom

'It was God who made me so beautiful. If I weren't, then I'd be a teacher.'

Linda Evangelista, supermodel

St Luke's parish church is less than a hundred yards up the road from Bev and Sean's front gate, and in all the years that the Croziers have lived in Bluestone Rise, the sign outside has always remained the same. Over time, the sign has weathered badly and what was once printed in bold black letters on white paper has gradually faded to dark-grey, barely legible print on yellowing parchment, with the corners curled in like an ancient script. A collection of dead insects has gathered at the bottom of the display board behind the dirty glass, a miniature graveyard of decomposing flies and bugs, spindly legs all akimbo and inert little wings folded and fractured. One of the dead insects has expired over the ancient notice in such an odd position that the word 'flock' looks like 'fuck':

> Acknowledge that the LORD is GOD.
> He made us, and we belong to him;
> We are his people, we are his flock.
> Psalms 100:3

Next to the biblical quotation, also unchanged over the years, is the touchingly illiterate:

> This Church of GOD freely open it's doors to lost soles who seek to find the path to HEAVEN through Jesus CHRIST the LORD.

Underneath this, some evidently 'lost sole' had scrawled *GOD SUX*, and, in a different spray-can colour (electric blue), *SKIN UP FOR JESUS* and *KELLY IRWIN IS A SLAG*. Other than these relatively inoffensive little ditties however, the church noticeboard and the building itself were unusually and mercifully devoid of the typical blasphemous graffiti that decorated most other available surfaces in and around Rivington Hill.

In the caretaker's yard at Willow Lane Primary, for example, an admonitory and preposterously optimistic sign on the brick wall said: COMMIT NO NUISANCE. The caretaker, a cranky and reclusive widower in his fifties, was responsible for the creation and erection of the sign. Arguably, he was equally responsible for its prompt desecration because, as the ten-year-old graffiti artist later argued in his own defence, 'I'd never of written *piss off you old cunt* if he hadn't put the sign up in the first place.' At the bus stop, on the Ilford route, further decorative scrawls of colour vividly conveyed the empty thoughts and vacuous declarations of the masses. *I shagged Jamie ere*; *Dagenham Posse Roolz OK*; and the unfathomable *Spades go home and boil yer bums*, the origin and meaning of which will likely forever remain a mystery (although the general sentiment behind it was acknowledged and duly ignored by the black people of the community). On the wall of the Barley Mow, by the front door: *I love Kelly Irwin* (she was a favoured subject of many spray-can musings, both vituperative and desirous), *West Ham FC 4EVER* (courtesy of Billy Crozier after his first alcoholic binge in 1982), *Matt Evans is gay* and *D. Frampton has no dick and shit hair.*

Sometimes the graffiti hinted at a potentially poetic leaning, a frustrated and sensitive artist lurking somewhere behind the guise of anguished vandal: *Fuck the teachaz/Fuck the police/Fuck the guvament/Fuck me, please* (as sprayed outside the gates of Willow Lane Primary). Most of the time, though, it was just wanton abusiveness and indiscriminate filth, ad nauseam. Private property was not safe, and even the most safely guarded wall, garage, shed, fence or car was highly likely to find itself on the receiving end of an impromptu paint job, or worse.

Like many outer-city suburbs, then, Rivington Hill was perhaps not the ideal place to grow up in, and certainly didn't produce a noticeable number of well-balanced and law-abiding citizens. Some were immune to the pervasive atmosphere of despair, but most were in agreement that there was only one way out of the grime: crime. Of course, it was not so much a 'way out' as a short-term coping strategy that ultimately wedged them even further 'in'. The 'us and them' divide became not so much an issue as an all-out crusade against which there was a united front, intent on rebelling with full pugnacious force. And the rebellion took on an augural, irresistible force within such communities, so that you were left with two stark choices: join in or get out. It was gang mentality, false security, but it was the only security most people knew. Even the few ostensibly decent and principled families who attended St Luke's every Sunday were unlikely to turn down an opportunity to earn a quick and highly illicit bob or two. The vicar himself, who appeared so deceptively unassuming and sweet-natured in his chunky-knit cardigan and dog collar, was something of a notorious 'Delboy Trotter' type and he made no apology for his shady dealings. After all, it was probably his 'old mucker upstairs', a.k.a. the Good Lord Almighty, who put the good deals his way in the first place, so who was he, a humble servant of God, to turn down such kindly deific gestures? A bit of divine intervention never went amiss, and divine collusion was even better.

Between the hours of ten and midday on Sundays, Father McKinley was indeed the very picture of holy rhapsody, sermonising from the pulpit to the hard-core faithful of Rivington Hill (his congregation seldom amounted to more than half a dozen pensioners, two pathologically quiet families and a mangy dog). But there was another side to Father McKinley, and he would display an even greater enthusiasm when flogging his ever-changing array of knocked-off items to members of his parish, pronouncing each of them, not untruthfully, to be a 'ruddy steal'. Sometimes he would have the audacity to advertise his wares on the noticeboard in the vestibule, bold as brass, among the *St Luke's News* updates, the latest Girl Guide events, charity raffles and Gardening Club memos. He was a born salesman, and would often try to convert strangers in the street with the hard sell. His approach was simple and direct: 'Do you want to go to Hell when you die, my friend? Or do you want to find a friend in Jesus Christ and reserve your place in Heaven among the righteous souls?' If they showed no interest in Christianity and in saving themselves from the infernal bowels of Hell (as was the usual and expected response), he would gleefully seize his moment and say, 'Oh well, never mind squire, never mind. Tell you what. How about this? Can I interest you in a genuine eighteen-carat gold-plated diamond fascia Cartier watch, still in its box with a guarantee? Genuine, mind. One hundred per cent, mate. Kosher. Trust me. For you, because I like you, call it a ton. Come on, can't say fairer than that. These beauties are over a grand down 'arrods. Rare as you like. Swear to you. On me mother's grave. Would a man of the cloth lie?'

Father McKinley was no ordinary vicar, and the churchgoers of Rivington Hill were no ordinary congregation. Few people on the estate had time for religion, even the slightly perverted breed of religion that the wheelin' dealin' cheeky sneaky Father McKinley upheld. They were far too busy eking out their own existence through drink, drugs and money-spinning scams to worry about the existence of God. To them, the very idea of God was arbitrary at best, dull and contemptible at worst.

I knew all about 'love thy neighbour' and 'blessed are the meek', but similarly, religion seemed pointless to me. Bev suggested I accompany her to St Luke's after I expressed a passing interest in Christianity, but even after attending a couple of Sunday sermons, hosted in Father McKinley's inimitable ebullient style, I was still unable to grasp the true meaning and motives behind it. Why look forward to redemption in death when it means spending your whole life repenting? What a waste of time and energy! Why did religion have to have such strict rules and why did people hate other people just because they believed in different things? Everything seemed so paradoxical and hypocritical.

It was during a wedding ceremony at St Luke's church, little more than a year after that much more famous wedding, that I first encountered the Bible. After a single wistful gaze at the frothy white dress and wispy tulle veil, I turned my full attention to Proverbs, and memorised all the verses that struck a chord, for whatever reason:

Wealth protects the rich; poverty destroys the poor.
Beauty in a woman without good judgement is like a gold ring in a pig's snout.
Help others and you will be helped.
The righteous have enough to eat, but the wicked are always hungry.
Better to eat vegetables with people you love than to eat the finest meat where there is hate.
Homes are made by the wisdom of women, but are destroyed by foolishness.
No one, not even his neighbour, likes a poor man, but the rich have many friends.
Intelligent people want to learn, but stupid people are satisfied with ignorance.
It's stupid to get drunk.
Children are fortunate if they have a father who is honest and does what is right.
The rich and the poor have this in common: the LORD made them both.
Poor people are the rich man's slaves.

Children just naturally do silly, careless things, but a good spanking will teach them how to behave.
Pay attention to your teacher and learn all you can.
Make your father and mother proud of you; give your mother that happiness.
Don't be envious of evil people, and don't try to make friends with them.
Rich people always think they are wise, but a poor person who has insight into character knows better.

The Bible was the longest, heaviest and strangest book I had ever seen. It had hundreds of flimsy, diaphanous pages and dozens of simple black-and-white illustrations of fish and donkeys and angels and men with beards. A strange, musty smell billowed up from the pages; it reminded me of Oxfam clothes. There seemed to be no plot to speak of, far too many characters, odd chapter titles and silly little numbers dotted all over the place. And it all seemed so ... contradictory. Nothing actually *happened*, it just *told* you things. Apparently God loved everyone and everything but there were a lot of exceptions, and many things he just wouldn't tolerate. I couldn't be sure whether, as a relatively plain-looking and occasionally naughty (but basically nice) little girl with an active mind and a kind nature but a dubious family background and no known or confirmed father, I was in God's favour or not. God seemed to dislike a lot of things, given that he was supposed to be a God of Love. Drunks, loose women, envy, laziness, wealth, adultery, poverty, arrogance, vanity, ignorance, wickedness, hunger. It made me wonder what kind of Christian you needed to be in order to secure your salvation. Perhaps God should try living in Rivington Hill for a while, then maybe he'd realise that goodness and righteousness comes easier to some people than others.

It was at the same wedding, September 1982, that I fell in love with Mark. I was seven, he was nine. I didn't ask for it to happen, he just looked over at me briefly from the adjacent pew at the end of the service and something in his eyes, however subliminal, made my heart swell with a sudden, passionate and absolute love for him. It was a connection that only I could have been aware of, as sudden and breathtaking as a punch in the guts; something I had never experienced before and felt utterly certain I would never experience again with such an incandescent intensity. Of course, he was that little bit older and I had always considered him very handsome and suave, and these are always factors precipitating a massive crush for an impressionable little girl. But all at once, the fiery little flutter was something more, and it frightened me. It felt like fate, but at the same time I knew, deep within my heavy bursting heart, he could never reciprocate the feeling. He would never love me, not like this. Never like this. Nobody could ever love anybody the way I loved him. It was an impossible love; it overpowered my body and simultaneously dispirited my soul. It would remain unrequited, and that simple truth only made the passion all the more intense. Such was the masochistic nature of my intense passion. And so it remained.

The bride at this particular wedding was Bev's god-daughter, Christine. She was only nineteen and her chosen husband was much older: 'getting on for forty', according to Bev. I thought this was weird. Why would anyone want to marry someone old enough to be their dad? The guy even had grey hair. And worse, a moustache. Nevertheless, true to my status as Bev's unofficial honorary daughter (which had taken me very little time to assume), I had been more than happy to attend the wedding and look the part. I wasn't given many chances to dress up, and this was the first wedding I had ever been to. Bev had even bought me new shoes and a smart dress with a ribbon at the waist; yellow and blue, with a hat to match.

As respectable as I appeared in all my finery, I stole something that day – the only substantial thing I have ever stolen. While the congregation were enthralled in the melodic throes of 'Joyful Joyful We Adore Thee', I tucked the Good News Bible under my white lambswool cardigan and resolved to read the whole thing cover to cover. Throughout the evening reception, I would disappear every now and then beneath one of the long tables with a plate of sausage rolls and cold quiche to read it in secrecy – I scanned the first part of Genesis then became bored and flicked forward to the New Testament. I knew that stealing from a church was very bad, but thought it was quite possible that God might forgive me because I was reading His Special Book now, and that could only be a good thing. I was learning stuff from the Good News Bible. And I was determined to find some good news in there somewhere before the last dance.

Failing that, I tried to find some advice in it about unrequited love, but instead referred back to the Old Testament and amused myself for the most part with the Song of Songs ('Like a lily among thorns is my darling among women'). I dreamed of how good everything would be when I was grown up, when handsome men like Mark would say such things to me without irony or vomiting.

Eventually, after a period of being frustratingly stand-offish and supercilious toward me, Mark became a little protective, and even (I think) fond of me. I tended to greatly amuse and bemuse him on occasions, albeit mostly unintentionally. I was the annoying little sister he had never had and never really wanted. And he was just the Boy of my Dreams.

I was invited to join the Crozier family on their annual holiday to Clacton-on-Sea in the summer of 1982. During subsequent summers, half-terms and other school breaks, not to mention practically every weekend and most weekday evenings thereafter, I effectively transferred myself from the hard, dysfunctional bosom of my own family to the much more welcoming and congenial comfort of the Crozier family. Bev used to fold out the sofa bed and cover me with a blanket, and before too long I slept over on such a regular basis that I almost viewed their lounge as my own bedroom. Every night after the rest of the family had gone to bed and all was dark and quiet, Norman the dog would pad in and lick my face and lie across my feet. Sometimes one or two of the cats curled up on my chest, or sprawled beside me, purring hypnotically as I stroked them. Even on the coldest winter night, I felt warm and secure and utterly content on my foam guest bed in that cosy room.

Like many of the pets in that house, I was the stray that stayed. And never went away. Just as I was glad for the refuge the Croziers provided, my mother was merely grateful for the fact she rarely had to feed me and seemed quite willing to transfer responsibility. After she met Bev and Sean at a PTA meeting at Willow Lane, she told me that she only wished Kev and Shaz and even baby Jolene would find a nice, 'do-gooding' family like the Croziers so that she might be granted some peace and quiet once in a while. I wasn't really sure how sincere she was, but then I never really knew very much about her at all.

Sean's parents, Barbara and Jack Crozier, lived a simple, rustic life in a quaint, cosy little whitewashed cottage that had an outside toilet and a wonky chimney on a sloping red-tiled roof, situated on the Newquay coast, overlooking a small farm. They were a sprightly, slightly unorthodox but immensely sweet and gregarious couple, whose long and successful marriage worked because of, rather than in spite of, their individual quirks. Barbara had long, straight, silver hair and hardly any wrinkles. Jack had no hair at all, with a protuberant head and comical horn-rimmed glasses that looked too big for his small face, which was the colour and texture of a mouldy peach.

Sean was the middle of three boys. Charlie, the eldest, was certifiably mad and lived on his own in a mobile home in Dublin. Barbara and Jack would periodically receive letters from him and the odd garbled telephone call, but sadly hadn't seen their beloved first-born since he left home to 'discover new highs' in 1964 and instead ended up finding a new low. There he had remained ever since, his mental state progressively deteriorating until a road accident in 1976 lost him a leg and an eye – from which point, curiously, he appeared to stabilise. Richard, the youngest, worked for the BBC and lived in Dorking in Surrey with a wife called Natalie and a son called Josh. There was little contact between him and either of his brothers, not so much through choice as lifestyle demands and a lack of common ground. The more time passed, the wider the gulf grew. A card at Christmas, and maybe one on birthdays, if memory and time permitted.

For the first year of their marriage, Bev and Sean earned most of their money by busking (banjo, harmonica, tambourine, tin drum), 'freelance palmistry' and, when they got the chance, flogging fake antiques from the back of Sean's car. They lived happily in their caravan for a time, and ate baked beans straight from the can and watched the sunset behind the sea every night, sitting huddled together on the back step wrapped in a rug. They had William in 1968, moved nearer London to seek out a more profitable and conventional family-focused life, and the rest is history. Bev jettisoned her tie-dye sari and essential oils in favour of an apron and a can of Pledge. Liberation and latitude were sacrificed for comparative security and a safe and predictable home life in the suburbs. I learned nearly all the Crozier family history from browsing through family albums with Bev and engaging in discussions with Ned, and the more I learned, the more fascinated I became.

From the first time I stayed with Jack and Barbara Crozier, sleeping on a squashy camp bed in the small back room at their cottage, with the scent of roses wafting through the open window, I knew all I wanted was to be a part of this family for ever. Those holidays in Newquay, just one week once a year, made me feel glad to be alive. Waking up to the sound of the cockerel in the morning, Barbara bringing me breakfast in bed on a silver tray; bacon and fried bread with the eggs done 'sunny side up – just how you like them m'darlin'', spending most days idly exploring the rock pools on the beach with my net and bucket until the sun went down. Eating deliciously greasy fish and chips with Billy and Mark at the amusement arcade, losing all my money within minutes and then losing all the two-pence coins that Mark gave me on the penny-drop machines.

Although with hindsight there wasn't anything objectively extraordinary or remarkable about them, there seemed to be no end to the wonderment that the Crozier family provided for me. Still, I continued to find it odd and a little frustrating that I always managed to ingratiate myself with most of the grown-ups, while people from my own generation rarely had much time for me. I would have done anything to have Mark on my side. Anything.

Sometimes I felt like he was. Sometimes I even felt that there was hope; that my love was not entirely in vain. Another memory comes to mind.

It was a Tuesday morning at school, a very crisp late-October morning with a sky that was practically pure white, whisked up like ice-cream. Outside was freezing cold despite the absence of a breeze, and the birds sulked and shrilled and puffed up their feathers, guarding their eggs in twig nests high in the bare branches of spindly trees. The year was 1984. Our teacher was called Mrs McLeod, a highly spirited little Scottish woman with a unique approach to the curriculum and an even more original dress code. The children respected her authority more than any other teacher's, simply because she was a little bit deranged and there was always the simmering threat that her profound eccentricity would burst out unexpectedly into full-on hammer-wielding psychosis. That morning she was wearing magenta pedal pushers and a red zip-up hooded jacket that said BROOKLYN, NY on the back. She was taking her class outside for a 'nature walk', on the tenuous premise that she was going to show us 'one of life's small miracles'. To Mrs McLeod, a 'small miracle' could be anything, from a feather to an acorn to a snail's shell to a fresh mound of canine excrement. So her pupils did not have high hopes about the miraculousness of this small thing, whatever it might be. Nevertheless, Mrs McLeod had successfully instilled a little bit of enthusiasm and mental vigour within at least two of her charges, I being one and Amber the other. After leading us all past a copse of trees along the tarmac path towards the playing field, Mrs McLeod suddenly stopped, flinging out her arms dramatically, crucifixion-style, so the straggling line of children behind her stopped, one after another, like dominoes.

I had left my cardigan back in the classroom and stood shivering and rubbing my arms. Mark, who liked very few people in the class because he found them young and crass and annoying, was fully ensconced in his parka jacket, zipped up to the chin, and hung around on the periphery of the group, looking aloof and uninterested to the point of mental catatonia. He had been moved down a year when he was nine due to protracted spells of chronic idleness, truancy and feigned illness, and so he had little time for the lessons and for his classmates – even less so than he had done before.

Amber noticed me shivering and put her arm around me. Amber had her new coat on, and I was deeply envious – it was a midnight-blue colour, warm and long with a wonderfully soft lining, and the hood was trimmed with black synthetic fur. Amber's 'deputy father' Patrick had picked it up for a fiver in a charity shop, and it was the kind of coat I yearned for. I coveted a beautiful coat like that with all my heart, but instead I had inherited Kev's ugly old green parka jacket, which was full of holes and smelt of boys. Conversely, Amber's coat was in practically perfect condition and smelt of nice washing powder and tangerines. I encircled Amber's skinny waist beneath the coat and we cuddled up together as Mrs McLeod launched into a rhapsodic eulogy about the miracle of nature she was about to reveal to us. Douglas Frampton and Michael Blundell poked me in the back and made a snide comment about 'ebony and ivory'. Amber – once such a sweet, shy, quiet little thing – turned around sharply with a furious flick of her braids and told them to kiss her butt. I sometimes worried about my influence over my friend's usually placid demeanour. But at the same time I was pleased that Amber was picking up all my best points (a feisty 'take no shit' attitude never did anyone any harm after all), while still retaining all that mysterious serenity, integrity and feminine composure that I so admired in her.

'Caroline's got fleas,' Douglas hissed at Amber. 'And she smells like shit.'

'Douglas!' Mrs McLeod trilled, interrupting her spiel when she realised, to her profound indignation, that there was a member of the class who was not providing her with his undivided attention. 'Do you have something to share with us? Hmm? If so, out with it please, and mark my words, young man, it had better be good.'

Douglas, unlike most of the bullies and other general dickheads I had hitherto encountered during my primary-school years, had at least been blessed with an honest and plucky character. And as much as I despised him, I had to concede that he was at least consistent and behaved in an equally brazen and unpleasant way in solo as he did in the naturally emboldening company of friends. I admired that consistency.

'I was just telling Amber that her lesbo lover is smelly and has fleas, Miss,' he said. 'I just thought she needed to know.'

'I see.' Mrs McLeod stood before her restless charges and contemplated the best way to react to this puerile but disarmingly direct assertion. 'Well, may I suggest you impart such pertinent information in your own time? Hmm? Please, children, I am *trying* to –'

My hand flew into the air and I called out, 'Miss! Miss!'

Mrs McLeod blinked at me wearily through her thick, beige-tinted glasses. With a sigh, she said, 'Yes, Caroline?'

'It's not true,' I blurted out.

'What?'

'I don't have fleas, Miss.'

Mrs McLeod was beginning to get flustered. 'Listen, I don't think . . .'

'*And* she doesn't smell,' Amber piped up, tightening her arm around me protectively. 'Douglas just picks on people because he knows he is the ugliest and smelliest person in the world.'

At this, I almost fell over with surprise. Amber never spoke in class, at least never more than 'yes' and 'no' and 'I don't know'. This was encouraging progress.

'Fuck you, Sambo,' Douglas sneered, his fetid breath and brutish expression doing little to disprove the plausibility of Amber's accusation.

'*Please*, enough of this!' Mrs McLeod pleaded, clapping her hands before raising them skywards, the soft Celtic cadence now warbling slightly, as it always did when she became over-anxious or excited. 'When you are older you might come to realise how much beauty this world has to offer us, and you will cease this silly talk of fleas and smells. Now!' She clapped her hands together again, aware that her eccentricity was beginning to get the better of her. Twenty-six pink, black or brown faces, half of them inquisitive and half of them bored, stared back at her expectantly, or else listlessly, down at the ground. On she went, unable to stop herself.

'As I was trying to say, before I was so rrrudely interrupted . . .' She rolled her 'r' and exaggerated her accent, a sure sign she was getting carried away. 'We have come outside, children, into this crrrisp, brrracing autumn air to witness for ourselves how indescribably wonderful and extraordinary Mother Nature really is. How, every now and then, lest we forget, she provides us with splendid little examples of her power and beauty and resilience. Things the untrained mind may consider commonplace and unremarkable, but no! Noooo!' She shook her head ferociously and pointed to the ground by her feet. 'You see?'

Our curiosity slightly whetted, but hopes still realistically low, we all looked at the spot she indicated and saw nothing more splendid or extraordinary than a mushroom, not dissimilar from the everyday mushrooms available in bulk at any supermarket. It had obviously emerged overnight from the tarmac, in what Mrs McLeod reverentially described, in hushed tones, as a 'glorious, triumphant, fungal eruption'. She gazed around at the class, her eyes wide and pellucid. Every expression she met was blank or contemptuous.

Michael Blundell was outraged. 'You dragged us out here to show us a *mushroom*?' he moaned. 'A bloody *mushroom*?'

Mrs McLeod pursed her lips, refusing to rise to the provocation. She straightened up and looked at him. 'Tell me, Master Blundell, what do you see every morning when you look in the mirror?'

I grinned to myself, sensing that a well-deserved and timely put-down was imminent. Nothing can compare to the sadistic sense of glee that comes from witnessing the public humiliation of an avowed enemy, and nobody doled out public humiliation as effectively as Mrs McLeod did. All eyes turned to Michael.

He hesitated, glanced at Douglas, and said, 'I see . . . my . . . face, Miss.'

'Your face. Right. Of course. Anything else?'

Michael was getting a little nervous now. 'Well, I see me. Just . . . me.'

'And you're happy with that, are you?'

'Er . . . yeah.' Michael was feeling unfairly victimised, and this of course is a feeling that bullies are particularly uncomfortable with, so he then rashly added, 'And I'd rather look at my face every morning than *yours*, Mrs M, that's for sure.'

Douglas chuckled and clapped his accomplice on the back, and Michael relaxed, knowing this moment of bravado had given him that all-important opportunity to realign the teacher–pupil hierarchy. No teacher should ever be granted the upper hand, not even a mad Scottish one.

Mrs McLeod sucked a long inhalation of breath between her teeth and remained portentously composed. 'Is that sooo?' she said. Mrs McLeod rarely lost her temper, but when she did, God help you. The class waited for Mrs M to launch into her attack – even Mark became slightly more alert as we all watched her facial expression adjust itself into a smile of formidable sangfroid.

'Do you consider yourself to be a handsome young man, Mickey?'

Mrs McLeod rarely shortened the names of her pupils, so this informality was something of a surprise, especially to Michael. He much preferred to be called 'Mike', as he was of the opinion that only overweight builders and cartoon mice were called Mickey. Judging by the expression on his teacher's face, though, he wasn't going to argue with her. Not even he was stupid enough to try.

'Dunno, Miss,' he muttered.

'Shall I ask the girls what they think?'

Michael must have known that any attempts at cheeking her would almost certainly backfire badly at this stage, so he hunched his shoulders, stared at the ground and mumbled, 'No.'

Boys who are *objectively* ugly often overcompensate for their facial shortcomings by being loud, brash and outrageous, or perhaps by cultivating their own personal brand of detracting humour. Douglas and Michael, the class clowns, got away with one hell of a disservice to the human form, but sadly the older they got, the less their comic capers amused. So they were just objectively ugly and objectively annoying with it.

'In that case, would you kindly shut up, or I will be forced to do something nobody here but you will regret. You understand?'

Michael dug his hands in his pockets, frowned, and muttered something unintelligible that Mrs McLeod accepted as grudging assent. She stared him out for a few more seconds (another one of her unnerving powers), and turned back to the mushroom. She crouched down beside it and recommenced her appraisal, almost as if it had never been interrupted: 'Victorious! Glorious! Triumphant! Beautiful little mushroom!'

Mrs McLeod, bless her, was in the wrong job. Or rather, she was in the right job, but she was stuck with the wrong kind of pupil. The average Willow Lane pupil was not likely to provide the captive, creative audience she craved for these odd little forays into hyperbole about Nature.

'Look, children,' she enthused, 'marvel at how it has veritably *exploded* forth from beneath the hard, intransigent ground, displacing that tarmac in its trajectory. Simply stunning. What beautiful, awe-inspiring determination, for such a little, delicate thing! What natural wonder!'

Either she didn't know that her pupils were as yet unable to understand words of more than two syllables, or to appreciate phenomena beyond Atari computer games and cunningly marketed Hasbro and Mattel products, or she was merely talking to herself at this stage. I for one was certainly more than a little perplexed as she continued to ramble, but nevertheless I found her enraptured rhetoric quite touching.

'Against all odds, it has burst forth its fabulous umbrella head, arching toward the sky, tasting daylight, soaking up the air. The triumph of fragility over brutality, like . . . like . . .'

My hand shot up when I suddenly remembered something I had recently read, and I called out before Mrs McLeod had even noticed my frantically waving arm.

'Please Miss,' I said, 'do you mean like that Allsop fable about the wind and the sunshine?'

Mrs McLeod looked fit to pop with excitement. 'Yes! Yes, exactly that, Caroline. Well done. When did you read that?'

'When my Uncle George was last on day release he came to visit my mum and he brought presents for everyone, and I got a pack of playing cards and the book of Allsop fables and I read all the stories before bedtime, because they're not very long really. Then I beat my brother at pontoon three times in a row.'

There was a silence then, during which I turned and noticed Mark staring at me from the other side of the crowd, and for the first time it seemed he was looking *at* me and not through me. I tried returning the stare, but it was so intense that I had to look away quickly, blushing like mad.

'Well well, you *are* a clever wee lass,' Mrs McLeod beamed eventually, presumably referring to my speedy reading pursuits rather than my pontoon skills.

'God, you're such a crawler, Shaw,' Douglas Frampton said, shoving me in the back again.

'Yeah, a stinking, flea-ridden crawler,' Michael Blundell added, snorting into the cuff of his shirt.

Mark pulled his hood down and retaliated on my behalf, using his usual medley of obscene epithets. 'For fuck's sake, just leave her alone, wankers.'

I was amazed by this vehement and open defence of my honour, such as it was. Mark only ever stood up for himself and had never really paid much attention to my classroom spats and tribulations. I instantly flushed with affection and gratitude, but belied this female vulnerability by turning around quickly and punching Michael in the podge of his paunch, just to show I was more than capable of sticking up for myself. Meantime, Douglas, Michael and Mark bandied insults between themselves until they ran out of original ideas and had to resort to the standard 'gay'.

'*You're* gay.'

'No, you're the fuckin' gay. Faggot.'

'Bender.'

Etcetera.

Mrs McLeod was now hyperventilating with anxiety and impatience, until finally she squealed at the top of her substantial Highland lungs, 'Rrrright, that's *enough*!'

Michael, who always insisted on having the last word, yanked my hair and muttered, 'Shitface crawler,' but Mrs McLeod was not going to allow him the last word this time. She surged forward and pounced on him, pulling him out of the crowd by the collar and declaring him to be 'the most irritating, snotty little boy' she had ever had the misfortune of working with (I thought she was going to say 'bugger' instead of 'boy', but Mrs McLeod managed admirably to restrain herself). By way of a penalty, Michael was made to sit cross-legged on the ground a few feet away from the rest of the group, with his back to his classmates.

'And you can stay behind after school today and write me a poem about why mushrooms are much more beautiful organisms than cocky little boys,' Mrs McLeod told him, rounding off the punishment perfectly. 'Preferably in handwriting I can actually read, not the usual illegible scrrrribble.'

Satisfied that this would give Michael some 'precious wee moments on his oon to contemplate his disruptive misdemeanours', and that the insurgency had now finally been quelled, she continued once again, oblivious to Michael making faces and rude gestures behind her back. 'Yes,' she murmured, closing her eyes, 'the wind and the sunshine. Yes . . .'

We looked at each other in bafflement as Mrs McLeod lost herself once again in the arcane and unfathomable depths of her private thoughts. 'Most of you will, I assume, be familiar with the fables of Mr Aesop,' she said, opening her eyes again and squinting around at each of the children in turn. She looked at me for the longest time, obviously hoping for a little cooperation, but I didn't want to show off any more than I supposed I already had, so I kept quiet and looked down at my shoes.

'You see, children, sometimes even the tiniest things can win battles against the apparently insuperable,' Mrs McLeod went on. 'Gentleness against brute force. This mushroom is testimony to that, is it not? David and Goliath, remember them?'

The religious among us – that is, one painfully shy blonde girl called Ruth who was from a decent Church of England family – nodded vigorously and found the courage to say something.

'David won,' she whispered, barely audibly, with an accompanying blush.

'Yes, that's right Ruthie, little David tossed the wee stone from his catapult and it knocked the great giant Goliath oot cold.'

Otherwise preoccupied with throwing pine cones and pebbles at Michael's head and dodging the return volleys, Mark made a contemptuous noise. 'Yeah, and who believes *that*?' he jeered. 'What a load of bollocks.'

Mrs McLeod's head swivelled round, not unlike an *Exorcist* extra. 'Master Crozier, as the oldest pupil here, I expect a little more decorum from you. Your behaviour leaves a lot to be desired, young man.'

'Well this *lesson* leaves a lot to be desired. I thought you were supposed to teach us stuff, not go on about mushrooms and boring shit. It's such crap.'

'Rrrright, that's it, I've had enough of your cheek, young man . . .'

'Oh, save it, if you're going to make me sit on the ground or write some shite poem or just go on and on at me like a broken record, then I don't care. Do your worst. For *fuck's* sake.'

There was a horrified silence. I spun round and looked at Mark with an ambivalent mixture of awe and revulsion, and he stared straight back and again he didn't take his eyes off me. He remained just as cool and calm as ever. The effect took my breath away, and I consciously cursed myself for being so bowled over by him. Since when did I find stupidity and arrogance so impressive?

Since forever, it seemed.

When Mrs McLeod found her voice, it was surprisingly controlled and subdued, although she had become pale and ominously motionless. 'Go back to the classroom, please Mark,' she said. 'We'll talk about this later.'

'Yeah, right, don't worry, I'm off. Jesus *Christ*.'

I watched him go – swaggering gait, shoulders hunched, hands thrust in pockets, hood pulled up, shoes untied, so utterly vainglorious – and I wondered how someone with so much still to learn could be so full of disdain and self-assurance.

And yet I still loved him, and hated myself for it.

In early December that same year, Mark and I were doing some ill-advised peak-time Christmas shopping together in Chelmsford. Bev and Sean had dropped us off in the morning and ordered us to meet them in the Debenhams restaurant at lunchtime, provided we hadn't been 'crushed to death' by then (Sean's macabre but not entirely implausible scenario). Sure enough, it did seem that the entire population of south-east England had gravitated toward that comely little corner of Essex on that particular Saturday, swarming around with their assorted bulky carrier bags and rolls of wrapping paper, sticking out at all angles like gaudy bayonets. Impatience and avarice had long since quashed the festive cheer that was presumably supposed to be promoted by the endless, nerve-grating piped music which played round and round in the shopping centre, the aural equivalent of Chinese water torture.

We had arrived at ten in fairly high spirits, but by midday both of us were rapidly losing the will to live.

'Why do you suck up so much at school?' Mark had asked me.

'What are you talking about? I don't suck up,' I replied, perhaps a little too tersely. I narrowly avoided a collision with a poker-faced teenage mother, formidably armed with a child-crammed twin pushchair, who, like most similarly encumbered mothers, was walking with the unheeding fury and destructive determination of a dalek. Pushchairs as ammunition – it was all the rage, especially at Christmas time.

Deliberately changing the subject, I wailed, 'God, if I hear "Winter bloody Wonderland" one more time I will scream! And how many people live in bloody Chelmsford anyway? It's driving me *mad*!'

Mark ducked into Our Price and I followed him. We were silent for a while, Mark browsing the rock and pop section, while I feigned interest in the singles chart. Tears for Fears. Frankie Goes to Hollywood. Thompson Twins. Wham! (CHOOSE LIFE) Band Aid. 'Do They Know It's Christmas?' How could anyone *not* know it was Christmas, I thought grimly.

'I just don't get it,' Mark continued, presumably still addressing me but not looking at me, instead selecting a cassette to study the track listing on the back. 'School is like, totally shit, and you seem to love it. Sorry Caz, but that ain't normal. And you're good at everything, like a natural fuckin' genius or summink. You *know* stuff.'

I was unable to defend myself adequately against Mark, and my respect and admiration for him ran so deep that I felt both obliged and compelled to agree with just about everything he said, even if this meant contradicting myself in some cases. In spite of this, I secretly objected to the way he talked; deliberately and exaggeratedly drawling mockney, with the typical lazy habit of inserting expletives at random and unnecessary intervals in every sentence. He never used to talk like that, not when I first knew him. True, he had never really had a 'civilised tongue in his head', as Ned would say, but he hadn't been as coarse as this a year or so before.

'I don't love school,' I asserted defiantly. 'And anyway, I'm not good at PE.'

That much was very true.

Even Mark couldn't deny this. 'I mean the brainy stuff. Maths and that shit. And the creative stuff. Reading and writing. I can't be fucked with any of that. Fuck it.'

Like most other estate boys, Mark's favourite word was 'fuck'; its versatility and inherent applicability in any conversation was indisputable, no matter what the theme. As a noun it was perfect and punchy, as a verb it was suitably dismissive and crude, as an adjective or simple conjunction it added a certain *je ne sais quoi*. In short, as a word, it was pretty much indispensable.

Mark decided to buy the tape, and gave a tenner and a briefly flirtatious smile to the moderately attractive adolescent girl at the till. She rang up the purchase, fingered her nose ring, stuffed the cassette into a bag and gave him his change without even glancing at him. I didn't have very much money, and the little I did have was supposed to go towards presents for every member of my family, *and* something nice for the Croziers, preferably a small gift each for everyone. And of course, a nice little greeting card for all my friends – Katie, Amber, definitely one for Mark, possibly one for the new Pakistani girl who had just started in my class. I felt sorry for her because Mrs McLeod couldn't pronounce her name properly, and Michael and Douglas frequently taunted her by pronouncing it deliberately very wrong.

I had seven pounds and eighty-five pence to spend.

'What do you think I should buy my mum for Christmas?' I asked Mark, still anxious to divert the topic of conversation away from that of school.

Mark shrugged. 'How am I supposed to know? A bottle of meths?'

I ignored the dig and tried a different tactic. 'Well . . . what are you getting for *your* mum?'

Again, he shrugged. 'Nothin'. She told me not to bother.'

'But . . . but . . . you have to get her *something*.'

'Why? I haven't got her anything before. I'll get her a card, that'll do. She's easily pleased anyway.'

I felt curiously enraged by Mark's indifference. 'You're so selfish,' I snapped. 'She deserves more than that.'

'Oh, get a life, Caz. Fancy a milkshake or something before we meet my folks? My shout.' He nodded towards Burger King and smiled at me in his typically infuriating/ingratiating way.

My stomach had been grumbling for a while now. I had skipped breakfast because the bread was stale and the milk was sour and my mum had not found the time or the inclination (or indeed the cash) to get more provisions in. Two or three days of every week I would stay at Arcadian House with my real family; not so much because I wanted to, but because I felt I *should*. In a way I was scared *not* to. Bev kept drumming it into me to never take my family for granted and often gave me the 'blood is thicker than water' speech. For reasons that took me a while to grasp, she had absolute respect and admiration for my mother, and was even unable to find anything bad to say about my brother when she met him.

So part of me almost felt tempted to spend my seven pounds and eighty-five pence on some basic groceries instead of silly Christmas gifts. That would help my mum out, show her I cared. Just a litre of semi-skimmed, a small loaf of cheap medium-sliced white, a packet of own-brand cornflakes, some cheese maybe, a bit of streaky bacon, some tinned stuff, a packet of custard creams. That would still have left me with enough for a pack of greeting cards, at least.

My mum collected the family benefits every Tuesday at the Post Office, about half a mile away, and most of it was gone before the weekend. I thought it was mean that we weren't entitled to any extra at Christmas time, especially considering that all the food seemed to be so much more expensive, even though there was so much more of it. A recent visit to Sainsburys with Bev had made my eyes pop out of my head in amazement – the aisles had been stuffed to capacity with huge tins of luxurious assorted biscuits, snack selection boxes, massive bars of chocolate, bulging net sacks of brazil nuts, ice cream in every imaginable flavour, frozen turkeys so huge that I couldn't even get my arms around one to lift it from the freezer. Food, glorious food, everywhere, masses of it, sweet and savoury, healthy and delicious, wholesome and indulgent. Calories screamed at you from around every corner, each and every shelf heaving under the weight of innumerable bounteous delicacies. All the people in Sainsburys had filled their trolleys high, some people even had *two* trolleys. It was simply breathtaking. I had asked Bev how there could possibly be so much food in the *whole world*, let alone just in one fairly modestly sized Sainsburys store, and Bev had laughed and explained, 'It's just that time of year, sweetheart.'

It's that time of year. Consumerism gone crazy. Wherever I looked, all I could see was people wanting, pursuing, choosing, purchasing. Christmas: a time for giving, but make sure you get what *you* want first, before someone beats you to it. The greed was astounding. Surely, I thought, the starving in Ethiopia would die of shock if they could see the brightly lit interior of just one British supermarket. Gazing around in rapture at the seemingly limitless choice, I remembered the recent images on television of the terrible, scrawny babies with their hollow eyes and distended bellies, flies landing on sad brown faces, the skewed skeletal limbs, so much suffering. Although it was in a country far away and still far beyond my own understanding, the images had stayed with me, stuck in my mind like visions from a nightmare. I had been entranced by a particularly brutal news bulletin, those endless expanses of desolation and deprivation. *Real* desolation, *total* deprivation. But before I had a chance to learn *how* and *why* the world could be so cruel and unjust, my mother had lit up a Mayfair and changed channels in favour of *The Price is Right*.

'You spendin' Christmas up in Liverpool again this year I s'pose?' Mark enquired, offering me a sip of his Coke. He had bought a burger and a large portion of fries as well, although Bev and Sean were supposed to be treating us to lunch and had ordered us not to spoil our appetites. I sucked on the straw and studied him for a few seconds. Mark ate like a pig, both in the quantity and quality of what he ate, and the manner in which he ate it. He chewed with his mouth open and spoke with his mouth full, spraying food fragments all over the place, totally without shame or self-consciousness. I studied him quite closely in an attempt to stave off the burning passion in my heart, perhaps to convince myself that he was actually quite repellent, not worthy of my admiration and certainly not of my love.

Even after witnessing the remarkably rapid disappearance of half a quarter-pounder down Mark's gullet, the passion still burned, although possibly a little less ardently than was normally the case. Mark possessed a rakish attractiveness. He had intense eyes – dark brown, heavily lashed and deeply expressive, even when he was in a characteristically vacant frame of mind. They were narrow and deep-set, and he had the unerring ability to make the recipient of his smouldering glares and gazes either melt with desire or shudder with dread. Mark essentially had three different kinds of stare: lusty, listless and confrontational. Mark's lips also fascinated me – they were full and sensuous and slightly too pink, giving the possibly misleading impression that he knew damn well how to kiss and that he did a lot of it. I longed to discover whether Mark's lips tasted and felt as good as they looked. I found myself staring helplessly and longingly at his mouth while he talked, and stared even when he was eating, like now, with those luscious lips smeared with sauce and grease. I had spent enough time in his company to know the difference between a genuine smile (rare) and his favoured smirk/grin, an expression I had privately named the 'smark'. This was utilised whenever he felt proud, smug, uninterested, baffled or contemptuous. Needless to say, it was one of his typical expressions.

I sighed and took another sip of Coke, the smell of the burger making my empty gut groan ravenously.

'Yes,' I replied, helping myself to a couple of Mark's French fries. 'Patrick is giving us a lift up there in his van the day before Christmas Eve.'

I felt no excitement whatsoever at the prospect of this annual jaunt up north. Another Christmas in Liverpool. The same as it always had been, for as long as I could remember. Another week spent in my grandmother's horrible little house with the tatty artificial tree slanting at an odd angle in its little red pot in the poky front room, cracked baubles and tin-foil trinkets dangling from every threadbare branch, ugly grimacing fairy stuck on the top. Cards on the mantelpiece and the windowsill, blown over by the breeze that whistled audibly through the flimsy sash windows. Tinsel on the door handles, fairy lights at the window, a shabby plastic holly wreath on the door, no hot water last thing at night or first thing in the morning, weak sugary tea and cold porridge with jam for breakfast, overcooked vegetables for dinner.

And Christmas Day was always the ultimate anticlimax: reading out the same lame cracker jokes and wearing silly paper hats that ripped too easily, and drinking too much Panda Cola while my grandmother pottered about in the narrow kitchen and swore at the radio, or stepped on the cat's tail while she left the vegetables to stew for too long on the hob.

Fighting with Kev over who got the best presents (always him). The same row between my mother and grandmother, because they reliably bought each other exactly the same present every year (monogrammed hankies and hosiery of some description). Fighting with Kev over who would have the sofa bed or who would end up on the floor, neither of which were remotely comfortable anyway. Arguments over whether to watch the inane film on BBC1 or the inane quiz show on ITV. My grandmother always got the last word because it was *her house*. After the Queen's speech, my mum would spend hours on the telephone to friends and/or the latest man in her life, i.e., people she 'actually fuckin' liked', while her children would be reprimanded for some boredom-driven misdemeanour by an increasingly irate grandmother. ('That's my phone bill, Eleanor, get the cheeky shyster to call you back, and will you do something about your bloody kids, they're driving me round the bloody bend.')

Oh yes, Christmas. Quality family time; the usual sanity-draining Yuletide ritual. By New Year's Day, homicidal instincts between family members would have reliably reached an all-time high. The television would be left on at all hours just to give everyone something else on which to focus their frustrations and murderous compulsions. The ultimate communal opiate, suitable for all the family. *Essential* for all the family.

'Patrick? As in Amber's dad's bit of rough?' Mark wheezed sardonically.

I frowned at him. 'Yes. He has family on Merseyside. Amber and Gordon are staying at her Auntie Janet's for Christmas. That's Gordon's sister. I met her once. She's weird. She lives in Braintree.'

'That whole family is fuckin' weird, if you ask me,' Mark muttered dismissively, otherwise occupied with the last morsels of his burger. He chewed noisily, regarding me through his eyelashes until I felt quite uneasy and self-conscious. After a moment, he swallowed a final mouthful and asked me, 'Caz, d'you sometimes wish you were someone else?'

This startled me. Mark wasn't the type to ask questions any more far-reaching and profound than 'Fancy a biscuit?' or 'Did you see the size of that bird's arse?'

I considered a response. 'Yes, of course I do,' I said eventually. 'Do you?'

'Who would you like to be?'

'Oh, I don't know . . .' I continued to evade his interrogative stare. I decided to keep my answer fairly diplomatic and obvious, although there was a whole list of girls we both knew at school with whom I would happily have exchanged places. 'Some beautiful famous actress, probably,' I said, taking the easy option. 'Kim Basinger, or maybe Daryl Hannah. Anyone famous and glamorous, really. Maybe Madonna. Or Debbie Harry.'

Mark nodded in approval. 'Yeah, cool. I'd be . . . James Bond.'

'He's a fictional character,' I protested. 'Who would you be in real life?'

'Oh, I dunno. The bloke out of that shit Norwegian band that all the girls fancy. A DJ, maybe. Or some fantastic footballer. Tony Cottee, yeah, I'd definitely be him. Anyone rich and good-looking, really.'

We continued sitting there in silence and relative gloom. Mark drained the last of the Coke, belched and finally concluded, with a heavy sigh, 'Shit, it's so fuckin' boring being us, innit.'

'Yeah.' I acceded with a rueful nod. 'But we can dream.'

4

Love You To Pieces

'In the little world in which children have their existence, whosoever brings them up, there is nothing so finely perceived and so finely felt, as injustice.'

Charles Dickens, *Great Expectations*

Puberty exploded on to the scene, totally uninvited and about two years too early, in the spring of 1985. It gatecrashed my body with all the invasive presumption of a drunk and over-affectionate aunt at an anniversary party, smothering me with its excessive bumps and bulges and pumping me full of hormones and alien thoughts and desires that disgusted me almost as much as they excited me. The smooth, pink body that had suffered and healed itself through so many childhood injuries, that nimble and pliant girl's body with which I was so comfortable and utterly unselfconscious, all of a sudden transmogrified into something altogether different and weird.

It began with hair.

I more or less knew what to expect, but really, so *early*? And so *much*? I was only nine years old, and already weird things had started happening to my hitherto bald little girlie parts. I was repulsed, overwhelmed, intrigued, dismayed and thrilled. I asked my mum: 'What's this hair for?' And I showed her my premature sproutings: three or four dark-brown hairs curling from my plump, pink pudendum. 'Why's it there, Mum? Am I going to have one like yours?'

She didn't explain very much to me at the time, but stopped bathing me with Shaz and Jolene from then on. I was glad about that. I needed my own private bathtime to get to grips with what was going on, to explore my mysterious new folds and protuberances, the parts of me that I was now starting to view in an entirely different light. The pubes didn't stop at three or four of course, and I gave up counting before too long. Kev meanwhile discovered a new way to inflict ultimate pain on his sister – aim for the nipples. As far as I was concerned, getting punched in the nipple could have been no less painful than a full-pelt thwack in Kev's groin. My nipples became an endless source of anguish and delight – just the right amount of pressure (I discovered, late one night, beneath the cover of my duvet) was actually quite pleasurable and tingly; a prod, poke or tweak or anything harder than the softest touch was unspeakable agony.

Sex education inevitably encroached on our otherwise dull and uneventful lessons. Many hundreds of questions had been forming in my ever-curious mind, and the sex-education class, conspicuously inadequate in both its duration and its thoroughness, managed to address few if any of them. Mrs McLeod, under normal circumstances our most liberal and unabashed teacher, had been given the unenviable task of explaining the intricacies of sex to a class of over thirty unruly nine- and ten-year-olds.

She had an hour to do it.

'Okee-dokee girls and boys,' she had begun, unpromisingly, standing next to a dusty old television set on an antiquated stand and clapping her hands together with great authority. 'I'm just gonnae pop on a wee video for you all to watch, and if you have some questions at the end of it, I'll do my utmost to furnish you with the answer.' She asked Jason Baxter to turn the light off and pull the window blinds shut, and then bent down to study the television set and the brand-new VCR positioned underneath, which blinked its blank LCD display at her like a mocking chant. After a few moments of close scrutiny and a confused frenzy of fruitless button pressing, Mrs McLeod silently accepted defeat.

'Yes, well . . .' She coughed and stood upright again with a slight creak and peered at our expectant faces in the gloom of the classroom. 'Jason, if you could turn the lights back on for a wee while, so I can work out how to turn these daft contraptions on . . .'

'Try strippin' Miss! That'll get 'em well turned on, haha!' called out Douglas Frampton, the obligatory prat at the back, whose tireless heckling of teachers was such an everyday occurrence that it was often, to his pique, totally ignored.

Mrs McLeod's only reaction to this was a terse and weary, 'It's "Mrs", Douglas, not "Miss",' and she didn't even look at him. Douglas Frampton was easy to spot and learning to blank him took years of professional practice. He had a messy mop of red curls and a huge pair of goggly blue eyes that stared out gormlessly from a podgy, anaemic face overcrowded with freckles. He was the most annoying and least attractive boy I had ever met, not counting Kev.

Jason obediently flicked the low-voltage lights back on, and Mrs

McLeod pushed her glasses to the end of her nose and, within a minute, discovered the power button on the telly (a large rectangular thing on the bottom right of the control panel that said *on/off*). With a triumphant flourish, she jabbed it with her index finger. 'Now,' she said, as *TV-am* slowly emerged on the screen and the room became filled with the unintelligible drone of earnest adults waffling amongst themselves about current issues. 'If you could all be quiet while the video is on, because there'll likely be a lot to take in . . .' She peered closely at the VCR again, seeking out the *play* button. 'And we'll have no gigglin' or messin' aboot, please children. This is an important . . . er . . . thing. So pay attention, please.'

Eventually, after consulting Martin Pollock (the class technology whizz) once or twice, the video commenced with a crackle and a flicker and the class was confronted with the words: WHAT IS HAPPENING TO MY BODY? in large white letters on a dark-blue background. A couple of the boys tittered. Douglas Frampton hollered, 'My dick's gone all long and hard, Miss!'

Mrs McLeod responded to the mischief by turning the volume up on the telly, and this had the desired effect. Not even Douglas could compete with a seventies sex-education programme with the volume level cranked up and the embarrassment factor on maximum. And watching a suited, sombre, moustachioed man with a mullet standing in front of a detailed diagram of the human body and using preposterous words like 'penis' and 'pituitary' without a discernible twinkle of humour or shame is enough to subdue even the bolshiest pupil.

Mrs M sat at the front of the classroom with her eyes facing forward, unblinkingly watching our reactions with a wry smile. Her expression was a mixture of perverse enjoyment and empathetic chagrin. Similarly, part of me felt compelled to sit and view the entire thing through to the bitter end while a larger part of me wanted to run away screaming. Every time the word 'vagina' was mentioned you could feel, deep within your very *soul*, the burning embarrassment of every little girl in that room. As for 'testicles', well, the boys made valiant attempts at turning their acute mortification into a bit of a nudge-nudge male-bonding session, but it was a pretty unconvincing show all round. There wasn't an unblushing face to be seen anywhere. It was purest cruelty from beginning to end.

To be honest, there must be a better way of teaching boys and girls about sex. Cramming a load of them altogether in a room with an outspoken yet out-of-touch teacher to elucidate all the ambiguous threads of belated info they might glean from a diabolical, out-of-date video – well, it's hardly the ideal approach for such a sensitive subject. Especially when they're at 'that age' – somewhere delicate in between infancy and the start of the onset of puberty. But what is the best way to teach them? And what is the best age? Girls as young as thirteen were pushing prams around Rivington Hill (all over the country they were at it of course, but Rivington Hill was a bit of a hot-spot area for children having children), while boys as old as twelve started to fancy themselves as real men once they had experienced their first productive wank. Instantly, a favourite (and in many cases, *only*) hobby was born. And when those amenable young girls with their active ovaries and those cocksure old boys with their active fists and wrists got together, an even better hobby was discovered, on couches and floors and park benches; feverish and frequent, fast and furious, and all too often fructuous. It was kind of fun, and most important of all, it was *free.* Little more incentive was required. Procreation for recreation.

In the four years I had been attending Willow Lane, my class size had almost doubled, from twenty-one to thirty-seven. Mark was one of the additions. Having been made to repeat the year, he was the eldest by far in our year at eleven and a half, and probably the cleverest except he pretended not to be. As far as I was concerned, he was the best-looking and certainly the most suave and sophisticated boy in the class, if not the world. I felt brave enough to glance over at him just once (his presence made me flush and tremble even in the best of circumstances), and he was calmly ripping pages out of his exercise book and making paper aeroplanes while all the other boys around him buried their faces in their hands or glanced uncomfortably from floor to ceiling. *I bet he knows it all already,* I thought to myself. *I bet he knows everything there is to know about sex in the whole wide world.* Then an exciting idea occurred to me. *Maybe he's already done it!* This fabulous possibility sent a lascivious shiver up and down my spine. *Maybe he can teach me what to do, if he's already an expert.* I felt like my insides were melting as my imagination ran riot over a tantalising series of highly improbable scenarios. I wanted to glance at him again, to check for any outward indication of his sexual mastery, but I couldn't bring myself to do so, and wouldn't even have known what telltale signs to look for anyway. Mark was a bit of an enigma to me, and I kind of liked it that way.

The final agonising moments of the programme depicted four naked bodies – a girl's body juxtaposed against that of a woman, and a boy's compared to a full-grown and unnaturally hairy adult male. The stoic voice of a male narrator explained, with the aid of pop-up arrows, how the girl's body would soon outwardly change as she became a woman ('the nipples will enlarge, and the breasts will fill out, *thus*, and the hips, thighs and bottom will be padded with extra fat with the onset of monthly menstrual periods . . .') and similarly, how the boy's 'testicles will drop and grow hair and produce millions of sperm every day, with as many as three hundred million in every ejaculation'.

This made me sit up and take notice. Three hundred million was a big number. It was one *hell* of a big number. I had once counted up to one hundred when I played hide and seek with Amber, and that had taken so long I thought I would fall asleep with boredom. But *three hundred million* – surely nobody had ever counted up that far. Surely it wasn't even *possible*. That number was like, infinity, practically. I ventured another sneaky peek at Mark and wondered if *he* had three hundred million sperm swimming about inside *his* testicles, or whether three hundred million was just a maximum figure that boys had to work up to until they became proper big men, and they started off with only about half a dozen or so at first. Then I found myself wondering what Mark looked like naked, whether he had hair and muscles yet. Whether he suffered from 'nocturnal emissions'. Whether he touched himself in a special way, 'down there'. To my mortification, Mark caught me looking at him and he stared back intently, furrowing his eyebrows as if to say *what's your problem?* (He was *so* cool!) I turned my head away, feeling on fire.

'Rrright, everyone!' Mrs McLeod exclaimed, standing up suddenly and placing her hands firmly on her fleshy haunches. She indicated to Jason to turn the lights back on and to Martin to stop the VCR and turn off the television, and they both obliged, rather too readily. There was an inward sigh of collective relief now that the video had finally come to an end, and the boys relaxed into ritualistic chortles and conspiratorial asides, while the girls stared at their shoes and wished themselves somewhere else.

'Are there any questions at all?'

Dead silence. Not a single hand went up.

'What, nothing?' Mrs M looked around incredulously. 'That wee film gave you all the information you'll ever need, did it?'

A couple of coughs and a tinkling peal of laughter from Douglas and his cohorts at the back. Molly Broom, the second prettiest girl in the class, hesitantly raised a finger and dangled her arm out at the elbow, trying to be inconspicuous, and failing.

Mrs M pounced. 'Yes, Molly! You have a question?'

'Er . . .'

'Come on, deary. Don't be shy.'

'It's about . . . periods . . . ?'

'Yes, yes. Periods.' Mrs M enunciated the word as if to prove it was not dirty, nothing to be ashamed of. 'Go on.'

'Do they . . . hurt?'

'Och, my dear child, do they hurt!' Mrs M let out a strange high-pitched sound and Molly blushed until she was the same colour as her hair (she had the exact same colour hair as Douglas, except he was ugly with it, while Molly had been blessed with big green eyes, creamy skin and a perfect rosebud mouth). 'Noo, nothin' more than a bit o' a bellyache for a day or two, that's all,' Mrs M assured her with a comforting smile. Having been menopausal for some time, she obviously recalled precious little about her distant adolescent years of monthly hot-water bottles, disabling cramps and tears of anguish over stained sheets.

My hand shot up, almost against my will. Visibly bracing herself for one of my dreaded interrogations, Mrs M sighed and said, 'Yes, Caroline?'

'What's ejaculation mean, Mrs McLeod?'

The words escaped out of my mouth before I was aware of saying them, and Mrs M looked a little taken aback. Somebody tittered, and somebody else broke wind reasonably loudly, and then there was more tittering. Mrs M blinked patiently.

'Well,' she began hesitantly, 'it's . . . it's . . .' She faltered, desperately trying to think of a suitably succinct and sanitary description.

'I know what it means,' Douglas chimed in, waving his arm in the air. 'It's when mess comes out yer cock.'

Mrs M sighed and rocked back on her heels. 'Douglas, any more of your cheek and I'll send you to Mr Sheridan's office.'

Mr Sheridan was the headmaster at Willow Lane; he was very tall and thin and smelled of potatoes and glue. He didn't like Douglas and the feeling was mutual.

'But that's what it *means*, Miss,' Douglas protested.

Mrs M ignored him and instead attempted her own definition. 'Yes, the video did rather skirt over certain issues, didn't it?' she began, clearing her throat. 'Now, yes, let's see, *ejaculation* . . . it's kind of like

... well, the *productive* part of the male orgasm.' She pre-empted the next question and quickly continued: 'And an *orgasm* is ...' Her eyes became glazed and she paused for a little too long, with her hands folded together over her rounded stomach. 'Oooh. How would one describe it? Deary me. Well. It's the very *pinnacle* of sexual fulfilment ... it's kind of like ... a sneeze, I suppose.'

This easy analogy provoked knee-jerk reactions among the restless pre-pubescents. Beside me, Amber raised her hand and spoke up at once in an uncharacteristic show of boldness. 'My dad has hayfever and sneezes all the time!' she blurted out.

Mrs M rushed to put Amber's mind at ease, hurriedly backtracking. 'Aw, noo! When I say "sneeze", I just mean ... och, deary me ...' She trailed off and looked helplessly around, twiddling her thumbs in nervous agitation. 'It's *powerful*, like a sneeze is, you see. You know the way a sneeze builds up and up to an explosion ... ?'

The analogy was sadly lost on us, and Mrs McLeod bit her lip and shrugged her shoulders in helpless dismay as we gazed passively back at her, waiting in vain for enlightenment.

''S'alright, I know where you're comin' from, Mrs M,' someone said, finally breaking the awkward silence. 'If you'll pardon the pun.'

Everyone swivelled around to look at the speaker. It was Mark, of course. He nonchalantly flicked a paper aeroplane into the air, then put the rubber end of his pencil between his teeth and regarded Mrs McLeod with an unsettling stare and the faintest of smiles. I wanted to leap on him and kiss him like they did in the movies. I wanted him to show me, in a practical and hands-on way, what ejaculation *really* meant. Every part of me ached for him. He was *so* cool. So different from the other boys. And he was my *friend.* I hadn't quite ingratiated myself enough to warrant the honour of being considered *his* friend yet, but he was definitely *mine.* He had no choice in the matter of course, because his mum said I was like the daughter she never had and I spent every available minute at their house, assuming that glorious role, wallowing in it. But that only meant he had to acknowledge my existence from time to time, whether he liked it or not. At the very least, I was an annoying surrogate sister who kept getting in the way. But God, I adored him. I absolutely adored him.

'That Mark boy is like, *so* weird,' Amber whispered at me, jolting me out of my oneiric trance.

'Oh yeah, I *know*,' I said. '*So* weird.'

'Well. Thank you, Master Crozier,' Mrs M beamed. 'Now, will there be any more questions or shall I just press on?'

'Er, yeah, hold on, I've got one actually,' Mark said, flicking pages in his exercise book, pretending he had made some notes. Amber rolled her eyes at me and we both giggled furtively behind our hands. He looked up, raised his eyebrows and, with the greatest solemnity and composure, he said, 'How can you tell if you've made a girl pop her cork?'

Two or three of the boys instantly folded with mirth, while everyone else was stunned into dumbfounded silence. Amber looked at me and I looked back at her, and we were both lost for words, although quite possibly for different reasons.

Mrs M opened and closed her mouth, but no words came out. Mark's menacingly placid expression didn't change; he just carried on staring poor old Mrs M out, in silent expectation of an answer. Finally, she found her voice and, with all the false brightness and bravado she could muster, chirruped: 'Now, I think we may be racing a wee bit ahead of ourselves there, Mark dear. Perhaps we should start with the basics, yes?' She adjusted her specs, took a deep breath and consulted a book on her desk, licking her fingers and turning some pages, trying to regain a little of her former composure. 'Now, the reproductive system . . .'

She valiantly battled through the next half an hour or so, using vague terms and euphemisms and doing her best to answer questions that generally revealed a level of knowledge and experience far higher than she could have anticipated. Finally, I was satisfied that I wasn't the only one suffering from 'hair down there' trauma and Mrs M assured all us girls that we should shortly expect some obvious proof of our fecundity, and advised us to be well prepared for it. Similarly, the boys were told to expect 'frequently embarrassing and untimely tumescent episodes' (baffled looks all round), and to 'always treat your female counterparts with the respect they deserve' (more baffled looks).

In the ensuing years, a few quality moments alone with my mum's copy of the arcane *Sex and the Single Woman* and an edition of *Sunday Sport* surreptitiously snaffled from one of her current fly-by-night boyfriends taught me considerably more than any of my sex-education classes. Likewise, progressive discussions with female school friends created and exploded myths along the way.

Piece by piece, I increased my knowledge of all things sexual, propagative, perverse and libidinous; my mind was broadened, future experiences were planned and dreamed of and prepared for and regretted accordingly. And my body did all the things it was supposed to do.

Up until the age of about eight or nine, I was a pretty scrawny kid. There was never very much to eat at home, and I always got plenty of fairly intensive exercise since we walked everywhere and my mum always needed help with the buggy and the shopping. So I was always very active, probably verging on hyperactive. Skinny, but feisty with it. Exuberant.

Then something happened. As happens to females all over the globe, growing pains set in and the blueprint of my genes dictated how my body would react to the continuous swirl of active hormones, every fleshy part under attack from the arbitrary deposits of fat distribution. Puberty filled me out, just like the video had promised. Suffice to say, I *grew.* I grew upwards, but most of all I grew outwards. Bosoms ballooned. A number of my female friends became slightly jealous, describing me as 'shapely' and (in awed tones) 'voluptuous'. Backside blancmanged, bulging out of size tens, then size twelves, then, eventually, halfway through secondary school, size fourteens. Female friends became slightly less jealous, describing me as 'very shapely indeed', or much worse when my back was turned. Fat deposited itself excessively and tenaciously in all the 'right' places, rendering me, for all intents and purposes, normal and natural and every inch a functional woman. Hips: not so much child-bearing as hippo-bearing. Abdomen: sometimes I wondered if there was a hippo gestating in there already. Thighs: strong and sturdy, to put it politely. Female friends' jealousy rapidly waned, turning at once into pity or disdain, or often an uncomfortable combination of both, still disguised as unconvincing admiration – we were all pseudo-feminists, of course.

As my skinniness turned to chubbiness, so my exuberance inverted. Day by day, bit by bit, those mates who I saw as my equals and my allies, that television that had once so amused and enlightened me, all the things I had once unquestioningly trusted seemed to start strategically chipping away at my ego. Yet the illusion of comradeship was maintained throughout. A smile and a kind word here, a stab in the back there; false flattery and snide swipes, underhand tactics, bitchy appraisals and backhanded compliments. It was all part of growing into a woman, surrounded by other female bodies in all their many and varied forms, constantly competing superiority and inferiority complexes in their many guises. How, *why* do we change so irreversibly from happy-go-lucky and carefree little girls to neurotic and bitter young women? For me, it practically happened overnight.

Young kids naturally, *necessarily*, have hardy little egos. From the most timid and shy to the most brash and outgoing, all kids essentially have one person to look out for: themselves. Each and every child is the centre of his or her own world, and that world is a blissfully simple one, because everything is defined solely in terms of how it affects him or her. The perspectives and feelings and motivations of others rarely feature in their simple, egocentric minds. Growing up, growing out of it, means accepting that other people matter too, and ultimately perceiving them as equals, or at least as fellow human beings. This is the good, functional part of growing up: taming the ego, learning one's place.

Some people don't get this. Those who have been humoured and indulged since birth might have trouble with this part, stage one of the ego-shaping process. It's what makes you sociable, tolerable, well adjusted. It's what makes you realise that the world doesn't revolve around you, that you have to make allowances and compromises in order to maintain maximum harmony as part of a civilised society.

Stage two is quite different. Stage two is subtle, virulent and, for some vulnerable people, tragically unavoidable. If you get through stage one and stop there, you are lucky, because stage two is when the healthy ego, the adult ego with its realistic self-love still intact, becomes a prone target. It's all very well being a consumer, what becomes important is maintaining the belief that, as a consumer in a materialistic society, who you are, what you do, what you own and everything you aspire to will never be quite good enough. Even beneath my childish rumbustiousness, even despite the sizeable chip on my shoulder, despite my diligence and determination and academic achievements (not to mention an arguably pleasant personality), I firmly believed that I was never quite good enough, and probably never would be no matter how hard I tried. This was all acknowledged and accepted without actually knowing exactly what 'good enough' meant, what it entailed. Perfection becomes the only goal, and that hopeless ideal haunts the daily lives of all teenage girls, as they are taunted by the unattainable, until it drives them mad and alienates them from everything true and real that they once believed in.

My crippling inferiority complex was not fully realised until I went to secondary school, in autumn 1986. Up until then, school was sufferable and absorbing by turns, although towards the end of my Willow Lane years it was certainly more the former than the latter, and eventually I became so desperate to get out of the place I was practically climbing the walls. I had been recognised as 'gifted' and 'highly advanced' by a number of the teachers, but to be frank I think I only excelled because I was competing with a class full of dolts, in which any child who could spell their name and recite the seven- and eight-times tables was considered a potential genius. Willow Lane was not renowned for its child prodigies and the teachers did not go to work each day brimming with enthusiasm and hopeful of imparting knowledge to bright and receptive young brains. The school was located in the midst of a notoriously rough area where too many parents took little or no interest in their offspring's intellectual development, and where children took even less interest in learning anything constructive beyond defacing school textbooks and backchatting teachers. I didn't consider myself especially intelligent; I was just enthusiastic and curious. I soaked up new information like a sponge, regurgitated it, built on new knowledge, speeding through class exercises and homework assignments until the teachers weren't sure what to do with me.

And I read books, hundreds of them. I got through books in the same way that most people of my age got through cigarettes and lighter fuel. I couldn't get enough of them. I was like the robot in *Short Circuit*: Input! Input! Must . . . have . . . input! My appetite for books – fiction, non-fiction, academic, poetry, anything – was voracious, insatiable. The school library wasn't well equipped (the school was seriously underfunded in just about every way) and my mum couldn't even afford the *Beano* every week, so I wrote my own books when I ran out of reading material.

When I got really desperate, I would sneakily borrow some of my mum's second-hand dog-eared books and read them by torchlight under my duvet, while Kev snored and fidgeted in the bunk above. Mum had a sizeable collection of seedy, formulaic novels penned by shockingly wealthy and unimaginative American nymphomaniacs and socialites, bored out of their numb skulls and apparently no longer adequately satisfied by a formidable arsenal of dildos and twenty-four-hour cable television.

Every plot was the same, a bland mirror image of the author's own empty life, with just a few barely distinguishable tweaks here and there. Poor little rich girl rattling about in deceased daddy's or absent husband's mansion, her unrivalled beauty (they were always, *always* beautiful) attracts a host of amorous suitors, and 'something' predictable happens in between the decadent dinner parties and gala events (a cancer diagnosis perhaps, or a family bereavement or 'surprise' pregnancy). A whole host of vapid characters help to smooth over or spice up the various plot 'issues' until it is 'somehow' resolved via numerous and preposterous sexual awakenings and/or a shrewd career move involving lace underwear and a healthy bit of back-stabbing. I must confess that before I knew everything there was to know about sex and stuff, many of the scenes in these novels had me very befuddled. For example, for a long time I agonised over a passage that went something like this:

> With slow sensuous movements, Gianni laid Clarissa's slender, naked body gently upon the soft pile of the bathroom carpet, tenderly kissing her face, her throat, her breasts until, no longer able to stave off the inevitable carnal yearnings after so many years of temperate asceticism, she yielded to him readily, naturally . . . He then proceeded to part her honeyed thighs, licking hard at those fragrant, moist folds until she came, bucking rapturously against him with the trembling force of her excitement . . .

I tended to skirt over such scenes at first and although I knew they were most certainly rude I didn't have the inclination to scrutinise the finer details. The immediate questions that did come to my mind, however (and which remained unanswered for some years, some even to this day): *Can* a bathroom be carpeted? If so, what was the point? Temperate asceticism? Pardon? How can thighs be 'honeyed'? Fragrant? What? How is it that she 'came' when she was already there? I read and reread this passage, but the more I went over it, the less sense it made. People in these books were 'coming' all over the place, when as far as I could tell, they were quite simply *already there.* It just didn't make sense. (After my first few sexual experiences, I revisited these scenes and found myself wondering where on earth I would find a man who would be kind enough to make me 'buck rapturously'. Did such a man exist? I mean, *really*?)

In the absence of anything substantial and intelligible to fill the hungry nooks of my mind, I hoarded a vast collection of exercise books and started writing my own stuff, naturally avoiding all mention of honeyed thighs and rapturous bucking on bathroom carpets. In many ways, my fables were slightly more realistic. To me at least, they provided a welcome escape from the ordinary until they seemed literally to *become* more real.

I invented my own little fantasy world, and so I had an inexhaustible supply of things to write about. Riding a magic carpet to another world where I was the only revered human being and I ruled over everyone and everything and they all loved me, and I had to kiss a lot of frogs so I would get my choice of perfect princes. I had a magic book of spells and could get big like Alice in Wonderland and small like Little Miss Pepperpot whenever I needed to. Similarly, I could fly and make myself invisible at will, and also had telekinetic and incendiary powers at my disposal. Just like in cartoons, nothing could hurt me and anything was possible. It rained cold cherryade, and the trees and lush fields were made of chocolate and candy.

In my imagination I lived in a luxury palace with an all-singing, all-dancing, aerodynamic unicorn, and the people at school who annoyed me were my servants. The teachers were my maids and butlers and were obliged to curtsey and do whatever I asked without question. I would sit on a huge velvet and gold throne and be entertained by a jester who looked like Timothy Claypole out of *Rentaghost.* I had big banquets with endless silver platters of gourmet food, and I invited lots of people but I was always the most beautiful of all. My banquets were like the one in Adam Ant's *Prince Charming* video, and naturally, Adam Ant* himself (my first pop idol and hero) was the guest of honour. I flirted with him all night but I refused his frequent requests for my hand in marriage no matter how much he begged (and believe me, he begged) because I was too young and already promised to someone else. Yes, even in my fantasies I had a sense of righteousness and loyalty to the mere mortal who had stolen my heart. Mark was always at the centre of it all, the Object of my Fantasy. My Hero, Anti-Hero, Villain, my Everything.

I kept Kev in the dungeons and fed him leftovers. He had to call me 'Your Royal and Supreme Highness' and grovel at my feet before I let him play with my many millions of wondrous toys and games. If he did anything remotely naughty I'd threaten to kick him into the moat, which was full of crocodiles. I slept in a plush four-poster bed and I had a wardrobe crammed with gorgeous new dresses of tulle and guipure lace and organza and floating silks in all different colours that swished along the marbled floors. As in Narnia, I could access the real world whenever I felt like it by going to the back of my wardrobe and zipping down a giant, winding rollercoaster, back to Essex, in a majestic flurry of glitter and confetti – not forgetting to take my magic carpet with me so I could return promptly to Fantasy Land when my

* After 1982, the interchangeable star guests of these fantasies (depending on my mood) were: Morten Harket, Mickey Rourke, Simon Le Bon, George Michael, 'Face' out of *The A-Team*, and 'the guy in the Levis ad'.

assignment at home was done. Even when I was in the real world I still had my magic powers at my disposal, and so everyone wanted to be my friend and all the boys thought I was amazing and pretty and they wanted to kiss me. But they weren't good enough for me, I was royalty and they were only Essex Boys. They had to admire me from afar and make do with kissing the ground I walked on, and Adam Ant would swing at them from the chandeliers or jump out of the trees in his highwayman's mask if they tried anything dodgy.

It was down to me to save my land from the occasional rogue evil wizard and witch and sorcerer, but my kingdom had a typically abundant population of benevolent imps and goblins and fairies who were all my friends and helped me out in times of trouble. My magic spells were always the most fabulous and good and effective, and although he was a mere Essex Boy like the others, Mark was always the frog I kissed the most. I was a princess, so it was my prerogative.

Plus, of course, he adored me to the point of helpless infatuation. How could he not? I did say *anything* was possible in my Fantasy Land.

During my final year at Willow Lane, a few unpleasant things happened. My fairy tale had been slipping away fast, and without warning, my imagination petered out and attuned itself to more mundane and sensible things. Making friends and influencing people was high on the agenda, and something of a challenge since I had finally accepted that I would never have magical powers, I would never be beautiful or powerful or remarkable in any way at all, and I was certainly not a princess of anywhere. My imagination had been my one constant, the one thing I had been able to rely on throughout, and now it had abandoned me, or at least it felt like it had. I suppose I just stopped believing in it, perhaps because I stopped believing in myself. I was just boring old Caroline Shaw, the clever and artless girl who spoke too much, knew too much and lived on a council estate with an alcoholic mother and far too many siblings. I had very little going for me except a strong desire to make a good impression on other people, but of course all the other kids had that desire as well, and most were considerably more adept at it than I was.

Likewise, my Mr Perfect had been a terrible delusion, confined to long-abandoned Roger Hargreaves tales and *Bunty* annuals. The idea of happy endings evaporated into nothing more than a tiny fragment of a figment, tossed aside with my twee Enid Blyton and the sublime Roald Dahl. I lost interest in my toys. Whenever I saw a big old tree I no longer investigated the trunk for any evidence of a secret door leading to a secret staircase to a secret world. I stopped making nonsense words out of Alphabetti Spaghetti. I stopped eating Alphabetti Spaghetti. I stopped believing in the tooth fairy (who never left me more than two pence anyway, when all my friends got at least ten) and I actually began to feel acute embarrassment that I had ever been foolish and gullible enough to believe in Santa Claus. And baby Jesus.

I was dispatched to the opticians when I was eleven after failing a routine eye test at school. I caused a brief scene in front of a heartlessly unsympathetic optometrist who blandly informed me that my vision was 'nowhere near' twenty-twenty, and, as if this wasn't heartbreaking enough for a self-conscious young girl, it was 'likely only to get worse over the next few years'. It ended with me walking out in tears, stepping out carelessly into the road and almost getting run over by a bus, stopped only by my mum pulling me back on to the pavement.

True to my worst nightmares, a hideous pair of spectacles was foisted upon me to correct a worsening myopia that I had valiantly but pointlessly been trying to ignore for some years (for example, by sitting within close proximity of the blackboard and still having to squint). My mum told me to pull myself together and bought me a bag of chips and a Fanta, but even Bev couldn't think of anything nicer to say than 'Never mind, dear' when she first saw me with my specs on. After I had worn the glasses once, of course, not wearing them made me realise how bad my eyesight had become. Even so, vanity compelled me to shove them in my pocket unless it was absolutely necessary to have sharp and accurate vision. I thought it was unfair that visual acuity had to come at the expense of prettiness, which had never been one of my strong points anyway. Why hinder me further when I was already struggling to be noticed? It was so unfair.

'It's so unfair!' I yelled, catching another glimpse of myself in the Croziers' hall mirror. 'I look *horrible*!'

'Don't be so dramatic, Caz,' Bev soothed. 'They really suit you. They make you look . . . intelligent. Very refined.'

This was blatant bullshit, but I always took what Bev said to me as gospel truth, no matter how biased and endearingly tactful she may have been. I looked at my reflection again, my head cocked to one side. Whatever angle I chose to view myself from, the same goofy, bespectacled image peered disapprovingly back at me. A silly little girl with emerging bulges and crooked teeth and oily hair and stumpy limbs and wide slanty eyes that blinked out vacantly behind ugly oblong lenses. I could never let Mark see me like this. I was already suffering from the first pangs of imminent heartbreak, as I had overheard Sean muttering something about Mark having a girlfriend – 'an' a right common little missy, too'. Wearing glasses simply compounded my misery.

My one true love was romantically involved with a local slapper, and my face, already fighting a losing battle against a premature onslaught of pimples and the final haphazard emergence of adult teeth, now had a pair of cumbersome and conspicuously unattractive frames to contend with. All in all, nature was not granting me much of an advantage in cultivating the sexy, sophisticated image I desperately wanted. The same kind of perfection that every girl of my age wanted more than anything else – more than brains, success, riches, and popularity. Because if you have beauty, you have everything – you are wise, knowledgeable, popular, brilliant, important. It is all automatically bestowed to you, attributed to you as a natural consequence of that effortless beauty. People assume everything just from the way you look, and how you present yourself. If you are beautiful to look at, you will go places, regardless of anything else. Everyone knew that. It was obvious. But I had been told – *guaranteed*, even – that I would 'blossom', that every part of me would soon ooze sensuality and mystique and unfettered gorgeousness. I would have every man at my mercy. How was this supposed to come about when I was speccy, spotty, studious and so utterly lacking in self-confidence?

'It won't happen overnight,' Bev had warned me, 'but it will be like the cute little green caterpillar changing into the glorious and magnificent butterfly. That will be you, Caroline. That will be you soon.'

I supposed I was in the chrysalis stage. And I hoped it wouldn't last too long because I already felt like I was suffocating.

'Men seldom make passes at girls who wear glasses,' Sean remarked, as he passed us on his way to the bathroom, a rolled-up newspaper tucked under his arm and a cup of tea in his hand. It was that time of day. Bev insisted you could set your watch by Sean's bowel movements. 'Now, does anyone need the loo before I launch my turd missile?' Sean was generally a man of few words, but what exquisite words they were.

Bev admonished him for being coarse, then wandered into the kitchen to make a salad. I followed her. 'Don't be mean about

Caroline's specs,' she called out to Sean as he thundered up the stairs. 'I was just telling her how clever they make her look.'

I sat at the kitchen table and flicked through Mark's *Smash Hits* magazine, marvelling at how clear the print looked, but then remembering that it only looked clear because *I* looked ugly. Bloody glasses. In a wilful and self-defeating gesture, I took them off and brought the magazine close to my face, kidding myself that I could see just as well without them.

'Yeah, they do actually,' Sean bellowed back from the bathroom, now comfortably enthroned. 'You'd make a sexy little secretary for someone some day.'

'Sean!' Bev chastised, proceeding to slice a cucumber on the chopping board with a little too much vigour. 'You can be such a sexist pig sometimes.'

'I'm not going to be a secretary, actually, Sean,' I retorted emphatically, waddling to the bottom of the stairs and shouting up to ensure he could hear me. 'I'm going to teach English as a foreign language and live in a beautiful villa on a beach with lots of animals. Maybe South Africa.' Yes, I had it all planned out – absurdly optimistic, perhaps, but more an admirably pragmatic ambition than a fanciful dream, surely?

'Ha! Alright then love, you go for it.'

'*And* I'm not going to get married,' I went on, heedless of his bemusement and gentle mockery. 'Because women waste too much time on the wrong man when they should be doing better things.'

Bev stared at me disbelievingly, dropping the vegetable knife with a clatter. 'Well, well. I have a little disciple,' she said finally, beaming with pride and admiration. 'How about a hot chocolate?'

I beamed back at her. 'Yes please.'

'Christ on a rickshaw, Beverley, you've got that kid well trained,' Sean commented, emptying the last dregs of his lower intestine with a satisfied sigh and a resounding quack of flatulence. 'Before we know it, we'll be bombarded with a new breed of ruddy feminist. You women wouldn't last five minutes without us, and you know it.'

'Ignore him, love,' Bev whispered. 'He's just an old grouch.'

'Where is Mark tonight?' I asked, trying to sound as if I didn't really care.

'Out with his brother somewhere. They should be back soon. Are you staying for dinner?'

Usually Bev didn't even ask, because by now I was practically a full-time full-board lodger, gracing my unfazed biological mum with my presence only when it had been specifically called for. And that wasn't very often. So this question threw me a little. Perhaps I had been outstaying my welcome and was too obtuse to pick up any subtle 'for Christ's sake go home and leave us alone' hints.

'Er . . .'

'You see,' Bev began, stirring hot water into the pink Barbie cup she had bought me for my tenth birthday, 'not that it really matters I suppose, but I think Mark's bringing his girlfriend back with him this evening.' She gave me a sidelong glance, testing my reaction.

I felt as if someone had ripped me open. My head filled with fire and my throat filled with bile and the rest of me turned cold, as if ice was running through my veins. 'Oh, that's nice,' I stammered, choking back my sorrow and repugnance. 'What's her name?'

Bev hesitated, slowed her stirring and dropped her gaze. 'Oh, Caro . . .' She placed the cup on the table in front of me and took my limp hand in hers. 'You've really got a thing about my Mark, haven't you love?'

I shook my head defiantly, scattering a couple of tears that had managed to squeeze their way out of my overbrimming eyes. It's not like I hadn't made it obvious. Girls know that obviousness repulses boys – they always go for the obviously pretty, but the obviously pretty can afford to be aloof and hard to get and so not obviously bloody attainable – pick me! pick me! But there was nothing I could do about it. I couldn't help but laugh out loud at Mark when he tried to be funny, adopt some of his mannerisms and phrases, take a sudden avid interest in his football team and eye him hungrily whenever I thought he wasn't looking. I was so smitten I actually wanted to *be* him. If I could only be him, then I would marry me. Because we belonged together. It was only right.

'Oh, you silly thing, come here.' Bev pulled me to her in a close embrace and I sank my face into the fragrant fabric of her dress and blubbed unashamedly. 'What was it you said not two minutes ago?'

'I can't remember!' I wailed pathetically, flinging my arms around her sturdy hips.

'About wasting too much time on the wrong man . . . ?' she prompted, holding me by the shoulders and pulling away. She held my chin and tipped my face towards her. 'Honestly. What are we going to do with you?'

I was too overcome with emotion to feel embarrassed about my outburst. It just seemed so *unfair*. Mark was mine. It felt like I had staked my claim on him long ago, that I should be rightfully entitled to first dibs on his affections. Whether he liked it or not, I had imposed myself on him and by doing so, surely I excluded the need for him ever to want any other girl? Why *would* he want anyone else? He knew me better than anyone, and I knew him. And I loved him – like a persistent sickness. I loved that boy with all my strength, with every fibre of my being. More than just a temporary ache inside me, more than a momentary throb, a pulse of desire, a torrid flush in the groin. More than a crush, a passing phase, more than a schoolgirl's swooning passion, this was *real*. So yes, I was a schoolgirl, and yes, I swooned over him, but it was *more* than that, really and truly, it was greater than that. It was so blindingly bright and strong, so utterly important and monumental. It felt like I could die from it if it remained unrequited and unnoticed. I didn't just have the hots for him, I was *boiling over*. It was Love with a capital 'L'.

Wasn't my Love good enough? I felt outraged and affronted that so much burning passion could remain so inconsequential – irritating, even – to its object. Couldn't he just hang in there a bit longer, wait until the gawky little caterpillar became the glorious and magnificent butterfly? It would be worth the wait. We would be so good together. Mark and Caroline. Caroline Crozier. Already, in my sillier and most exquisitely lovesick moments, I had industriously signed my new name, putting a little heart above both the i's in place of a dot. Over and over again I had written it, on class exercise books, on pencil cases, on the back of my hand, ignoring the lessons droning on in the background, whatever the subject. Perfecting my imaginary new signature took precedence over everything. Apart from the fantasising itself, of course.

'You're just a little girl still, sweetie,' Bev said, stroking my hair. 'You've got better things to worry about. There'll be plenty of time for all that when you've grown up.'

My myopic vision was further disabled by a blur of fresh tears when I tried focusing on her face. I knew she was trying to be kind, but the words were like bee stings on my bruised heart. It was as if she was deriding my emotions, dismissing the adoration I had for her son as nothing more than a little girl's daydream. I didn't have the composure – or the vocabulary, for that matter – to tell her how I was feeling, so I merely took a deep breath and blurted out, 'Little girls have feelings too.'

'Of course they do. Of course.' She handed me a piece of kitchen roll to wipe my eyes and blow my nose. 'But there'll be plenty of time for all this nonsense later on, when you've grown up and seen what the world is really about. Enjoy your childhood, Caroline. Make the most of it. Don't get carried away by romance. Life isn't about that. It isn't romantic. Believe me.'

Bev was always saying 'trust me' or 'believe me', but I wanted to find out these things for myself. I didn't want to just take her word for it; I craved the experience, even if it turned out to be painful and horrible. How could I ever know something for sure unless I experienced it for myself? For the first time, I felt an intense surge of bitter resentment towards Bev. I wanted to scream, to throw things, to lash out, but I just clenched my fists and held them in my lap, fighting back further sobs. 'I'll go home now,' I muttered, wondering where that was exactly. 'I – I don't think anyone wants me here . . .'

This was a desperate bit of assurance-seeking, and as I hoped, Bev was quick to alleviate my burgeoning sense of desolation and dejection. 'Come on, don't be daft! We love having you here, you know we do. Listen, how about you help me make the dinner? I think I'll do my vegetarian special tonight . . .' She popped a cherry tomato in her mouth and turned the radio on.

I ceased my girlish snivelling and sank into miserable silence. Bev gave me the salad bowl and asked me to toss in the vinaigrette dressing, which I did, with great fury.

'Mark doesn't like your vegetarian special . . .' I muttered, poking at the lettuce leaves half-heartedly with a big metal spoon.

'No, but *you* do. And I do. And Sean and Billy eat anything that's put in front of them. So that's four against one, isn't it?'

'What about . . .' I was going to say 'What about his girlfriend?', but the words stuck in my throat. I sprinkled the last drops of the vinaigrette haphazardly onto the salad, soaking it completely, and nibbled on a cucumber slice. There was another long silence. Eventually, no longer able to take the suspense, I asked her again, 'So what is her name?'

Bev leaned across the hob and prodded something that was bubbling and sputtering in a saucepan. 'Who?'

'His . . . er . . . you know.'

'Rosie, I think.' She turned to me with a faint smile and, as if to console me, added, 'Mark is far too young for girlfriends, anyway. Billy didn't have a girlfriend until he was fifteen. And that didn't last long.'

I squished a tomato with the back of the spoon, with some considerable vehemence, imagining it was Rosie's eyeball.

Rosie. God, she even had a pretty name, the cow. I put the two names together: Mark and Rosie. Rosie Crozier. Damn. It sounded *poetic*, even. She was probably signing her new name already, complete with two little hearts over the i's. I felt myself steam with animosity, and started to breathe noisily and erratically.

I pushed the salad bowl away and said, 'There. Done.'

'Thank you, love. Don't you want your hot chocolate?'

I peered into the cup at the sweet brown liquid, which was now more lukewarm than hot, and forming a milky skin on the surface. 'Can I have a biscuit as well please?' I asked, taking a tentative sip.

'What happened to "no more chocolate or crisps or biscuits ever again"?'

True enough, I had openly announced my determination to stick to yet another low-cal diet earlier that week, for the umpteenth time choosing to deprive myself of all my favourite foods in an attempt to minimise the unruly fat splurges that persistently targeted my thighs, my paunch and my buttocks. But my willpower shrank as my body swelled, and so the vicious cycle, familiar to countless other developing girls everywhere, established and maintained itself. I was just eleven years old and I had already convinced myself that I was the fattest and ugliest pubescent girl on the entire estate, if not the entire planet. The most successful diet I had managed so far was one whole week of shunning desserts and snacks, which was a monumental achievement as far as I was concerned, but nevertheless seemed to do little to change the somewhat spherical shape of my body.

'What's the point?' I grumbled. 'Why *can't* I eat nice things if I want to?'

Bev ruffled my hair and planted a wet kiss on my forehead. 'That's the Caroline I know and love,' she said kindly. 'I mean, look at me,' she added, running her hands over her stomach. 'I've always been a bit on the plump side, but Sean wouldn't have me any other way.'

'He's a bit fat anyway,' I commented bluntly.

'Well, yes,' she conceded, 'that's true, but it's more of a middle-age spread in his case.'

'Just like all of this is only puppy fat?' I asked, jabbing a finger below my ribcage. Bev put two chocolate digestives on the table in front of me and gave me an encouraging smile. 'Of course it is. You have been blessed with a lovely face and an intelligent mind. You're a pretty girl, Caro. And you will be a beautiful woman in just a few years. Trust me.'

I was almost heartened by this (having pinned so much desperate hope on the fable of the Ugly Duckling), but then I remembered that Mark and Billy would soon arrive with their respective girlfriends and, whatever Bev might say, I didn't really want to be around for their grand entrance. All those couples . . . and me. If I stayed for dinner, I would be a gooseberry. A gooseberry with glasses. And I doubted I would be able to suppress the urge to pick up Bev's vegetable knife and plunge it into Rosie's pretty little head when she was just sitting on the other side of the table hand in hand with Mark, with *my* Mark. I had little doubt that Mark had kissed her in the way that I had dreamed he would some day kiss me. Tongues and everything. He was probably kissing her right now, while I was sitting there preparing dinner with his mother in the kitchen. The very thought made me feel sick to the stomach. I was Cinderella without the Fairy Godmother. *I* was the one turning into a pumpkin, and I didn't even have an elegant glass slipper to impress him with, just a pair of mouldy plimsolls.

I was doomed.

After a brief internal fight with my common sense and volition, I scoffed the biscuits and immediately felt even more depressed.

Bev turned the radio up and hummed along to 'Absolute Beginners', seemingly unaware of my immense inner turmoil. Quietly, I slipped down from the chair and made some mumbled excuses, and was both relieved and dismayed when she didn't try hard enough to convince me to stay.

That night I cried myself to sleep while Mum and Kev stuffed themselves on oven chips and bacon butties in the room next door, their hollow laughter echoing through the flimsy walls as they watched *Only Fools and Horses* in glorious full colour on our new television set.

Girls are effectively *trained* to be bitter and hysterical and jealous and neurotic, I suppose. That may sound cynical or maybe even a little histrionic, but there's a grain of truth in there somewhere. It's a slow, pernicious and inevitable progression; from the very earliest stage of child-to-woman development they are conditioned to stop believing in themselves, or at least to stop assuming natural contentment with themselves. They begin to pre-empt disappointment and inadequacy, until it becomes auto-suggestion.

The unrealistic expectations that set them up for the ultimate downfall are engendered, almost certainly, with the presentation of the first Barbie doll. Barbie represents everything the little girl aspires to, and she wants to provide that Barbie of hers with all the necessary accoutrements – a dream home with all mod cons, a full glittering wardrobe of tailored clothes, a pink jeep, a pink moped, a handsome dark-haired companion called Ken. Barbie can have it all, because she's Barbie. When I finally received my first Barbie, my joy was tempered by a slight sense of despondency, because I knew I couldn't provide her with all the things that Barbie was permitted, indeed *expected*, to have – the pink palace and accessories, the wonderful dresses, not even the ready-made man with his plastic smile and jointed limbs. This probably meant I didn't really deserve to have a Barbie at all. All I could do for her was brush and plait her lovely blonde hair, acquaint her with my brother's nasty old Action Man, and perhaps undress her, then dress her again, in the same outfit she came boxed in, over and over again. It hardly seemed right that a perfect doll should be subjected to such an inadequate and bleak existence.

The boy-toy equivalent – Action Man – was frankly quite inferior. The conspicuous absence of a male organ (well it just wouldn't be *right*, would it?) does make you wonder if the word 'action' is an entirely appropriate description. Certainly he had 'fully moveable parts', better than Ken's, and his hair (such as it was) was slightly less effeminate than Ken's, plus of course he had those odd shifty eyes, facilitated by a somewhat crap 'pully-string' mechanism in the back of his head. But these features barely constituted any real 'action', and didn't come anywhere near to compensating for the *dicklessness*.

Yes, I admit it, up until the age of eleven (by which time I should really have known better), I would strip Action Man of his trendy camouflage slacks while Barbie would wait compliantly naked and primed in the luxury shoe-box bed I had made for her. And yes, I have to confess that I would position the two undressed amorous dolls in a variety of *Kama Sutra*-esque predicaments, after play-acting all kinds of absurd seduction scenes between the two of them. But poor old Babs must have been a mite disappointed. There she lay, in all her tiny, delicate slimness and smoothness, with that pert, pronounced bosom and unfeasibly long skinny legs, catatonic plastic smile and big blue eyes. And there was Action Man, with his built-in flesh-toned irremovable pants and boring, angular body, with no curves or bulges (or orifices, even) to explore with inquisitive fingers. The romantic scenarios I dramatised and dreamed between Barbie and Action Man required maximum imagination and improvisation. Even so, I had been told by Amber that Ken, Barbie's official partner, was an equally unsatisfactory sexual prospect. His 'package' was even more disappointing (those dreadful pants!), plus he didn't even have a 'pully-string' mechanism. All in all, not much of a boyfriend for the sublimely nubile Barbie.

Still, my Barbie made do. Just the one outfit and a bed made out of cardboard and rags, but she still smiled prettily. And Action Man was better than no boyfriend at all. Even if he was pretty inactive, and essentially androgynous.

I started secondary school that autumn, glasses and protuberances and wiry sproutings and all. Against the encouraging advice of teachers, the insistence of Bev and the indifference of mum, I declined the magnanimous offer of a place at the 'decent and highly respected' all-girls grammar school, St Jude's, located some ten miles from Rivington Hill, just outside Billericay. I had been referred there after sitting an unofficial entrance exam, but at that time I wasn't really interested in the 'academic excellence' and 'outstanding track record' of a school. Especially one that was renowned for its stacks of compulsory homework, populated by loads of girls with ponies and ponytails and posh accents and, worse, no boys. Although most boys got on my nerves, admittedly, a school without them just wouldn't have been right, somehow. It all sounded a little too *Malory Towers* and jolly hockey sticks to me. Plus the headteacher was called Mr Marigold, which just made the whole idea seem even sillier. Mr Marigold actually took the time to write a letter ('Care of Mr Sheridan, Willow Lane Primary School') specifically to invite me and my 'undoubtedly proud' parents (!) to an open evening at St Jude's, in the light of my 'excellent academic progress and exemplary test results to date'. Vaguely intrigued and quietly flattered by this unprecedented gesture, I had shown the letter to mum, who merely sneered 'What kind of a name is Mr Marigold?', and then to Bev, who cooed over it joyfully as if it were a personal request from the Queen.

In the end, though, I plumped for the notoriously indecent comprehensive school for the obnoxious and disrespectful, a sombre turn-of-the-century building situated less than one mile away. It was the obvious choice: most of my old friends and acquaintances were going there (including Mark of course), it was within walking distance, and its appalling track record was certainly not enough to put me off. One school was much like another, right? At any rate, I didn't really care, because the most important thing to me was still being with friends and having a good time. If I could get educated along the way, so much the better, but it wasn't my main concern by any means.

The Mason Tyler School was, to put it mildly, a miniature borstal. Whereas at Willow Lane the clusters of insolent kids that loitered in the playground would rarely get up to anything more mischievous and unruly than clandestine cigarette dealing, football-card swapping and the occasional scrap, the same could not be said of the Mason Tyler pupils. Their favourite hobbies included arson, vandalism, teacher taunting, carnal and chemical experimentation, swearing, brawling, thieving, smoking and skipping school. And that was just the more demure pupils.

Naturally, my first day at 'big school' was a scary experience. I defiantly repudiated my glasses again, stuffing them into my new school bag along with my new pencil case and a Golden Delicious that was more brown than golden, and well past being delicious. Kev had already started at Mason Tyler the year before, so I inherited some threadbare hand-me-downs from him, as well as the free cautionary advice: 'Don't ever try to fucking talk to me in front of my mates or I'll kill yer.' This was advice I had every intention of observing at all times, as I made a wise policy of maintaining a healthy distance from Kev even at home.

Eager to ensure that I attended my first day at big school looking just as smart as Mark, Bev kindly purchased a complete uniform for me from a 'bring and buy' sale at the local church: skirt, shirt, woollens, tie, gym kit, lace-up pumps, awful socks, the lot. All in very good condition too. I was obviously very keen to give a good impression on my first day, so I secured the scratchy navy blue pullover around my waist to conceal the bulges, brushed my freshly washed hair into two tidy plaits and buckled my white-socked feet into nearly-new patent leather shoes. I squinted appraisingly at my reflection and was gratified to be met with a vision, albeit a blurry one, of exemplary smartness. In fact, I was so soignée I was practically symmetrical. I smiled into the mirror, gave a little twirl and viewed myself from all sides, including from behind – a perspective I had usually chosen to overlook in recent months, for obvious reasons. The regulation uniform was newly laundered and ironed by Bev, clean shirt collar folded down over neatly knotted blue-and-red-striped tie, pearly buttons fitting nicely right up to the throat, pleated skirt skimming my knees; just the length a school skirt was supposed to be. The whole ensemble was perfect, if not particularly comfortable or stylish. I was a big girl now, and I was going to big school. I had to look the part, even if it meant looking and feeling vaguely absurd.

Bev gave me fifty pence before I set off, although I told her there was no need because I still got free school lunches (that said, their edibility was questionable at best). She gave Mark fifty pence too, and a Tupperware box containing sandwiches and crisps which she said he was to share with me, and he scowled and complained loudly when she tried to kiss him goodbye. He slouched off petulantly, pulling his shirt out of his trousers and trailing his new bag along the ground, head down as he scuffed along the pavement. I happily returned Bev's kiss and clung to her on the doorstep, staring down at her fluffy slippers as she told me not to worry and that everything was going to be all right.

I met Amber outside the park and we linked arms as we walked nervously through the estate and up the main road towards the school. Mark was way ahead of us by this time, and had joined up with some other lads, talking and joking with the usual brash over-confidence that comes from the gang mentality. You always knew when you were approaching the Mason Tyler school, because you could hear the raucous ruckus from the bottom of the road. It was not a particularly large building, but something about it reminded me of the scary old Victorian schoolhouses I had been reading about in Brontë and Dickens novels. It was situated just on the far edge of the Rivington Hill industrial estate, opposite a second-hand Ford garage and a small printing factory. It was probably the most unattractive part of Rivington Hill, and that was saying something.

That first morning, minutes before the first bell sounded and the kids were herded into a dismal assembly hall, my hopes were illogically, insanely high. My apprehension was jumbled up with hope; hopeless hope that this school, this educational institution, would be my springboard into the big bad world of reality. OK, so maybe it wasn't a great school, maybe it wasn't attended by noticeably pleasant people, and yes, maybe it did make Grange Hill look like Eton, but surely I was bound to learn lots of great things and make lots of interesting new friends? Isn't that what school was *for*?

Yes, in theory, but most of the local kids had different ideas. For them, as a largely homogenous collective of disparate discontents, school had no function, because the very idea of education repulsed them and the thought of submitting to any kind of authority was well beyond the realms of their limited understanding. For them, school represented nothing more than a place for meeting up every now and then, idling and making the teachers' lives a misery. Loitering behind the science block ankle-deep in cigarette butts, snogging outside the smoggy cafeteria, an unmistakable enclave of permanently stoned would-be pharmacists with their apothecary scales and precious clingfilm wraps, busy little hands exchanging bad goods for dirty cash in the secluded spot behind the sports hall.

More often than not, however, school was something to be avoided at all costs, because only *losers* went to school and these kids were not losers, no way! They were busy, busy little bees and they had much better things to do with their time. Who else would so jealously guard the street corners and dangle from railings and amble and smoke and chatter for hours on end outside railway stations and bus depots and shopping malls? It was a duty. It was their *right.*

A typical day in the life of a typical Mason Tyler School pupil rarely, if ever, actually featured school. The various gangs would casually saunter straight past the school gates most mornings, stripping off their uniforms to reveal much funkier daytime attire beneath, often stolen from older siblings. Then they would challenge each other to see which of their fresh-faced throng would be cool and brave enough to successfully acquire fags or booze from one of the local corner shops and off-licences. Any wily proprietor who refused to serve them what they wanted would surely get their comeuppance – a stream of insults, a door kicked in, a few articles stolen in retaliation, perhaps even a cheeky home-made fire-bomb chucked through a front window if the offended pupil was feeling especially temperamental. If these kids didn't get their fags and their booze, there was hell to pay. Just as the individual's life revolved around being a gang member, so the gang's existence relied on the liberal consumption of nicotine and alcohol.

If they weren't terrorising shopkeepers, there were plenty more prime quarries and idle pursuits. They packed their days with everything and nothing. They took the euphemism 'behavioural problems' to the limit. Expelling them from school as a punishment was like giving someone a tenner for nicking a quid, so ultimately there was no obviously effective way of dealing with their misbehaviour. There were too many of them for a start. It was out of control, and the sad fact of the matter was, each one of those kids was almost certain to have kids of their own before they even made it to their twenties. Usually with each other: double the trouble, quadrupling the problem.

I found out about the Mason Tyler ethos early, during the first assembly to be precise. Most schools have some kind of motto, usually stitched proudly in Latin on the school badge; the all-defining emblem of academic virtue. Mason Tyler's motto was: 'Do your best and you will triumph.' This had been universally interpreted as meaning, 'Do your worst because nobody gives a shit.' The headteacher, Mrs Daphne Sawyer, had the look of a prematurely aged, once-attractive woman who, at some point in her no doubt dispiriting career, had drawn the short straw. Big time. That is to say, she looked haggard and exhausted and perpetually pissed off. My heart went out to her as she stood up on the stage at the front of the assembly hall and welcomed the new pupils to the school and, in the same breath, respectfully requested that the old pupils did not try on 'a repeat performance of last year's "flour and eggs" debacle'.

'This is the start of an important year for many of you,' she went on wearily, as if reading from an autocue, 'and last year's exam pass rate was even worse than we had . . . feared.' She averted her eyes, clasped her hands together and sighed deeply. 'I only hope that, with the right guidance, and with the help of a new influx of specially trained teachers, some of whom are up here on stage with me and will introduce themselves later, we can eventually . . . somehow . . . re-establish the reputation of Mason Tyler as a school of great . . . potential.' Another sigh, and what sounded like a little sob, choked back and feebly disguised as a cough. She didn't sound very confident, even to me. Sitting on a row of chairs behind Mrs Sawyer, grim-faced teachers stared forward blankly. One of them had tears in her eyes.

'So, another year begins,' Mrs Sawyer continued, ignoring the conspicuous restlessness of some of the older pupils at the back of the hall, 'and I wish all of you well. I'm sure I speak for all the teachers when I say we are here for you, to guide you through the most important years of your education. I cannot emphasise enough how vital it is, in this day and age, to work hard throughout school, and to achieve the very highest grades to the best of your ability. It will pay off throughout your adult life, more than you can possibly know. Naturally, peer pressure is a powerful thing, and believe it or not, I too was your age once . . . ' Here she permitted herself a short, humourless burst of dry laughter. Somebody shouted out: 'Get on with it, you fuckin' old witch', then was promptly dragged away, to his scornful indifference, by a necessarily heavy-handed male teacher. The tyranny did not end there.

Mrs Sawyer attempted a Bible reading, which is a little bit like reciting Latin poetry at a village idiots' convention. She started it and she didn't stop or even falter once, in spite of the stink bomb released by a tenth-grader halfway through, and even after one of the older girls threw an unidentifiable missile onto the stage, missing her by just a few feet.

She persevered, through the potent sulphuric fug, reading to the end of the passage and even asking, 'Does anyone want to tell me the moral to be gleaned from that?' Mrs Sawyer was not a simpering, pathetic teacher. She had just been belittled to such a soul-crushing degree over the years that the bright, energetic woman who had no doubt started off brimming with confidence and authority was now reduced to a nervous wreck. She had obviously once possessed a deep love and zeal for her job (for some people, after all, teaching is considered a vocation of sorts), but teachers teach only because they hope some day, somewhere, a pupil will latch on and *absorb* something. The whole venture would all seem rather futile and self-defeating otherwise. Teaching a class of children who have no aspirations whatsoever, no interests, no respect and no desire to try and carve out a future away from the dole queue and daytime-television lifestyle of their forefathers must be the most disheartening job in the world. Even the most hardened and plucky candidate must end up losing their spark. What is there, after all, to make the job rewarding?

At nine-thirty in the morning of my first day at senior school I realised I wanted to get out of there. I *had* to get out of there. As soon as possible. Nearly every pupil in that hall had the glazed, acrimonious and derisive look I already recognised all too well. It was the look that said *couldn't-care-less-so-fuck-you.* It was the look that reflected the mentality of every weak-minded wastrel who pretended to be strong and important, in an ocean of near-identical nobodies who were each set on rebelling against a system that had successfully crushed every one of their equally pugnacious predecessors.

All things considered, the Mason Tyler route was not looking too hopeful.

I was assigned to the same form as Mark and Amber and, less happily, Douglas Frampton and a sociopathic Asian kid called Jeffrey Zamani who had some weird kind of hyperactivity disorder and a habit of biting people. There were a couple of others in my new form that I also knew from Willow Lane, but most of my new classmates were people I had never even seen before – most of whom I had no desire to associate with, if their hostile glares were anything to go by.

The form teacher was a thin-lipped, slab-nosed, stumpy-limbed, hunchbacked woman who insisted on being called 'Mzzzzzz' Johnson (*not* Miss, *not* Mrs), and made it clear from the outset that she would take no shit from anyone. She added, with a sharp slap of a ruler on the edge of a desk, that she used to be a prison warden so she knew how to deal with mischief-makers, but I had a feeling that this may have been a little white lie, or at the very least an exaggeration. She was certainly ugly enough, though. And she looked like the type of woman who had no problem with the idea of corporal punishment. I decided to keep on her good side.

We were each obliged to write our names and form numbers on the front of a series of exercise books, one for each subject, and were given a separate 'notes and homework' book, which we were told to use as a diary and general reminder book. By the end of that first day, mine was the only one that did not have 'Bollox to skool' or 'Fuck off shitty arseholes' or some such vulgarity scribbled with flagrant rebelliousness on the front and back covers. A sullen, underweight girl called Tamara Erskine did not find this acceptable and so kindly took the time to decorate mine for me with 'you're fanny stink's of piss' just before the final bell went. It seemed to be a rule that every pupil had, as a sign of basic respect to their peers, to have something offensive and/or meaningless written on their exercise books. Who was I to argue? Not wanting to go against the majority rule, I added (for want of something ruder), 'MC IS SEXY' in red pen, and then scribbled it out and wrote 'SKOOL SUX' in bold black, just to be on the safe side.

It became apparent to me that things were changing, and fast. Too fast. I felt the same inside, but everything else – including my own body – was different. Everything and everyone seemed to be ganging up on me, and it takes precious little for a pubescent girl to become insanely paranoid about all manner of ridiculous things. A number of educational pamphlets and Judy Blume novels had hinted, gently but unequivocally, that the teenage years were not likely to be easy. But I was only just eleven years old! If all of that was to be believed, I still had two years to wait before the *really* bad shit started up. The possibilities were too terrifying to contemplate.

At primary school I had often tried to ensure I was sitting next to Mark, or at least within close vicinity. If I sat close enough to smell him, I would be able to fantasise and daydream more vividly about how things might be when we were grown up and he would want to kiss me and be naked with me. The thoughts that would go through my mind would sometimes appal me, but generally they would always compel me to dive beneath my duvet every night and do the nipple thing. But from the first day of senior school, I couldn't help noticing that it was Mark who voluntarily sat close to me, quite blatantly seeking me out and choosing a desk adjacent to mine, or at least directly behind. Especially during maths and history lessons.

Although we had established a good friendship by this stage, it was more of a private mutual understanding, and I never expected him to bestow me with open displays of affection and warmth. The hopeless amorous yearning I still harboured for him was only a hindrance to a friendship that was otherwise fairly uncomplicated and solid. After all, he found it hard to perceive me as anything more than a silly little girl – even if he had to admit that I was likeable enough. Having someone like me as his friend would not do much to augment his ego or enhance his status, both of which were at a crucial and highly sensitive stage in their development. Whatever history we had, however many pleasant moments of platonic togetherness we had shared over the years, none of it seemed to matter when we were at school – boys had their priorities and their preferences, and Mark was quite clear about what his were. Suffice it to say, they didn't involve me. I was a mate, quite possibly even a 'great' mate (at least when it suited him), but I was still just a kid to him. Just a kid. And an unpretty kid at that.

Yet I continued to burn for him, despite everything. And I wasn't so witless that I failed to realise his true motivations for wanting to sit close to me during the lessons he found the most tedious and difficult. I was the one with all the answers. I knew everything, apparently. I didn't like it when people copied my notes and borrowed my homework, but it was different when Mark did it. Pathetically, I was consoled that I was at least able to offer him *something*, and that he relied on me for that one thing: my knowledge. My hard work. My brains. My intelligence. Which was, paradoxically, the main thing I started getting bullied about. Nobody likes a square, after all.

Yes, what I lacked in beauty I more than made up for in brains. I suppose I should have counted my blessings – a vast number of the Mason Tyler pupils had a definite deficit of both, and generally this didn't appear to be too much of a hindrance (indeed in some cases it was something of a boost). But instead I cursed myself for it. I carried on writing my stories, my poetry, my diary, my homework (always on time), and in the absence of more constructive pursuits, I even wrote soppy sonnets and love letters to Mark. Love letters that I would never, ever show to anybody, least of all to him.

His reaction, if he were to read them, would almost certainly be one of purest contempt. At best he would laugh at me, dismissing them as some kind of stupid joke that only soppy girls understand. At worst he would never speak to me again, never even ask to copy my homework, actively avoid me forever – and so the already tenuous ties between us would be severed. I knew that if I was to share these letters with my reluctant and bemused muse, all I could realistically hope for would be the peace of mind brought by confessing my true feelings at last. I knew that these unbearably intense emotions were destined to spill out at some point. I couldn't hold it all inside me indefinitely; it was only a matter of time.

But my worst nightmares played through the same old scenario: Mark would find and read my secret letters and romantic poems; so many ardent, earnest, romantic words poured out straight from my heart on to paper, so plainly and shamelessly, my curly, heart-studded handwriting nestling between the feint lines. And just as I thought my eloquence and passion might have him spellbound and helplessly love-struck, he would rip the pages up and throw them back in my face, and I would only be able to watch in sinking despair as he turned and walked away from me, the tiny pieces drifting on the air like confetti.

5

Something Borrowed

'To be without some of the things you want is an indispensable part of happiness.'

Bertrand Russell

Going to Mason Tyler turned out to be one of my less astute decisions. After two months, I had still failed effectively to inveigle myself into a single one of the school's many gangs and splinter groups, and this failure (along with my unforgivable penchant for learning) was a direct and sure-fire route to alienation and misery. Maybe it was because I never actually actively *tried* (most gangs do expect a little bit of effort – a shaved head, a specific tattoo, the passing of an obligatory initiation test, a love bite, sworn allegiance to a specific football team or indigenous tribe perhaps), or maybe it was because I quite simply didn't fit in anywhere. Naturally, this was distressing: when you are not comfortable with being called a 'child' and yet are still certainly a long way from adulthood, the need to fit in with your contemporaries overtakes every other aspect of your life. It becomes your *raison d'être.* How your peers perceive you is, quite simply, who you are. It is what you are. And, until you grow up and start to know better, it is *all* you are. Acceptance is the key.

I certainly wasn't the only outcast at Mason Tyler – the reasons for rejection in a community as volatile and cruel as a secondary school are many and varied and far from rational – but I didn't much fancy the idea of half a decade of being a pariah. I was essentially a social animal, but socialising within this particular school took on a distinctly sinister edge, as it relied on certain questionable personal qualities and whatever uncertain place you were awarded in the school hierarchy. Bullying and savagery was rife even *within* gangs, let alone between them, and anyone who wasn't in a gang at all didn't have a leg to stand on.

Amber – sweet, lovely Amber – hooked up with a gang of mouthy black girls and started having sex and smoking. Being neither black nor sexually primed, I was left on the periphery, and although Amber still talked to me and occasionally still interacted with me after school hours, our friendship petered out quickly, simply because we no longer had that wonderful, innocent connection between us. It died the minute Robbie Brookes lowered himself onto Amber's budding, twelve-year-old body in a shady copse at the back of Rivington Hill Park.

As for Mark, well, he fitted in with ease. Of course he did. Being older than the rest of the people in his form, he tended to mix with the ninth and tenth-graders and this gave him instant cred. He wasn't a member of any particular gang; rather, he was an honorary member of any and every gang that tolerated white, working-class, good-looking, ostensibly confident and easily adaptable boys. And naturally, that left his options pretty much open. His laid-back complacency turned into unashamed cockiness, and when his voice broke and his balls dropped and the girls started throwing themselves at him, that cockiness turned to grotesque arrogance. My love for him became a terrible, dissonant throb – but it was always there in the background, pricking at my heart, even when I realised that he had become, in essence, the most unlikeable person I had ever known, even including my brother.

Katie, my last hope of a lasting alliance, had been sent to another school, one that I had never heard of. I sometimes saw her around the estate, but sadly found that I no longer had anything much to say to her. Again, a lost connection. My new classmates, for the most part, were either intensely and openly antagonistic, or withdrawn and equally unapproachable. So basically, I was alone, or at least I *felt* alone. Not just alone, but hopelessly lonely with it – utterly on my own, sequestered from everybody else.

PE lessons were quite simply insufferable, and I tried every trick in the book to get out of them, including forging a letter from my mother:

> Dear Mr Bakewell
>
> Caroline has a rare and unfortunate disease which means she can't do any kind of activity that involves running. Or swinging a bat or a racket. She is allergic to grass and has a phobia of communal changing rooms. She also has a hole in her heart and suffers from brittle bones and so I suggest she utilises her PE lessons as an opportunity to catch up on her reading.
>
> Yours truly,
> Eleanor Shaw (Miss)

That didn't work. I feigned illness to such a compulsive degree that I ended up convincing myself that I had created a whole new disease called PE-phobia. But more often than not, I didn't get away with it, and was forced to endure those hellish twice-weekly PE lessons with the rest of them.

The worst times were when Mr Bakewell, the sadistic PE teacher, gleefully selected two of his favourite budding athletes and told them to 'pick their teams'. I was nearly always one of the last three or four, whittled down from a class of over thirty. The mortification was intense: we would all loiter in a hopeful bundle as the two hale and hearty team captains would pick and choose from our ever-decreasing number. The cream of the crop would be appointed first, one by one, with disheartening predictability: Tina Hartley (didn't like sport, but was renowned for her blow jobs and looked great in the tight little red PE pants and sky-blue Aertex shirt), Kevin Yates (tall and lanky and a little uncoordinated but could outrun a cheetah), James Howard (a touch on the porky side, but quite a good laugh and all the boys fancied his older sister), Katrina Peach (a supreme and undisputed champion at tennis, netball, volleyball, drug-dealing and the full spectrum of sexual athletics, with long legs and prematurely pronounced tits), Tamsin Botley (could do very interesting and innovative things with hockey sticks, apparently), Mark Crozier (the one all the girls wanted to be with and the boys wanted to be), Julian Headingley (a rugby player's physique and temperament). Loretta Gibbons was the worst chain-smoker in the class but she was always chosen before me, just because she was skinny and sassy – never mind that she couldn't run from the corner shop to the nearest bus stop without having an aggravated asthma attack. Michael Blundell was always chosen before me because at least he could be vicious if the team needed some underhand tactics. Sandra Woodcock was nearly always chosen before me, even though she was extremely short and wore glasses ten times more powerful than mine. And every time, *every damn time* without fail, I would be left feeling foolish and red-faced along with the other poor dismal rejects of the class: Emily Willis (small and ginger with spots and a nervous tic), John Hardy (couldn't catch, kick or run after a ball to save his life) and Beth Lambert (mousey and a little bit smelly). I had 'loser' stamped all over me.

My isolation at Mason Tyler felt all the more pronounced when I thought about the way things had been before, and how everything had changed so completely within just a few short months. I missed the primary years, my ingénue years of true infancy. It was as if I had somehow imagined them, or they were themselves merely a part of the whole elaborate fantasy world I had created for herself. Being a senior was just not the same. I missed sitting in play-time rings with other little girls, plaiting hair while having my hair plaited; the unassuming company of those innocent, chattering friends with their quick little hands and garrulous tongues, and the simple exchange of dreams and ideas. Hopscotch and skipping games: 'England, Ireland, Scotland, Wales', and 'Underneath the Apple Tree'. Endless games of make-believe acted out routinely in private dens and tents and tree-houses and underneath beds; makeshift castles where I was able to live out another life, fresh from an imagination unblemished by the tedious pragmatism of the real world.

Even though my own birthdays usually went by without a party to mark the occasion, I missed the birthday parties of classmates – the colourful paper invites that confirmed and arbitrarily strengthened friendships, pass-the-parcel, musical chairs, treasure hunts, balloons on the front door. I missed the comparative kindness of the soft-spoken, gentle-mannered primary teachers who made me feel special; their home-time stories and the smell of coffee and mint imperials on the breath of dinner ladies. Messy finger paintings on the classroom wall, gold stars as rewards for hard work, pegs in the cloakroom with name labels and pictures ('C for Caroline, C for Cat').

I missed racing Mark and Amber to the park when the last bell sounded; the winding route we took via the sweet shop, bypassing the centre of the estate where the lairy kids had taken to hanging out in their droves. Leapfrogging around the trees in the park, handstands against the wall and paddling in the river with my skirt hitched up into my knickers in the sunny days before the water got too polluted by rubbish and sewerage. Throwing sticks from the little foot-bridge, catching frogs in jars, daisy chains in summer and conker competitions in the autumn, kicking up the fallen tumbles of umber and russet leaves that piled up by the kerb. Halloween and bonfire night; toffee apples and facepaints, sparklers and Catherine wheels. The sound of the ice cream van in the background from April until August; that old familiar jingle that prompted me, like a Pavlovian dog, to salivate in anticipation of something cold and sticky and sweet and brightly coloured that would stain my lips and clothes.

I even missed the school dinners – the thick bright custard, as yellow as the crude smiling suns in my classroom paintings, ladled out over cold apple crumble or spotted dick, and the toad in the hole that tasted quite literally like its name. And the school trips to various uninteresting places of educational interest, the boredom of the return coach journey eased by Mark and the other rowdy boys pulling moonies out of the window on the back seat.

I would never forget those lazy Sunday afternoons in the Barley Mow with the Croziers, beating Ned at darts only because he let me win, and then getting bloated on crisps and Coke up until bedtime. Messing about with the other kids in the beer garden when the weather was good, or else hiding in the dank little beer cellar where we knew we weren't supposed to go, and telling each other ghost stories. Sitting under the tables among the rows of adult legs and sharing pork scratchings with Norman. Routines that became so joyful in their simple predictability that I could never imagine anything else, or anything better. Running half-naked around Bev's back garden and gleefully leaping through the water sprinklers to cool down when the summers got too hot, with the dogs lolloping at my heels.

Those glorious summers, hot days sweating on doorsteps with endless home-made lollies and bottles of lemonade, or lying on my back in Ned's allotment with a stem of grass in my mouth and the sun on my face, the hypnotic buzz of insects and lawnmowers lulling me to sleep. Watching the plump, pollen-drunk bees struggling to stay airborne, butterflies flitting with effortless grace between shrubs and flowers, the gorgeous smell of rosemary and thyme, and the fruit, the fruit! Ned's allotment, with its lush greens and succulent reds, the strawberries in the basket, juice down my chin, challenging Mark to see who could eat the most.

And the winters, building snowmen and getting mine desecrated by Mark and Billy, which always instigated a snowball fight, which I always lost. The day I finally got to glide down Bluestone Rise in a sledge all of my own, fingers icy blue, clenched inside woollen mittens, with Mark and Billy racing close behind me, pulling my scarf. The hours Mark and I spent together down the park with a sly bottle of scrumpy and a stolen packet of Sean's cigarettes which I only pretended to smoke, even in the pouring rain, *especially* in the pouring rain.

All those family days out, so spectacular and awesome that I wished they would never come to an end. Those were the days that whipped by quickly like a dizzying fairground ride and can now only be recalled in quick, tantalising snatches. The trip to Thorpe Park when Mark threw up all over Billy's hair and new jacket and we all got soaked on the log flume, with a picture at the end to keep the memory intact for ever. A small, fleeting moment of unexpected intimacy in the reptile house at Whipsnade Zoo, when Mark's previously undisclosed phobia of snakes was revealed and I was granted a rare and wonderful glimpse into a more vulnerable side of his nature. And afterwards, when we fell asleep against each other on the back seat of Sean's car during the long journey back home, I secretly watched with one eye half open as the passing lights in the road outside slid over Mark's face, creating an illusory glow through the slivers of shadow, which made my heart ache for him all the more.

The Saturday evenings indoors; the mouth-watering smell of Bev's cooking wafting from the kitchen. Eating dinner together on trays in front of *The Dukes of Hazzard* or *Knightrider* or *The A-Team* or *Jim'll Fix it.* The letters I wrote to Jimmy Saville, always the same, and always unanswered: 'Dear Jim, please can you fix it for me to be marooned on a tropical desert island like in *The Blue Lagoon*, with my best friend Mark and loads of ice cream. And a big freezer so it doesn't melt . . . and please no cameras.'

Going to the live football matches, the few I had been allowed to attend with the male Croziers, as a special privilege; even though I didn't much like football, I soon learned to appreciate that supporting West Ham FC was a kind of religion, not just a hobby. West Ham versus Aston Villa, February 1985 – I enjoyed every minute of that, seated next to Mark, watching him intently, every minute movement, the familiar outline of his profile, white breath clouding from his lips in the cold rain, damp tendrils of hair across his forehead, cheeks mottled pink. The spontaneous whoops of glee and guttural splutters of pointless encouragement every time West Ham got possession, the deafening bellows from the stands every time a goal was scored, the crestfallen droop in Mark's posture and his enraged protests when the full-time whistle went and West Ham had officially lost at home against 'a bunch of fuckin' wankers'. I liked to join in with the occasional *Go on my son*, or *REFE*REE!, although I rarely knew why I was saying it or what exactly it might achieve over such a deafening clamouring noise from an excitable crowd of thousands.

Mud fights in the glade under the swing rope in the middle of the park; sitting in a lukewarm, soapy bath hours later while Bev scrubbed my back and scolded me, though angrier with Mark because he was older and should have known better. I enjoyed that abdication of responsibility, even though nine times out of ten it would be me who had suggested the fights and games. Mark heroically took the blame every time, with few protests, and I liked to think that it must have been because, deep down, he loved me and so didn't mind getting in trouble for me.

Short escapades to the coast; long weekends in a colourful caravan in Clacton with the whole family, sharing a fold-out bed with two dogs and being kept awake by the sound of Ned's snoring on the other side of the room. Midnight feasts with Billy and Mark when all the adults were asleep; sneaking out with a picnic rug and a box of matches, running down past the wooden perimeter fence beyond the campsite to the beach, Billy lighting a fire in a secluded spot while Mark and I skimmed stones by moonlight and talked about silly things.

Camping out in the Croziers' back garden with the impromptu gatherings of Mark's friends, me being the only girl in an obnoxious sea of boy-filled sleeping bags. One of those nights, alone together for a change, trying to get to sleep on a slowly deflating air mattress beside Mark beneath a hot canvas canopy at the end of August, just talking and talking until we heard the first wood pigeon somewhere high above our heads. I remember his first kind words to me like an euphonious psalm, almost exactly three years after we had first met: 'You know, you're not so bad after all, Caz.' I felt as if I was walking on air for the rest of the day, replaying those few simple words over and over again in my head, imparting improbable hidden meaning to the statement.

There had been special, private moments with Mark, and I missed those times, the Mark I knew – before he became a geezer, one of the lads. Before he became so utterly tiresome. He had shunned me, then accepted me, then made time for me, and now I found myself back at square one again without knowing why or how. I was competing with bigger and better fish now. People were no longer equal, no longer operating on an equal basis. The goalposts had been shifted, inexplicably, inextricably. I was not one of the Important People. The struggle to get noticed was only the start – once you have been noticed, you then need to get accepted. Once you are accepted, far from the struggle being over, it has only just begun. You have an image to maintain, a personality to polish and uphold, a reputation to establish. It's not easy being a grown-up kid. You've got to look straight ahead and over your shoulder at all times.

Real childhood, the days when you are a child and you don't presume yourself to be anything else, was now more or less over. When I was five, being six had seemed like an eternity away. Being seven was simply far too long to wait, and as for making *double figures* – surely by that time the scientists would have invented flying cars and robots with superhuman powers. The notion of ever becoming an adult was incomprehensible. Time dragged its feet, but looking back on the prime of childhood – those priceless years between five and ten – they are remembered as the quickest years of your life. It is easy to pick out certain isolated moments and specific vivid details, but even those more lucid fragments are jumbled up with the rest, so that ultimately your childhood represents nothing more than a frenzied blur of school, play-time, birthday presents, favourite films and songs and toys, special days, exquisite moments, journeys and excursions, sleepovers, holidays and Christmases, each rolled into the other. Reminiscence becomes almost painful, because even an unhappy childhood has a rarefied glimmer of magic about it; a magic that can never be imitated or replicated in later life.

I was not keen on the idea of getting big. I had already outgrown so many things – not least the tiny, overcrowded flat I shared with a family that also just kept on growing. Jolene was now five, Sharon was seven, and at thirteen, Kev was already being marched in and out of juvenile detention centres following a perpetual succession of pick-pocketings, drug possessions and dealings, car thefts and break-ins. To top it all, my mother had finally found the 'man of her dreams', and this particular relationship seemed to be based on genuine companionship rather than mutual stupefaction and common aimlessness. Indeed, the man who would father the last of my siblings was a rare jewel: he devoted himself to Eleanor Shaw and her brood with ease and even eagerness. He blatantly adored the strange, elfin, disillusioned little lady who had bewitched him from across the bakery aisle at KwikSave. She was rough around the edges and hard as nails on the outside, but he had discovered a soft centre that was quite easily probed and provoked, hinting at an almost childlike need to love and to be loved. Yes, underneath it all, I knew my mother was just as romantic, emotional and vulnerable as all the other women from her generation – even those who had got their lucky breaks, embarked on powerful careers, or found good husbands and produced a matching set of genetic triumphs to fill their warm, suburban homes.

The new man's name was Ray, and everyone except Kev (who hated everyone) liked him enormously. Even my cantankerous grandmother had to accept that there wasn't anything particularly offensive about him, other than his 'nasty, lank hair' and 'suspiciously large feet'. Ray had a soft and simple heart and, less fortuitously perhaps, a similarly soft and simple mind that facilitated a natural, instantaneous rapport with the younger of his girlfriend's children. When he arrived on the scene the Shaws at last descended into some comfortable semblance of normality, and after a while Ray became a permanent fixture.

Ray had moved to Essex after being made redundant from his old job in Bristol, where he had been sharing a similarly cramped council house with his sister and her family. For reasons beyond my own humble understanding, he had voluntarily opted to move to Rivington Hill, where an old friend offered him a floor to crash on, and social services provided the dole money while he searched in vain for another job. Any job. This is the way it always seemed to operate. When you are blessed with none of the usual societal requirements – brains, brawn, beauty, accolades, confidence, experience, gumption, focus, ambition, agility, innovation, motivation, initiative and a mind-boggling standard of IT literacy – you may as well ditch your dreams of a high-flying, high-powered and highly respectable career. Ray certainly had none of those things, but he was enthusiastic and willing to learn, which – God bless him – was a start, at least.

His specialist subject was fruit and vegetables and fresh produce in general, and he was especially dextrous at constructing cardboard boxes and then putting things into them. He had worked in various packing factories, local stores and warehouses since the age of sixteen, and so had numerous basic manual skills, not least of which was a certain indispensable wizardry with cardboard and polystyrene. The job he landed in Rivington Hill was a little bit of a step up from his previous one (the straightforward and pretty much self-explanatory 'groceries delivery man'), but not what you'd call 'career progression', exactly. His new job was the rather more mysterious 'production line assistant', although the duties attached to this job title were still basic enough. It involved clocking in at dawn wearing the incumbent white nylon hat, plastic gloves and blue overalls, packing fruit into crates and sticking labels onto tins all day inside a noisy warehouse under the supervision of a 'line duty manager'. Ray did this for ten hours every day, including regular weekends, and earned enough per year to keep him in council housing and shabby clothes. The perks of the job included free bananas at lunchtime, all the out-of-date prunes his digestive system could cope with and a maximum of three ten-minute fag breaks per day, to fumigate his sorrows away. Other than that, there was little security and satisfaction to be derived from what the local Job Centre had fraudulently described to him as 'a wonderful opportunity where you will be working with friendly folk, and no two days are ever the same'.

Still, it kept the wolves from the door. And it kept Eleanor Shaw happy. And her kids. For a time, at least.

Teresa Annabel Jade Gilbert-Shaw was born on New Year's Day 1988, in the Arcadian lift of all places. Her birth took just twenty minutes from the first pang of pain to the last pop, and Ray had only just finished frantically dialling for an ambulance when, to his disbelief, he heard the first cries of his first child from just outside the front door of the flat. (Followed by 'Jesus Christ, it's another bloody girl' from my mum a few seconds later.) By this time, we had been living in our squalid little flat in Arcadian House for almost fourteen years, and as a home it was barely sufficient for two people, let alone a burgeoning family of seven. In addition, Arcadian House itself had been the subject of three drug raids in as many years and had quickly become overrun with squatters and jail-breakers, to the extent that it had even made a brief appearance on national news. (Headline: 'The sick and sorry state of the impoverished way of life in Britain today.')

All things considered, it was not the ideal place for a parent to nurture five inquisitive and impressionable children. Beggars can't be choosers of course, but I was increasingly aware that sharing a small bedroom with an older brother and two younger sisters was beginning to take its toll on my sanity. Especially now I had reached the age where privacy was important – vital, in fact, on some occasions. Now that there was *another* baby on the scene, it was clear that the family needed, as a matter of supreme urgency, a little more living space.

The patter of little feet chez Shaw had now become a deafening canter of outgrown shoes, and the situation was getting quite intolerable, even for a docile man like Ray. My Mum finally agreed to be sterilised after an astute bit of tit-for-tat (or 'tied-tubes-for-new-flat') bargaining from a persuasive social services representative who insisted that there was no way she could 'just keep on having babies willy-nilly' without any means of supporting them herself. So Teri was to be the last in a series of government-funded 'willy-nillies', and after my mum had been sterilised, at the ripe old age of twenty-nine, my family was moved into a bigger and better place. Three hundred yards away.

So it was goodbye to flat number fifty-nine at Arcadian, hello to a three-bedroomed, vaguely run-down but undeniably superior maisonette on the other side of the estate. Everyone was happy. At least, as happy as it is possible to be, given the circumstances. Mum and Ray and baby Teri had the second biggest of the three bedrooms and Kev was awarded the smallest, all to himself – with a mattress on the floor and an old bed sheet at the window instead of a proper curtain. As far as he was concerned, however, the seven foot by six foot box room was simply perfect. It was his own personal space – his heaven, his sanctuary, a private place where he could console himself in clandestine solitude with bad music, Superkings, White Lightning, Space Invaders, Penthouse, his imagination and innumerable boxes of man-sized Kleenex. And so the inevitable 'Fuck Off' sign was Sellotaped to the door. And just in case that message wasn't quite unequivocal enough, stuck between a Metallica poster and the teenage boy's current favourite, Miss Cindy Crawford, another sign stated 'Keep Out'. The message was loud and clear, and I – along with every other member of the family – had no intention of disobeying. The possibilities of what went on behind that closed door were too horrible to contemplate, and the realities doubtless much worse.

I was therefore granted the largest room, but only with the somewhat unwelcome proviso that I share it with two noisome under-tens, both of whom I found irritating at best, nauseating at worst. I attempted to make the most of an only slightly improved situation by creating my own sectioned-off area: a barely adequate length of chipboard served as a room divider, and I pinned pop posters and other paraphernalia on my side of it. I had also been granted a 'proper' bed – a wooden frame as well as a mattress – which although rickety and old was also incredibly soft and comfortable, like a nest, a padded refuge. The springs had gone, the headboard was dented and stained and plastered with white peeling residue from countless ripped-off stickers, but when I sat or lay on my bed behind that flimsy chipboard screen, I felt wonderfully at peace. Even when Shaz and Jo were bickering a few feet away beyond the chipboard barrier, or the umpteenth family feud was going on just beyond the bedroom door, I was often able to switch off and transport myself far away, cut myself off from the noise and enjoy a rare moment of pseudo-solitude.

It wasn't that I hated my family, or even that I blamed my permanent feeling of resentment and churlish anger wholly on them. But when approaching the fractious teenage years, even the most understanding and compliant of families is perceived by the hormonal victim as a preposterous collection of intolerable embarrassments. I knew my family was subnormal, even in the liberal 'anything goes' context of council-estate families. But I also knew that, short of demanding that Bev and Sean officially adopt me, there was no escaping from my *real* family, those to whom I was inextricably tied by biology and obligation. I hoped that perhaps now my listless mother had found what appeared to be her 'ideal man' (that is, someone relatively self-sufficient, obedient, adoring, willing and weak-willed, good with kids and not addicted to anything), things might start getting better. And there was no reason to believe that things *wouldn't* get better.

Unlike the invariably inept and inadequate men my mum had met over the years, Ray relished being a stand-in dad for her children. He was neither inept nor inadequate – at least not in terms of devotion and kindness, which were the things that really counted. He bought us things – colouring books, jigsaw puzzles, sweet biscuits, comics, tiny trinkets – even when it wasn't our birthdays. He bought things for mum, too – roses, bath salts, teddy bears that said 'I love you', porcelain ornaments like the ones the Croziers collected – and he rarely came home from work empty-handed, even if it was just a punnet of peaches or a bunch of bananas. He would tuck Jo and Shaz in their bunk beds every night after reading them a story, no matter how late he got back from work and how exhausted he was feeling. He would sometimes even invent stories, just off the top of his head, magical and fantastical adventure stories that I would also secretly listen to from my quiet corner behind my makeshift partition, even though I was getting far too old for such things.

Sure enough, after Teri was born and we had finished decorating our new place, I felt happier at home than I had ever done before. It wasn't just the new surroundings – although it was undeniably good finally to be granted the coveted luxury of a proper place to live, with an upstairs and a downstairs and a little more space and light, and fresh colour on the walls. It was more a general feeling of contentment and belonging. Although my mum was preoccupied with the demands of her fifth and final baby, and Ray was at work all day and most weekends, I used to await the home-time bell at school with greater anticipation and longing than ever before. And it wasn't just because I hated school – in comparison to school anywhere else now felt like bliss, but previously I had always felt indifferent about home-time. Now something had changed. Home had become *homely*; I actually enjoyed spending time there. Weekends had become bearable – sometimes even salubrious. My mum was noticeably mellowing, becoming warmer and more affectionate; she doled out fewer frosty glances and irascible tirades, and far more uninitiated cuddles and smiles, even after Teri had deprived her of sleep for nights on end.

Our new place came complete with a new fridge, a separate freezer (to stock up on some *nice* food!), a new gas oven, and – best of all – central heating that worked. Tufted carpets that were still relatively pleasant underfoot and weren't too ragged and scuffed at the corners. Doors still just about hanging on to their hinges, albeit mostly by rust fragments. The tired old furniture from our old flat somehow looked less embarrassing in our new home: the ancient mock-mahogany seemed to take on a new sheen and the cheap plywood looked slightly less tacky, given the right light from the new fringed lampshade in the corner. We still had to traipse to the launderette twice a week, but Mum had been assured in writing that plumbing would be installed for her very own washing machine before the end of the year. My family finally had something to feel proud of, even if it wasn't – strictly speaking – ours.

These new-found home comforts alone would have been enough to boost morale. But with Ray on the scene, it wasn't just the central heating that warmed the place up. The honeymoon flush of love between him and my mum was, at first, almost palpable – as fresh and rosy as the paint in the hallway. Just before, during and immediately after her pregnancy, Mum was treated like a queen. Nothing was too much trouble for Ray. And this love blossomed and spread, mushroomed, extended outwards to her children, immersed us like a balmy bubble bath, filled the house with an ambient calm and peace. For a time, it was almost perfect.

Ray Gilbert and Eleanor Shaw became Rivington Hill's answer to Donnie and Marie Osmond, except without the singing and the white teeth and the American Dream. While cars were being furiously hot-wired and smashed up just feet from the front door, and pensioners were being mugged by dwarfish scowl-faced schoolchildren outside in the cold cruel world, Ray and Mum embraced family life with rapture. While other couples were hurling heavy articles and strong verbal abuse at one another with impassioned fury in the surrounding maisonettes, Ray and Mum baked brownies or snuggled up on the sofa in front of the TV or chatted in bed together. Mum cooked Ray economy meals that he imaginatively claimed to be 'the very best in haute cuisine', and then he would put the kettle on and jig Teri or Jolene up and down on his knee, like a proper dad, proud as punch and beaming all over his broad pink face. Sometimes we would go on picnics and big family days out, just like the Croziers always did every other Sunday during spring and summer when the weather was fine.

The relationship, the dream, lasted just over a year.

Then they got married.

It was Valentine's Day 1988. Barking Registry Office. It was the first time for both of them, but they had a budget of two hundred quid so it was by all accounts a low-key affair – for a 'big day', it remained pretty small-scale. But while the wedding may not have been big on showy romance or starry-eyed, confetti-sprinkled splendour, it was certainly memorable.

Ray had spent the previous night away from Mum at a friend's house, respecting tradition and enjoying an abundance of alcohol to celebrate/commiserate over his last hours as a single man. Mum, conversely, spent the whole night with a disgruntled six-week-old baby clamped to her breast in front of a low-budget action movie on ITV, while two of her older offspring clobbered the hell out of each other in the room next door and her only son failed to appear back home for the third night in a row.

'Don't pick your nose.'

'I wasn't.'

'Yes, you were, Sharon. It doesn't look very ladylike. Certainly not the way for a bridesmaid to behave.'

'Don't care.'

Mum had twenty minutes to dry and style her hair into a dramatic bouffant, get changed, do her bridal make-up, feed the baby, change a nappy and make the rest of her children look presentable. The registrar had warned both of them to be on time. Not even five minutes late.

'Come away from the door, Caroline. There's no post on a Sunday anyway, you know that, you're not stupid. Come and help me with this, will you? Or at least go and polish those shoes.'

I was loitering by the front door, eyes focused optimistically on the doormat, and had been loitering there ever since I had sprung out of bed at a ridiculously early hour. I was hoping, with all my hopeless heart, that Mark might hand-deliver a Valentine card to me first thing in the morning, like the poor lovesick fool I knew he secretly was. Or else maybe, just maybe, there would be a single red rose waiting outside in a clear plastic tube, with a note attached: 'To My Darling Caroline, I have been in denial for all this time, and I want you to know you are the only girl for me and you always have been.'

So far nothing, but I knew it was just a matter of waiting.

'For crying out loud love, you're not going to get anything from Mark, the boy wouldn't know romance if it bit him on the arse,' Mum quipped. 'Just forget it. You're too good for him, anyway.'

I glared at the enormous bouquet of red roses Mum had received from Ray via Interflora that morning. They seemed to be mocking me, lying there on the table in all their magnificent full-bloom scarlet loveliness, within their luxurious layers of dark-purple tissue paper and crinkled plastic, the attached card saying 'For Ellie, My Beautiful Wife-To-Be'.

I wanted to weep when I saw them. I had never received flowers in my life, not once, not ever. Not even a sympathy bouquet from Beverley to compensate for her son's indifference. Not even a Valentine card. Not one poxy card for the entire twelve years I had been alive and female on this planet. Too young, Bev had said, still too young. Better things to worry about at your age, Ray and mum had commented, offhandedly, curled up together on the sofa in front of *EastEnders*' happy half-hour. All right for them, I had thought bitterly. They were adults and they had each other, they had no problems. They had it so easy.

'Kev's back,' I said blandly, watching through the kitchen window as my brother approached the front door, limping and staggering along like a wounded dog. There were streaks of blood down his white shirt, his eyes were puffy and red and his cheek was bruised purple-grey. In one hand he clutched a can of Super Tennents. His other hand was being held by a blonde girl in a grey tracksuit. 'And he's got a girl with him,' I added. Altogether not a bad night's work for a kid who had only recently celebrated his fourteenth birthday, I supposed. 'Stupid wanker,' was what I said.

Mum ignored the remark and raced to the door, flinging it open with a flourish. 'Kevin!' she exclaimed, heedless or possibly uncaring of the fact that she was standing in full view of the outside world wearing nothing more substantial than a damp hand towel, a super-support girdle and a nursing bra. 'Where the bloody hell have you been? You've been gone since Thursday, for God's sake. You knew it was the wedding today. As if I haven't got enough to ... Jesus Christ, what happened to you?'

'He got ... done in,' his companion answered for him, eyeing Mum through a messy fringe.

Mum blinked at the girl for a few seconds. 'And you are ... ?'

'Julie,' she replied, as if it was obvious.

'Julie. Of course.' Mum turned stiffly to Sharon, who still had a finger up her nose.

'Get my dressing gown, will you? It's on the sofa, I think.'

Sharon obliged sulkily, and Mum wrapped the faded, threadbare towelling robe around herself and impatiently ushered Kev and Julie inside, muttering about brass monkeys and pneumonia before slamming the door closed.

'Fuck's sake, I have to be at the registry office in less than an hour. You've got shitty timing, as ever,' Mum snapped. 'We've been out of our minds with worry about you, Kevin.'

This wasn't what I had been led to believe. In fact this wasn't the impression I had got at all since Kev's latest unexplained disappearance. 'Out of our minds with worry' was surely an exaggeration. Certainly there had been a few 'Where the hell is the little shit?' musings and maybe one or two 'Cheeky bastard treats this place like a drop-in centre' comments. But nobody had expressed deep concern over Kevin's protracted absence. I hadn't missed him, that was for sure. In fact, if he hadn't stunk out his bedroom with the peculiar 'Aroma de Kev', a smell unique to unwashed priapic adolescent boys, I would have chucked his stuff out and moved my stuff in there without too much deliberation – I felt entitled to my own room after so many years of sharing.

'I mean, is it too much to ask,' Mum went on, extracting Teri from her crib and placing her distractedly on a frayed changing mat, 'to pick up a phone? Hmm? Is that really asking too much? Where the hell have you been all this time?'

Kev's companion answered for him, a little too readily. 'He's been with me.' She had the rattling, gravelly voice of a chain-smoking woman in her forties, not a fresh-faced young girl in her early teens.

Mum was short-tempered at the best of times, and this was not a good time. 'Did I ask you?' she snapped, tearing impatiently at the sticky tabs on Teri's soiled nappy.

'Kev can't talk,' Julie explained.

'Oh? Is that so?' Mum lifted Teri's pliable little pink legs and stained bottom off the changing mat and removed the offending nappy with expert speed and efficiency, stuffing it into a bag and dropping it unceremoniously into the wicker basket by her feet. 'Kevin?' She had not once looked down at the writhing infant; her eyes were fixed firmly on her eldest. She continued to stare at him until he felt compelled to make a noise.

'I arnt alk,' he gibbered, pointing to his mouth. I noticed he had a split lip and one of his front teeth was broken. Somehow, strangely, the injuries made him look less unattractive. I thought my brother actually looked quite grown-up with the crap kicked out of him. It gave him a certain ruggedness. Manliness, or some vague promise of it at least. He had been beaten up before, of course, more times than I could remember. But this time he seemed to be wearing his injuries well, almost heroically.

Mum sighed. 'I don't have time for your silly games,' she said, with a dismissive shake of her head. 'Or the friggin' patience. Now, either go and get yourself ready if you're coming to the registry office, or stay in your room and stop wasting my time.'

'You getting married, Mrs Shaw?' Julie asked, coy and polite all of a sudden.

Mum cleaned up Teri's backside with a succession of cotton-wool balls and exhaled heavily. 'Yes, if I can ever get out of this bloody place. Pass me the wet wipes, Caroline. No, not those ones. The yellow ones.'

'Er . . . Mrs Shaw?' Julie ventured, timing her moment just as Teri's rear end defiantly exploded with another torrent of mess.

'Shit!' Mum exclaimed, not inappropriately, as a projectile dollop caught the edge of her dressing gown in its trajectory. 'Shit shit shit!'

'Mrs Shaw?' Julie said again, undeterred.

Mum stood away from the changing mat with her arms outstretched and looked at me in despair; in such situations the eldest daughter is always, by default, the second-in-command. I was now sitting on the arm of the sofa, attempting to clean my dirt-ingrained black patent shoes with tissues and spit and vainly hoping she wouldn't ask me the question I was anticipating.

'Finish this off for me, will you, Caroline?'

I looked up and grimaced. 'Ugh, no!'

'Listen, do I look to you like someone who will take no for an answer? Hmm? Do I?'

I thought about it. 'No,' I reasoned, not wanting to start an argument.

'Well, then. Nappies are there, cotton-wool balls are there, baby wipes are there, nappy-rash cream is . . . in that bag. I want her wearing that new little white suit I got from Mothercare, the one with the pink flowers. And stick that little hat on her as well, it's freezing outside. Go on. It won't take long. Make sure you get all the poo off her feet too. The stuff gets everywhere.'

'But *Mum* . . .' I knew that resistance was futile, so even as I whinged I was rolling up my sleeves and reaching for the Pampers.

'No buts, I've got to get ready,' Mum snapped, dabbing at the stain on her dressing gown with a wet wipe. 'God, when will any of you ever cut me some slack? You don't make my life any easier, you know. It's my *wedding day*. I'm getting married in . . .' She looked at the clock on the wall in the entrance hall and her voice escalated to a squeal. ' . . . Forty minutes! Jesus! Forty bloody minutes! The taxi will be here at quarter past. Look at me! Sharon, brush your hair and put your new shoes on. And *stop picking your nose*! Is Jolene still in the bathroom?'

'Yes, she's conspikated,' Sharon explained, dragging a hairbrush lackadaisically through her knotted brown hair. 'She says she can't get it out. And I need a wee!'

'Oh brilliant, that's just what I need,' Mum sighed. 'One who can't stop shitting, another who can't go at all.'

'Er . . . Mrs Shaw?' Julie persisted, unaccustomed as she obviously was to my mother's ferocious and potentially explosive moods.

'Look, love, it's not "Mrs Shaw", alright? At some point today I'm hoping it will be Mrs Gilbert, but until then I'm just a "miss". Call me Ellie. Just Ellie. OK?'

'OK, Mrs . . . Miss . . . Ellie. Er . . . can me an' Kev talk to you a minute?'

'Does it look like I've got a minute to spare?'

'Well, maybe we can tell you while you get ready.'

'Fine, just don't expect me to listen.' Mum bustled off to her bedroom and retrieved her hairdryer and brand new cream-coloured suit with matching pill-box hat. I didn't have the heart to tell her that Jolene had 'accidentally' decorated the hat the night before with her chunky-nibbed pen set, in the absence of a new colouring book. Or that she had pulled off one of the shiny brass-coloured buttons from the jacket.

'We do really need . . . to talk to you . . .' Julie went on, raising her voice slightly. She still hadn't let go of Kev's hand, even though he had repeatedly tried to wriggle out of her grasp.

From her porcelain throne in the bathroom, Jolene whimpered and grunted and then began to cry.

'I . . . cannot . . . believe this is happening,' Mum muttered, reappearing and plugging in the hairdryer, and folding the suit across the back of the sofa. She was beginning to shake, and I sensed it would be only a matter of minutes before she reached for the bottle. 'I feel like the old lady who lived in the fuckin' shoe,' she went on. 'I need a holiday. I've got to get away from you lot, you're doin' my head in.'

Teri was happily sucking her fingers and gazing blankly at me. I tried to stuff her soft, stumpy legs into the babygro, but she was not being cooperative and kept bending them and kicking out.

Mum yanked on her tights, and her fingernail ripped right through the gossamer fabric, laddering it all the way from the ankle to the knee. She was so exasperated at this stage that no expletive was adequate to convey her feelings. She paused, stuttered over some menacing fricatives, and took a few deep breaths.

I finally managed to imprison all of Teri's wayward limbs inside the babygro, and did up the poppers with a triumphant smile. 'Cup of tea, Mum?' I asked, picking Teri up and putting her back in the crib.

Mum put the back of her hand against her forehead. 'Coffee. With brandy,' she said, her voice now a sinister whisper.

Kev and I exchanged glances.

'No, on second thoughts, make it just straight brandy.'

'Ummm . . . OK.'

'Look, I know it's not a good time, but . . .' Julie persisted, pulling at Kev's arm and making him wince. I had to hand it to her, the girl had balls, and she was certainly persistent.

'No, it's the worst possible fucking time. This, *this* is supposed to be the happiest day of my life!' Mum gave her hair a blast with the hairdryer, combing it through hurriedly with her fingers while the rest of us simply stood dumbly and watched her.

'Considering the competition, it shouldn't be too fuckin' much to ask for really, should it?' she demanded over the strained drone of the hairdryer.

'You'd better get her brandy,' Kev said to me quietly, suddenly rediscovering the power of speech. 'I think she needs it.'

Five minutes later, Mum was seated on the sofa in her suit, the suit that had been brand new and immaculate the day before. The suit that had given her a brief jolt of excitement and hope when she first tried it on. Now, having applied Tipp-Ex as appropriate to the stains on the hat and given up the brief hunt for the missing button to a rather rumpled jacket, she hoped her strategically positioned faux sapphire-and-pearl brooch might serve to distract from the suit's imperfections.

Jolene was still on the toilet, clinging white-knuckled to the seat, and her punishment for ruining her mother's wedding attire was to be doled out at a later date. Mum assumed, rightly I think, that Jolene was already experiencing enough discomfort to partly repay her for her hat-scrawling and button-pulling misdemeanours. At length, Mum managed to find another pair of tights – too thick and itchy and the wrong shade of blue, but they would suffice. They would have to. She tied her hair at the back with a dozen floral fabric grips that I helped her to secure in place. I don't think it was as neat or as striking or 'bridal-looking' a result as she had hoped for, but her hair was still a little damp, so an understated, slightly limp coiffure would have to do. She put the hat beside her on the sofa and lay back against a mound of dirty baby clothes, looking across at Kev and Julie, who were still standing rather uncomfortably by the window. Kev was staring at the ceiling, Julie at the floor.

'OK,' Mum sighed, finally giving in, 'so what's so important? I've got a spare minute now before my next nervous breakdown, so come on, spit it out. And sit down, for fuck's sake, you're putting me on edge.'

Sharon wandered in and moaned about her dress being too tight around the neck.

'I'll give you tight around the bloody neck,' Mum threatened. 'Just leave me in peace for a bit will you, Shaz? Put your shoes on. Get yourself an orange squash or something. Where's your new velvet Alice band?'

'Dunno. Mummy, I need a wee and Jo's still . . .'

'I don't care! Just . . . go in the bath or something if you're that desperate.'

'Gross, Mum, don't let her go in the bath. That's horrible,' I objected. In truth the bath hadn't been cleaned for months and so it would probably have made little difference. I had my suspicions that it had been used for much more unsavoury purposes than occasional urination.

'You can shut up an' all, make yourself useful and get me another brandy.' She held out the empty glass and glared at me from under her fierce overgrown eyebrows, the plucking of which was yet another chore that had been overlooked.

I did so, grudgingly.

'So,' Julie began, watching Mum gulp down two thirds of the second glass without drawing breath, 'have you got your something old, something new, something borrowed, something blue?'

Mum stared at her blankly. 'What you talking about?'

'That's the tradition.'

'Is it now? Really. Well I never.' She tapped her nails against the glass as if in contemplation and gazed out of the back window at the communal garden. The communal garden was nothing more than a patch of yellowing lawn, but it was *our* patch of yellowing lawn. Partly ours, anyway. At least for now. The maisonette had even come with an en-bloc garage – all we needed now was a car to put in it. The latest council offering was the closest my mum was ever going to get to luxury, unless she got lucky in Ladbrokes or down the bingo hall. In ten years all she'd ever won was a weekend in the Lake District, a year's supply of cat food, a set of scented coat hangers, a Boots voucher, a basket of bath pearls and a bottle of Chardonnay, so my hopes weren't high.

'We're havin' a baby,' Julie blurted out, breaking the brief silence.

There was another silence after that announcement, a much longer one. Mum lit a cigarette. Sharon headed for the bathroom. I sat down next to Mum, on the hat. I looked over at Kev, who was squirming and blushing as he edged towards the door, pulled back by the firm hand of Julie.

'You're sitting on my hat,' Mum said to me, in a flat monotone. I stood up at once, picked up the squashed, misshapen hat and tried, valiantly but pointlessly, to manipulate it back into shape.

'Mrs . . . er, Shaw? Did you hear me?' Julie said.

'I heard you.' Mum blew out a stream of smoke and tapped the ash into a tea cup before clearing her throat and saying, 'Looks like I'll have to do without the hat, doesn't it?'

I looked at her apologetically, then back at the crumpled hat. It was, alas, quite beyond hope.

Julie was determined to get her speech out of the way. 'Me and Kev . . . we're like . . . together, yeah? We've been, like, serious, for nearly three months now, on and off. He says he'll marry me as soon as we're sixteen. We've already told me mum . . . and me stepdad.' She began to look uncomfortable now.

'Hmmm . . .' Mum regarded her battered son through the gathering smoke. 'So I see.'

Kev sniffed and I noticed blood seeping from his nose. I grabbed a box of tissues from the sideboard and offered it to him. He flapped his hand at me impatiently, but Julie took them from me with what could have been a conciliatory smile, or perhaps a sneer, and made Kev hold a wedge of them under his nose.

I felt disposed to say something at this juncture, perhaps just to break the icy silence.

'But Kev's only fourteen.'

It was a simple bald fact that in truth held little significance – the average age of first-time fathers in Rivington Hill was not that much older than fourteen anyway. But the very concept of my *brother*, my revolting brother creating a miniature version of himself – well, it was simply too horrible to contemplate. Surely there should be some law against that? Ugly, thick, socially useless people should of course be at liberty to masturbate on an almost continual basis if they so wish, but using their frequent urges for procreative purposes should be banned. Full stop.

'It was an accident ... we was just messin' around,' Julie prevaricated.

Procreation for recreation. Again. 'But me mum's brought me up to not believe in abortion an' all that,' Julie continued. 'So, I'm packin' in school and as soon as we're old enough, we'll get us a place together.'

My mouth dropped open, but Mum sat motionless, seemingly impassive for a time, the cigarette held loosely between her fingers, burning away a crumbling length of ash half an inch from the filter. Julie's emphatic opinion on abortion was not an unusual one – *nobody* agreed with abortion, and every estate-dweller believed that the creation of life was unimpeachably sacred even if it did all begin with an intoxicated knee-trembler round the back of a pub with some anonymous fly-by-night. This view was perhaps slightly incongruent with the fact that the murder and grievous assault rates were sky-high in the area. How utterly distinct and separate are love and life.

'How old are you, Julie?' Mum finally asked, dropping the remainder of her cigarette into the tea cup and lighting another one.

'Fifteen in April.'

'I see.'

A car outside blasted its horn, and everyone except Mum jumped in surprise. 'That'll be the cab,' she said, still not moving, not even blinking.

'Mum, we'd better ... go ...' I suggested.

'Get your sisters, make sure they're ready,' Mum said. 'Give Jolene some of those out-of-date prunes Ray put in the fridge – they should do the trick.'

'She'll never eat them.'

'Just do it, Caroline.'

'Sorry about the hat, Mum.'

'Just ... don't even talk about it, OK? It doesn't ... fucking ... matter.'

I sensed that a volcanic eruption was imminent, and I didn't want to be the catalyst, so I wandered to the bathroom and attempted to untangle Sharon from the shower curtain and to heave Jolene's bottom from the toilet seat. Neither of them seemed enthusiastic about being bridesmaids – Jolene had already smeared blackcurrant jam down the front of her silky cerise dress and Sharon continued to probe her nostrils and pull at her collar – but they cheered up a little when I offered them a Milky Bar if they remained silent for the next hour.

'This is a special day for Mum,' I reminded them, tucking them both into their knee-length winter coats and cleaning Jolene's grubby face with an even grubbier damp flannel. 'Just be on your best behaviour.'

'Will Ray be our daddy now?' Jolene asked, perking up a little at the mention of chocolate.

I stopped rubbing my sister's cheeks and considered a suitable answer. 'He's as good as we're gonna get,' I eventually replied.

'What do bridesmaids have to *do*, Carry-line?' Sharon asked.

'Speak properly for God's sake,' I snapped. 'They just stand there and look pretty. Which means the pair of you have a tough job ahead of you.'

'Oh. Is Kevin in trouble?'

I sighed and peered into the mirror. 'A whole shitload of trouble,' I assured them. 'A whole bloody shitload.'

For their honeymoon, Mum and Ray spent a rainy but pleasantly serene week in Jersey, followed by a weekend in the south of France. In a rare show of generosity, my grandmother paid for it, and she also travelled all the way down from Bootle to be with her daughter on her special day. As if that wasn't enough motherly munificence, she stayed to look after the kids while her daughter and new son-in-law honeymooned the best part of their marriage away in one or two three-star hotel rooms and one or fewer starlit beaches.

I didn't like my grandmother very much – she rarely smiled and she always talked about her life in terms of what 'could have been' had she not been unfortunate enough to have had too many children and disappointing husbands. She was not a great believer in marriage. 'I give 'em two years,' she said to me one evening, having already concluded a venomous verbal crucifixion of the Conservative party.

'Who?' I asked.

'Your mother and that Ray. Two years, max. Listen to me, young lady, take some advice from someone who knows. Love, this thing *we* call love, is very different from what men call love.'

I looked up from my latest book with mild curiosity. 'Do you think so, Nan?'

'Think so? I know so!'

'But Mum seems happier with Ray than I've ever seen her before.' By heart, I was just as cynical, but the perverse romantic in me often shone through when I was instigating an argument with my grandmother. 'I think it will work out for them. I hope it does.'

'Hah!' the old woman scoffed. She had investigated her daughter's drinks cabinet and discovered an old bottle of sherry at the back, behind the multitude of gin and tonic bottles. She emptied the last drops of the sherry into Jolene's plastic Mr Men beaker – the only clean receptacle she could find – and took a couple of sips.

I frowned, and my grandmother put the drink back on the sideboard, folded her knitting in her lap and took her glasses off. 'Understand, Caroline,' she began, rocking back in her chair and putting her swollen, arthritic feet up on the coffee table, 'I love my kids, all of 'em. Your Uncle Terry has made a few mistakes in the past, yes, as has your Uncle George. Pretty big mistakes an' all, some of 'em. But it doesn't change the fact they're still me kids. Your Aunt Linda, well, we all know about her and it's very sad, but I still love her. Course I do. Now, your mum, she's always been the wild child. Stubborn as a mule, and bloody stupid with it.'

I felt compelled to defend my mum, but couldn't think of anything substantial to back up my defence at the time, so I kept quiet.

'Now, she's had some men in her time, all bad,' the old lady went on. 'They use her and throw her away like a piece of rubbish . . .' She shook her head and sighed. 'Not her fault I suppose, but she falls for it every time.'

'You've been married *three times*, Nan,' I pointed out. 'If I remember rightly, the last one ran off with your pension and the Avon lady.'

Not quite true. 'Ran off' was a slight exaggeration – he hadn't been able to walk without the aid of a Zimmer frame and a pair of super-strength spectacles, so maybe a better verb would be 'doddered'. Or 'shambled', perhaps.

My grandmother's small blue eyes bored into me angrily. 'That's enough about that,' she snapped. 'We're not talking about my life, we're talking about your mother.'

'All I'm saying,' I retorted patiently, slipping into idle rumination, 'is that you won't get anywhere in life unless you make a few mistakes. Everything is all a bit hit and miss really, when you think about it.

Mum does her best. She really does, Nan. It's not like she's had an easy time. It's been really hard for her. She's just taken what chances she had, whenever she could. Same as anyone. She's just been unlucky.'

Unlucky. Yes. That was perhaps something of an understatement.

My grandmother appeared quite taken aback by my unusually eloquent and considered argument, and was momentarily lost for words. Diplomacy and intra-family loyalty were not strong points among the Shaws, after all. She pursed her lips and grabbed a ragged copy of *That's Life!* from the sideboard. She had already read it dozens of times, completed the crossword and entered all the competitions, but she always referred back to it in the absence of any other numbing stimulus, or even simply to remind herself, through the readers' letters and 'exclusive' real-life accounts, that there were many others out there who led similarly inane and meaningless existences. After disinterestedly scanning through 'I found my husband in bed with my best friend's daughter' and 'I wasn't overweight – I had a five-stone ulcer!', she sighed and continued from where she had left off.

'Ray does seem to be a good deal nicer than the others,' she eventually conceded. 'But what I'm saying is that you can *never be sure*. You might think that someone feels exactly the same way about you as you do about them, but how can you know for certain? It's a matter of finding the genuine ones, Carrie. Genuine. That's what you want. An' it's rare, that is, believe me, it's rare.'

I was tempted to get up and finish off my book in my own room, away from the garrulous drone of a bitter old woman, but even there I was unlikely to get very much peace with Shaz and Jolene fighting over my hand-me-down Etch-a-Sketch. Besides, I was in an unusually mellow and lazy mood, so I curled up on the sofa with my head against a cushion and half listened. When I was younger, I had entertained the possibility of setting my grandmother up with Ned. They were both lonely and widowed (be it literally through death or effectively through errancy), and I believed, deep within my naive young heart, that a man and a woman who were both old and lonely would naturally match up perfectly together.

I could see now how wrong I was.

'I'm not saying I don't *believe* in love . . .' my grandmother continued, 'just that it's not this two-a-penny flash in the pan that some people seem to think it is.'

'Mum wouldn't have married Ray if she didn't think it was going to last,' I said. 'And they make each other happy, which must count for something.'

'Of course it does! But Caroline, you're a clever girl, can't you see why so many relationships simply fall apart? It takes *time*, and that is something I haven't got. But that's because I'm an old lady now. I'm beyond caring. Others don't have that excuse. People are so impatient these days. And so greedy! They want the world on a plate, and they want it now.'

'What are you getting at, Nan?'

'I mean, it's all very well and good *now* – she's only known the man five minutes!'

'Are you talking about Mum and Ray again?'

'Yes, of course I am. Who else?'

'They met just before Christmas 1986, Nan. Hardly five minutes ago. Well over a year.'

'Pah! What does she know about him? Nothing! Of course it's all hearts and flowers now, but what about next year? Further down the line it will be a whole different story. What about when little Teri gets older and more demanding? And all the others – I mean, the man is taking on a hell of a lot, isn't he? Not only his own child but the children of four other men. Four! And what about when he starts coming home late or when Ellie gets bored? You know as well as I do that your mother has a natural tendency to get bored. Yes, she does, Carrie, don't try denying it. She just loses interest. Just like that.' She clicked her fingers and paused for dramatic effect, lowering her voice before carrying on.

'It won't last, that's all I'm saying. They'll start to really get to know each other, and they won't like what they find out, underneath the surfaces. It takes time, but it will happen. Disillusionment, that's what it's called.'

I was growing increasingly irritated. 'Can't you just be happy for her? Mum hasn't exactly had it easy, you know.'

'You were a mistake, I know that much,' my grandmother sniffed, tilting the subject slightly, and hoping that I might rise to the provocation.

Despite myself, I did. 'What?'

'Your father was the worst of the bunch. Big, burly man with . . .'

'A metal plate in his head and loads of tattoos down his arms, I know, I know,' I finished impatiently. 'I don't really care, and I don't want to talk about him. It doesn't really bother me.'

'Just as well that's all you know about him,' she said enigmatically, picking up her knitting again. 'He was a dodgy one, that Brian. Took advantage of your mum, a sixteen-year-old girl at the time she was, and him a ruddy great man of thirty! Old enough to be her father. That's disgusting, that is. In and out of jail all his bloody life. Got your mother pissed and had his way with her in the park down the road. She trusted him. Don't know why she trusted him, but she did. And then he goes an' knocks her up. Poor little scrap, only sixteen and with a little 'un already.'

I felt a knot of sickness and tension in my stomach, and swallowed it down with some tepid lime cordial. 'Please talk about something else, Nan,' I said. Then under my breath, I added, 'Or preferably just shut up.'

The old woman eyed me suspiciously. 'Remember that time you came to stay with me, years ago when it was just you and your brother? Must have been 1980 or thereabouts. No, I remember, it was just after your fourth birthday. August 1979. Do you remember?'

I shook my head. 'I only really remember that time a few years ago when Kev fell out of a tree and your cat had kittens. And last summer when you took us on a boat ride across the Mersey and we went to the Maritime Museum and Kev got bored and Shaz wet herself.'

At this, my grandmother allowed herself a little smile. 'No, maybe you're too young to remember the time I'm thinking of, it was a while back. I sat you on my knee in the back garden and you looked at me and you said, *Nanny, what was my daddy like?*'

'Did I? I don't remember that at all.' I had never been curious about my father, and had always presumed that the less I knew, the better. Ignorance was indeed bliss, in this case at least.

'Do you know what I said?'

I sighed and turned to the last page of my book. I remembered reading *George's Marvellous Medicine* several years earlier and had wondered about the logistics and practicalities of poisoning my grandmother. If it was good enough for a Roald Dahl character, it was good enough for me. I had eventually concluded that the disadvantages would probably outweigh the benefits, and so in the end decided just to put a spoonful of pepper in her tea instead of sugar.

'I had to lie to you,' my grandmother said, taking a last swig of the sherry. 'How could I tell the truth? You were so young, so full of hope and innocence.'

'So what did you say?'

'I told you he was dead.'

'I see. And was I OK about that?'

'Oh, you were fine. I assured you he was a very nice man when he was alive, and that he loved you very much.'

'Hmm, I bet that put my troubled little mind at rest,' I muttered.

'Well, he may as well be dead,' she reasoned.

I wanted to shout out loud that I couldn't help who my father was, and I wasn't to blame for how things had turned out (that common petulant teenage phrase: 'I never asked to be born!'). I suppose what I really wanted was reassurance that I wasn't really a 'mistake'. Or maybe that I started off as one but now nobody regretted or resented my existence. Was that too much to ask for? But just at that moment, there was a piercing wail of agony or possibly rage from one of the bedrooms.

'Sounds like Jo playing up again,' my grandmother said. 'Check on the kids, will you, Carrie? I don't want them beating each other up all bloody night. Must be nearly time for Teresa's feed, too . . .' She tapped the baby monitor and brought it close to her ear when it failed to produce any discernible sound. 'Can't hear a bloody thing,' she moaned, putting it back on the sideboard.

'Try switching it on,' I grumbled, throwing my book to the floor. 'It's alright, I'll put them to bed. And I'll feed Teri. And change her. Then I think I'll go for a walk.'

'You will do nothing of the sort, young lady,' she croaked, fumbling in the pocket of her tartan dressing gown for her Silk Cut. 'You have school tomorrow. And your mum and Ray get back from France in the afternoon, don't forget. It's already quarter past nine.'

'I'm not going to school tomorrow. Mum said I could take the day off so you could get back to Liverpool before it gets dark.'

'Did she now?' She lit up a cigarette and blew the smoke out in a vicious cloud, her eyes scrutinising me sceptically. 'Well, it's not right that you should miss school. Look how Kev turned out – always skiving, that boy, and now he's got himself into a right pickle.'

'Nan, one day off isn't going to make any difference.'

'That's the thing about you lot, you're so damn ungrateful.'

I groaned with impatience. 'What are you talking about *now*?'

'When I was your age, we had no time for school anyway. Oh we *wanted* to go, we wanted to learn, more than anything, but we could not allow ourselves that luxury! We had to *work* to put bread on the table. Me an' Hazel, me sister, we could of been someone, we could of gone places, but no, we had no money, both our parents were sick, and so what else could we do? Just thirteen and fifteen years old we were, up at dawn, scrubbing people's doorsteps and cleaning their homes for half a crown, collapsing into bed at the end of the evening, and just a bowl of gruel and a slice of bread to eat the whole day.'

I had already had this lecture, countless times. 'But I wouldn't *mind* that!' I exclaimed. 'Anything is better than school. I hate it!' How could anyone with even a glimmer of sanity define school as a 'luxury'? For me, it was anything *but* luxury. It was hell.

My grandmother extended a finger and began wagging it in admonition. 'Now, Carrie, of all my grandchildren you are the one who has been born with some intelligence, some real, you know,' she tapped her forehead with the filter of her cigarette, 'common sense.' She took another drag and leaned forward in her seat. 'Know what I mean? I would hate to see you throw it all away. You have a future. I never had that. I never . . .'

'Oh for crying out loud, Nan, spare me all this endless self-pity. What kind of future do *I* have then? Look around. I mean, come on, get real. At least your parents made a go of it. At least you *had* parents, a family, for however long. I have three sisters and a brother, all of us have different dads, mine being the biggest shithead of them all. We're living in a place with rising damp and dodgy electrics and sagging ceilings and it's barely big enough for four people, let alone seven. We don't own it anyway and we don't own most of the things in it. We don't really own *anything*. We have no money apart from what the government doles out to us, and most of that goes on mum's gambling and drink and fags. Mum has never worked and never *will* work, all she ever does is . . .'

'She *has* worked!' Nan interjected. 'She had that party-organiser job for a while. And she was a waitress down at that café in Eastman Street.'

I laughed bitterly. 'She held a couple of Ann Summers parties and served fry-ups to builders and hung-over students for a month or so. The Inland Revenue are hardly going to be rubbing their hands with glee over those little ventures, are they?'

The bony finger started wagging again. 'Now, that's enough of your cheek. Your mum has had a tough life, show her some respect.'

I sighed in despair at the old woman's misplaced piety. 'Well, I'll see to the baby I suppose,' I said, standing up and walking towards the door. 'Then I'm going round to Mark's. At least *his* mum actually *listens* to me. I wish *they* were my family. You lot are all just . . . crap!'

I slammed the door behind me; as I stood out in the hall, quivering with rage, I heard my grandmother mutter one of her favourite catchphrases, 'Bloody ungrateful kids.'

Then there was the clack of needles as she resumed her knitting, uncaring as she usually was about the odd dropped stitch.

I literally sprinted to the Crozier house. Ned answered the door.

'Was wonderin' when you might make an appearance. Haven't seen you all weekend,' he said. His mood was more sombre than usual, but I didn't notice at first because I was struggling to get my breath back. I stumbled into the hall and Ned put his hand on my shoulder. He waited a few seconds for my panting to subside.

'Bev went into hospital on Thursday night, love,' he whispered finally.

My heart rate surged again and I felt the sweat turn cold on my skin. 'W-what for?'

'She's upstairs in bed now, but they wouldn't let her out until this morning. She's . . . quite ill, I'm afraid. Very weak.'

'How come? W-what's wrong?' My knees buckled and I fell with a thud onto the bottom stair. 'Why didn't someone tell me?'

'Bev said you have enough to worry about at the moment. Mark was going to come and get you or at least call you, but . . . it's a family thing. You understand. We're glad you're here now, though. She'll be grateful for some female company. And she's on the mend now, so don't you worry. I'll put the kettle on.'

It's a family thing. The words stuck like thorns.

'Can I see her?' I stammered. I held on to the banister and slowly got to my feet. 'W-would she mind if I went up?'

Ned smiled and patted my arm. 'No, of course not. I'll bring you up some drinks in a moment.'

Still gripping the banister, I slowly made my way up the stairs. The spiral pattern on the burgundy carpet seemed to swim before my eyes, a whirling volution, as if I was drunk. Mark appeared suddenly at the top of the stairs, and I almost fell into him.

'Hi Caro.' He noticed my panicked expression and said, 'Hey. It's . . . nothing to worry about really.' He forced a smile. 'You know my mum, she bounces back.'

I could see through his smile, and, almost like an automatic reflex, I put my arms around him and hugged him close to me. It wasn't the first time we had embraced, but such moments of physical closeness between us, even the briefest of hugs, were undeniably few and far between. Mark tended to avoid bodily contact as a rule, unless he was playing football, instigating a fight or trying to convince a girl to go that little bit further. As far as he was concerned, anything non-sporting, non-violent or non-sexual was for wimps, weaklings and women. So the hug didn't last long. He pulled away and avoided my eyes, playing it cool as ever.

'What's wrong with her?' I asked. 'She's gonna be OK, isn't she?'

Mark shrugged and lowered his head. 'It was so sudden, she just . . . kind of collapsed.'

Norman the dog appeared from Mark's bedroom and bounded excitedly over to me, almost knocking me over. I patted him distractedly, trying in vain to establish eye contact with Mark. He was always so evasive, and it irritated me. 'Did they say . . . at the hospital . . . I mean, it's not like . . . cancer or anything?' I could barely bring myself to say the word.

He shrugged again. 'No, I don't think they know what it is. She's making out she's OK, but . . . well, you go in and see for yourself. Me dad's in there with her at the moment. Sorry I didn't . . . let you know. I just thought, what with your mum getting married and your gran being an old bitch and the rest of your family giving you hell . . . you prob'ly had enough to worry about . . .'

Part of me wanted to hit him, but I also wanted to hug him again, and never to let go. I wanted *him* to initiate an embrace, for once.

'Don't you know me well enough by now Mark?' I mumbled, pushing past him and creeping towards Bev's room. He pursued me, grabbing my arm and pulling me back towards him.

'Please understand, Caz,' he said. 'I know how you feel, and I was gonna call you, but she *is* my mum. She's *my* mum. Understand?'

I finally met his eye and glared at him in disbelief, then wrenched my arm from his grip. 'Why don't you start acting like her *son*, then?' I said. 'You've always taken her for granted, you don't know how lucky you are to be so . . .'

To my astonishment and horror, I tasted the salty onset of tears in the back of my mouth, and before I could do anything about it, they welled up into my eyes and spilled over, choking me with sobs. I covered my face with my hands and bowed my head, my shoulders shaking, unable to hold it back any longer. Mark just stood there, watching me dumbly, obviously acutely discomfited by the unexpected outpouring of female emotion. Slowly, after a strained pause, he stretched his hand out towards me and touched my back, then began tentatively stroking my hair, but I shook him off irritably, unable to relish the contact I craved, too distraught to welcome it or reciprocate. The tears were long overdue; I had been feeling pent up and fragile for weeks, and had now finally reached breaking point. I didn't need comforting, I wasn't looking for sympathy, I simply needed to lash out, to scream, to let myself go at last.

'You're so lucky,' I finally managed to blurt out, 'your family, your house, your friends, *everything* . . . everyone loves you. And you don't even have to *try*.'

'Caz . . .'

'You just have no idea. Do you?' I glared at him through my tears, and like a dam bursting inside me, those fervid, torrential emotions finally overpowered me. I felt the last of my self-consciousness slip and before I knew it, the words were gushing out, an avalanche of inane, terrible, heartfelt words.

'*Do* you? I'm a human being too, Mark, I have feelings, and I'm not like you, I'm not going to hide them or pretend they don't exist. I hurt. I need. *I feel.* I . . . love you, I can't help it, I always have loved you, and I always will. And . . . and I hate you, too. I do, I really do. I hate you so much for not loving me. For being so damn . . . *cold*.' I ran out of breath and dissolved into more tears, shame and burning regret adding to my misery now. How could I be so stupid? What would Mark know about love? What would he care? I'd really blown it this time.

Mark stood motionless, facing me but looking at the wall, the door, the dog, unable to rest his eyes on anything for longer than a split second. He tried touching me again, a half-hearted gesture, but I waved him away, impatient with myself, with him, with everything.

'Caz . . .' he began, lost for words but wanting to fill the terrible void of silence with something, any old drivel. He inched forward uncomfortably, his arms twitching at his sides. I was torn between wanting to kiss him and wanting to spit on him. He was so bloody useless, so dense, so insensitive, so inexplicably adorable. 'Shit, Caz . . . I . . .'

At that moment, Bev's voice drifted from her room, saving her son from an awkward situation: 'Caroline, is that you, love?'

I rubbed my eyes with the sleeve of my jumper and breathed in deeply, trying to gain composure. 'Yes, I'm here,' I replied, steadying my voice. 'H-how are you?'

'Please come in, it seems like ages since I last saw you.' Bev's voice was faint and reedy, as if she was having trouble breathing.

I swallowed back another sob. 'It's . . . only been a few days, Bev,' I called back, attempting to sound chipper despite the catch in my voice.

Mark thought of a very good idea, and went to the bathroom, emerging shortly with a fistful of tissues and offering them to me. I took them from him and blew my nose, then gave the soggy bundle back to him. We exchanged one last glance, but I was unable to read anything in his eyes. It could have been affection, concern, love, even – but equally it could have been contempt or mere mortification. I had used to want to be able to tune into Mark's innermost thoughts and feelings; now I felt quite grateful that I had no clue. His impenetrability, rather than making him seem more mysterious and exciting, now just bored and frustrated me. What was the fun in having barriers if they couldn't be knocked down? And God knows I had tried for long enough by now.

'Just forget what I said,' I hissed, leaning close to him as I reached for the door handle.

He still couldn't look at me. 'Whatever,' he sighed.

'Yeah, whatever. That's right, Mark. Just forget everything. You're good at that, aren't you?'

And I turned away, pushing the door open and disappearing inside, leaving Mark in the corridor with only the dog for company.

The curtains were drawn and the dimmer switch was on low in Bev's room. It smelled strange. The radiator must have been on full whack, because I immediately felt uncomfortably warm. I shut the door behind me and approached the bed. Sean was sitting on it holding Bev's hand. On the cabinet by the bed there was a vase of yellow and pink carnations, and a jug of water. I couldn't see her face properly in the dim light, especially through the blurry barriers of tears and myopia, but I was able to see even from a distance that the delicate, ashen little woman lying against the pillows didn't look like the Bev I knew.

'That was some little speech you gave my son,' Bev murmured, holding out her free hand. I took it and perched sheepishly on the edge of the bed.

'You heard?'

Bev closed her eyes and smiled. 'I heard enough.'

'I'm sorry.'

Bev squeezed my hand gently. 'I think maybe you did him a favour.'

I glanced across at Sean. He winked at me and said, 'Alright, love?'

I nodded, tried to smile, felt the sting of tears prick my eyes again. 'I just . . . wanted to talk to someone . . .' I said, feeling pathetic. 'I didn't know you were ill, Bev. I'm so sorry, I just . . .'

'Shh, don't worry. I look much worse than I feel.'

'Really?'

'Really. I did feel like death for a while, yes, but I'm getting better. Be back to my old self in no time I'm sure.'

'But w-what's wrong? Why did you have to go to hospital? You were fine when I saw you last week.'

'They did some tests and they couldn't find anything. They thought it could be diabetes, or even MS, but all the tests came back clear. I think I just had a funny turn. My body had just had enough. Needs a rest, that's all, I think.'

'Is that *really* all it is? You're sure?' I was dubious, as I'd never seen Bev look so ill and tired. She had grey circles underneath her eyes, her cheeks were sallow and sunken and her hair, pulled back away from her face, looked thin and colourless. Maybe it was just the light in the room, or lack of it.

'Why did they keep you in hospital all weekend then?'

Sean cleared his throat and muttered, 'Just a precaution, she'll be fine now. Don't worry.'

'Honestly?'

Bev squeezed my hand again, a little tighter. 'Honestly. Anyway, what's with you? Why are you looking so down in the dumps?'

There was a knock at the door. 'Only me, love,' Ned called from outside in the corridor. 'I've brought up some tea and a hot chocolate for Caroline.'

Sean got up to open the door for him.

'Our Mark's stormed out in a huff,' Ned chortled, coming in and placing the tray on Bev's dressing table. 'Said he'll be back by eleven, but I'd say he's gone round to whatsername's house.'

Bev and I looked at each other knowingly. 'You've obviously given him something to think about,' Bev whispered.

'I doubt it,' I said. 'He never listens to a word I say.' I didn't want to know who the latest 'whatsername' was, and I told myself that I didn't much care. Mark could shack up with every slapper in town as far as I was concerned. They were welcome to him.

But my heart plummeted further.

'You'd be surprised how much actually sinks into that tiny brain of his.'

I couldn't help smiling at this, but remained doubtful. Mark knew the scores of every West Ham match since 1978 and the names, dates of birth, marital status and red-card quota of every key player, but this left very little room for any other knowledge, and certainly seemed to preclude the possibility of any deep introspection and erudite conversation. I had forced myself to learn the bare minimum, just so that Mark and I could share some basic football-related opinions. But the simple truth, if I was being *really* honest, was that I didn't really *have* an opinion on football. Football was just football. Twenty-two blokes kicking a sack of air about in a field. Sure, *now* I took more than a passing interest in West Ham's progress, but only because I knew how much it meant to Mark. I had to demonstrate that I, too, cared. I remained confounded as to how anyone could care about the game to the extent that it became an obsession. But football *was* Mark's obsession, and he was mine. So who was the real sad case?

'Pass me my tea will you, Sean love,' Bev sighed.

'Wait, let me just . . . make you comfortable first,' he said, plumping her pillows and helping her sit up. I had never known Sean to be so attentive. He picked up her cup from the tray and handed it to her, telling her to be careful and not to spill it.

'For God's sake, I'm not a bloody invalid!' she said, half laughing. She looked at me and joked, 'Maybe I should get sick more often if this is the treatment I get!'

'Don't you dare,' Sean grunted.

'Well, me and Sean will be downstairs if you need anything, Beverley,' Ned said, sensing that a bit of female bonding was possibly in the offing. Sean got the hint and kissed his wife before following Ned out of the room.

After they had gone, Bev waited a while before saying, 'Now my dear, forgive me for prying but I think there's something you need to get off your chest. She looked at me closely. 'Am I right?'

I didn't respond, and couldn't return her stare.

'Tell you what,' she said, 'if you tell me what's wrong with you I'll tell you what's wrong with me. Is that a deal?'

'So you *do* know what it is?'

Bev sipped her tea and let go of my hand. 'Well, yes,' she said. 'And it's certainly not life-threatening so take that look off your face!'

'Not at all?'

'Not any more.'

'So it was?'

She shrugged. 'Potentially, I suppose. It was my own stupid fault for ignoring my health. You know me, the opposite of a hypochondriac! But these things have a habit of catching up with you . . .' She began to cough tremulously, spilling a few drops of tea over the quilt before she managed to put the cup on the bedside table.

'It's . . . just . . . well, women's trouble, basically,' she explained. 'Nothing wildly exciting. There are other things, that winter flu bug I got just after Christmas didn't help matters for a start. It all adds up, you know.'

'Women's trouble?'

'Well, you know I've been having migraines and dizzy spells on and off, and some mobility problems ... just moving around, lifting things, simple things like that?'

I knew that sometimes Bev complained of a bad back, but I never thought it was serious because she had always been so offhand about it. 'Is that why they tested for MS?' I asked.

'Yes, my mum developed it when she was about my age, you see. It usually starts off with just a few symptoms but slowly gets worse. They thought perhaps that I . . . well, never mind. It's not that serious. I was feeling tired all the time and losing weight too, that's why they tested me for diabetes. I've got that in the family too. I tell you, I've had enough blood taken out of my arm to feed a whole colony of vampires!' She rubbed the inside of her elbow, and I noticed a little circular plaster.

'So . . . ?' I prompted.

'So, that's it really. I just kind of blacked out on Thursday afternoon while I was doing some shopping . . . keeled over without warning into the frozen fish and that was it. A bit embarrassing, really. When I woke up I found myself in a hospital ward.'

I eyed her dubiously. 'You've only told me what's *not* wrong with you.'

'Nothing more to tell, Caz love. Early menopause, that's all. It's just causing some complications. I'm deficient in some nutrient or other and feeling a bit ... weepy and weak. Risk of osteoporosis as well, which means no more coffee or salt for me, and these here tablets twice a day.' She fished in her bedside drawer and rattled a box of white pills. 'And I've been told to slow my life down. Give up one of my part-time jobs. Take a holiday. Get rid of a few pets, maybe.'

'You can't get rid of your pets!' I exclaimed.

She smiled and patted my hand. 'Course not. I'd sooner be rid of the boys than any of my pets,' she mused light-heartedly. 'A right pair of bloody teenagers, they are, it's them that's turning me into a grey and decrepit old lady. Anyway, enough about them. Have I put your mind at rest now?'

I wasn't entirely convinced or placated, but muttered, 'I suppose so.' I collected my hot chocolate from the tray and studied my reflection in the ornate mirror above the dressing table. My eyes were red and puffy and I almost didn't recognise myself, until I moved nearer and my focus adjusted. I was so bored with that same expression, that same face, gazing vapidly back at me every time, pre-empting dissatisfaction. Still too fat. Big apple cheeks and shapeless chin. Slouched, stumpy gait. Short little neck. Still not pretty enough. Oh yes, the eyes could be very striking if they didn't always look so sad and if they weren't set in such an oddly proportioned face. And if they were only just that little bit closer together. My nose wasn't big enough, it didn't have character. It looked like a snout. My mouth wasn't right; my lips were too thin and pale and looked even sillier when I made efforts to improve them with lipstick. I wanted full, sexy, pouting lips like Tina Hartley. Lips like my ex-best friend Amber. Succulent lips that said *kiss me* without even moving. And I wanted whiter than white teeth, straight and shiny, for a dazzling smile like all those gorgeous pop stars and actresses who beamed from the front pages day after day. I would be smiling all the time then, even if I didn't feel like it. If I was that gorgeous to look at I would never stop smiling! *Eye candy*, Mark and Billy called it. I wanted to be eye candy. But my teeth were kind of beige; inadequate like the rest of me. And the two at the front were a little bit wonky. My hair looked dull, it was long and thick but it just hung down over my shoulders, lifeless and greasy, with the tops of my ears poking through. Another thing – my ears were too big. Getting them pierced hadn't detracted from their size, it had only made it more noticeable. Besides which, I couldn't afford a nice pair of earrings. I didn't have a nice *pair* of *anything*: breasts, buttocks, thighs, feet . . . all deformed somehow, in some way or other. Unsightly, horrible, freakish.

'You admiring yourself again?' Bev asked. 'Teenage girls and their vanity! I remember what I was like back then!' She began to cough again, and poured herself a glass of water.

'I'm an ugly fat fucking bitch,' I muttered, under my breath. It had become my mantra. 'Ugly, ugly, fat, *fat*.' My reflection sniped back at me, and I tried staring it out, and failed.

'What was that?' Bev said, swapping the water for tea and clicking on her lamp.

I turned and forced a smile, even though fresh tears had begun to slide down my face.

'I was just thinking, you're only about fortyish, Bev,' I said, refusing to let myself break down again. 'You're way too young to have your menopause.'

'Forty-four next month. But bless you for being so sweet.' I think Bev was about to make a joke about being over the hill, but she noticed the shine of my tears as I approached the bed again. 'Oh, Caro, sit here, take my hand . . . here, come on.'

The soothing tenderness in Bev's voice was all it took to set me off again. She held out her arms and let me cry onto her shoulder. Bev always had a palliative effect on my sorrow, no matter how deep-rooted or irreconcilable I believed the sadness to be.

'Remember our deal,' Bev whispered, once my sobbing had ceased. 'I tell you, you tell me. Yes?'

I felt exhausted and dehydrated. It had been so much effort holding back the tears, disguising my heavy heart with a brave face for such a long time. Now the tears had finally come, I felt drained. My throat hurt. My eyes stung. I reached for the tissues and managed to knock the box to the floor. Bev leaned down and picked them up for me.

'Even if I did tell you, you wouldn't understand,' I whimpered, pulling out two or three tissues and holding them against my hot eyes. 'Nobody understands.'

'How can you know when you won't even tell me?'

I tried to speak clearly but it came out as a whine. 'I just . . . hate life. I *hate* it.'

Bev sighed. She clearly already knew about the trials of adolescence, with all its pitfalls and acne scars. She sometimes described her two boys as 'vile juveniles', brooding and uncommunicative at best, obnoxious and hostile at second best. A phase that just had to be endured, not so much by the adolescent as by all those who have to live with the adolescent. I suppose Mark was currently going through the same stage as me, just in an entirely opposite way. He seemed to love life almost as much as he loved himself, and made the most of every moment, surrounding himself with his loyal gang of friends and a pick 'n' mix selection of casual girlfriends. Bev once told me that she wished some of Mark's *joie de vivre* and confidence would rub off on me, and at the same time that a little of my self-effacement would rub off on Mark, just to strike a balance between our two seemingly diametrically different personalities. 'A little bit of healthy interpersonal osmosis', she had said.

'Oh love, we all feel like that sometimes,' Bev finally responded. 'You're at that age . . .'

'Please, *please* don't tell me I'm at that age!' I pleaded. 'I've heard it a million times already!'

'But . . . it's true. You won't always feel like this.'

'Bev . . . please try to understand . . . I want to die. Every time I look in the mirror it reminds me that I am a failure.'

'Excuse me, young lady, but when did you decide that?' Bev demanded, raising her voice slightly. 'A failure? *You?* Do me a favour!' She held me by the shoulders and forced me to look her in the eye. 'You're the smartest kid on the estate! Probably in all of Essex!'

I frowned at the total lack of consolation that was conveyed by this supposed compliment.

Bev continued. 'You're funny, you're sweet, you're pretty, you're . . .'

'No, no, no!' I interrupted, standing up and pacing impatiently to the other side of the room, avoiding the mirror this time. '*No!* I'm *none* of those things. I'm *nothing.* I try so hard, but I have no friends any more. I used to, but something happened and I don't understand what I did wrong. I hate school, I hate it so much I can hardly bear to think about Monday morning. I hate practically everyone there, and everyone hates me. Amber used to be my friend but now she's a . . . she's a . . . *slag.* She doesn't speak to me much any more, and we never see each other after school. It's like I'm not good enough for her. We have nothing in common now. And she was my *best* friend! My best friend in the whole *world.*'

I paused to force back another sob, and almost succeeded. I carried on, my voice cracking more and more with every statement until I became virtually unintelligible.

'I am sick of the way I look. If I was beautiful Mark would want me. Everything would be different. But Mark can have anyone, and everyone wants him and most other girls are so much prettier than me. And thinner. And stupid, stupid, *stupid!* He loves *stupidity,* he's drawn to it like a . . . like a fly to shit, every time. I don't know why, but can't you see I have nothing to offer him? He'll just never be interested in someone like me. You know, Bev, I disgust myself. Sometimes, *sometimes* I can forget about it and for a short time I might be able to convince myself that my life will work out alright, that I'm a good person at heart and that's all that matters.'

'That *is* what matters . . .' Bev chipped in, looking slightly taken aback by the force of my diatribe.

'But it isn't!' I shrieked, totally hysterical now. 'It *isn't!* Look at me! Look at me! I've just got fatter and fatter even though I only eat as much as everyone else. And it's not just that I hate myself for what I look like. Not even my own family have time for me. It's like I'm insignificant, less than a nothing. My own Nan told me I was a mistake. Tonight she told me that. Like I need reminding. And my mum still sometimes acts as if she'd rather I didn't exist. Can you imagine how bad it makes me feel? What do I have to live for? My own family don't want me around, and as for school . . . School makes me feel sick. You have to have the right kind of everything. You need the attitude to fit in, the clothes that everyone else wears, the face, the figure, you have to be something so . . . so *false.*'

'And why would you want to be like that?' Bev's voice was remarkably equable and soothing, while I was just getting increasingly uptight.

'Because I want to be *part* of something, of course! Can't you see? I want to be *included.* I want to feel less . . . worthless. But . . . I can't pretend. I can't fit in.'

'You're better than that, Caro. You're not worthless. You know that.'

'But I don't think I'll fit in *anywhere.* Ever. I'm so alone. I feel like a freak.'

There was silence, except for the ticking of a clock and my indelicate periodic snuffles.

'Have you finished now?' Bev asked.

I nodded, feeling quite humble, and slunk back to the bed, head down.

'Firstly, let me assure you, you are *not* a mistake,' Bev whispered, taking my hand in hers. 'I'm sure your Nan didn't mean what she said. You are an asset to your family, and I don't see how your mother would cope without having you around. Your family do love you, of *course* they do, it's just everyone has different ways of showing it.'

'I always thought there was just the one way of showing it . . . by being *loving*?'

Bev held up her hand. 'You've had your say. Now let me have mine. Secondly, you are not a freak. You are a little girl who is very quickly turning into a woman, and you're scared and unsure of yourself, which is normal. Don't you think every other girl at your school is going through exactly the same emotions?'

I shrugged and looked at my feet.

'Of course they are', Bev went on 'They just have their gangs to make them feel less insecure. Group mentality weakens the individual, Caroline. You only have yourself to answer to. That makes you strong. You're independent. You'll have no problem when you're grown up.'

Bev seemed so wise and knowledgeable and rational at times like this, but I was unable to latch on to the words and attach any real meaning to them, or make them truly applicable to me. I felt like such a hopeless case that nothing could be of consolation.

'Do you know what I'm going to do?' Bev said, opening her drawer again and leaning across to look for something inside.

'What?'

'I'm going to phone up that other school and get them to take you.'

There was a brief silence. 'W-what?' I stammered.

'That's where you belong, my dear,' Bev went on. 'You'll be so much happier there. You have a brain, something most of the poor scraps at Mason Tyler can only dream of having. Had they the intelligence to dream of such things.'

I felt confused. 'Do you mean St Jude's?'

'Of course I mean St Jude's. It's one of the best schools around here. I don't know why you didn't go there in the first place. You'll have no nasty boys to distract you, and you can really knuckle down and realise your potential in a place like that.' She removed some papers, pills, pens and a diary from her drawer and then found what she had been looking for. 'A-ha! Here we are. That letter Mr Marigold sent you, remember? Nearly two years ago now.' She pulled out a rather crumpled piece of paper and unfolded it carefully. 'As soon as I'm back on my feet, I'll give them a call. It will be a fresh start for you.'

'Do I not get a say in this?' I asked, half horrified, half excited.

'Yes. Of course you do. No more Mason Tyler, no more dreading Monday morning, no more feeling so unhappy. So. What do you say?' Bev put her reading glasses on and scanned the letter proudly. 'Or shall I answer for you?'

I clambered into the bed beside Bev, reading the letter over her shoulder. If nothing else it reminded me that I had made an *impression* on somebody. A *positive* impression. Someone was willing to give me a chance to succeed, to become someone. How could I not grab that chance, when golden opportunities in my life were so rare?

The two words Bev had uttered so casually bounced about gleefully inside my head: fresh start, *fresh start*.

'You'd do that for me?' I asked Bev meekly, cuddling up closer to her and pulling the quilt tightly around us. Bev smelt of lavender water and cinnamon. I buried my face into her cotton nightgown and she put her arm around me.

'You silly old thing,' she said. 'You're like a daughter to me. I want you to be happy.'

With that, I felt an exquisite rush of warmth rise up within me. I felt my bottom lip tremble. 'Really?' I peered up at her through my fringe.

'You know you don't even have to ask. Now, we're agreed, yes?'

I nodded dumbly. 'It's not too late, is it?'

'Oh, I shouldn't think so. Leave it with me.' She folded the letter and put it back in the drawer, pushed her glasses on top of her head and closed her eyes. 'Now, after all that excitement I feel rather exhausted. You don't mind if I have a little nap, do you?'

I shifted onto my stomach and we were both quiet for a few moments. I too felt exhausted, although more emotionally than physically.

'I don't know what I'd do without you, Bev,' I eventually sobbed into the fragrant pillowcase.

'You'd probably manage, dear,' Bev murmured, stroking my hair.

Two minutes later, we were both asleep.

6

What Was the Question Again?

A new uniform (burgundy, not navy blue), a new gym kit, a hockey stick, a new pencil case, a ring binder, three HB pencils, a fountain pen and ten blue cartridges, a new school bag, three A4 refill pads, a compass, set square and protractor, a calculator. Thus equipped, and with a snazzy new geometric haircut and resolutely optimistic demeanour to boot, I began my new existence at St Jude's Grammar School.

St Jude's motto was 'Excellence, diligence, eminence', and the school was firmly focused on ensuring that every one of their eight hundred and fifty perfectly packaged, crisply uniformed pupils adhered to each of these three principles with conscientious loyalty. Trading in Mason Tyler for St Jude's in pursuit of personal happiness and fulfilment was, on the face of it, quite a logical move. But then so is the condemned man's choice of hanging over slow torture. It was perhaps best described as a hybrid of *Prisoner Cell Block H*, Monty Python's *Castle Anthrax* and *Malory Towers*. And yet it stood firm by its conviction – however well deserved – that it was 'among the best of Britain's intermediate educational institutions'.

I was in over my head right from the start.

The unnatural environment created when several hundred lethally hormonal, bitchy and bewildered young girls are crammed together in a confined space can never be imagined; it has to be experienced to be believed. Mark used to say that simply imagining it was good enough fuel for many a cold lonely night with only his right hand for company. But it was easy for him to be flippant. He didn't have to go through a culture shock like the one I experienced on that appropriately dismal and dreary April morning in 1988.

Bev put forward my transfer application and argued my case, very eloquently and convincingly, backed up by encomiastic references from Mrs Sawyer and a number of my subject teachers, even Ms Johnson. This surprised me because Ms Johnson never seemed to have a nice word to say about anyone, hardened as she had become to the unlikelihood of anyone under the age of twenty possessing a single agreeable trait. Even my mum gave me encouragement in this new academic venture, telling me it was 'about bloody time someone in this family showed the world what they were really made of'. Whatever she meant by that, anything resembling a compliment coming from my mother always sent my hopes soaring.

Despite all this support, a needlessly lengthy but ultimately unanimous referral process had ensued, during which I was bandied about from pillar to post, psychologically assessed and rigorously examined, both behaviourally and mentally. I was finally deemed a suitable candidate and permitted to join the intellectual elite smack in the middle of the spring term. The contrast between the two schools was a shock to the system that not even Mr Marigold's belated 'Welcome to St Jude's Grammar [Glamour?] School for Girls' brochure could have prepared me for. Whereas the female Mason Tyler pupil got by quite well thank you very much with her tits, tongue and caustic attitude, the average St Jude's pupil had breasts and brains and breeding on her side – a lethal combination of irresistible traits, to be sure. They were, in every way, a cut above me. A different species.

And did I fit in any better there than I had done at Mason Tyler?

Well, I was arguably two thirds of the way there to start with – I had breasts and I certainly had brains. Several authoritative people had already assured me of the latter, and the former was pretty much elementary. Unfortunately breeding is something that cannot even be faked. You've either got it or you haven't. My idea of 'class' was admittedly very naive back then, simply because I had never really been in such close proximity to so many 'posh' people. That isn't to say they were *all* posh, of course; just as not *all* the pupils at Mason Tyler were 'common'. But the majority of these girls had undoubtedly been conditioned in the inimitable ways of the privileged throughout their short lives. Silver spoons and all that. They were *classy*. Slutty, yes, some of them, but nevertheless classy with it. Another lethal combination. Many of them were classy, slutty *and* pretty. These were the ones to respect at all times, no matter what. As Important People went, you couldn't get a higher rank. The combination of looks and class and sexual suggestibility was the most lethal of all. It was far, far beyond my reach.

Talking of lethal combinations, my first lesson at St Jude's was chemistry. The teacher was called Mrs Farquharson. She was scary.

'Now girls, please can you refer to page 217 – the cobalt chloride experiment that we started last week, as I'm sure those of you who remained awake will recall . . . oh, Celine, share your book with the new girl, will you please?' (That was me – the new girl.)

The sweetly scented body beside me shifted slightly and, with a heavy sigh and an air of implacable surliness, opened her book and pushed it towards me. I muttered 'thanks', and ventured a quick glance at her, but she had a shiny curtain of sleek hair hiding the side of her face and her head was turned away, so all I could deduce was that she was brunette and petite, and seemed to have a penchant for the smell of synthetic orange groves and vanilla. The smell was making me feel quite nauseous, but it made a change from the mould, tobacco and halitosis aroma of most Mason Tyler pupils. She rested her chin on her hand, tilted her face slightly and flickered her eyelashes, but she didn't deign to look at me. I wondered if I was so invisible or so unimportant that I wasn't even worth looking at, let alone speaking to.

Mrs Farquharson was excitedly scribbling something on the blackboard; a diagram with labels and a brief description of an experimental method involving a Bunsen burner and several test tubes. She had vicious, jagged handwriting and the chalk kept snapping in her grip with every vigorous stroke and stab. Somebody to my left passed me a note. I looked down at it. It was a piece of lined notepaper folded in half with the letters 'CJ' written on it in red biro.

'Pass it on,' a voice hissed at me. The breath smelled of Juicy Fruit – chewing gum was categorically prohibited, so only the most rebellious pupil dared to indulge. That was most of the girls in my chemistry class: twenty sets of jaws were obstinately chomping away all around the room. Thinking it foolhardy to ignore or to retort, I dumbly slid the piece of paper across the top of the desk towards Celine; the sweet-smelling, brown-eyed girl on my right. She made a huffy noise, and snatched the piece of paper without looking at it.

'Now, remember that the element cobalt can form compounds in two different oxidation states. Who can tell me what I said about equilibrium, and the anhydrous and complex ions?' Mrs Farquharson had already launched into the language of chemistry teachers, a hybrid of gobbledegook and equations.

'The aim of the experiment was . . . what?' she went on. So many questions, so few answers. I didn't have a clue what she was on about. The nearest I had come to practical chemistry at Mason Tyler was fending off the podgy little hands of a toad-faced ninth-grader called Thomas Wickitt.

Mrs Farquharson sighed impatiently when no pupil ventured an answer. 'To investigate the effects of temperature and concentration upon the position of equilibrium in a solution of cobalt (II)' (she underlined it on the blackboard and the fifth piece of chalk broke) 'containing excess chloride ions. Am I jogging some memories yet?'

Silence, except for the periodic snapping of a hair band, a bra strap and/or some gum.

'Come on girls, I know it's a Monday morning but really! Make *some* kind of effort will you?'

The Juicy Fruit girl leant in towards me. 'Oi, put your hand up and tell her you weren't here and so you don't know what the feck she's going on about.'

Did I say these girls were classy?

'Pardon?' I whispered back.

'Well, I can't understand a bloody word of this, and the book isn't helping much neither.'

I glanced at her; she was classically, casually pretty, with big chocolate-drop eyes and long vanilla hair flowing around her shoulders. 'Why can't you ask her?' I hissed back indignantly.

'She'll kill me,' was the simple response.

Fair enough, I thought. Don't want to start off on the wrong footing with this lot. I put my hand up.

Mrs Farquharson placed her palms flat on her desk and sighed, blinking at me wearily. 'Yes?'

'Could you please . . . er . . . run through it again, just quickly, because I wasn't here and I don't actually know what cobalt chloride is?' I ventured nervously. I didn't want to get on the wrong side of my peers, but equally I didn't want to piss the teachers off either.

She averted her eyes and muttered something under her breath. 'Anyone else need reminding?' she asked, picking up another piece of chalk.

Slowly, one by one, hands ascended into the air. Not everyone, but the overwhelming majority. This made me feel slightly better.

'Very well,' Mrs Farquharson said, 'I will go over it one more time, and then you can all get into pairs, grab your overalls and goggles from the box at the back, carry out this experiment for yourselves, write it up in detail and hand in your findings by the end of the lesson.'

Groans all round.

The words every new girl must dread on her first day at school: not 'overalls and goggles', not even 'write it up in detail', but '*get into pairs*'. Get into pairs? But I didn't *know* anyone. Who would want to pair up with me, anyway? I looked and felt shabby and inferior to just about everyone else there. I didn't have any chewing gum. I reeked of council estates and bad taste. I was scared shitless. 'Get into pairs' was only slightly less humiliating than that cruel PE ritual which entailed two of the fittest and most attractive pupils being told to 'pick their teams'. A ritual with which I was only too familiar.

'Here, you can join up with us two, we know absolutely nothing about chemistry anyway so we'll just bodge it up together, yeah?' Juicy Fruit girl offered, looking over at Celine, who was engrossed with plaiting her hair. 'That OK, CJ?'

'Whatever.' She didn't look up. She was now reading the note that I had passed to her.

'Juicy Fruit?' Juicy Fruit girl offered, thrusting a packet in my face.

'Cheers.' If you can't beat them, join them. I was pleasantly surprised by her casual friendliness – but somehow it didn't make me feel any more at ease.

'Go get the overalls and goggles from the box over there, would you?' she asked, nodding towards the back of the room where a riot of nasty blue polyester garments was being hurled about. 'White overalls for CJ, she won't wear the blue ones. I'll get the Bunsen burner and stuff.'

I hopped down from my stool and wandered over to the box, chewing briskly on the gum and accidentally biting my tongue out of sheer nervousness. I waited patiently while a group wrangled over some geeky-looking plastic safety goggles, then waded in, extracted two blue overalls and frantically dug about in a search for white ones.

'All the white ones have gone now,' a girl's voice informed me. 'They always go first. Gotta be quick. Nobody likes the blue ones.'

Blue, white, they were exactly the same except for the colour. Could vanity really run so deep as to extend to the colour of the compulsory overalls they wore in the chemistry lab? Surely not. I grabbed another blue one and scampered back to the desk. Juicy Fruit girl was setting up a load of test tubes, and Celine (CJ?) was sticking her finger into a pot of lip balm.

'Er, they didn't have any white ones left,' I said, putting the overalls on the desk. CJ looked at me as if I was retarded.

'I always have white ones,' she drawled. The accent had a soft American lilt to it, or possibly Canadian.

'Where are the safety goggles?' Juicy Fruit girl demanded.

'Oh, sorry, forgot,' I simpered, hating the pathetic nervous edge in my voice. 'I'll get them now . . .' I wanted to add 'Any particular colour choice, madam?' but of course, I was in no position to ridicule these high priestesses of fashion. So I slunk off again and collected three pairs of goggles, feeling even shorter than I was.

'I'm Rebecca by the way,' Juicy Fruit girl said, tying the overalls and snapping on the goggles. 'Becca. That's CJ.'

I smiled and tried to get CJ to look at me, but she was cold as ice. 'Right, let's get on with this stupid bloody experiment then,' was all she said, popping her lip balm into a tin pencil case. The pencil case had 'CJ' scratched onto it, and there was a photo-booth picture of herself with a floppy-haired boy of about sixteen Sellotaped to the inside of the lid.

'So you're Caroline?' Rebecca went on, clamping a test tube to a contraption above a Bunsen burner and slipping the rubber pipe into the gas tap. I had never seen such a set-up before and wondered what it was all for.

'Yes,' I said, thankful that she had the decency to remember.

'Have you only just moved to the area then?'

'What? Oh . . . um, not exactly.'

'Where do you live then?'

'Riv– er, Hornchurch,' I bluffed.

'Oh yeah? Which road? My boyfriend lives there.'

'Oh, well, not exactly *in* Hornchurch, but near it.' My hole-digging operation was already well under way, but the lies were automatic: they escaped from my mouth without first consulting my common sense. What I was telling her now wasn't exactly *false* – Rivington Hill wasn't far from Hornchurch, distance-wise. But I sensed a whole series of heinous falsifications was imminent.

'How many cars does your dad have?' was the next question. Understandably perhaps, this threw me a bit.

'Pardon?'

'My dad got a new one at the weekend,' she half laughed, flicking some pages in her exercise book. 'This one is silver, his other two are dark blue. Well, the Toyota is kind of more purple than blue I suppose. I always wanted a silver one. It's really nice. It's even nicer than my brother's. He drove me to school in it this morning. I just *love* the smell of new cars, don't you?'

I thought I managed pretty well to keep the conversation going, considering we were obviously living on different planets. 'What make of car is it?' I asked, trying to keep a normal, casually interested tone of voice.

'A convertible Jag,' she said.

This meant nothing to me of course, but it sounded pretty good.

'Oh God, he only got that because *my* dad has one,' CJ piped up, taking a break from the strenuous task of filing her nails.

'Yeah, but yours is an older model, my dad got an F-reg.'

Had I entered some strange alien planet? What were they talking about? What is an F-reg? Why would *anyone* need three cars?

'So what? My dad has *four* cars, and my mum has a land rover, so that's five altogether, so we beat you.'

Why would anyone need four cars *and* a jeep?

'Oh shut up, CJ,' Rebecca said. 'Who cares anyway?'

Well, quite. I was beginning to prickle with anxiety. What would they say if they knew I had zero cars and, come to think of it, zero dad? What would they say if I told them that the nearest I had been to a car, apart from occasional rides in Sean Crozier's ancient banger, was watching my older brother smash up and set fire to a neighbour's ancient rust bucket (as a favour, so the neighbour could claim the insurance)? What would they say if I asked them what the difference was between an F-reg and a G-reg? What would they say if I told them I lived on a council estate and for the past eighteen months had attended a rough school called Mason Tyler that had been threatened with closure three times since Thatcher was voted in as PM? What would they say if I told them my mother had been on benefits for fifteen years and was about to become a grandmother at the age of thirty? Would any of it actually mean anything to them?

'Have you set that up properly now?' CJ asked irritably, extending a varnished fingernail to disinterestedly tap a test tube of strange powder. This turned out to be her entire net contribution to the experiment. 'God, this is boring,' she grumbled, shaking her hair back with a loud sigh, like a film star tired of the applause.

If I had had my very own beauty adviser, my hair might have looked something like CJ's. It was more or less the same shade of chestnut, just a little bit longer and much, much glossier. I gawped at it in envy and admiration, resisting the temptation to touch it, then removed my ponytail band and loosened my own hair, dragging my fingers through the knots in a somewhat risible attempt to demonstrate that I, too, had flowing tresses. Then I remembered: my hair didn't flow, it had never flowed, it simply hung limply like seaweed off a rock. I put my ponytail band back in despondently.

'CJ, you're so *impatient*,' Rebecca snapped. 'Why don't you do it then, if you're so damn clever?'

It was beginning to dawn on me that Rebecca and CJ were best friends. Their bickering and petty competitiveness gave the game away.

'Will you girls over there keep the noise down!' Mrs Farquharson barked from the other end of the room, looking up from assisting a diminutive pair of curly-haired girls with their equipment. 'If you need a hand then wait your turn. I'm coming round to check on everyone's progress so keep the gossip to a minimum, and the work to a maximum if you don't mind.'

'That's the Jordan twins over there,' Rebecca confided to me, nodding towards the curly-haired girls. 'All the teachers love them because they suck up, and their dad is some local councillor or something. Don't trust them, they're both slags and they're liars too.'

I wasn't wearing my glasses (as usual), but as far as I could tell the twins were identical and both of them looked a little bit sad, with dainty downturned mouths and droopy eyes. I heeded Rebecca's wise words – after all, she was currently my only connection to this strange band of fellow pubescent females, and I wasn't going to do anything to jeopardise even this most tenuous of links.

'So what school did you go to before? Where d'you live? Did you have to pass some kind of genius test to get in here?'

I thought it was very possible that Rebecca wouldn't have heard of Mason Tyler, so I told her and, dodging the second question, confirmed that I did indeed have to take a few numeracy and verbal-reasoning tests and that Mr Marigold had personally invited me in light of my 'exemplary results'. I personally thought the tests had hardly been the stuff of genius, but I decided to keep that opinion to myself. I got the impression that Rebecca fancied herself as a bit of an intellectual purely by virtue of her St Jude's status, and I was loath to cast aspersions on this conviction.

'Mr Marigold! Ha!' she said. 'The old twat, he's going senile.'

I wondered if this was just a wickedly humorous opinion she wanted to share with me, or whether it was intended to insinuate that a personal invite from him wasn't worth the paper it was written on.

'I haven't met him yet,' I said.

'Don't bother, he won't even remember you. He's going to retire by the end of the year, that's what me and CJ reckon anyway. Then we're hoping Mr Anderson will take over. He's the deputy head and he's . . . nice.'

'Are there many male teachers?' I asked cautiously. Surely it wasn't natural to have so many young women enclosed in one building without injecting a little bit of testosterone here and there, just for balance? Surely it wasn't *healthy*?

She shook her head. 'There's Mr Thornalley, he's also a geriatric fart. He teaches maths, but mostly to the older girls. He stinks too. Never washes his trousers. Check out the stains if you ever get lumbered with him. Mr Singh teaches physics, but he's married and a Muslim anyway, I think. Apart from that . . . no male teachers. If you're lucky we might get Mr Anderson for English Literature. He's nice-looking and CJ's sister used to go out with him and she says . . .' She dropped her voice so low I could hardly hear what she said next. '. . . She says he's got a *massive* dick.'

How should I react to this? I searched for a pithy reaction. 'That's nice,' I said eventually. 'Does that influence his teaching skills at all?'

She furrowed her perfect blonde brow. 'You what?'

'Never mind. Two, by the way.'

She still looked confused, which was what I wanted her to be. I clarified the crafty fib with shameless aplomb. 'My dad has two cars but I've been nagging him for ages to get another one because both of them are at *least* a year old.' I said it quickly, with a certain nonchalant savoir-faire, as if I was bored with the subject of dads and cars already. Which I categorically was.

'Oh, right.'

I didn't know if my elaborate web of lies would mean acceptance or not, but it was a damn site better than admitting the truth. No cars, no executive home, no mod cons, no dad, no money.

No chance.

And still the gangs, the gangs. They were everywhere. St Jude's teemed with them. Except now they were called *cliques*. It's a natural herd mentality, an instinctive need to form a clan of like-minded peers, and the St Jude's girls may generally have been from a different class to the Mason Tyler rabble, but they were still social animals with a strong desire to bond and gossip. The girls within the same gang often classified themselves as 'friends', but when backs were turned the claws came out. There is no stronger and more lethal emotion among teenage girls than jealousy. And jealousy, in all its sick green leviathan inevitability, was everywhere. You could smell it. You could taste it. You could hear it whispering through the voluble assembly rows. The air was heavy with it, like an oppressive humidity shot through with the aroma of musky perfume and Juicy Fruit.

I was happy on the periphery for a while, because I was neither scorned nor welcomed. More importantly, I had nothing to be jealous of, nothing for them to feel intimidated or threatened by. There was no pressure on me. I had no fixed identity. I could flit. But it was apparent that I would soon have to find my niche and make some attempt to get a grip on this brand-new social circle. It was either that or accept my doom: a pariah forever. Bev had always told me I was more a 'chameleon' than a 'black sheep' – that I had the ability to adjust and stabilise myself to any given environment. Natural resilience: that's what she called it. That's what I had, apparently. But resilience doesn't count for much when you lack the confidence to back it up.

The cliques terrified me more than the gangs. Their sheer volume was overwhelming. The dynamics involved within a clique are fairly straightforward and yet impossible for an outsider to fathom. As Bev had rightly maintained, single gang members become feeble and pitiable when taken away from the safety of their pack, but I rapidly formed the opinion that the same could not be said of the cliques and their individual members. Every clique member was formidable in solo, only to become utterly indestructible when within her clique. And the older they got, the more awe-inspiringly untouchable they became. Even the unattractive ones possessed an elusive quality of immaculate beauty and distinguished grace. To me, the eleventh and twelfth-graders were goddesses, pure and simple. In my eyes, there was no higher being on the face of the planet, not even the well-groomed, well-bred eleventh and twelfth-graders from the boys' school who were all desperate to lose their virginities and (invariably) hearts to these spectacular sirens.

The eleventh and twelfth-graders carried their chunky files and folders around with them everywhere, with a funky little bag slung casually over one shoulder – just about big enough to accommodate their make-up, a trashy novel, some glitzy novelty keyrings, some emergency pads and a hairbrush. All the older girls had the natural, palpable assurance that comes from emerging from the bowels of puberty into full-bloom womanhood. Contrary to the extensive and apparently pointless school rulebook, they dyed their hair and wore make-up and body jewellery – glittery nail polish, purple or red highlights, heavy eyeliner and thickened lashes, lipstick, shaped eyebrows, powdered noses. Their surgical steel rings flashed bijou gemstones in various anatomical nooks, and every fleshy (even bony) part of their ears was studded with jewellery. In summer, it was all exposed navels, kitsch sunglasses, tinted lip balm, shirts left open, smooth Impulse-misted armpits, supple breasts almost visible beneath thin cotton.

I remember thinking to myself that once I reached that age, I would possess enough beauty, charisma and confidence to bewitch any man, and even Mark would be spellbound.

And I couldn't wait.

At the end of my first day at St Jude's, I took my seat at the back of the school coach and pondered my fate. The coach took a meandering route and only went through the outskirts of Rivington Hill – the nearest bus stop was ten minutes' walk from the estate, and I was grateful for that half-mile distance. Nobody needed to find out I was an estate girl. Some of the other St Jude's girls often bandied the word 'estate' about, as if it was actually something to be proud of, using weird expressions like 'my father deals with real estate' (I wondered, is there such a thing as *unreal* estate?), and 'my father's Spanish estate'. Of course, I knew there was more than one meaning of the word 'estate', just as there was an alternative and quite starkly different meaning of the verb 'come' (one that made those strange, enigmatic passages in my Mum's rude novels suddenly make more sense).

The school coach took us past and around the shopping centre that the Mason Tyler pupils favoured. When the bus stopped at a red light outside the main precinct, I looked out of the window and spotted Mark with a bunch of Mason Tyler girls and boys, sitting on a wall in their blazers and crumpled shirts, swigging White Lightning and munching fries out of brown paper bags, scornful of the spitting rain that hadn't let up all day. I sank lower in my seat, trying to make myself inconspicuous, and hoping he wouldn't look up and see me. I prayed for the lights to change. A girl with bleached hair and an extremely short skirt sauntered up to Mark and they began to kiss in a most unattractive but strangely transfixing fashion. I watched his hands slide from her shoulders to her buttocks and under her micro-skirt, while her hands wandered all over him: bony, quick little hands, a ring on every finger and a different shade of polish on every nail.

Something inside me snapped at that moment, and for the first time

I saw Mark through new eyes: not the myopic, love-glazed eyes I had seen him with for as long as I could remember, but the hardened, jaded stare of someone who had finally had enough of being second-best. Almost without knowing what I was doing, I turned to the girl sitting beside me – a slightly younger girl with a severely short haircut but a pretty, elfin face – and said, 'Do you have a boyfriend?'

She looked at me, slightly aghast, and in a very refined accent she replied, 'Of course not! I've only just turned twelve!'

The lights went green and the coach lurched forward again. With deep gravitas, I told her, 'I've just dumped mine.'

'I beg your pardon?'

I pressed my forehead to the window and my eyes flickered rapidly across the row of shops and restaurants as we passed: Gregg's bakery (where Mark had once bought me a chocolate eclair because some bullies had nicked the money Bev gave me), Clinton Cards (where I had purchased his birthday, Christmas and Valentine cards for the past five years), McDonald's (where we sometimes used to meet and eat after school), Next (where, after months of careful saving, I had recently acquired a pink top and some frayed blue jeans in the hope that Mark would find me more attractive in them – he hadn't noticed), Dolcis (where, after stashing away further savings, I had bought my first decent pair of shoes), and Pizza Express (where the Croziers had taken me for my twelfth birthday).

Everything I saw, every facet of my life, I could only perceive in relation to Mark, the times we had shared together and how deeply and irrevocably I loved him.

It was only now that I was beginning to realise it was about time I got a life. Starting now.

'Yeah, I dumped him,' I repeated, more to myself now. 'He was no good for me.'

Seeing Mark on my way home from school became a regular event. If he wasn't on that wall outside the precinct with his gang and his girls, I would be sure to spy him in McDonald's – just a quick, fleeting glimpse as the coach sped past. Always the same gang, about six or seven of them altogether, including two or three girls. Tina Hartley was usually there, seeming to get skinnier each time I saw her, and sometimes Billy Crozier would be there with an older gang, ignoring the plebs. All they seemed to do for hours on end, day after day, was sit and smoke and snog and sneer. Sometimes there would be fights, but they would usually kick off much later in the evening. Sometimes I would look at them with awe, envy, disgust, horror, condescension, admiration, bafflement, resentment . . . usually a combination of all of those feelings. My heart still leapt when I saw Mark, but it wasn't love any more – I told myself it could be hate mixed with a residual hopeless lust, and I accepted that explanation as perfectly plausible.

The longer I was at St Jude's, the greater the gulf grew between me and my former contemporaries at Mason Tyler. Now I truly was in limbo. I wasn't one of them and I never had been, and I wasn't one of the St Jude's lot, and I felt uncertain that I ever would be. Now the best I could wish for was supercilious smiles, the odd shared joke or opinion and grudging pairings up (often with HRH Princess CJ and loyal subject Becca) during the more taxing practical science lessons.

Nobody went out of their way to befriend me, but then nobody showed me any real animosity either. This is not to say that the girls in my form were unfriendly – generally they were pleasant enough – but I arrived on the scene long after the groups and factions had been established. And it is not to say they didn't have their moments of unprovoked bitchiness either – they were, after all, hormonal females. To be fair, I had probably already resigned myself to solitude; it was conditioned deep within me. At Willow Lane I had been the most robust and sociable little scamp in the entire school, which, given the competition, was no mean feat; now, within such a short space of time, I had become withdrawn and self-conscious. And things only got worse.

Puberty was continuing to ravage me: there was not one inch of my body that had not expanded, extended or exploded. Teenage angst had taken control of my brain, exacerbated by my sense of desolation. I despised myself and, for a time, I despised everyone else with equal passion. Oh, passion – I still had too much of that, passion with no real object and no reason and no obvious source. It was passion for passion's sake, and it burned on and on and on.

My first period came in the middle of the night two months before my thirteenth birthday; perhaps overdue considering I had been sprouting for a good two years by that stage, but nevertheless not exactly a convenient development and certainly not a very convenient moment. When I returned to St Jude's after the summer holiday, I went to the doctor in the hope that something could be done about my acne, which had spread like wildfire. I sat there and moaned and moaned about my various problems – not just medical and cosmetic, but personal, psychosexual, familial, existential, emotional, menstrual and mental. The doctor listened patiently to my tirade for the first ten minutes, then sighed, looked at her watch and scribbled out a prescription for the Pill.

Home soon reverted back to the usual council-estate domestic hell within four walls. My mother and Ray were now way past the honeymoon stage, and Ray was made redundant from his job in July 1988, which did not ease the tension between the newlyweds. Around this time, Teri was teething and would not stop crying. The noise in the house was relentless. My mother was about to become a grandmother, but Kevin wasn't remotely interested in fatherhood and had already found another enamoured ignoramus to call his girlfriend. Julie, the girl who was to be the mother of my first niece, ended up spending more time at our place than Kevin did. Her parents had more or less disowned her, and I think my mum must have seen a little of herself in Julie, because she began to treat her like her own daughter. That is to say, she occasionally fed and watered her, frequently shouted at her, cursed her, insulted her, and every now and then, perhaps under the influence of drink, threw her arms around her and offered a precious moment's counsel and consolation. I too felt sorry for Julie – any girl who was prepared to bear my brother's child must surely have been in desperate need of professional help.

She would sleep alone on the mattress in Kev's room while he was out, doubtless sowing more wild oats and committing more crimes against humanity, and I'd hear her crying in the night, even over the sound of Mum and Ray arguing in the lounge. One night I crept in and slipped under the quilt beside her and we cried together, and she confided in me that she had no friends and felt alone and I confided much the same in her, so we resolved to be best friends from then on. A simple, childish agreement between two scared children, complicated only by the birth of my niece two weeks later.

Something quite unexpected and unprecedented happened when I returned to school in September. Rebecca was having a party at her house that Friday night and was handing out invitations like fliers, making wide-eyed promises about chocolate cakes and 'eighteen certificate' videos. This in itself was not unusual; there was a party every other weekend at some house or other – usually when the parents had escaped to their second home in the country or their villa abroad – and the invitations were strewn about among classmates and clique members with great enthusiasm. When Rebecca handed an invitation to me – a silver envelope with my name written on it in black – I wasn't exactly *shocked*. Yes, it was my first official invitation to any kind of social gathering since starting at the school, but Rebecca was one of very few who I considered a potential friend, even though the kindest thing I could remember her ever saying to me was 'Here, you can pair up with us if you like.'

I was, however, mildly taken aback, and extremely grateful. Incredulous at first.

'Is this for *me*?' I spluttered.

'D'oh, *yeah.*' Rebecca often put on a goofy voice to get her point across more effectively. 'It does, like, have *your* name on the front, unless you changed it over the summer?'

I tried to underplay my inordinate gratitude to avoid sounding pathetic, but somehow I just couldn't quite do it. 'Oh, thanks Becca, that's really sweet of you. Thank you. Thanks so much.' I ripped the envelope open and pulled out the official invite:

Rebecca Hermione Delaney
is cordingly inviting
CAROLINE S.
to her party on
Friday the 9th of September 1988
at
2, Manor Gardens, Billericay (on the corner)
from 5 p.m. until VERY LATE!!!
Bring a sleeping bag and a ***present*** (it's my birthday on Sunday)
RSVP

'So will you come?' she asked.

Nobody ever said 'no' to Rebecca, not even CJ, who was revered and adulated by everyone because she was so flawlessly attractive and cool. (It hadn't taken me long to suss out the hierarchy of our form, and CJ wasn't the type to let you forget that she was up there at the very top.) It was understood that certain people just shouldn't have to take no for an answer. They had never had to throughout their childhoods, and they sure as hell weren't about to start now.

I wasn't going to break that rule.

'I'd love to,' I said. And it was true, I was delighted about it. And then, just in case she hadn't heard me the first time, or the second or third time for that matter, I added, 'Thank you very much.'

'You're welcome.'

'It's cordially, by the way.'

'What?'

'Rebecca Hermione Delaney is *cordially* inviting . . .' I said, innocently and erroneously assuming that she would be grateful for my correction.

'Are you saying there's a mistake on my invitations?'

'Well, not really . . .' I noticed something in her eyes, and it wasn't a friendly twinkle, more like a sinister glint. I decided not to press the issue. 'No, the invitation is lovely, really great, and thank you for thinking of me.'

Then I suppose I must have stumbled away somewhere to bludgeon away the last surviving minuscule molecule of my dignity.

So all I had to worry about was what to wear, what present to buy her, where I was going to get the money from and how on earth I was going to get back to Rivington Hill from Billericay on Saturday morning.

According with tradition, I turned to Bev for advice.

'Oh Caroline, even if I had a nice dress to lend you, it probably wouldn't fit you! I put on so much weight after having the boys and was never able to shift it . . .' She opened her wardrobe and pondered for a while, hands on hips. 'Surely it doesn't matter what you wear? It's only a sleepover, isn't it?'

Damn, that was another thing. I had to get some decent pyjamas. My discoloured, misshapen nightshirt would cause no end of scornful laughs among the pretty brushed tartan cotton and pastel satins. I slumped down onto Bev's bed and put my face in my hands. 'It's never going to work,' I mumbled.

'What isn't?'

'Me . . . and them. I'm not one of them. They're so *different*. They're so . . . perfect.'

'What *are* you talking about? You've been invited to a party! Of course you're one of them. You wouldn't have been invited otherwise. And of course they're not perfect, nobody is.'

'Rebecca and CJ are,' I muttered.

The seed of jealousy had been planted, there was no denying it. Being female and self-effacing and slightly mixed up, I knew that by fraternising with similarly oestrogenised females who all seemed to possess everything I could blatantly never possess, that seed would soon grow into one great big fuck-off green tree of jealousy. It had already started. The budding roots of deep-rooted envy seeped into my waking thoughts, it infiltrated my dreams. It mingled with my myriad insecurities and made me sick. It ate me away inside.

'Come on Caz, don't be stupid, you just haven't given them a chance. You haven't given *yourself* a chance.'

'I have got *some* friends. Kind of. I mean . . . there are a few girls in my form who are really nice and everything. It's just, Becca and CJ . . . they're so . . . it's like, they think they're so clever but neither of them seems to *know* very much, and yet everybody hangs onto them like . . . like . . .'

'The popular girls, eh?'

'Popular? They're like celebrities.'

'Pretty, too?'

'Sickeningly.'

'Well, there you go. And you've been invited to a popular, pretty girl's party. So what's the problem?'

'That *is* the problem Bev. I'm not popular, I'm not pretty, I have no nice clothes, I have no money to get Becca a present, I have nothing in common with them unless I lie about every single aspect of my life and tell them I have rich parents and talk about cars and swimming pools and horses and . . . boyfriends.'

'Well, there it is you see,' Bev said.

'There what is?'

'Boys. You do have something in common. You're all young women with obsessions. Just because you have a different background and different circumstances doesn't mean you can't be friends with them. You'll be fine. Just be yourself. You're all human beings, you're all essentially the same inside. Just . . . be yourself.'

Bev had an infuriating knack of making impossible things sound simple.

'I hate being myself,' I muttered. 'I hate everything about being myself.'

'Listen, you made a promise to me, remember? You promised me you would stop being so negative all the time and start looking on the bright side of life.'

'I know I did, it's just . . . the sun has gone behind a massive great cloud and I don't think it's coming out again.'

Bev didn't smile at my childish metaphor. 'Sometimes you've just got to pull yourself together and be thankful for what you *have* got, not resentful for what you haven't,' she said sternly. 'Don't expect sympathy from me, Caroline, I've had a hard life myself and I wouldn't change what I've got – and what I haven't got – for the world.'

'I know you wouldn't, but that's because . . .'

'Because I have my family, my friends, my lovely pets, and my health . . . well, just about anyway. And they are the most important things. Aren't they?'

I sighed. 'I suppose so.' I wasn't going to add, *but my family are dysfunctional, my friends are imaginary, my only pet is a cockroach I rescued from the kitchen, my health is questionable and, in a nutshell, my life is a big splat of shite.* But that's what I was thinking.

'Now, the thing to do is to have a look in the second-hand shops and see if they have anything suitable . . .'

'For a present for *Becca*?' I squeaked in horror. 'No way, I can't get her a present from a second-hand shop! She'll never speak to me again. I'll be a laughing stock for ever. I'll never be invited to anyone's party ever again, not even an unpopular girl's party.'

'Calm down, I meant *clothes*. You might be able to find a nice little dress for the party.'

'Oh. Hmph. I doubt it. It's all old ladies and tea cosies and boring jigsaw puzzles and flowery blouses . . .'

'Oh my goodness, you *are* a grump. Time of the month is it?'

'No, it *isn't* actually.'

'I don't know, we're a right pair, aren't we? I'm just winding down and you're just starting up.'

I blinked at her solemnly.

'Tell you what,' she began, 'I'll meet you after school on Wednesday. I can take the bus up after I've finished my cleaning shift at the community centre. We'll have a look in the charity shops in Chelmsford and Billericay, they're bound to have loads of lovely stuff in there.'

'Do you think so?'

'Oh yes. I used to take Billy down there to get him stuff for school – the old St Jude's Boys uniform was almost the same as Mason Tyler, just a different tie and obviously a different badge on the blazer. But all I had to do was pick it off and sew on the right one. The St Jude's mothers can afford to get their sons a different uniform every five minutes, so the charity shops were always full of school shirts and trousers and sweaters, all of them in practically perfect condition. Most of the clothes I got for Billy were still good enough for Mark to wear when he started at Masons a few years later.'

'But . . . I've got no money . . .' I said, knowing that this was rarely a problem because Bev didn't mind treating me every now and then.

Sure enough, she smiled knowingly and said, 'That doesn't matter. If you see something you like and it doesn't cost too much, I'll get it for you. It will also give us a chance to have a nice little private girlie chat. We haven't had one of those for a while. I might even take you out for tea somewhere after we've shopped. Would you like that?'

'You don't mind?'

Bev studied me for a while, her grey eyes scanning my face, my nylon shirt, my polyester A-line skirt, and my thick fluffy tights that made me sweat but were preferable to exposing my naked corned-beef legs.

'As long as you stop feeling so bloody sorry for yourself.'

Bev to the rescue again. I wondered what I had done to deserve such a saviour. Then I remembered my other problem.

'How am I going to get back home from Billericay on Saturday? It's eight miles away.'

She pondered this. Eventually she brightened and said, 'Yes, well we'll just have to worry about that when it comes to it, won't we?'

That was one of the things that perplexed me most about adults: they didn't see *anything* as a problem unless it was directly affecting them right now. If it wasn't, it could always wait until tomorrow. My brain could not work like that. It latched onto a problem – real, imagined, unlikely, potential, piddling or probable – and wouldn't be able to think of anything else. I always had something to worry about and my mind was like a whirlpool of stress: had I done my Science homework? What excuse was I going to use this time to get out of double PE? And what was going to be my excuse for not giving my form teacher the parental-consent form and twenty-quid cheque for the geography field trip? Was I ever going to understand long division? Why did the music teacher hate me? Was my eyesight going to get even worse? Would I never get a boyfriend? Would I ever get out of Rivington Hill? Why did the older girls look at me in such a hostile way? Did I *have* to take maths as a GCSE option? Would I ever have the courage to get myself measured for a proper bra, the necessity of which was now really quite undeniable? Did I have a personal hygiene problem and yet remain unaware of it because I was so accustomed to the smell? After the Mark saga, would I ever be able to love anybody else? Would anybody be able to love me? Was there anything lovable about me at all? Should I have had that bar of chocolate?

And so it went on, round and round, on and on, relentlessly. At this age you can only hope and pray that things will get better the older you get, little aware that you will probably never have it so good as when you are still young enough to worry about those little things that you will only laugh about – or forget entirely – in years to come. My inexhaustible propensity to fret meant that between now and Friday I would have recurrent nightmares of being stuck in Billericay all day on Saturday, with Rebecca wondering where on earth my dad and his two cars were. Strangely, and somewhat foolishly, I was not particularly worried about the party itself.

From the outside, Billericay's Oxfam didn't look much different from the others I'd been to: the East Ham Oxfam, the Ilford Oxfam, and the one in Bootle with my grandmother. The smell inside was certainly no different: wax polish, ancient books (like the Bibles in churches) and mothballs. And the clientele didn't differ much, either. Mostly over forty. The ladies in here were a little different, though. Something in their manner. Impeccably dressed and a little sombre-looking. Like librarians.

Leaving Bev to investigate the 'teenage clothing' rail, I wandered over to the eclectic 'crafts' section and reached up to touch a dreamcatcher that dangled from the ceiling. It spun slowly around, and the little bells tinkled. I thought it was lovely, but rather pointless. The price tag on it said £3.99, which I thought was very expensive considering it performed no real function other than to spin and tinkle and look pretty.

I rummaged in a wicker basket filled with tapestry purses and wallets. Then I considered a row of strange wooden ornaments placed on a top shelf in a row: an owl with green gemstone eyes, a family of ducks on a small plinth, a dog standing on its hind legs. I liked the dog and if I had had any money, I would have bought it for Bev. It was just the kind of thing she would appreciate.

On the shelf underneath, there was a collection of candles, some big plain pillar ones and some tiny scented ones in lots of bright colours. I picked up a 'jasmine and orange' one and sniffed it. There was a plain glass vase filled with incense sticks in paper packets and next to that, lots of other vases and bowls. Some had plastic flowers in them, some had coloured glass pebbles. I wondered if Becca might like one of those for her birthday. A bowl with some pebbles in it. Very useful, I mused. No self-respecting teenage girl should be without one.

'Hey, Caroline, how about this?' Bev called out from the other side of the shop. I looked up: she was holding aloft a pale-blue ankle-length skirt in one hand, and a white skinny-fit T-shirt with a blue hearts and silver stars design in the other. Curious, I wandered over and felt the fabric of the skirt.

'It's lovely,' I said. 'But it will never fit me. And that T-shirt will never get over my head, let alone over my horrible fat boobs.'

'You're talking nonsense. They will look lovely on you. Wait a sec . . .' Bev turned around and, to my acute mortification, loudly asked the lady behind the counter whether there was a changing room I could use. The lady put down the magazine she had been engrossed in, and said, 'There's a little room in the back. How many items?'

'Two,' Bev said.

'Fine, alright.' She waved her hand dismissively and resumed reading.

Bev handed me the skirt and top and pushed me towards the changing room – a tiny little cubicle with a grubby mirror and a heavy brown curtain. 'Go on then,' she said, 'let's see what they look like on you.'

I felt self-conscious and embarrassed, but stumbled in and pulled the curtain across. I had experienced the horror of changing rooms before. First it was the indignity of getting undressed with the knowledge that there were *other people* beyond the curtain . . . being semi-naked in a strange place was not my ideal scenario, even in the absence of other people. Then it was the lighting. The lighting in changing rooms is never – and by never I mean *never* – flattering. The only light in this particular changing cubicle was the sickly trickle of fuzzy electric light that filtered through the brown curtain, and the gloomy rain-smeared daylight from the window at the front of the shop.

Unsurprisingly, my dishevelled reflection in the mirror after I had shed my school uniform was not a vision that delighted me. My breasts were clamped in, squashed up and misshapen by my tight training bra – the same tiny bra I had bought when I was eleven years old and had still not upgraded, despite swelling at least two sizes since. My stomach – once streamlined and flat – was now fleshy and globular and, just as bad, hairy. Hair didn't seem to appreciate its boundaries and tended to carry on merrily growing wherever it could. From the top of my knicker elastic to my belly button, I had a line of downy hair that no amount of painful plucking had yet managed to conquer. It kept coming back, thicker and darker and more tenacious than ever. So I had resigned myself to just leaving it. It was becoming a jungle down there. Never mind razors and Immac and waxing. I needed a machete.

Then there were my legs – thickset, stubby little legs to which I had previously given very little thought. But since starting at St Jude's, those two pink little stumps had become objects of great weight – both literally and figuratively. They had also become the bane of my life. And my bottom was my nemesis. Everything about the lower part of my body was wrong – I didn't even know where to start. Then, of course, there was cellulite – yes, it did exist, according to the wise ones at St Jude's, though I could only offer a baffled expression during the great 'cellulite' debate. Of *course* it existed.

'What exactly is it?' I had gone on to enquire, aware that I ran the risk of public ridicule.

'Ha! You of all people should know!' Geraldine Thompson had remarked (to which I silently took objection, as she was not one of The Beautiful People and therefore had no right to be so callous).

CJ had patiently explained the gory facts to me, and qualified her lurid description with: 'Of course, I don't have any because my mother takes me to the beauty parlour in Brentwood every Saturday morning and I get a special fat-draining treatment on my thighs after my facial.' I think it was at this precise moment that the realisation of CJ's full vacuity really hit me.

Oh yes, cellulite existed all right and it was alive and well on *my* thighs. I examined my reflection for far too long; obsessed, fascinated and disgusted all at the same time. This was the usual mixture of emotions I experienced when studying my body for any length of time. Disgust was usually the strongest of the lot. I wondered what it must feel like to be Becca or CJ – to be able to strip off all my clothes in one glorious flourish and gaze rapturously into the mirror, throwing my glossy head of hair back and laughing out loud for sheer joy at my unblemished beauty. The freedom of it, the pure delight they must derive from being so physically fantastic. If only I could have just a little of what they had – even if it was just the confidence that naturally came with their beauty.

'What are you doing in there?' Bev demanded, tweaking the curtain. 'Come on love, we haven't got all day!'

'I-I'm coming, won't be a minute!' I called back, yanking the skirt off the hanger and stepping into it, dreading the *Can I get the waistband over my thighs?* moment. Amazingly, because the waistband was slightly elasticated, I did manage to hoist it up, and once it was around my hips it dug into my paunch, splaying out the flesh into three rolls and clamping onto my behind like cling film around a joint of meat. It was too much to ask to be able to do the zip up, so I left it, and the button at the top of the zip had less chance of meeting the buttonhole than I had of meeting the Princess of Wales by the Oxfam bargain bucket.

'What size is this skirt supposed to be?' I asked Bev, not daring to breathe out.

'It said age thirteen on the little tag,' she replied.

'Either they were lying,' I huffed, 'or I'm a fat cow.'

'Oh, maybe it said age twelve, I can't remember. Can I see?'

'No! Hold on, I've still got to try the top on!'

'Hurry up!'

'OK, OK, just a minute . . .' I forced my head through the T-shirt and then tried shoving my arms through the sleeves. There was an inauspicious ripping sound, but after a brief struggle I was finally able to present myself to the mirror, bulges and tight fits and rucked waistlines and all. The vision was not glamorous – the 'through a hedge backwards' hair and uncomplementary ensemble made sure of that – but nevertheless the look had potential. Possibly.

I pulled the curtain back and grimaced. 'I don't think it's . . .' I said, squirming uncomfortably. '. . . quite me. I'm way too fat for the skirt. And the top is much too tight.'

I felt as if a thousand pairs of eyes were on me, even though there was now hardly anybody else in the shop apart from Bev, the uninterested assistant and a middle-aged mother with a pushchair and a fake tan.

Bev stepped forward and cocked her head to the side, making some vague evaluative noises.

Then, tacitly admitting the screamingly obvious, she said, 'Well . . . do you want to choose something else? I could adjust the skirt if you like, but . . .'

'Why don't you try something from the ladies' range?' the shop assistant suggested, without looking up from her magazine. 'There's some lovely new frocks and stuff just come in this morning.' She flapped her hand towards the rail on the opposite wall.

'Thank you,' Bev said. Then to me, she said, 'Get out of those silly little girlie clothes, and we'll find you something truly fabulous and sophisticated. Alright?'

My hopes were not high, and the distressing changing-room experience hadn't left me in the most compliant and cooperative of moods, but sure enough, a little later, we walked out of Oxfam with our spirits raised, and a bag each. For me, Bev had purchased a pair of black velour trousers and a purple glittery top, both of which I loved and both of which fitted me perfectly. For herself, she bought the dreamcatcher I had admired, and said she intended to hang it above her bedroom window in the hope that it might bring pleasant nocturnal thoughts – or that, at the very least, the annoying tinkling sounds would induce Sean to get out of bed first to put the kettle on in the mornings.

I didn't think our afternoon shopping escapade could get any more successful, but before we popped into a sandwich shop for tea, Bev suggested a quick sneak around Woolworths and Mister Pound. Among the assorted bric-a-brac in Mister Pound, I discovered a cotton sleepsuit that was baggy enough to disguise my bulges and yet not so oversized it would make me look like the Michelin Man. And yes, true to the Mister Pound promise it was indeed just one pound, so Bev bought it for me, even though she thought the cute bunny-rabbit and tortoise design was too childish for such a 'sophisticated young woman'. In Woolworths, Bev suggested a flowery photo frame and Sade cassette album might make a good gift for Becca, and by this time I was quite tired and the shops were closing up so I agreed. Having been horrified at the suggestion of getting Rebecca's present from a charity shop, I found no logical flaws in the idea that a gift from Woolworths would necessarily be of superior quality.

'On the whole, I'm sure you'll agree, a most satisfying afternoon.' Bev beamed at me over her brie-and-tomato baguette and I sipped Fanta through a straw and contemplated my cheeseburger. 'We got you a nice party outfit, a lovely present for your friend, and an unusual spinning thing for my bedroom.'

'And some new pyjamas,' I added. 'For a pound.'

'Yes, quite a bargain.'

I lifted up the bap on my burger and looked at the cheese melting into the meat.

'Thank you, Bev,' I said meekly. 'I'm so grateful. You're so good to me. My mum would never have the time or the money or the patience to take me shopping. Maybe to KwikSave to help her with the food shopping, but never for stuff that *I* wanted.'

Bev was silent for a while. 'Your mum has a lot to cope with,' she reminded me pointedly. 'Especially now she's a grandmother. And with . . . everything else.'

By 'everything else' she meant a failing marriage, a delinquent son, debts up to her eyeballs, and three demanding under-tens. It seemed absurd to me that my mum was now a gran – some of the girls at St Jude's had siblings who were practically the same age as my mother, and mothers who weren't much younger than my Nan.

'I know . . .' I sighed. 'But it's not my fault.'

Bev put down her baguette and wiped her mouth with a napkin. 'Nobody ever said it was your fault, Caro. But it's what you've all been lumbered with. It's your life, and you should try to make the best of it. So pull together. Try to help your mum, not resent her. It's not her fault either, you know. You must try to work as a team. If you don't, it will only make it worse. Much worse.'

'As a team?' I echoed blankly. 'We all hate each other.'

'Now that is *not* true,' Bev said. 'Your mum loves all of you very much and I know for certain that she's particularly proud of her eldest daughter . . .'

'Yeah, right.' So emphatic was my disagreement with this statement that it was all I could do to restrain myself from uttering a few unnecessarily strong four-letter words. But Bev was adamant. 'You'd better believe it, young lady. Remember the last parents' evening at Masons?'

I scowled. 'I'd rather not think about that. It was a disaster.'

Bev sat back. 'Yes, maybe your mother shouldn't have had so much to drink and maybe she shouldn't have said what she said to poor Mrs Sawyer. But it was only because she was so nervous about showing you up.'

'She did show me up.'

'Yes, but she didn't mean to. You know what she said to me, after she had spoken to your teachers, once she'd sobered up a bit?'

'I don't want to know.'

'She said she was so glad that you'd met me, because she felt bad for not being a proper mother to you.'

I was quite surprised by this. It wasn't the kind of thing my mum would say, even in her more tender alcoholic moments. 'She said that?'

Bev nodded. 'She told me she was extremely proud of you and knew that she was probably a disappointment to you. She really is a very sensitive woman, you know.'

I swallowed hard. 'She really said that?'

'Of course, I reassured her that she was doing a brilliant job of bringing all of you up, and that you weren't disappointed in her at all. Because you're not . . . are you?'

I suddenly felt quite ashamed. 'No,' I mumbled. 'I'm not

disappointed. I just . . .' I searched for the appropriate phrase and finally settled for: 'I wish my family were just . . . normal.'

Bev found this amusing. 'Good grief, what do you define as a *normal* family? Do you think *my* lot are normal? Do you think I don't sometimes wish they'd all bugger off and leave me alone? Families aren't like the ones in the daytime soap operas, you know.'

I chewed my burger and fell silent. Bev wasn't finished. 'You can't choose your family, but you can choose how to deal with your family. No family is perfect, for goodness' sake! You can't just reject them because they don't conform to what you want. If you go on feeling ashamed of the woman who brought you into the world, what hope is there of you ever finding peace within yourself?'

She had lapsed into what Mark affectionately called 'hippy-babble', but I was listening to her anyway. She did make sense, and she always made me feel better and curbed my self-pity, which had a tendency to spiral out of control. Bev saw good in everyone, and hope in even the most hopeless situations, but I remained convinced that if she was ever forced to spend a full twenty-four hour stint at my place, with my entire family around her, she would have no hesitation in concluding, *OK, you were right all along, Caro, your family really do suck.*

'Can we not talk about my family any more, please?'

'Alright, alright. We'll talk about something else,' Bev conceded. She paused and then asked, 'How is little Teri getting on, by the way?'

'She's got most of her front teeth now.'

'Oh, good, that must be a relief.'

'It will be Chelsea's turn next,' I grumbled.

'Chelsea?'

'My niece. Kev's . . . daughter.' Even now, I could hardly bring myself to confess out loud that my brother had fathered a child. Not only that, but a child called Chelsea.

'Oh yes, of course. So she's living with you too?'

I nodded grimly. 'And Julie.'

'Julie is . . . Kevin's . . . girlfriend?'

'Ex.'

'Oh, dear. And how old is she?'

'Fifteen.'

'Oh, dear. What about Kevin? Is he still causing trouble?'

I finished my Fanta noisily and stabbed an ice cube with the end of my straw. 'I haven't seen him since last week. The police are after him again. They called round twice yesterday.'

'That's a shame. He used to be such a nice boy.'

'What? Kev doesn't have a nice bone in his entire body!'

Bev lapsed into misty-eyed reminiscence. 'When you were all young, you all used to play together in the beer garden at the pub, remember?' she said. 'Ned would take you down to the Barley Mow on Sundays after lunch and meet up with all his old friends at the bar. You lot would disappear somewhere with your crisps and your bottles of pop and we wouldn't see you for hours. It was you, Mark, Kevin, Mark's friend Ashley from down the road, and your little black friend from the estate. And the very tiny one with the glasses would be there too, sometimes.'

'Katie.'

'Yes, that's right, Katie. Do you still see her?'

I suddenly felt a gigantic wave of depression sweep through me. 'She must have moved away. She was sent to a special school and I haven't seen her around the estate for ages.'

'She was a lovely girl. Very shy.'

'Yes.'

'And your other friend, that pretty black girl . . .'

'Amber.'

'Yes, Amber, she was a sweetheart, wasn't she? So well behaved. It's a shame you two don't get on any more.'

I didn't want to tell Bev that Amber was now a chain-smoking, glue-sniffing, trainee prostitute with nail extensions and a pierced tongue. Or that one of Amber's dads was critically ill in hospital as a direct result of worrying about his errant daughter's numerous follies. So I merely said, 'Yeah, I don't see much of her either now. She's got even worse since I left Masons.'

Bev regarded me sadly. 'You had such lovely friends at primary school. Isn't it a pity that friends drift apart?'

I looked at the remaining half of my burger and realised I didn't feel hungry any more. 'Can we go now?' I said.

There are some truly defining moments in any person's life – moments of revelation, which can and probably will change the course of your life for ever, somehow, in some way.

Childhood doesn't just end, it slowly dies, and I couldn't come to terms with that death – I was unable to adjust. Logically, this surely meant I was 'maladjusted'? Yes. Maladjusted would be a good word to describe me at this point in my life: thirteen years old, a few pounds overweight, more than a few pounds poorer than everyone at my school, mentally confused, emotionally frangible and physically inadequate.

Thirteen. Unlucky for some, they say.

Friday came round. I had wrapped up Rebecca's present with a metallic silver bow and tucked it in my school bag, along with my new pyjamas, a toothbrush, a comb and my glasses that I wasn't going to use unless an emergency required perfect vision.

At home-time, Rebecca's brother picked her up in a car that was shaped like a phallic missile, with a roof that went back at the touch of a button and a loud stereo that played relentless electric guitar. His name was James, he was eighteen and the minute I saw him my entire body went spasmodic with lust.

'You'll have to excuse my brother,' Rebecca announced ceremoniously, pretending to be embarrassed, but obviously flushing with pride that she was related to a god in a platinum chariot. 'He tends to show off.'

No shit.

'Hello, girls,' he said, slipping his sunglasses to the end of his nose and winking lazily, like a pop star drunk on fame. His voice was suffused with all the velvety wit and charm that went with his manly good looks. Standing there outside the school gate, barely ten feet away, I was unable to tear my eyes away and was unaware that my mouth had dropped open.

'Your parents gone already?' CJ enquired, leaning into the car and shoving her bag underneath the passenger seat.

'Yeah, I drove them to the airport this morning,' James said, lighting a cigarette and looking at himself in the rear-view mirror as he blew the smoke out. 'You've got the house for tonight, but I'll want it tomorrow, so you can piss off to CJ's place for the rest of the weekend, alright Becks?'

Rebecca got in the passenger seat and slammed the door. 'Mum and Dad put *you* in charge, *Ja*mie. You're supposed to look after me, remember?'

He sighed impatiently. 'Look, I'm leaving you lot alone tonight, aren't I? For Christ's sake, Beck, it's only one night.'

'Suppose you'll be with *her* again?'

'None of your business. Now, who's coming with me and who's getting the bus?' He looked over at us curiously. I watched his fingers twist around the steering wheel and imagined those same fingers touching me in intimate places, coiling around my wrists, holding me down, entwining with my own fingers, slipping inside my clothing.

CJ didn't hesitate. 'I'm coming with you,' she asserted, springing into the back without first opening the door.

The rest of us – twelve altogether – remained silent. Perhaps we were all equally overawed. Certainly nobody could have felt any more overawed than I did at that time.

'Come on, I haven't got all day,' he said, readjusting his sunglasses and facing forward. 'I'm not that bad a driver, am I?'

Feeling myself redden, I stepped towards the car and stammered, 'C-can I come?'

His eyes met mine, and even through the tint of his shades, the connection made my heart flutter madly like trapped birds.

He smiled, held out his hand and said, 'Don't think I've met you. New girl, Becks?'

'Oh. Yeah. That's Caroline,' Rebecca said, preoccupied with brushing her hair. 'She's good at History and English.'

'And Biology,' I simpered, accepting the proffered hand and resisting the urge to clutch it forcibly to my heaving bosom.

'Really? No wonder she's invited you then. She'll probably lock you in her room with all the homework she's got behind with,' he joked, taking another drag of his cigarette and smiling with only the left side of his mouth. Yes, this was said in a light-hearted fashion but still it was horribly plausible. I wouldn't have put a stunt like that past Becks. She was capable of anything, and she got away with everything.

'Oh, ha-de-ha James, now just shut up and let's get out of here,' Becca sneered. She turned to all the other party guests and said, 'See you back at my place, everyone. James is going to get us some booze, so if you have any special requests, tell him now.'

'No I'm fuckin' not,' James objected.

'Don't worry girls, he will. White wine, Malibu, Archers, and ... whatever. The usual. Don't be late, yeah?' Rebecca called out as the others started walking away towards the bus stop.

After a quick and surreptitious hunt for the handle, I meekly opened the door of the back seat and slipped in next to CJ, who shot me one of her acidic smiles. I had never been in a car like this one before. I had never even *seen* a car like this one, apart from on the telly, which was only a colourful box of dreams to me in any case. The car smelt of newness, of leather and musk. The seats were quite slippery but amazingly comfortable, like a moulded nest with armrests. There were flashing lights above the gearbox that reminded me of the *Knightrider* series that I used to watch on TV. I wouldn't have been completely shocked if the car had started talking to us in a robotic female voice. I had never seen anything so ludicrously luxurious in all my life. I never even imagined that such a car could exist. It was like a space shuttle. Not even James Bond could hope for something this fantastic. I kept my bag on my lap and tried to control my breathing.

CJ leaned over and whispered, 'You'll want to put the seat belt on.'

'Seat belt?'

'Yeah, James drives fast. And I mean, *fast.*'

I obediently strapped myself in after fumbling clumsily for the catch. James turned down the volume on his stereo a fraction and revved the engine. 'OK girls, let's go,' he said. I gazed at his hands as they turned the steering wheel – strong, large hands, the hands of a man, not the groping little paws of a boy. And this car was the car of a man. A man who always got what he wanted and didn't have to beg or steal. A real man. The subtle fragrance I could smell in the air, just a faint whiff every now and then, was the smell of a man. I was delirious with Man Sensory Overload. The car built up velocity quickly, and as it thundered down the road, the force of it threw my loose hair back over my shoulders and my school tie flapped behind me in the wind. It was the most exhilarating ride I'd have with a man for quite some time.

As impressed as I was with the car, there were still further objects of unspeakable wonder awaiting me inside the enormous mock-Tudor castle that Becca laughingly called her family's 'main place of residence'. To add to my burgeoning sense of inadequacy, she ushered us in saying, 'Welcome to my humble abode'. This 'main place of residence', this 'humble abode' was set out over three floors, each floor being well over twice the size of my own family's entire maisonette. Except I couldn't even make that comparison – this was something so beyond my own reality, way beyond even my wildest fantasies, that I was unable to take in the details at first. Just the sheer magnitude of it was more than enough to blow me away. In the enormous expanse of private driveway at the front of the house there were two other cars parked parallel outside a double garage, each car almost as spectacular as the one James was driving; metallic paintwork and shiny hubcaps and gleaming trimmings.

It was the kind of house you would expect to see on *Through the Keyhole,* outrageously opulent and so big you could get lost in it. I could imagine Loyd Grossman admiring the shiny brass lion's-head door handle and then stepping into the wide, marbled entrance hall with punctilious grace, carefully closing the solid oak and stained-glass front door behind him. He would then gaze around respectfully at the surroundings and remark in his nasal tones on the 'extraordinary' staircase with the 'marvellous' mezzanine gallery above, the plush-carpeted downstairs cloakroom, the 'enormous' farmhouse-style kitchen with its capacious stainless-steel larder fridge and electric tin opener and shiny food processor and Soda-Stream machine (how I *longed* for a Soda-Stream, every time I saw the telly ads!). Then there was the 'magnificent' drawing room with its upholstered armchairs and scroll-legged desks, the 'tastefully decorated' dining room with its eight-seater mahogany table, and the 'divine' domed conservatory overlooking the most 'fantastically well tended' landscaped garden. (These are all the words I would probably have used, had I not been rendered speechless for the entire duration of my guided tour around Becca's home.)

And all that was just the ground floor.

I had always assumed that houses like this only belonged to the wealthiest and most prestigious superstars, and that such unadulterated luxury could never be sampled by anyone who wasn't a major celebrity or a member of royalty. All along, I had been sharing my homework notes and limited science knowledge with a girl who lived in a mansion fit for a king. And even a king might wonder how to operate a wall-mounted electric tin opener. This house was not only huge, it was filled with *things*. Amazing things. A shiny microwave, a brand-new home entertainment system with *surround sound* (I had never even heard of such a thing before), a tropical aquarium set into the wall, an Aga oven, a fax machine that sporadically beeped.

The kitchen floor at my house wasn't fit to walk on: Becca's shiny tiled kitchen floor looked clean enough to eat off. My head was spinning and James hadn't even got back from the off-licence with the booze yet. (CJ's powers of persuasion had worked in the end: he must have known it was pointless trying to deny the wishes of two wilful young women.)

'Do you want to see my room?' Becca asked gleefully, opening the enormous fridge and extracting two kiwi fruit, a banana, half a watermelon and a pot of fromage frais. As huge as the fridge was, it was packed to capacity, and not a KwikSave or Sainsburys Economy label in sight.

Prompted by what could only have been morbid curiosity, I said, 'Yes.'

CJ grabbed the banana and began peeling it. 'Nice house, innit?'

I was still only capable of monosyllabic, brainless responses. 'Yes.'

'It's bigger than my house,' CJ said offhandedly. 'But my room's bigger than Becca's.'

'Oh.'

'Come on,' she chirruped, biting the end of the banana in an almost sexual fashion, 'let's go upstairs.'

I couldn't move. Now I was thinking about what Lloyd Grossman might make of *my* home, back in the putrescent hamlet of Rivington Hill, eight-point-five miles and three million light years away from this heavenly chateau. In my mind's eye I was imagining a peasants' version of *Through the Keyhole*: Sir David Frost sitting expectantly in the bright studio in his sharp suit, asking a visibly horrified Loyd what evidence he might find for the home and studio audience this time as he intrepidly goes ... *Through* ... *the* ... kicked-in front door ...

LOYD: Even before we are granted an internal viewing of this home, the first thing that strikes one is the extraordinary, almost *exquisite*, shabbiness of the front door. At once, one's sensibilities are affronted by the total lack of a front-door handle, a doorbell of any description or indeed even the most basic of knockers to assist a visitor in heralding their arrival to the occupants. But when one studies the immediate surroundings, one does wonder what sane person would want to visit this home at all. I haven't even dared venture inside and already I have had my wallet stolen by some pre-school urchins and been verbally assaulted by a knife-wielding drunk woman in a tartan tabard. Perhaps I should overlook the disintegrating front door with its peeling paint and busted lock, and silently pray that whatever awaits me therein isn't quite as ghastly as the immediate vicinity. [*Pushes the door open and strides boldly into our living/dining room, cautiously sniffing the air with a look of disgust.*]

Ah yes, not so much an entrance hall as a case of finding oneself plunged straight into the very bowels of Hell. For the benefit of the home and studio audience, one feels compelled to convey to you the highly offensive smell that is immediately evident: one feels incapable of an adequately graphic description, but suffice to say, the stench of public urinals, warm milk and stale bread does seem to be the overriding bouquet. This room, one can only assume, is a communal family area one would normally call a drawing room or perhaps a sitting room, and I think I can safely speculate that a good deal more of the latter goes on in this particular area. Indeed, you can even see the buttock imprints worn into the cushion of this mangy old sofa! And see how the soft furnishings have become so threadbare over time that it would appear only the stains of ingrained dirt are holding them together. And look at the floor! If I kick away some of the discarded detritus that litters the carpet, like so, you will see that these floors have not been cleaned for what could be months, possibly years. The extent of the accumulated filth is really quite breathtaking. One would be impressed if only one wasn't so appalled.

I believe it was Quentin Crisp who asserted that there is no need to do any housework after the first four years, because the dirt doesn't get any worse. A maxim to which this family evidently subscribes. Observe the shelving unit to my left. Surely, this was assembled by a gang of excitable chimps. See how unusual the design is – each shelf actually slopes at a somewhat severe angle – quite, quite unique. It is nothing short of a miracle that these flimsy, slanting planks should manage to support the random assortment of junk that fills every available space. Let's investigate . . . [*Minces across the cluttered carpet with exaggerated vigilance.*]

Ah, yes. Miriam Stoppard's *Mother and Baby* book, minus front cover; a motorcycle helmet; a teat from an infant's drinking bottle; a yellow crayon; two Jackie Collins novels; a collection of scratched country-and-western records; a broken record player; a heinous porcelain ornament and various other knick-knacks; an old edition of *TV Times*; a knitting needle; two somewhat dishevelled copies of *Take a Break*; a photo album; an empty bottle of Polish vodka; a floral cosmetic bag that appears to be empty apart from a cotton wool ball and a defunct lipstick; an egg-stained bib; a severed doll's head; an overflowing ashtray; three packets of 'Lambert and Butler' cigarettes, all empty; an out-of-date telephone directory . . . and all this just on the one shelf. One dares not progress further.

Two short strides take one into what one can only presume to be the kitchen area. The cream-and-brown-checked lino is sticky underfoot and stained by an unimaginable multitude of splattered fluids and ground-in solids. A different texture underfoot with each step. Quite extraordinary. The view through the cracked and grimy window looks out onto some garages and two or three dismal high-rise blocks just opposite. See, on that small patch of ground over there, a gang of youngsters kicking a ball about – or is it a dead cat? – and inhaling lighter fuel . . . a delightful, innocent scene that must surely make the inhabitants' hearts sing for joy as they contemplate their deprived little existence over their economy-brand morning coffee. On the mildewed draining board, just here, the dirty plates and rusted cutlery are piled high beside the kitchen sink, as indeed they appear to have been for quite some time, given their suspiciously adhesive qualities. The sink is full of greasy grey water, and the oven, situated but a cup's throw away, is black and green with fat drippings, mould, cremated residue and unidentifiable spillages over untold years. A creature no bigger than my fist lies quite, quite dead in the far corner, and one almost feels sympathy for it.

One surely does not have the courage to ascend the stairs to investigate the bathroom and bedrooms. One shudders to imagine what horrors await beyond that badly lit first-floor hallway. David, we must surely have all the evidence we need in these two ground-floor rooms, and one is now far too nauseous to proceed. In conclusion, then: the ghastly front door, the sickly smell, the unkempt furnishings, the embedded filth, the wonky shelves, the lifeless rodent left to rot in the kitchen . . . David, I ask you, who, or indeed what, in their right mind, would live in a place like this? It's over to you . . .

'You can get changed in the en suite if you like,' Becca offered, putting a music tape on and slipping out of her school skirt. I recognised the song – it had been on the radio in the Crozier kitchen once or twice. It was by a band called Fleetwood Mac and I had seen the video on *Top of the Pops* only a week or so before. Bev said Fleetwood Mac had been her favourite band in the seventies. I liked the song – it was romantic and sad and reminded me of Mark. Loads of songs reminded me of Mark. Too many. In fact, there were very few songs I could sit back and listen to without having some thought or memory of him transmitted subliminally through the melody.

I watched dumbly as Becca unbuttoned her shirt and began hunting through her wardrobe with exaggeratedly frantic movements.

'Go on, then,' CJ said, glaring at me through her fringe. She was already down to her bra and knickers and had pulled a collection of different outfits from her school bag and laid them out across Becca's bed. 'What are you waiting for?'

'Erm . . .' I began, unsure of how to phrase my question. 'What's an en suite?'

Becca looked over at CJ and they both started giggling.

'You're so funny,' Becca said finally, taking my bag from me and leading me from her bedroom into an adjoining room that contained a toilet, a shower cubicle, a basin, countless liquid-filled bottles and colourful tubs and sprays. '*This* is the en suite,' she told me. 'You can even have a shower if you like. Feel free to use any of my stuff. What clothes have you brought with you?'

'What . . . clothes?'

'Don't tell me you've forgotten, Caroline!'

The penny dropped. 'No, oh, no! I've got . . . clothes . . . in my bag.'

'Good. I'll leave you to it then.' She smiled at me and I thought: *can we be friends? Can we really be friends, you and me?* There was a sound downstairs. 'Oh, that will be Jamie back from the offie,' she enthused. 'The others will be here soon, too . . . so hurry up. OK?'

She slammed the door behind her and I gazed around me, wondering if this was all just a dream. Becca's bedroom was way bigger than I'd even dared to imagine. And she had her own bathroom. Her own *bathroom.* It was all too much.

Should I have a shower? Dare I have a shower? Becca was the one who suggested it, so maybe I smelt. Maybe that was her 'polite' or 'subtle' way of telling me. So dare I *not* have a shower? Hurriedly, I locked the door and took my blazer off.

Which towel should I use? They were so clean and warm, fluffy and purest white, hanging over the radiator, one small, one large. Would she mind if I used those lovely towels on my unlovely body? Should I wash my hair too? I didn't want to appear rude. But I did want to be as fragrant and fashionable as the rest of them. I wanted my hair to swing, to shine, to look *touchable.* I wanted to look like a girl who could afford to say no and never have to say please or thank you.

There was only one thing for it. I began frantically sniffing the various gels and lotions Becca had lying around. This took some time. Then, appropriate toiletries selected, I double-checked the lock, undressed, and pulled back the shower screen before stepping in among the sparkling chrome and shiny white tiles.

Ten minutes later, I was damp and aromatic, my hair wrapped up in the smaller of the two towels, as I experimented with perfume sprays and a basket of Body Shop cosmetics that I discovered while nosing about in the cabinet underneath the basin. I tried a spritz of something called 'Eternity', then glossed my lips with a pinkish roll-on tube. Then I discovered an antiperspirant and tackled my armpits, with a quick spray down the front of my fresh knickers, just for luck. I had used mascara before, but only my mum's stodgy old ninety-nine-pence one from the market, so when I found a more upmarket brand called 'Extra Lush & Curly Lash' I had no hesitation in whizzing the wand quickly over my lashes. The effect was really quite pleasing. Once I had put on my new trousers and top and checked myself in the mirror for a final time, there was now a faint pulse of excitement deep within me, and this was starting to become stronger than the foreboding sense of doom that had permeated my thoughts all day.

'You don't scrub up too badly after all,' I told my water-misted reflection.

A voice outside called my name.

'I'm coming, sorry!' I yelled back, stuffing my creased school uniform deep into my bag.

'It's present time,' Rebecca grinned, as I emerged from the en suite in a trail of vapour and eau de toilette. 'Then it's get-pissed time!'

Everyone cheered. They had all arrived now, and they were already in their party gear – buttressed décolletage and skimpy skirts matched up with glitzy shoes and flashing jewellery. My faint pulse of excitement weakened slightly.

'Now, as you all know,' Becca announced importantly, standing on her bed, revelling and resplendent in her status as The Centre of Attention, 'I am fourteen on Sunday, and that's the main reason for this party. My *bloody* parents have gone away to bloody Prague . . . again!' (She rolled her eyes dramatically as if having an entire mansion at her disposal was some kind of chore.) 'But they will be back to take me out on my birthday and have agreed that while they're away I can have a little gathering tonight . . . just a *quiet* one of course . . .'

A few girls laughed, a ripple of awful falsetto titters.

'. . . But please don't destroy anything, and in particular don't go into my dad's study as that's where he keeps all his precious bloody books and computer and golf clubs and stuff. Just don't do anything silly! Or I'll have to bribe my brother to clean up the evidence tomorrow!'

More laughs.

'Anyway, whose present shall I open first?' She bounced up and down like a little girl on Christmas morning.

'Mine! Mine!' came the euphoric refrain. I did not join in. I now doubted very much that Becca would appreciate my gift. A crappy acrylic photo frame and a budget-priced music cassette which – I noticed, browsing her impressive collection – she already had. I watched Becca's joyful face light up as she was bombarded with presents, one after another, and I felt an uncontrollable wave of contempt rise up inside me. Then I felt guilty for feeling so antagonistic toward the hostess – after all, it had been good of her to invite me, and surely I wasn't even worthy of such an occasion. Then I felt angry with myself for feeling guilty and unworthy, and felt antagonistic all over again. This tautologous reel of impotent emotions continued to confuse me for some time, or at least for as long as it took Becca gleefully to rip off several acres of pretty foil paper from a number of superbly superfluous and yet distinctly pricey-looking presents.

Suddenly I was brought back down to earth.

Right the hell back down, and buried alive.

'Goodness Caroline, where *did* you get those trousers from?' Polly Warner-Topping (yes, her real name) asked me, thrusting a silvery package adorned with purple ribbon towards Becca. Polly was probably the poshest girl in the class – at least she looked it and, with her plummy English accent, she sounded it – but CJ had assured me that her house was in fact a 'very basic' semi in a less salubrious area of Billericay. Nevertheless, I perversely revered Polly and was a little intimidated by her horsey manner and relentless pronunciation of 'proper' English words, all emphatic plosives and rounded vowels. I wasn't sure what she was insinuating by stressing the word 'did'. But I was pretty sure that I didn't like her tone.

'Er . . . where did I *get* them from?' I echoed stupidly. What should I say? Good grief, what the hell should I say? 'Oh, oh,' I improvised madly. 'Oh, these old things . . . I've had them ages.'

'Really?' She raised a cynical eyebrow. 'They look just like the trousers my mother gave to the charity shop last week.'

Silence descended immediately, like the toxic dust after a nuclear bomb has exploded. Even the wrapping paper stopped rustling.

There it was, a major defining moment in my life.

I'd define that one as pretty soul-crushing.

Believe it or not, the party actually didn't turn out so badly. Once I had got over the mortification of confessing that yes, the trousers I was wearing probably were the selfsame trousers that Mrs Warner-Topping had dismissively tossed into a bin bag for Oxfam. And once I had got over the abject humiliation of being grilled about how often I bought stuff from 'proper shops' and how much pocket money I got. (The average, we concluded after a quick poll among us, was a fiver a week. I went along with that, although five pence a year would have been much closer to the truth in my case.)

After a few glasses of wine, however, and an hour or so of watching a ludicrous, gory and loud horror film on Becca's immense television set, my tension eased, and I thought: Sod it. Just sod it. Who cares? These girls were born rich, I was born poor. They had plenty, I had nothing. So what? So what? Why should they feel fortunate, and why should I feel *un*fortunate? It's only money. It's only *stuff*; possessions, that's all. What difference does it make? We're all the same, really. Underneath it all, we're just the same vulnerable mortals.

No matter how much I drank that night, though, I couldn't completely relax.

They were *worthy*. What did I have going for me? What did I have that they could possibly envy or covet or at least admire? Precisely nothing. And they all seemed so blasé about their worthiness, all of them were naturally, *obviously* important. It wasn't even an *issue* for them. It was just a natural fact, and that was that. So why should it be an issue for me?

I was analysing things too much. I was beating myself up over something to which I had already resigned myself, long ago. But still the thoughts went on, more powerful and all-consuming than ever.

What made it worse was that none of these girls was intrinsically despicable; I couldn't even allow myself the dubious consolation of possessing a nicer personality, whatever that was worth. I tried to imagine how exactly they perceived me, what kind of impression I gave of myself. I was certainly unrefined. Unsophisticated. Uncivilised. And there wasn't much I could do about that, other than unconvincing attempts to fake it. But then, I wasn't the only one who felt obliged to fake certain aspects of my character – as far as I could tell, the very essence of being a teenage girl involved some degree of dissimulation. Lunchtime chats with certain classmates had confirmed this in no uncertain terms.

'Your turn, Caroline,' someone said, prodding me in the back.

'What?'

I had been so engrossed in my own inner turmoil of self-deprecation that I was oblivious to the party game that had been going on around me.

A girl called Millicent Havers handed me a plastic tumbler with two dice inside. I took them from her dumbly and sat there in the midst of the fragrant pyjamas and empty wine bottles, just staring down at the carpet.

'Come on, we haven't got all night!'

I realised I was acting like a bit of an arse, stranded there on my own private planet. I threw an eight. Becca squealed and consulted a piece of paper. 'Question number eight . . .' she muttered to herself, '. . . are you ready?'

'Er . . . yes?' I replied hesitantly, completely confounded as to what I was supposed to be ready for.

'Question eight . . . ooh, this is a good one . . . what's the furthest you've ever been . . . with a *boy*?'

More strained peals of laughter resounded as another bottle of sparkling perry was passed around our excitable collective.

I remained silent.

'Can I answer this one please?' Gemma Powell piped up, lying back across the luxuriant cream shag-pile in her cute and needlessly sexy negligee. For a thirteen-year-old, she was pretty advanced in terms of sexual knowledge, experience and – if her frequently hair-raising tales were to be believed – expertise.

'No you can't, we already know you're a dirty slut,' Becca snapped, half bitchy, half respectful. Such is a fellow female's perception of a sexually enlightened peer: sure she's a slag, but, hey, we want to befriend her on a superficial level and we sure as hell want to hear all about it please. In detail.

'I bet Caroline hasn't even *kissed* a boy yet!' Gemma sneered, running her immaculately manicured hands over her slim shaved legs in a needlessly provocative way. I wondered if she might be a lesbian in denial. She always seemed to be making a conscious effort to appear sexy and desperately attractive, but what was the point, at an all-girl school? The big bad green seed inside me sprouted an emerald bloom of empty jealousy, just for her. I felt it open up and spray out its poisonous pollen as I watched her deliberately feline movements, those big kittenish eyes and the frisky svelte limbs. I hated her, with a passion and without real reason. And my hatred for her only reaffirmed my hatred for myself.

'I *have* kissed a boy,' I found myself objecting, tearing my entranced eyes away from Gemma's mocking smile before the triffids took over inside my head. 'And my best friend is a boy and he's going to be fifteen in December so he knows *everything*.'

This sounded, and objectively *was*, a pathetic statement. What was more pathetic was the ludicrous blush of pride that spread within me as I said it. (And yes – I *had* kissed a boy, incidentally. Not Mark. And not really a proper kiss. And OK, if I was being honest, not really a boy. Does a poster of George Michael count? Or an uninvited and wholly unappreciated peck on the cheek from Thomas Wickitt?)

'So . . .' Becca began, exchanging looks with a couple of the other girls, '. . . what you're saying is . . . correct me if I'm wrong here . . . but the furthest you've been is . . . kissing?'

Millicent Havers touched my shoulder gently and passed the bottle of perry to me, now half full. Or maybe half empty. I accepted with a weak smile and took a swig, then another one, before saying, 'I haven't met a boy I like enough yet, that's all.' This was fair enough, surely.

'Fair enough,' Gemma said. 'I lost my virginity when I was eleven, and he was a right bastard. Best to wait, Caz.'

There was something so patronising about this that I simply couldn't leave it there. But equally, I couldn't think of an apt comeback or pithy putdown so I just said, 'Don't call me Caz.'

In truth, I didn't mind being called Caz at all, but I didn't like the way Gemma bloody Powell called me Caz. So offhand, like I was a rough council-estate girl or something. She arched an eyebrow and curled her strawberry-glazed lip in bemusement.

'Whatever,' she sighed.

'Ladies, ladies,' Becca soothed, taking the bottle of perry from me and holding it aloft as if to quell the brewing hostility; the teenage Essex girl's equivalent of waving a white flag. *Steady on folks, at ease, this one's got a bottle of Babycham!* What a hostess this girl was. There was nothing she couldn't do, and she knew it. 'I think we're all getting a bit pissed and feisty now!' she exclaimed, polishing off the bottle and wiping her mouth with the back of her hand. 'CJ, your turn to roll the dice, then we'll watch another movie and eat all the leftovers from dinner. And drink some more booze, yeah!'

I started to think that Becca would make an excellent manager someday – she was so forthright, so bossy and self-assured. She commanded respect, and, unlike CJ, who was vain and unreservedly selfish as well, most people genuinely liked her and didn't have to pretend. Becca was going to make it in life, she was a winner; even at the tender age of fourteen this was more or less a foregone conclusion. She must have had it stamped on her from birth. Success. *Success.*

CJ threw a four and was asked to reveal a number of semi-interesting sex-related factoids, and ventured a few more that she was not necessarily required to share with us. I soon realised that I had some catching up to do. Gemma divulged various lurid intricacies about what she had got up to with her latest boyfriend, because she had been 'really crazy about him at the time'. This provoked incredulity, intrigue and horror in equal proportions from most of the congregation. ('You mean you put your mouth where the guy *pees out of*?' Tanya Bletchley had squealed, covering her hand with her mouth as if she was about to throw up. 'No way! I could never . . . I mean *never* do that! Not even to save my family's life. No way. Not even if I really, like, *loved* the guy.')

We began wilting shortly after that; Gemma monopolised the largest and comfiest of the two settees and fell asleep, spreadeagled and glamorous on the ivory leather like a Hollywood starlet, long before the second movie had finished. One by one most of the others curled up in their sleeping bags on the floor and followed suit. When the movie was finally over, Becca – the hostess with the mostess – turned to me, the beast with the least, and asked me where I'd like to sleep. I hadn't brought a sleeping bag with me – not because I had forgotten, but because I didn't own one. Bev had offered to lend me Mark's or Billy's, but they were both quite old and shabby and had their names sewn into the lining, so I had declined, assuming Becca might have some spare linen or blankets for me to crash out on anyway.

'Well, me and CJ are in my bed, obviously,' she said. 'But Jamie's out at his girlfriend's tonight, so you can have his bed if you like.'

She must have seen my expression change and she hurriedly added, 'Don't worry, it doesn't smell that bad! He's quite clean and hygienic . . . for a boy.'

I wasn't quite sure how to react. 'I'm not really that tired right now,' I said, which was a bit of a lie. The thought of sleeping in a stranger's bed – that is, a beautiful, *male* stranger's bed – filled me with a mixture of apprehension and extreme excitement. As tired as I admittedly was, I doubt I would have been able to get very much sleep anyway.

But Becca was in manager mode, and the law was laid down.

'Come on, Caro, we're going upstairs now anyway, everyone else is dead to the world and CJ gets grumpy if she doesn't have at least eight hours' sleep. See, it's already gone three in the morning!' She pointed to the gold-rimmed clock on the wall behind me, whose shiny black roman numerals confirmed this. 'Do you want a drink before bed? Tea or something? We've got Earl Grey and Darjeeling as well as the normal stuff. And lots of biscuits still left in the cupboard if you like.'

I had already eaten so much that night I was ready to pop. I shook my head. 'No thanks, Becks, maybe it is best if I crash now, too,' I conceded.

She smiled at me, and I smiled back, wondering if she considered me a real friend yet, or if she ever would. Or even if she *could*. I wanted her to be mine, at least I certainly sought her approval, although I still wasn't sure what we had to offer each other exactly. I craved the security of genuine friendship, and I knew I wasn't the only one. We were all united by that basic need. The need to be part of something subjectively special and worthwhile.

CJ stretched and yawned and Becca made a start on clearing up the debris from the floor and the table – paper plates, half-eaten morsels, plastic wrappers, miscellaneous junk.

Realising that CJ had absolutely no intention of helping her, I got up and offered my own mess-cleaning services, which were politely declined. Then she changed her mind, however, and gave me an armful of litter, asking me to dispose of it in the bin in the kitchen. The bin was stainless steel, with a push-button mechanism to open the flap, and even inside it was cleaner and more fragrant than the damn *fridge* I had at my place.

And so it came to pass that I ended up sleeping in the bed of a god that night, listening to the sounds of Becca and CJ giggling in the room opposite until they finally flaked out. After that, the only sound I was aware of was my own heavy breathing and, much more acutely, the total and complete silence outside. Lying in my own bed at home, I had become accustomed to all kinds of disturbing nocturnal noises outside in the estate, beyond the thin, rattling glass of my bedroom window. Dogs barking, glass smashing, cars crashing, fists flying, footsteps clattering, windscreens shattering, sirens shrieking, babies crying, grown-ups crying, kids shouting, tyres screeching, cats fighting.

Here, in this bed, in this room, in this beautiful, magnificent house, the only sound outside in the secluded cul-de-sac was the sound of perfect silence. Even with the window open. Hardly a breeze. The curtains barely moved. The silence was so absolute it made me paranoid. It made my head ache. But my unease may have had more to do with the fact that I was lying there in a state of quasi-rapture, sniffing the pillow of Rebecca's older brother and doing the nipple thing like crazy, without even being conscious of it at first.

When I did eventually realise that my hand was on my breast beneath the polyester of my pyjamas, I paused and allowed myself a small moment of panic and horror. I was in a stranger's bed touching my nipples! I had my top wrenched right up under my chin and my breasts were in contact with James Delaney's quilt. My breasts were touching where his hands (and possibly, oh yes, *other* body parts) had touched. That thought alone was, to me, at that moment, nothing short of the very zenith of my puerile passions. My small moment of panic and horror soon passed, and I carried on with the Nipple Thing – both hands, both nipples, now with some enthusiasm. I felt like a hussy but I knew for sure that what I was doing was nothing in comparison to what my contemporaries at Mason Tyler got up to. So I continued, inhaling the smell of the sheets, gazing at a poster of Bob Dylan on the opposite wall and feeling my arousal escalate, wave against wave of helpless desire, almost entirely against my own will. The smell of the sheets was not really erotic in itself of course, but the promise of manliness suggested deep within that scent shot a powerful aphrodisiac straight to my brain, and I lost control. I didn't know who Bob Dylan was but the face depicted in that A2 sepia poster in the semi-darkness, brooding and pensive and almost certainly artistic and anguished, was the face of a *man*, and that was good enough for me. I studied it, squinting in the semi-darkness, and imagined the face of James. Then Mark. Then James. Over and over the face warped, shifted.

My left hand crept down to the elastic of my waistband, pulled at it, then quickly disappeared underneath. I tentatively explored the coarse tangle of hair at my crotch, the feel of which was still alien and unpleasant to me. Descending still further, down between my legs, I was distracted when I heard a noise from Becca's room. More giggles, interspersed with whispering. If Mark were in my position right now, he would almost certainly be imagining Becca and CJ engaged in a mock-lesbian pillow fight. Two pretty girls in the same bed, one blonde, one brunette, half-dressed, wrestling playfully among the soft cotton sheets, going hell for leather with their pillows, then their hands, then their tongues . . . Yes, if Mark were in my position right now, he would almost certainly be vigorously jerking off.

Jerking off. That's what they all got up to these days, the boys at least. It was no secret. There was no shame. It was as natural as breathing and eating and going to the toilet. Mark even talked quite openly about it, but possibly only to revel in my blushes.

'Nothing to do on Sundays except wanking,' he had once said. 'No better way to start the day. Or to end the day, actually. And if you're stuck for something to do in between . . .'

I didn't quite understand the whole masturbation thing, but at that moment, in that scenario, the motives behind such an act were becoming clearer by the second. Mark had even gone one stage further in his masturbation monologue, overstepping the line, asking me, 'Do you bring yerself off too, Caz? Do yer? Do you finger yerself till ya come? Yeah, bet yer do, filthy girl.'

By now of course I was familiar with the less decorous meaning of the word 'come', although I still thought it was a peculiar expression, and quite silly. But I did like the word 'orgasm'. It was suggestive and naughty. It rhymed with spasm. And chasm. I still couldn't say it out loud without dissolving into giggles.

Becca and CJ must have fallen asleep again, because all was quiet once more beyond the closed door. I pulled the quilt right over my head and put my hand back between my legs, experiencing a strange urgency to my usually benign gynaecological exploration this time. Thoughts continued to circulate inside my head. Gemma Powell had had a boy's willy in her *mouth*. And in her vagina. But nobody ever used that word. *Vagina.* Mark called it minge, muff, fanny, pussy, cunt. But he also called people who he didn't like 'cunt', which was apparently the worst thing you could ever say about someone. Worse even than arsehole.

I still had so much to learn, too much. My fingers continued probing and exploring, still my lust burgeoned. My finger could fit up there no problem, and I even ventured two at a time, which got me wondering about willies and the logistics of insertion. Sexual intercourse. Mating. Sure it sounded fine in *theory*, if slightly ludicrous, but really – *really* – what was the point? How did it all work? Why should something so objectively *unsexy* be considered so . . . fantastic? Everyone subscribed to it once they'd tried it. They said it was the best thing in the world. But putting a protruding body part inside a bodily aperture, what was so good about that? It wasn't like people got excited by picking their nose or sucking their thumb.

As I wondered about this, tedious and tangential as it was, I felt something unfamiliar overtake my body. I wondered what Mark's willy looked like. No, not 'willy'. That was a crass, childish word. Dick. Cock. That's more like it. Monosyllabic was so much more forceful, so much sexier. Was it so absurd, imagining me and Mark, naked and together? Even if it never happened, and I had little doubt that it never would, what was the harm in imagining it? Would I put it in my mouth? Could I? Or anywhere else? The thought terrified me, appalled me, but aroused and enthralled me more. Would I feasibly be capable of giving Mark an erection, a hard-on, a boner, a woody, even though he obviously didn't fancy me?

That was a prerequisite, apparently. Girls had to get warm and wet, boys had to get big and hard. Gemma had assured us that boys get erections even when they don't want to, sometimes *especially* when they don't want to, in fact 'they get them all the time really'. Perhaps as a result of this unpredictable erectile spontaneity, boys aren't fussy. The hard-on becomes, in effect, their brain. Most of them would do it with anyone. Gemma said the first time hurt, but not much. She said that you know when a boy wants sex because he kisses with his tongue and puts his hands under your top and down your pants. She said that boys will tell you that they love you but they don't really. They just want to put their dick inside you, that's all. When they do, the love will usually go away quite quickly afterwards.

My thoughts remained with Mark – naked Mark, hard Mark, lusty Mark. Mark beside me, on me, inside me. Mark's eyes looking into mine, Mark kissing me full on the mouth, Mark telling me I was beautiful, telling me he loved me, Mark's mouth where my hands were right now, all over me . . .

These thoughts drove me wild. Mark had done 'it' with Tina Hartley, and a couple of other girls as well. I knew that for sure. My passion became augmented by a new kind of jealousy, sexual jealousy, powerful and terrible. Three girls had performed intimate acts with the boy I loved, and he had never granted me so much as a kiss. I had established a rhythm by now, more rapid, in synch with my shallow breathing, too audible in my ears underneath that hot cover in that humid room. My right hand was still on my nipple, fingers brushing against it, running over the rounded mound of my breast as I felt my body temperature rise, sweat moistening my forehead, my inner thighs, my upper lip, the back of my neck. Was it disgusting, what I was doing? Was it shameful? The more I rubbed at myself, the less I cared. The sensations from this stimulation were unlike anything I had experienced before, and my imagination fuelled it further, pushed the desire to a whole new plateau.

Then another seizure of blind panic gripped me, suddenly, out of nowhere. During the grand tour of the Delaney home, I had noticed something. Becca had CCTV in her house, in just about every room. Security, she had explained. Her parents were strong believers in protecting their assets. There was a twenty-four-hour hi-tech burglar alarm system in operation, which was hooked up to a special police alert service, so if someone broke in, the alarm would go off automatically and the police would arrive there within ten minutes. And the cameras would catch the burglars even if the police didn't. *Cameras.* My hand stopped moving and I pulled the quilt back down and stared wide-eyed at the ceiling, trying to get my breath back. Was there a camera in this room? Had the Delaneys' trusty home-security system caught me playing with myself?

Oh My God.

The mortification would have been beyond endurance. Frantically, I looked around, searching for a blinking red light. I couldn't see anything. Still I remained frozen. The Bob Dylan poster seemed sinister to me now – like he was watching me. Dirty girl, *dirty girl*, he was saying. Mark's face, then James's face.

Mark's was saying, *Yeah right Caz, keep fantasising 'cos you'll never have me for real.*

James's was saying, *What the hell do you think you're doing, masturbating in my bed? Who do you think you are? Dirty girl!* I flushed with shame, straightened out my pyjamas and waited for my breathing to regulate.

The lust trailed off, dissipated as rapidly as it had arisen, and I was left feeling guilty and foolish and sweaty. The silence outside descended once again, heavy and oppressive.

I wished myself home and, to my surprise, began to cry.

7

Sky-diving, Stage-diving, Muff-diving and Other Cunning Stunts

> 'Is it inevitable that as women become increasingly adventurous and have higher expectations of life, they will find men less and less adequate?'
>
> **Theodore Zeldin, *An Intimate History of Humanity***

The sports scene at St Jude's was big business. The school had its own award-winning hockey team, lacrosse team, netball squad and synchronised swimming club. They took pride in their championship events, and there were official award ceremonies held every term, with every sporty and athletic pupil called up to the front time after time so the stodgier and less agile girls left on the floor would be deservedly shown up and shamed.

The gymnasium was a vast, fully equipped hall that played host to all kinds of regular strenuous activity, from circuit training to softball, from aerobics to badminton. Twice a year it would also host a disco in collaboration with the boys' school, and its quieter nooks would then be privy to a variety of other popular physical pastimes. The gymnasium was heady with the scent of mouldy old trainers, squeaky new trainers, a hundred intermingled perfumes, deodorant-sprayed armpits, Femfresh and sweat-drenched Aertex. The changing rooms were like a torture chamber: twice a week I would have to endure that terrible, terrifying ordeal of stripping down to underwear with too many other female bodies and braving the gym kit for an hour or two of enforced physical exertion. There are few experiences more disheartening for a teenage girl than undressing en masse in a communal changing room with mirrors on every wall and harsh lighting. The prettiest girls always vocalised the most concerns about their bodies, while merrily parading around in bra and knickers.

'Ugh, look at the cellulite on my legs,' Rebecca would openly grumble, standing in front of the largest mirror and squeezing her slim thighs, front and back, inner and outer, drawing attention to herself. 'And my fat stomach!' The taut little abdomen was prodded, and then

CJ and a couple of the other Beautiful Ones would join in, each of them bemoaning their imaginary flaws, in full view of all. Look at me everyone, *look at me*! You see, *this* is what you want to look like, girls! You want to be me! Admit it! But just to make you feel even worse, I'm going to put myself down, and pretend I am dissatisfied with this fabulously faultless figure!

This became a ritual, and a tedious one. Rebecca in her bra and knickers looked like the kind of girl you found on the fashion pages of the glossy magazines I had started reading out of masochistic compulsion – natural and absolute perfection. Supremely gorgeous. Sickeningly, unjustly attractive. Like the other genuinely insecure and self-effacing girls in my class, and mercifully there were others, I would undress as quickly and unobtrusively as possible, avoiding the mirrors and staying in the darkest corners, desperately trying to ignore the Beautiful Ones as they padded about conspicuously in their socks and undies.

No, PE was still definitely not one of my favourites.

English was my strongest subject. I was the best in my class. The teacher, a zany middle-aged cynic called Ms Quigley, recognised my potential immediately. I received an A+ for my first major English assignment. The set exercise was to write between five and ten alternative dictionary definitions for a number of words beginning with the same randomly allocated letter. I was given the letter 'M'. Bonus points were available for innovation and imagination.

MARRIAGE: a domestic agreement between two people who are temporarily compatible and/or permanently deluded.
MARK: a stain, standard, sign, score or arbitrary emblem. Used equally as a verb and a noun. Sometimes a proper noun.
MESS: something that needs sorting out.
MYSELF: (abstract noun) see 'mess'.
MULTIPLICATION: something tedious enforced on bored schoolchildren in theory and adopted by bored council-estate mothers in practice.
MIRACLE: myself (abstract noun) and Mark (proper noun) united together in a domestic agreement, either marriage (see above) or its typical prerequisite, *cohabitation.*
MISTAKE: see 'marriage'.
MINIMALIST: a person concerned with the art of making a modest amount look both adequate and tasteful.

MILLIONAIRE: an antonym of the above.

At first, Ms Quigley gave me a simple 'A', telling me it would have been an A+ if only I had bothered to alphabetise it correctly. I argued that this oversight was deliberate, and necessary for 'artistic licence', and Ms Quigley saw my point and awarded me the A+ without further comment.

While I was trying to secure myself in the highly charged, fiercely competitive but relatively safe and lawful little world of St Jude's, Mark bunked and flunked and drove his mother round the bend. His own schooldays were largely characterised by long spells of absenteeism and, on the rare occasions when he did grace the classroom with his unmistakable presence, reliable bouts of severely disruptive behaviour. His reputation became quite legendary. By the middle of his first term at Mason Tyler he was known to pretty much everyone, inspiring endless superlatives from teachers and fellow pupils alike:

'The cheekiest little bugger I have ever had the misfortune to teach' – Mr Ashford, Geography.
'No redeeming features that I can think of' – Mrs Jessop, Religious Studies.
'Mark Crozier? Yes, sure, his name's on the register but I don't believe I've actually ever had the pleasure of meeting him' – Miss Leeson, Home Economics.
'A stupid, hopeless waste of time and space' – Mr Richards, Physics.
'Incredibly foolish, ill-behaved and as inept with his mother tongue as he is with foreign languages' – Miss Beaumont, French and Spanish.
'Fit as fuck and good with his hands' – Tina Hartley, 9F.
'A right pisshead and a good laugh' – Paul Ingles, 10S.

Mark couldn't wait to get his schooldays over with so he could go out into the big wide world and seek his fortune – whether that fortune lay in a lifetime of dole money and dossing, or (at the opposite end of the reality spectrum) in fulfilling his boyhood dream of becoming a famous celebrity (or of marrying one). I had my own dreams too of course, and unlike Mark, I planned to achieve them via a more conventional route; by plunging headlong into scholastic pursuits and immersing myself in books and homework. That was the route I had been assured would inevitably lead to comfort and contentment.

Eventually, at least. *Just stick with it and your hard work will pay off. The rewards will be great.* And all that jazz.

It helps to have dreams when you are a teenager, just as an active imagination fired by fantasy is a prerequisite to a fulfilling childhood. From this point on, grim reality incessantly batters you into submission, but the anguish that this cruel process of disillusionment causes is never more pronounced than when you are a teenager. This is because you are not yet inoculated against it; you are still to be numbed to it, fresh as you still remain from the agreeable bubble of fanciful infancy. The refusal to be moulded, the reluctance to conform, somehow makes the whole process easier, purely by virtue of the fact that it alienates you from everything you feel compelled to reject: family, education, society, law and order.

Mark and I had begun discussions about career aspirations as early as our Willow Lane days, although at first of course it was all pretty much pie-in-the-sky stuff. After the last bell sounded, we would often go to the park or maybe to the tree-house in his back garden (this was quite an honour as it was strictly a 'boys only' zone), and there we would eat Space Invaders crisps, drink bottles of sweet, lurid-coloured fizzy liquid and talk to each other until it got dark. Surprisingly enough, it was usually Mark who did most of the talking. He had ideas, he had plans, he had real *ambitions*, and for a time I was the only person he wanted to share these with. That fact alone made me feel all warm inside, although his reasoning behind it was obvious – I wasn't about to tell him that he was a silly fool, and that his dreams would never come true. I was only ever going to encourage him, believe in him, and tell him what he wanted to hear.

He had first revealed to me that he wanted to be a pilot, ''cos they get to fly big cool planes and visit loads of cool countries and do it with sexy women all over the world.' As first dreams go, this was a pretty spectacular one. I retaliated with my own, slightly less fantastical ambition: 'I think I want to be a teacher, or a nurse, or an air stewardess.'

'Yeah,' he had responded, 'you'd make a good teacher, I reckon.'

'Really? You think so?' I was absurdly flattered by this seemingly genuine remark. I knew I wasn't really cut out to be a nurse (I didn't like the sight of blood very much for a start), and I doubted I'd ever be pretty enough to be an air stewardess, but I did feel that I could quite realistically make it as a teacher.

'Yeah sure Caz, I mean you're dead clever, aren't ya?'

And so, at seven and nine years old, we had it planned: he was going to be an airline pilot and I was going to be a teacher. That was what we were going to do with our lives, and nobody in the whole world was going to stop us.

A few months later, he had changed his mind. 'I wanna be a fireman.'

'A *fireman*? Why?'

'Well . . . they get to bomb about in a fire engine, put out fires, rescue people, and everyone thinks they're heroes.'

A career that demanded status and respect was all Mark wanted; all he had hoped for at that young, sanguine age. But the older he got, the more these feasible (if unlikely) ambitions turned to impossible dreams. The long-term future to a child is a fuzzy, abstract thing – inevitable, yes, but fairly irrelevant. But the future you think about and plan for all too quickly becomes the present that you waste and the potential that you squander.

The less asinine conversations I enjoyed with Mark weren't only about careers and aspirations. We shared fantasies sometimes, and memories. Preoccupied as we both became with our own delinquent predilections as we got older, quality moments alone with Mark became something of a rarity, and so whenever they happened I tried to make the best of them. Believe it or not, Mark was capable of initiating some fascinating and potentially philosophical discussions, although he never had the mental capacity or attention span necessary to see these through to a satisfactory conclusion, much to my frustration. At least he pretended not to, but I knew him better than that. Behind that impressive facade of swaggering confidence and fashionable ignorance, I knew Mark was swamped by the manifold secret insecurities that afflict any teenager. Underneath all that brashness and bravado, I recognised a common connection between us, that same connection that first set my heart ablaze with love for him on that day in September 1982.

Now, with his gang of similarly endowed friends, none of whom I was formally introduced to until I was sixteen, Mark fancied himself as King of Rivington Hill. He was King of Everywhere, as far as he was concerned. They had their own graffiti signature, their own code, their own way of walking and talking, their own unique sartorial style (bandanna, baseball cap, circus-tent trousers, headphones, motif T-shirts, branded jackets, branded trainers, sovereign rings the odd piercing or tattoo). They had their very own culture. They all felt like they had the world at their feet when they were together.

But I noticed the real Mark shine through when it was just him on his own, with nobody around for him to impress or hoodwink. He knew he could be himself with me, and he also knew that was more than good enough for me.

'If you could have any superhero power, what would you want?'

We were in our usual spot in the park. It was the day before my first mock GCSE exam, the very day Mark had chosen to formally announce his decision to leave school after the exams and seek his fortune as a mechanic (not a fireman or a pilot), and so he was in a very cheerful, ruminative mood.

I thought about this question for quite a while, and Mark filled the silence with a low, humming noise as he tilted his head back against a tree and swatted at a swarm of flies with his baseball cap.

I eventually turned onto my stomach and propped myself up on my elbows, watching the dancing shadows of the patulous branches flicker and criss-cross over Mark's face. It was a hot day and I felt a little self-conscious in my short sundress, my uneasiness worsened by the fact that Mark had taken off his shirt and was looking incredibly attractive and sultry.

I thought that the ability to fly and X-ray vision were the obvious answers and far too unoriginal, so I said, 'I suppose . . . I wish I could read people's minds.'

Mark was surprised by this. He wasn't aware of how longingly I was gazing at him as he put his hands behind his head and squinted up at the sky, his face creased in concentration. For some reason, the fact that Mark wasn't the sharpest tool in the box actually heightened my ardour, engorged my lust. His indolence, docility and benightedness added extra appeal to his simple charms. Especially at times like this, when it was just him and me. I didn't know why I was drawn to what was essentially a deficit, but such is the strange and illogical nature of attraction and love, I suppose.

'But would you *really* want to read other people's minds?' Mark said, still frowning. 'Like, find out what people really think about you and stuff? Don't you think that would be a bit . . . well, freaky?'

I plucked a couple of daisies and buttercups as I pondered this. After the St Jude's indoctrination had all but convinced me that life was all about petty competitiveness and personal attainment, Mark at least provided me with a crucial link to the real world and who I really was. I was unable to deny my roots, however far my branches were permitted to spread. Mark kept me grounded, although of course he didn't realise it. And neither did I at that time, at least not consciously.

'Well, I suppose you'd be able to tell who your real friends are,' I said. Then, sadly, I added, 'And everybody lies, you know. Even friends.'

Mark was not convinced. 'I think I'd rather not know what some people really think,' he murmured, closing his eyes against the sun, which had just rolled out brighter than ever from behind a cloud. 'Besides, the people who you really like, who you really trust . . . you can usually tell what they're thinking anyway.' He half opened one eye and peered at me inquisitively. 'Can't you?'

I hoped with all my heart that he couldn't tell what I was thinking, lying there beside him under a shady canopy of branches on a sunny summer afternoon in my skimpy sundress, ovulating like crazy. 'What would *you* want?' I asked him. 'What super-power, I mean?'

Mark obviously had his answer ready. 'I'd like to be able to make myself invisible,' he replied. 'Whenever I needed to.'

'What for?' I asked, knowing the answer probably had something to do with free entrance to West Ham matches and spying on naked females.

'I could sneak into the birds' changing rooms and check out all the tits and arses,' he explained, 'and I could get into any footie match I wanted.'

I smiled at his predictability. I didn't want to say that I already felt like I had the power of invisibility, because the implication would have been lost on him. But that's what I was thinking. Caroline the Amazing Invisible Girl. She's there all right, but you probably won't notice her.

He put his baseball cap back on and pulled the peak down over his eyes, lying back and using his rolled-up shirt as a pillow. 'You don't mind if I have a little snooze do ya, Caz?'

I continued to stare at him for a bit longer; the soft pale fuzzy curve of his belly above his belt, the flat, hairless chest, his nipples, his strong, broad shoulders, his throat, his arms. I wanted to kiss him, everywhere, all over that imperfect but spectacular body.

After what could have been some minutes, I tore my eyes away and said, 'Actually I'd better go and revise for tomorrow's exam now.'

I got up and brushed myself down. Mark didn't move and didn't acknowledge my departure, even though I said goodbye three times before I started to walk away. I left him to sleep, angry with myself for feeling so wretchedly enamoured, even now.

Over the years, Rivington Hill disintegrated. During the eighties, the estate expanded slowly, resulting in a gradual increase in crime rates and a directly proportional decline in living standards. The early eighties were afflicted by widespread unemployment and Rivington Hill was a particular hotspot. Morale was low, resentment and apathy were high. Around the time of the Falklands and Cold War hyper-tension, over half the families in the area were officially living in poverty. Two new blocks of council homes were constructed between 1987 and 1989, and by the early nineties, nearly four hundred new families had moved to the area – and then a more rapid deterioration got under way. The children swarmed the street corners like rats; neglected, rejected and bored. Year by year their numbers increased, the gangs grew stronger and more savage; common compassion and neighbourliness became extinct. I could remember when certain areas of the Rivington Hill estate may have been feasibly described as relatively pleasant (if not entirely serene and attractive). Beyond the high-rise blocks and purpose-built maisonettes, there were rows upon rows of tiny terraces, mostly on the outskirts of the estate. Every house had its own wheelie bin. One each. Green, with the house number painted on the front in white.

As I grew up, even these more pleasant houses became progressively dilapidated. Bev became concerned about the changes, about the seemingly never-ending invasions of new inhabitants, and she started to talk about moving out of Bluestone Rise, away from Rivington Hill. She told me it broke her heart to say it, but she no longer felt as safe as she used to in her own home. She said things would never be the same again, not now, not ever.

The first half of the nineties was, in every way and on every level, a coming of age for both Mark and me, although it had been clear for some time that we were veering off in different directions. That much had always been inevitable I suppose. Now the teenage years were in full swing, and sexual depravity and social delinquency in their many and varied forms had commenced in earnest. Mark, being an out-and-out estate boy and doggedly proud of this fact, entered his teens with clenched fists, gritted teeth and well-packed testicles. He was, from the outset, a boy with unshakable delusions of machismo and grandeur.

Mason Tyler, although decidedly second-rate as an educational establishment, was an ideal environment for Mark to meet like-minded people, and as a social base it was worth attending every so often. He soon became part of a notorious ten-strong gang, of which he was pretty much accepted as the leader, if not officially then certainly by an implicit consensus among the other members. His closest friends – that is, those with whom he indulged most regularly in various illegal pursuits – were Simon Tamworth, Thomas Flynn and Paul 'Kermit' Howard. (Paul was widely referred to as 'Kermit' because he had been amorously and relentlessly hounded since primary school by a loud, plump, besotted girl called Harriet Fraser, and she bore a striking resemblance to Miss Piggy.) I had known Paul before Mark did, or at least known *of* him, because he was caught shoplifting with my brother at age seven, not to mention numerous times hence, and the pair of them had been almost inseparable at Willow Lane.

These four plucky, bellicose boys constituted the very heart of the gang – they were daring, defiant and rude, and there was no low too low for them to sink to, and no high not worth striving for. Pills and thrills. If it ain't nailed down, nick it. That was the name of the game. One favourite pastime was stealing CDs, often under the influence of amphetamine and/or alcohol. As a collective, they managed to steal hundreds of pounds' worth at a time, then would rush back to the park or, if total privacy was required, to a bedroom, to assess their takings.

These experiences brought them closer together, united them in the all-important cause, confirmed their identity, both as individuals and as gang members. They all had everything to win, and nothing to lose except their boredom. Once they had got a taste for thieving, it became apparent that half the fun lay in the act itself, and of managing to get away with it; the fact that something was *attained* through the act was merely a bonus.

A very agreeable bonus, admittedly.

'I'll swap you Happy Mondays for that Wonderstuff album, Tam,' Mark said. It was just a few weeks before GCSEs were due to commence, and the lads were demonstrating their typically die-hard dedication to their education by bypassing the school gates every day in favour of tireless criminal activity and the old favourite, 'loitering with/without intent'. Now they were busy comparing their swags in Mark's bedroom following another raid at a Virgin Megastore.

I was sitting on Mark's bed reading *Pride and Prejudice*, ignoring them or at least pretending to. As usual, they were ignoring me too, which suited me fine. For a while now, I had been regularly turning up at the house on the flimsy premise that I was willing to help Mark with his homework and 'revision' (such as it was). Bev thought I might be able to motivate him (a bit of 'reverse psychology' perhaps), and encouraged me to persevere, even though it was a losing battle right from the start, as we both knew it would be. I nearly always ended up in the front room with the TV on and my hand in the biscuit barrel, exchanging idle pleasantries with Ned while one of the parakeets flew down and pecked the pages of a textbook I would be half-heartedly reading. Meanwhile Mark would just stay up in his room or go out, offering his mother no more than the usual 'Don't wait up' advice and me no more than a fleeting 'hello, goodbye'.

This time, however, Mark had invited me up to his room after sauntering in unexpectedly at dinner-time with the lads, assuring me that I 'wouldn't believe what fantastic shit' they had managed to extort between them. Also they had some 'amazing gear', and insisted I should try some. So who was I to argue? The impending English Literature exam could take a back seat for a few moments, surely. Indeed, I felt positively privileged and most taken aback to be welcomed into this happy little throng, albeit only to be almost completely blanked after the first joint had been rolled and passed around.

The conversation initially revolved around recent drug-fuelled misdemeanours and the sexual persuasions and proclivities of certain acquaintances, and then attention was turned to their latest batch of stolen goods. I had to admit, it was an impressive collection – well over a hundred CDs between them. I wondered how they managed it.

'Nah, already got that one, mate,' Tamworth said. 'It's alright, that is. You manage to half-inch that Stone Roses LP?'

'I got that one,' Kermit trilled triumphantly, opening up his jacket and emptying his deep pockets with pride, one CD after another piling up on the floor by his feet. Kermit was wily, and the most highly skilled thief and pickpocket Mark knew. He held him in great esteem. Even I had to admit that Kermit was quite a remarkable felon, and definitely an indispensable member of a gang set on mass looting. He was also their main source of drugs. He was The Artful Dodger of Rivington Hill, eluding police, store security systems, eagle-eyed shopkeepers and unwitting members of the public on a daily basis. There had been a few near misses, but he was more or less undetectable and had only ever spent one night in a police cell. And that had been for glassing a bloke who dared to look at him 'a bit funny'. But with his misleadingly innocent baby face and wide blue eyes, Kermit didn't even *look* suspicious. 'It's in there somewhere, I think,' he said. 'Fuck me Flynn, you sad bastard, you got Jason fuckin' Donovan!'

Flynn was quick to prevent a predictable outpouring of derision from his colleagues.

'It's for me sister, innit. What do you take me for?'

'Don't answer that, lads,' Mark grinned, inciting chortles from the other two.

Flynn was probably the best looking, although too chiselled and 'pretty' to be considered a really threatening sexual competitor to his more rapacious cohorts. The others mollified their slight unease about Flynn's aesthetic advantage by frequently insinuating that, despite an impressive history of all-female conquests, he may have been – just possibly – a little on the poofy side. Flynn reacted badly to the teasing, which naturally provoked further teasing.

At seventeen, Mark was utterly incapable of thinking of anything beyond tomorrow and outside his gang. His family was now perceived as a collection of tragically unavoidable people who lived in his house, with whom he communicated only when absolutely necessary and never in words of more than one syllable. His dependency on them would never be realised for as long as they continued to exist and cause him such anguish and embarrassment simply by virtue of that existence.

I, meanwhile, had been promoted (demoted?) from 'just a girl from the estate' to 'just a girl I know' until finally, after official introductions to the hard-core, Mark conceded that I was, in fact, kind of a 'mate'. At first, referring to any female as a 'mate' has certain awkward implications for a teenage boy who wants to maintain credibility with his closest and most shallow-thinking friends. Just as admitting that you love and need your family is beyond the pale.

A knock at the door animated the four boys into a sudden flurry of anxious activity. 'Hang on!' Mark called out, extinguishing the joint and flicking it out of the window then lifting his valance sheet so Kermit could kick all the lifted CDs under his bed. Once concealed, they each positioned themselves appropriately – Tamworth reclined against Mark's beanbag, Flynn and Kermit slouched on the bed pretending to read a discarded and obscenely defaced science book, Mark sprawled casually on the floor.

'Hello, can I come in?' Bev opened the door cautiously, just enough to poke her head around and greet her son and his friends in an unintentionally embarrassing manner. 'It's only me,' she said, smiling at the assembled youths. 'Hello boys. Oh, Caro, you're still here!'

'Not for much longer,' I assured her. We exchanged weary expressions.

'Afternoon, Mrs C,' the boys chorused; a familiar refrain by now.

'What do you want?' Mark demanded.

Bev had learned to ignore her son's hostility. 'Just checking up on you, darling. A small part of me still cares, you know. Would anyone like a drink? I've put the kettle on.'

'No ta,' Mark said firmly, answering for everyone.

'Nobody?'

'Can I just have some water please, Bev?' I asked.

'Sure.' She was about to close the door but then she flung it wider, sniffing the air cautiously. 'Are you lot smoking weed?'

'Shit Mum, as if we would!' Mark objected.

Bev's sceptical stare was outwitted by unblinking defiance. Bev sighed and said, 'Alright, well don't forget it's Grandad's birthday dinner tonight so I want you downstairs with the rest of the family by seven at the latest, please.'

'Yeah, yeah, whatever.'

'Preferably sober, if at all possible.'

'For Christ's sake Mum, leave me alone will you?'

Bev raised her voice, obviously getting a little irate now. '*Caroline* remembered grandad's birthday.' She glanced at me but I looked down at my book, unappreciative of the mention and of the attention it provoked. 'She even brought him round a card and a little present. Is it too much to ask . . .'

Well aware of Mark's burgeoning discomfort and impatience, I quickly cut her short.

'It's OK Bev, he'll be down later. Once I've introduced him to the joys of classical literature.' I waved my book at her feebly and she shrugged and shook her head before closing the door – not quite slamming it, but still a little harder and louder than usual.

We listened to her footsteps fade away down the stairs and then Tamworth blurted out mockingly, 'Golly Mark, you can't miss *Grandad's birthday dinner*!'

The other two were smirking uncontrollably, and Mark defended his slightly bruised dignity with a petulant and predictable 'Fuck you.'

'So Caz,' Kermit drawled, starting to roll another joint and using the ripped corner of the front cover of *Chemistry for Beginners* as a roach, 'when are you going to start giving shit-for-brains here some of that "extra tuition" his old woman keeps banging on about?'

'Well, given his capacity for learning and his enthused approach to all academic matters, I am assuming he will need very little guidance from me,' I quipped back, affecting a posh accent that I knew would only add to Mark's irritation.

Sure enough, he tetchily interjected. 'Oh just shut the fuck up, you're all doing my head in. Oi Flynn, stick on one of these will yer?' He picked a CD at random from under his bed, the latest 'acid house' dance compilation, the millionth in a seemingly inexhaustible series that year. 'Here, this one'll do.' He tossed it at Flynn, who was closest to Mark's hi-fi, the one appliance in the house to which Bev would gladly have taken a sledgehammer. 'Whack it on full volume, piss the folks off. And hurry up with that joint, Kerm, I'm on edge here.'

'Alright mate, keep your knickers on,' Kermit retorted.

Mark's mood was the sort that could only be alleviated by drugs and loud music. It was a fairly typical one for him. Flynn put the CD on and Kermit shouted at me over the din as he licked Rizla papers. 'Why do you always come round 'ere with yer books and stuff when you already know that Mark is a lost cause?'

'Good question,' I yelled back. Kermit lit up the joint and inhaled deeply, passing it to Mark at once because he sensed, rightly, that the poor boy needed mellowing out.

'Reckon it's probably for the absorbing discourse I always seem to strike up with him,' I said eventually.

Flynn chuckled gruffly as he cracked open a can of Tetley Bitter, no doubt assuming that 'discourse' was a posh word for sex.

'Yeah, that'd be right, you only have to look at the cunt to see he's an intellectual innit,' Kermit said.

Mark was choosing to ignore the teasing, having already found a happy plane of abstracted contentment in the herbal contents of Kermit's roll-up. 'Is this the same gear you had last week?' he asked him dozily.

'Nah, that was all gone by Sunday night. This stuff is better. Bought a gram of it off that geezer down Larry's bar last night.'

'Not Shady Dave?'

'Nah, some Asian bloke. The one who used to hang out with me mum's ex. Forget his name. He overcharged me but there was nuffin better going on.'

Mark took a couple more tokes and nodded his approval. 'Yeah, it's not bad.' He offered the joint to me and with very little deliberation I closed my book and accepted it. Mark had a detrimental influence on me. I had always thought I was much more impervious to peer pressure than Mark ever was and took pride in this conviction but the truth was, I caved in just as readily and easily. Anything to fit in. I already knew that marijuana had a degenerative effect on brain-cell development, but this seemed largely irrelevant to me as I took the intoxicating smoke deep into my lungs.

The boys tested out a couple more of their swiped CDs while Kermit packed and distributed a couple more joints, and before too long all of us were pretty much in a state of agreeable stupefaction. A little more progressively incoherent banter with four young men who inadvertently made me feel like the most intelligent and sophisticated creature on earth, and I decided that revision could wait for another time. Brain cells permitting.

Mark was right. There was more to life. Faking it. Making it. Allow some time in between to be yourself.

While Mark was nicking stuff and lying about his age in order to gain access to the best pubs and clubs in the area, I lied about my age in order to get a weekend job to pay for all the things my school friends incited me to possess, as a matter of necessity. And just as there were limitless things to want as a child, I found there were yet more things for the teenage girl to seek to possess; status symbols in miniature. My home life should have put things into perspective, but as far as I was concerned, the attainment of these superficial trinkets – jewellery, cosmetics, sundry fashion items – became a far more pressing issue in my selfish teenage mind than the fact that my mother couldn't afford to feed her five kids. Mark tended to steal something he wanted but couldn't afford, while I coveted from afar, yearned to the point of obsession, and sometimes – whenever I could – saved up for and ultimately obtained.

Similarly, the issue of boyfriends – of seeking, targeting and ultimately ensnaring a suitable candidate – also became something of a preoccupation, even taking precedence over the consistent attainment of 'A' grades for some girls. Balancing the pressures of school with the equally momentous pressures of being a teenage girl was proving something of a challenge.

I met my first 'love interest' in May 1990 during one of St Jude's legendary combined school discos, although there was no love and very little interest right from the start. His name was Stephen and he was in the year above me at the boys' school. He approached me, quite boldly, after we had exchanged a couple of suggestive looks from across the hall. The chat-up line had been neither persuasive nor remotely memorable, but he wasn't ugly or obviously lecherous, so when Rebecca approved of his shoes and advised me to 'go for it', there was little more to be said. Rebecca and I were 'friends' by this stage; that is, we managed to suspend hostilities between us enough to see the good in each other and spend time in one another's company outside school hours from time to time.

I think the truth was that Rebecca saw me at first as a 'project' more than a friend. Perhaps she perceived my vulnerability as a bit of a challenge, but she tended to play on it more than she tried to remedy it. For a teenage girl, a friend who is in awe of you and in contempt of herself is a true friend indeed. Conversely, I saw Becca as someone who I *had* to befriend because otherwise my bitterness would only have made me hate her. And Rebecca was not there to be hated. Admired, yes. Envied, certainly. But never hated.

Our friendship was reaffirmed when we both received detention for taking unauthorised absence together (it had been Rebecca's idea), on a Friday afternoon in the middle of my second spring term at St Jude's. The matron was a formidable, unsympathetic woman with a voluminous bouffant and a filing cabinet filled with a veritable arsenal of sanitary products and Band-Aids. She had her own room next door to the bursar's office, and this was where girls went when they were suffering from female problems or if they had done something naughty. It was therefore populated on a daily basis by moaning menstruating girls and slackers and skivers.

Rebecca and I were forced to sit side by side in the matron's office, under her hawk-like stare, and sort through the lost-property box and sew letters onto netball kits for two hours after school as punishment for our mischief. Giggling and talking was strictly disallowed. I stole a pair of trainers and a Walkman from the lost-property box and concealed them in my bag when matron wasn't looking. Rebecca deliberately sewed the letters on upside-down and scrawled surreptitious little notes and passed them to me, each one suggesting increasingly implausible but highly amusing theories about the matron's sex life. Once our detention was over, we arranged to bunk off again at the same time the following week.

Stephen and I slow-danced to Bryan Adams and Roxette; he got an erection for which he made no apology (on the contrary, he seemed resolved to bring it to my attention), and my bottom was subjected to a good deal of groping. Two dates later, having gone no further than kissing with tongues (an activity I initially endured rather than enjoyed), I was horrified when Stephen suddenly steered my hand toward his crotch and requested a wank – 'just a quick one, it won't take long.' It would perhaps not have been so shocking if we had been somewhere other than the Chelmsford ice rink, in full view of the Saturday skaters.

'Crikey, Caroline, I don't mean here!' he had protested, trying in vain to assuage his hard-on by pressing it hard against my hip, doddering an unsteady rhythm on his ice skates as his lips ineptly sought mine. With him at nearly six feet tall and me at barely five, kissing had not been so much a prefatory facet of intimacy as an experiment in forbearance and stamina – specially whilst wearing ice skates. 'I thought maybe we could go for a walk or something . . . by the river . . . through the park . . .' he persisted, still grinding against me.

This was when I remembered I was a young woman of integrity and discernment.

'Fuck off, Stephen,' I had replied.

The truth was, I still didn't actually know how to fulfil some of the more dextrous girlfriendly duties, and the possibility of cocking up – for want of a better phrase – petrified me. Hearsay and speculation from the other girls only petrified me more. I knew I would have to learn one day, and that the best and indeed only way of learning was through direct 'hands-on' experience, but I also knew that Stephen was not the one I wanted to practise on. There was no chemistry between us whatsoever; just the mere fact that I was female and he was male. Sexual curiosity on its own is sometimes not enough, not even if it's inflated by a degree of youthful desperation.

But it was all academic, in the end. Rebecca's New Year's Eve party a few months later turned out to be enlightening on many levels, and not just for me either. While CJ was occupied with losing her virginity to her long-term American boyfriend in the Delaney family bathroom, and the notoriously profligate Gemma Powell eagerly cornered James Delaney's best friend in the master bedroom, I became randomly acquainted with a skinny, spotty bloke called Gavin in the downstairs cloakroom. More specifically, I became acquainted with the sound of him panting in my ear and the feel and smell of his greasy hair as he stuffed his hand in my knickers and slobbered over my face and neck. Although I certainly didn't remember asking for such a rude invasion of my own personal space, it somehow seemed inappropriate and prudish to not reciprocate. Being drunk helped, naturally. The whole thing was over in five minutes. He got his fingers wet, I got mine wet – and his trousers, the front of my skirt, the pedestal mat and several sheets of Andrex also got a pretty raw deal. It was neither pleasant nor wholly repulsive, as can reasonably be said of most teenage sexual experiences, but it did at least teach me something about the nature of the male libido – it's a force to be reckoned with. Three hundred million was still one hell of a big number, but I was starting to believe it now.

I was unceremoniously deflowered in the back of a Ford Cortina in the early summer of 1991, by an eighteen-year-old called Peter who lived in Walthamstow. The first thing he had said to me, when we met at an East End pub in March, was, 'Dye your hair red darlin'. You'd look really sexy with red hair.' For reasons beyond my comprehension, I found him irresistibly attractive. My bastard-radar was on red alert, and I just couldn't help myself.

It helped that he had a car, of course. He took me out in it a few times, I dyed my hair ('Autumn Spice'), we discovered a secluded private parking spot, he told me that he had three ribbed Durex in his back pocket, I acquiesced. I feel I must apologise for such a bald abridgement of my first penetrative sexual encounter, but the details of it remain mercifully hazy. I remember 'Unbelievable' by EMF was on the radio while he 'rubbered up', and I can hardly forget that by the time the next song, 'Devil Inside' by INXS, had finished, the whole experience was over. I hadn't known whether to laugh or cry. We got dressed and I told him I was hungry. He patted my thigh and drove me home via a McDonald's drive-thru, and we only did it one more time after that.

This relationship was something of a distraction to my GCSE studies, which were well under way during this period, but Peter didn't demand too much of my time and he ditched me after the last exam was over and done with anyway. He had met a barmaid with naturally red hair and a nicer arse. I was neither surprised nor especially heartbroken, and by the time I collected my GCSE results I had almost completely forgotten about the burly Arsenal-supporting cretin who had deflowered me.

Straight As across the board, except Maths, for which I was grateful (and surprised) to get a B. I gave myself D-minus for Relationship Success, but I had plenty of time – the rest of my life, in fact – to work on that.

At around this time, my friendship with Mark was going through a transitional phase. Since I had started at St Jude's, I naturally tended to see him less frequently and the time we did spend together was often a little strained, and our conversations limited. We had less in common now than we ever had done. I began to find him boring and irritating, and I suppose he must have thought much the same of me – we had different priorities, different sets of friends, different ideals. Everything had changed.

I still treated the Crozier house like my second home, but neither Mark nor Billy had the respect to treat the place like anything except a 'doss-house', according to an enraged Sean. Even when Mark *was* in when I called round to the Croziers, he didn't venture out of his room unless it was to demand food or use the bathroom. Indeed, the only thing he said to me for almost four months was 'hey Caz, you've done something with your hair', when he met me by chance in Romford after I had just treated myself to a one-off 'beautification session' at the salon. (Aside from the cleansing facial and make-up, my hair had been dyed even darker red, with broad copper streaks, and then hacked into a bob. It sounds hideous and it was, but at the time I was deluded into thinking it fashionable enough to justify the forty pounds I handed to the hairdresser – never mind the additional twenty-five I gave to the 'skin and cosmetic specialist' for turning me into a 'glamour puss'.)

And so, given Mark's elusiveness, it was often the case that I would spend much of my spare time in the company of grown-ups – Bev in particular. She would offer me advice and sustenance, and consoled me for continuing to love someone so hopeless, even though I was by now well aware of the irrationality and inanity of it all and still unable to reconcile or justify my feelings ('Why *do* I love a wanker? Why? *Why?*'). I would offer Bev similar consolation, although she had an excuse for loving Mark; as his mother she had no choice in the matter. And so we despaired together.

Because he tended to stay out for nights on end, I'd sometime even sleep in Mark's bed, shower-fresh and hopeful in his West Ham football shirt and my favourite knickers with my hair washed and brushed and my legs and armpits clean and shaved. It was just a very small part of me that anticipated Mark returning home to find me there, thinking what the hell and getting in beside me.

Mark had taken to petty crime by day and trawling bars and clubs night after night, or at least the few bars and clubs that accepted his dodgy fake ID, and I was still hanging on in vain hope. Sometimes, when I had nothing better to do, which was more often than I would have liked, I lay awake wondering what he was getting up to.

Successfully installed in a suitably smoky and alcohol-misted venue, I imagined Mark seeking out his prey and attacking in the only way his untrained brain knew how, fuelled by lager and libido.

Even the shyest teenage Essex boy salivates after anything remotely female in such a cringingly obvious and obtrusive way that even the shyest Essex girl cannot possibly hope to hold onto her chastity for as long as her parents would ideally wish. And Mark was not shy. He was the opposite of shy.

As I discovered myself, the approach the teenage boy adopts is invariably that of a blundering primate, with no more sophistication involved than a witless one-liner and a lewd glance down the cleavage. The Essex clubs were heaving with kids who wanted to be grown-ups and so smoked and drank and took drugs and had fights and sex like it was going out of fashion. They were salacious, obnoxious and dull, all essentially replicas of each other and all out for the same goal . . . fornication, desecration, denigration, degradation.

Every Friday and Saturday night, you could spot the uninitiated a mile off, desperate gangs of boys loitering around perfumed female collectives like iron filings around a magnet. By the end of the night many of them would have successfully hooked up in pairs and drifted outside to the secluded seediness of a back alley or car park somewhere, frantically ridding themselves of their virginities in less time than it takes to boil an egg. After that first anonymous and intimately forgettable coalescence, it all goes downhill for most of them.

Now, having duly sampled most of the notorious local clubs myself, and even with the exams taken and passed and the virginity thing out of the way, something still weighed heavy on my mind, and it wasn't just the omnipresent weight issue. It wasn't even the fact I still felt unable to live up to the standards both real and imagined, set by friends. Now I had sixth form to look forward to. I was now officially one of those sirens that I had so admired when I first started at St Jude's; one of those untouchable young women who bedazzled the plebs with her vast experience and natural brilliance. Except my insecurities were still as overwhelming as ever. I didn't *feel* admirable, I didn't feel experienced or brilliant. I felt exactly the same, just very slightly taller, more voluptuous and knowledgeable perhaps, and marginally less naive. But not altogether a vast improvement on the awkward, awestruck little girl who had started there three-and-a-half years before.

My A-level options were chosen after not very much deliberation at all: English Literature, History, Human Biology and Business Studies. Quite a hotchpotch of subjects, but I figured it would provide me with a good solid background of pertinent wisdom and general knowledge. Besides which, they were the only subjects I found even remotely interesting.

In October 1991, Bev and Sean held a party at their house to celebrate their twenty-fifth wedding anniversary. Everyone was invited, and everyone turned up. Incompatible and potentially explosive mixtures of young and old, pissed and sober, married and single, happy and disgruntled made the occasion one to remember. Mark, disdainful of family events at the best of times, spent much of his time playing chords on his guitar in his room and ignoring repeated requests for his presence from downstairs. I got drunk on Sean's home-brew and found myself at the bottom of the garden with a similarly pixilated and ineffably dull middle-aged lady called Valerie. She was Mark's aunt, and she had been talked about in the Crozier family household for as long as I could remember. Just outside the back door Tamworth sat semi-comatose against the wall with his head between his legs, while both the dogs licked sick from his shoes. Billy's best mate was leaning out of the bathroom window and threatening to jump, and Billy was foolishly calling his bluff by telling him he didn't 'have the bollocks for it'.

'Y'see, I don't get to see Bev and her lot very often,' Valerie was explaining to me. 'I live in Bristol you see. I know it's not a million miles away, but what with my job, and Tony's job – he's a financial director of a telecommunications business – there is just so little spare time. And the years just whip by, don't you find? We did keep in touch for a while, like, every day I mean, when she and Sean first got married. As her older sister I understandably felt a bit protective of her. I'll be frank with you sweetheart, I thought she was making a mistake. I really did. She was only twenty-one, and Sean was even younger – barely an adult – and they were so terribly naive. She's always had her head in the clouds, has Beverley. The moment she met Sean, she said she knew he was the one. She said it was "destiny". Destiny indeed!'

I was half listening, but the threat of imminent sickness prevented me from offering the usual polite gestures. I held on to my stomach and breathed hard, looking at the pretty rows of flowers and shrubs that lined the back fence and searching for a convenient place to throw up.

'Well, it wasn't like that with my Tony. Not really. But I suppose love is something that grows over time, it's not just something that happens to you, just like that, out of nowhere. Is it? He's a financial director, you know. And Emma's studying medicine at King's. She took a year out in Africa. I wasn't keen on her going at first, but it turned out to be a fantastic experience for her. Well what can I say? I'm a mother. Mothers worry. But Emma is very independent, so I suppose I will just have to learn to let her get on with her own thing. She met her boyfriend out there. In Zimbabwe. He works for Saatchi's, you know. Advertising executive. Very nice young man. Neil. And such good manners! That's so rare these days, don't you find? He couldn't make it here today unfortunately. He's playing golf in Buckinghamshire. Have you met my Emma? Beautiful girl. We're so proud of her.'

Unbeknown to Valerie, darling Emma had long since escaped to Rivington Hill Park with Mark's friend Flynn and a litre of Strongbow and was probably, at that very point, being enthusiastically penetrated up against a tree.

I managed a weak smile before vomiting onto a patch of geraniums.

'That's right sweetheart, get it out of your system. Cigarette?' Valerie offered me a Silk Cut, which I declined with a wave of my hand. Valerie shrugged, lit up one for herself and continued rambling. 'Well, they've made it this far, I suppose,' she sighed, presumably referring to the party hosts. 'Twenty-five years. It's a long time. Not all plain sailing though, I'm sure. They'll be the first to tell you that much. Me and Tony will be celebrating our silver next year too. Course, we had a proper church wedding. Mum and Dad were so disappointed that Bev insisted on one of those silly little civil ceremonies. If you're gonna do it, you may as well do it right, understand what I'm saying sweetheart?'

I nodded vigorously and vomited again.

'You're a friend of Mark's, I suppose?'

Again I nodded. My legs had turned to jelly. I held onto the fence for support and took a few deep breaths.

'Not his girlfriend, are you?'

I shook my head and closed my eyes, willing this droning bore of a woman to disappear and leave me alone.

'He's a strange one, isn't he? Such a moody boy. But handsome, yes, there's no denying it. Billy too. I hear Billy's got a new job at the Post Office. He's a nice boy.'

She was impervious to the fact that Billy was sprawled just a few feet away from us on the patio, while his best mate emptied the contents of the laundry basket onto him from the window above. Valerie continued, blowing out smoke rings and gazing blankly into space. 'I don't know, Maybe Mark is just going through a weird phase. I suppose you know more about that than I do. Shame they gave up on school, the pair of them. But still, I don't suppose everyone's cut out for ... that kind of thing ...' She paused, sucking hard on her cigarette, and I hoped that the ordeal was now over and Valerie had finally run out of gas.

It wasn't, and she hadn't.

'It's like, take Tony's brother John,' she went on relentlessly, 'yes he's a good example, he was never into all that. They thought he had learning difficulties at first . . . *special needs* they call it now, don't they? But no, he wasn't *thick* or anything, no, God bless him, he just had no interest in school. He was bullied though, he was always a bit on the chubby side you see, and I think he found it hard to make friends. Anyway, you'll never guess how he ended up! At thirty years old he had a successful restaurant business in Dorset, and he had worked hard to build up that business, believe me, he really gave it his all. But in 1986, for some reason, he decided to throw it all in for a whole new life and off he went and opened up a nudist colony in the Algarve with his wife Gloria. It's the truth, as God is my witness. Unbelievable, isn't it? We all thought he was mad, of course, but he seems happy enough. And they've settled there now, with their kiddies and all. Having a whale of a time, it would seem. Hmm. Just goes to show.'

I was tempted to say, *Goes to show what? Flunk school and a nudist colony in a beautiful part of southern Europe can be all yours?*

Just in time I was saved by Ned, who wasn't keen on parties and, like me, had already tired of making idle chitchat with people he hardly knew. He stepped out of the back door, swerving around a now unconscious Tamworth, and ambled to the end of the garden with a pained look on his face.

'Here y'go, before you kill off any more of me geraniums,' he said, handing me a glass of water.

'Alright Dad,' Valerie mumbled. 'Was just having a nice little chat with Caroline here. It is Caroline, isn't it? That is your name?'

I confirmed that it was, silently contemplating the tempting possibility of aiming my next vomit splurge at Valerie's shoes.

'They're on the wacky baccy in there now, would you believe,' Ned told them. 'Bev and Sean and those two from next door. It's like a bloody Amsterdam coffee shop up in that bedroom, I tell you. Happy as sandboys they are, puffin' away like nobody's business.'

Valerie made a disapproving noise. 'Some people never grow up,' she remarked.

'Your Tony's in there too, love,' Ned was quick to point out. 'He's really coming out of his shell. I suppose the absinthe helped loosen him up a bit, too. Last I saw, he was doing his impersonation of Kenneth Williams with a soap dish balanced on his head.'

Valerie looked horrified, then incredulous. She finished her cigarette then threw the butt on the grass and stamped on it. 'I need another drink,' she snapped, turning on her heel and disappearing back into the house.

Ned turned to me and raised an eyebrow. 'I bet you thought you were going to die of boredom,' he said. 'Our Val does have a tendency to . . . go on a bit.'

'She's harmless enough.'

'Are you kidding? She don't know when to stop. Yap, yap, yap, on and on. Her phone bills are through the roof. And boring? Good Lord, you don't know the meaning of boring until you've had a conversation with my Val. And she talks about soap characters as if they're real people.'

'We hadn't got on to the subject of *EastEnders* and *Corrie*, thank God.'

'Be grateful for small mercies, my love.'

I drank the water and gave the glass back to Ned. 'I feel rough,' I muttered. 'I think I need to lie down.'

Ned patted me on the head. 'That home-brew was a bit much, wasn't it?'

'It certainly did the job.' I managed a smile. 'Is Mark still in his room?'

'What do you think?'

'I'll get him down.'

'Good luck.'

'I want his bed anyway.'

Ned chuckled. 'You're a brave little lady.'

Mark immersed himself in badly paid manual work and successive late nights, while I exhausted myself with A-levels and a weekend job in Woolworths. After his eighteenth birthday, when he assumed things would start getting better, things got worse for Mark. He was too idle to hold down a job for very long, and too greedy and proud to accept that he would have to start on a low wage in a menial role. He continued to live at home, rent-free, but dreamed of some day owning his own bachelor pad, replete with the latest technology and an oriental live-in maid to see to all his laundry, cleaning and miscellaneous needs. For as long as he continued living with his parents and earning £3.76 per hour (or seventy pounds a fortnight while he signed on), he reluctantly came to accept that nothing short of a lottery win would actualise his dream. The frustration was hard for him to bear. To console himself, he spent most of his spare time cavorting with friends. He passed his driving test and inherited the old family car, and this at least gave him an element of freedom; an invaluable asset to any young adult who feels trapped and resentful and anguished. So every now and then, on his own or with a friend or two, he would drive his car somewhere, anywhere, escaping from reality by whatever means possible with exquisite little snatches of imagined freedom.

Sometimes it would just be the two of us; short escapades to the south coast or to Southend or Harwich. After a four-year period of being quite cool with each other, we gradually rekindled our friendship, and the tension eased. This was just as well because when the time came for me to go away to university we might otherwise have lost touch altogether, and that old spark may well have sputtered out completely.

I had little time for boyfriends, although between two more hair-colour changes and several confidence crises, I did manage to squeeze in two relationships. Both had been relatively (perhaps mercifully) brief, and the 'L' word was certainly never mentioned. As much as I believed it would have been wonderful to have a steady boyfriend, particularly one who wasn't a complete arse, I witnessed the regular relationship highs and lows of my friends and that was enough to sway me towards choosing a simple single life.

Perhaps more accurately, the single life chose me. It suited me. I wasn't in love with Mark any more – not in the sense that I couldn't bear to think of life without him – but even so, I was still aware of that unambiguous pull, that irrepressible glow of recognition and longing, every time I saw him. The warm affection was now dampened by an equally uncontrollable sense of scorn. His mother still despaired of him; more now than ever.

'Even when he actually gets off his lazy arse and finds himself a job, he calls in sick most days, ends up getting fired and mopes about the house watching daytime TV,' she wailed. 'He eats all the food and never does a thing around the house. He won't even *talk* to me, unless it's to moan about something. It drives me mad. In the evenings I don't see him at all, he never tells me where he's going, often he's gone for days on end, sometimes he even brings some slapper back with him . . . oh Caro, I don't mean to sound so awful but I really can't stand him at the moment.'

I sympathised. 'He's a twat,' I said, naturally meaning it in the kindest possible way. 'But all blokes are twats at that age, pretty much. Look, he's only just turned eighteen. By next year, once he gets used to this whole adulthood thing, he might start to accept some responsibility and find himself a good job, stick with it and move out.'

'Oh, do you think so?' Bev looked ecstatic at the very possibility. Then her smile faded. 'I don't think I can take it for another year,' she said glumly.

'It could even happen tomorrow. I really don't think Mark is the type to just . . . let himself fester for ever. He does have ambitions, you know.'

Bev chuckled drily. 'Pardon me for being a bit cynical about that, he wouldn't know ambition if it bit him on the arse.'

I smiled. 'I think he'll get his lucky break soon.'

'Please don't give me false hope, I am a woman on the edge.'

'We'll just have to be patient with him.'

'Fine for you to say, you don't have to live with him. Now . . . tea . . . or wine?'

'Wine, please.'

'Red or white?'

'How about both?'

Bev smiled, for the first time that day, and rummaged in a drawer for the corkscrew.

Mark wasn't a drug addict, as his mum secretly feared, but he was thrill-chasing on a compulsive basis, and like most thrill-addicted young people, cared very little about the consequences of his actions. Perhaps it would be fair to say he was an adrenalin junkie. His favourite haunts were those frequented by drug dealers and promiscuous women – he felt at home in most nightclubs in and around the local area, with the odd illegal rave thrown in every so often.

He met his first 'serious' girlfriend on the last leg of a pub crawl/club trawl in Romford. An honorary geezer or 'token girl' among boorish males, I was fortunate and foolish enough to join them on this particular escapade. My participation in the revelry was not unprecedented but it was by no means commonplace. I took my chances when

I could, even if I didn't feel like it, because invitations to Mark's outings were few and far between.

Shortly after Kermit and Flynn had done their typical disappearing act, within minutes of us first arriving, Mark was on his third beer and ready to score. I was on my second glass of wine and ready for bed.

The women, or girls, who could often be found in this type of establishment were invariably in a state referred to by Mark and his mates as 'up for it'. A girl caught Mark's eye from twenty yards away, and she was no exception. He immediately thought she was the most beautiful woman he had ever seen.

He pointed her out to Tamworth and me, asking us if we had ever seen such a 'fine specimen' of a bird. Tamworth said, 'Not bad at all mate,' and I neither agreed nor demurred, merely holding his beer for him as he braced himself for the attack.

The clubbing females tended to wear little more than hair lacquer, lipstick, masses of cheap gold jewellery and a scowl. This particular girl was leaning against the DJ booth, chatting to two guys who were chatting back at her, or more accurately at her overcrowded bustier. Her skin looked tanned and her teeth looked impossibly white under the UV lights. A sheen of light perspiration, visible even from a distance, shone on her face and chest. And oh what a face. And what a chest. I took a seat by the dance floor and watched bitterly as she bewitched with her bosoms and perfect symmetry, wondering if she was as much of a tart as she appeared to be.

Tamworth put his arm around me and assured me, in his own words, that she almost certainly was. 'The sort of girl you wouldn't want to take home to your mother,' he whispered. 'Mark's on a safe bet there.' He noticed my glass was empty. 'Want another?'

I didn't, but I said yes anyway. Drinking gave me something to do to fill the time, and drunkenness made that time pass by more quickly.

When it came to chat-up lines, with this lot there were no limits and no boundaries of cheesiness, bawdiness, tastelessness or shamelessness. If the boys got knocked back with one line, they just went away and tried it on someone else. Or if they had a particularly strong attraction for the girl, they consulted their repertoire and tried another line. They never lost heart because they were confident of getting lucky eventually.

The safe 'n' standard: *Fancy a drink?* or *Fancy a dance?* obviously score no points for originality, but there's less chance of rejection or ridicule than a number of the riskier options, such as *Fancy a quick one?* or *Get your coat love, you've pulled.* Or, approaching criminal levels of brazenness, *This face leaves in five minutes, make sure you're on it*, which is only likely to work at the very end of the night when both parties are blind and paralytic. The one Flynn and Kermit favoured was *Nice shoes, fancy a fuck?* Surprisingly, they had received an almost hundred per cent success rate with that line. Flynn claimed it was because women took so much pride in their shoes.

'Never, ever underestimate a woman's vanity,' was his advice to the others. 'A bird's vanity knows no bounds. It's pretty much their weakness. Even the ugly ones. *Especially* the ugly ones. Use it to your advantage.'

The clubs were all the same, every Friday and Saturday night, the same rowdy groups amalgamating into one dense, sweaty, vibrating congregation, worshipping the DJ, filling the air with sodden pheromones, thick blue smoke, stale fragrance and acrid ethanol breath. After sufficient chemical intake, the quality of the club's music becomes irrelevant. However loud, however repetitive, it just becomes background noise, a rapid mix of beats to move about to. The typical dance technique of clubbers consists of a random repertoire of rigid, mechanical arm movements and uncoordinated leg twitching. If rhythm is achieved, more often than not it is quite by chance. Ecstasy and alcohol and sexual success were the primary eudemonic contingents to each and every clubber, all arbitrarily united by whatever communal sonic vibe the DJ was attempting, however ineptly, to enhance from his decks.

After polishing off his drink and accepting another from Tamworth when he returned from the bar, Mark finally summoned up sufficient courage to approach the Beautiful Girl. He tried to catch her eye, but she was looking elsewhere and seemed distracted. I observed from the sidelines as he sidled up to her until he was close enough to venture his chosen gambit of the evening, which was at least as honest as it was risible: 'You're the most beautiful girl I have ever seen.'

Of course, this *could* (theoretically) be a romantic assertion, given the right moment and the right context. Shouting it at somebody in skin-tight black leather trousers with a lovebite on her neck over the clamorous sound of DJ Judge Mental's megamix is probably not ideal. Nevertheless, she appeared to respond positively and after they had exchanged names (which was by no means a mandatory requirement in such situations), he offered her a dab of coke, a small wrap of which he had concealed in the pocket of his shirt 'in case of an emergency'. She told him she had already taken three pills and didn't want any more drugs. He bought her a drink and the next thing I knew they were kissing like crazy.

Ten minutes later they were in the back of a cab on the way to her place.

Not long after that I was in a cab back to mine, on my own.

'She was *filthy* mate, fuckin' 'ell, I've never seen anything like it.' Mark was chain-smoking excitedly as he related the previous evening's events to a wide-eyed Kermit, leaving out no embellishment or exaggeration. 'We got back to her place and she just lay down on the bed and took her knickers off, legs at quarter past nine, no messin'. It was like, *Do me this way! Now this way! Take me, take me! Fuck me, harder, harder! Flip me over, do my arsehole, deeper, more, more!* She knackered me. I shit you not. She was a right nympho. It was fantastic.'

'No way! You seein' her again?' Kermit was doubtless experiencing some perverse vicarious enjoyment from hearing about Mark's exploits, as his own Saturday night, by contrast, had consisted of copping off with someone else's bird, suffering the violent consequences from a somewhat irked boyfriend and finally passing out in a dish of chicken jalfrezi before being piled into a cab. I was experiencing no enjoyment at all as I had already been subjected to the full gruesome saga earlier that day when I made the mistake of calling Mark to check he had got home all right.

We were sitting at the bar in a rowdy pub in Dagenham, and I was the only one making a conscious effort to appear inconspicuous. It was late afternoon, but I had lost all track of time and the boys as ever had lost all track of everything. Kermit was wearing sunglasses to conceal his black eyes and blot out the daylight, and Mark was wearing a T-shirt with the pithy caption 'Real men eat pussy'. Kermit's hangover and cracked ribs were causing him some discomfort, so he was on the Jack Daniel's. Mark had given the last of his speed to Tamworth and was feeling dehydrated so he drank water and smoked his way steadily through a pack of twenty Camel Lights. I had ordered a sandwich from the bar and a pint of Diet Coke, but consumption of both was proving a slow and arduous process, punctuated at intervals by decidedly unfeminine belches and waves of nausea.

'What the fuck do you think?' Mark said, lighting up another. He studied Kermit critically for a moment. 'Take those stupid bloody glasses off, Kerm, you look like a prick.'

'I'm in pain,' Kermit grumbled. 'Everything hurts.' He touched his chest and winced. 'Reckon I should maybe get checked out down the

’ospital, me ribs are giving me gyp. That savage arsehole really laid into me, y’know. Built like a brick shithouse an’ all.’

‘Mate, I know about pain,’ Mark mumbled, fingering the recent knife wound underneath the collar of his T-shirt, which was still tender to touch even after two months. That was a night I had mercifully missed out on. Mark overdid the mixing and ended up getting seven shades of shit beaten out of him by an Arsenal fan with a flickknife. ‘But what don’t kill you only makes you stronger,’ he added.

Kermit cast him a contemptuous look. ‘You fuckin’ what?’

Mark shrugged. ‘Somethin’ me mum said once,’ he muttered, dismissing it.

Kermit took Mark’s last cigarette. ‘What’s ’appened to Tam? He’s been in the bogs for ages now.’

Mark shrugged again. ‘You know what he’s like. He takes half a day to lay a fuckin’ cable. It’s like some kind of bloody ritual to him.’

‘Nice, guys. Really pleasant. Some of us are trying to eat, you know,’ I complained, indicating my half-munched gammon ham and mustard pub sandwich.

As if on cue, Tamworth appeared from the toilets, wired up and wild-eyed. The sight of him did little to restore my appetite. He stumbled towards us and screamed, quite unashamedly, ‘Shit guys! You’re not gonna believe this! My fuckin’ dick has disappeared!’

Kermit took a sip of his JD and placed a conciliatory hand on Tamworth’s shoulder.

‘Mate,’ he said. ‘You’re hysterical. What are you on?’

Mark shook his head and laughed under his breath, and I was painfully aware that we were receiving some unwanted attention from a group of bemused young women at the other end of the bar. I instinctively affected my ‘I’m not with them’ demeanour.

‘My dick!’ Tamworth exclaimed, quite without self-awareness. ‘It’s gone!’

Kermit turned to Mark with some concern. ‘You didn’t give him *all* that speed I sold you on Friday night, did you?’

Mark signalled to the barman for another drink. ‘Not all of it,’ he said. ‘About half.’

Kermit lowered his voice. ‘Fuck me, Mark, you know what Tam is like with speed. He’s a wanker with Class As. He takes Es like they’re fuckin’ Smarties or somethin’.’

Tamworth was becoming increasingly incomprehensible. ‘You think I’m *joking*?’ he spluttered. ‘Well OK, yeah, I’m pretty wired but I’ve been worse than this before and I'm telling you, I just went for a jimmy and when I looked for my cock . . . oi, are you listening?'

Mark and Kermit nodded solemnly, trying not to laugh.

'Caz?' He looked to me for support but I was quite incapable of offering more than a bemused grimace, and perhaps a nibble of my sandwich.

Tamworth was in no mood for sandwiches. On he went, undeterred by the silence that had now fallen and the appalled looks he was receiving. '. . . I mean it hadn't just shrunk or whatever, y'know, it's not like it was just small or tiny or anything, it just *wasn't there.* Do you understand what I'm saying? There's nothing there at all. Nothing, man.'

Mark was beginning to see that his friend was in some genuine distress. He ordered four beers and told Tamworth to stop panicking. This only made Tamworth even more agitated.

'Panicking? Fuck's sake Mark, I've lost my cunting nob, wouldn't you be in a slight state of frickin' panic?'

Mark turned to Kermit. 'Sort him out, will you?'

Kermit was indignant. 'What do you want me to do about it?' he demanded. 'I'm not going into the kazi with him to help him locate his dick. No way.' He noted the torment on Tamworth's face and relented, pulling up a bar stool. 'C'mon, mate,' he said soothingly, now feeling a little sympathy for his friend's dilemma, 'sit down and let Mark tell you about last night. He got laid, you know. Some bird called Kylie.'

'Oh yeah, just what I need to hear about right now,' Tamworth grumbled.

'Come on mate,' Mark said, thrusting a beer bottle into his hand, 'just get pissed and chill out. Forget about it. Your dick might even make a guest appearance later on. Just wait for the come-down. Everything's gonna be OK. OK? Oi Caz, tell him, will yer.'

Dutifully, I intoned, 'Everything's gonna be OK Simon, don't you worry.' (Mark maintained that those words always seemed so much more convincing when they came from a woman.)

At length, Tamworth calmed down and the boys began loudly plotting their next social extravaganza, leaving me quietly to contemplate the remnants of my sandwich and dodge the sympathetic gazes of every other woman in the pub.

The glimpses I was occasionally permitted into Mark's weird little world made me wonder if I was missing out on something by opting for a more temperate, routine-driven existence. But Mark's lifestyle, as intriguing as it may have appeared to a relatively sedate outsider such as myself, really wasn't as exciting as he would have liked people to think. Passing out on floors, tussling with savage strangers with the minimum of provocation and maximum of bodily damage, waking up with hangovers in unfamiliar beds and wishing himself dead. Sprawling over urinals every night, forehead pressed against moist concrete, last year's catchiest singles looping inside his brain as he waits for piss to happen. Always just waiting for something to happen, anything. Acting on unnatural impulses to ease the boredom of waiting, lumbering toward the next inevitable error of judgement. Dirty grains of cocaine smudged onto a toilet cistern, paying for any old shit in powder or pill form from people who can't be trusted, days on end without sleep or food.

Dying was the new living.

Still, as a stark alternative to my own lifestyle, it retained a strange and enduring appeal.

When I was offered a place at Leeds University to study Politics and Modern World History, I had no idea how quickly the next three years of my life would pass. Rebecca also applied for Leeds, although on the advice of her father she opted for a law degree. My A-level results came through in August 1993, a fortnight after my eighteenth birthday. Two A's, two B's. So my place at Leeds was confirmed and the dream of starting a new life away from the squalor of Rivington Hill, away from the asphyxiating insularity of St Jude's, was now becoming a reality, well within my reach.

On results day, my mum wept, hugged and kissed me, and told me that she was extremely proud and would miss me very much. I was shocked to tears myself by the gesture, unprecedented and entirely unexpected. Mum had previously taken very little interest in my educational pursuits, dismissing exams as 'a waste of time', and the attainment of a university degree as 'a load of bloody old bollocks'.

'I know we've not always exactly got on,' she said, still hugging me close to her bony body. 'But all I can say is this . . .' She pulled away and I looked into those tired, tearful eyes and felt consumed by guilt and sadness.

'. . . Go for it,' she went on, 'just go for it, Caz, and do what you want to do and be a success. Be a better person than your mum ever was.'

Mum and Ray had divorced in early 1992. Perhaps wisely, Mum had not since been seriously involved with anyone else and was now on anti-depressants, which did not really go well with her alcohol habit. On the days when the booze didn't render her incapable or incapacitated, much of her time was taken up with looking after her three youngest daughters. Teri had just started school, Shaz was in the full swing of puberty and naturally putting everyone through merry hell, while Jo had an attitude problem that was almost as savage, and getting worse by the day. Kev was on remand, and not for the first time. Mum hadn't heard from Julie or seen her only known grandchild since 1990, when Julie shacked up with someone else on the other side of London. She had written a couple of times, enclosing a recent photo of Chelsea with the second letter, but not mentioning a forwarding address or even a contact number. The photo was put into a silver-plated frame and positioned on Mum's bedside table, and we can only assume or hope that Chelsea is as happy now as she looked at the moment that photo was taken.

Mark's reaction to my departure for university had been equally surprising. The day before I was due to leave, I packed my bags and went straight round to the Croziers. Bev, Sean and Ned had in turn wished me luck, plying me with hugs and kisses and hearty pats on the back and cups of tea and long-overdue advice relating to boys and alcohol. Mark came down from his room just as we were all initiating a game of Trivial Pursuit. He was spruced up and ready for a night on the town, reeking of musky aftershave and hair gel, stylishly primed in Ben Sherman and Calvin Klein and Levi Strauss – all set to subject his body to another barrage of physical and chemical excess. He stood in the doorway looking at me for a long time, not moving.

Bev made an impatient noise. 'For crying out loud, Mark, don't just stand there, come and give the girl a hug! She's going up north tomorrow, so you won't see her again for a while.'

I diverted the subject, feeling uncomfortable under his brooding scrutiny. 'Where you going tonight, Mark?' I asked him. 'Anywhere nice?' I returned his stare, trying to keep my voice casual and calm.

Mark didn't say anything. His eyes were wide and wild and suspiciously animated. I safely assumed he was on drugs. He shifted his gaze and looked at his mother.

'Can I borrow some money?'

Sean answered for his wife, emphasising his response by banging his fists on the table and making the Trivial Pursuit pieces bounce off the board. 'You cheeky little bastard, how many times do we have to say *no* before you understand? What, do you think we're made of money?'

Mark now gazed at his father, his expression insolent and scornful. 'I didn't ask you.'

Bev and I exchanged glances. Sean was visibly fuming but Ned patted him on the shoulder as if to restrain him, telling him to calm down. There was a silence.

'Say goodbye to Caroline, Mark,' Bev said eventually, as if talking to a tiresome young child.

Mark hesitated. Ned reached into his back pocket, sighing wearily, and pulled out a tenner from his wallet. 'Here you go, son. I want payin' back, mind.'

Sean shot his father-in-law a frosty look, but didn't intervene when Mark took the money. He would store his anger for the almighty pent-up explosion that was destined to occur at some point between father and son on the not-too-distant horizon. I had little doubt that it would not be pretty.

'Cheers, pops,' Mark said, folding the note and concealing it in his back pocket. Then he turned to me. 'Enjoy yourself, yeah? Have a good one.'

I felt my heart sink. I had expected, or at least hoped for, just a little bit more *emotion* from my oldest friend. Some display of *feeling*, no matter how brief or perfunctory.

But Mark was acting like he couldn't have cared less. Well, this *was* what Mark was all about, I supposed. Indifference had always been his middle name.

'Thanks,' I croaked. 'You too.'

What Mark did next surprised everybody. Shocked would be a better word. He threw his arms around me, kissed me on the lips for just a tiny split-second longer than a platonic relationship might deem appropriate, and said, 'Take care of yourself, mate. I'm gonna miss you.'

Then, as instantly as the embrace had been initiated, he drew away from me, grabbed his jacket from the back of the chair and left, slamming the front door behind him without another word.

Bev, Sean and Ned and I were all left in stunned silence. Giddy with the scent he had left lingering in the air, I realised then that love may well fade and mutate over time, but it never really dies, and at once I felt like bursting into tears.

8

The Earnestness of Being Important

'Only in our dreams are we free. The rest of the time we need wages.'
Terry Pratchett, *Wyrd Sisters*

Time whipped by while I was at university, accelerated by brand-new delights and discoveries that made days and nights blend into one another. I couldn't remember ever feeling so happy, and the poverty situation naturally never bothered me. Free overdraft, cheap booze, an interesting mix of new people from all walks of life, a library crammed with books about more or less everything, a cosmopolitan new city to explore, great social events, no obligations. I was in my element. This is the time during which my memory starts to become a bit of a blur; a merciful haze perhaps. Mark told me that the late eighties through to much of the early nineties was a complete blank to him and he maintained that he couldn't be sure of where he went, how he got there, what he did, who he did it with and why. Now, having been comparatively temperate in terms of lifestyle, I was beginning to subscribe to a similar routine of interminable oblivion, and loving every minute of it.

I feel that this episodic amnesia is a blessing. Certainly the few memories I can retrieve from this period are largely inane, like lurid freeze-frames from a terrible tragi-comedy, the kind of subliminal recollections that make me cringe with remorse even to this day, no matter how much alcohol had been involved at the time and no matter how many years have since passed. But as Mark always said, that's what being young is all about. Make the most of it while you can.

When Mark called me, out of the blue, late on a Thursday night towards the end of April 1994, I hardly recognised his voice. For the whole time I had known him, he had never once instigated a phone call, and I therefore didn't have much trouble deducing immediately that he had a pretty important reason for doing so on this occasion.

Mark was not big on emotions, but I could tell at once that he was choked up and I braced myself for the worst.

'Mark? Are you OK?' I prompted him gently, after a terse exchange of salutations.

He paused; the slight crackle of interference down the phone line was deafening. 'I thought you might like to know . . .' he trailed off, and I remained silent, waiting anxiously for him to come out with it.

'My Grandad died this morning.'

He let out a little sob, disguising it as a cough. 'Erm . . . yeah. He's dead,' he went on, trying to sound composed. 'Thought you might want to know.' He cleared his throat and steadied his voice. 'The . . . er . . . funeral is next Tuesday. Mum says she'd like you to be there if you can.'

I was too shocked and distressed to respond at first. I merely listened to Mark battling against tears as he continued talking. 'And . . . well, er . . . I reckon it would be good if you could make it, too. Grandad would have . . .'

At this point he lost control, and for the first time, I heard Mark properly weep – big, hearty, wet sobs. It was more than enough to set me off. Mark never referred to Ned as 'Grandad', it had always been 'pops', 'old timer' and sometimes more offensive terms of endearment. Through my own tears, I managed to stutter, 'I am so sorry, Mark . . . really I am. I don't know what to say. Was it . . . sudden?'

Mark took a few seconds to calm down, and didn't speak until he felt confident that he wasn't going to lapse into maudlin sentimentality again. I wanted to hug him. I was absolutely overwhelmed by the urge to be with him, to comfort him. My heart went out to him. I thought it was tragic that Mark had never really let his Grandad know how much he cared about him. But Mark was like that – emotionally distant as best, emotionally frigid at worst. He closed himself off, reluctant to let anyone get inside to know the real person. It infuriated me, but equally it fascinated me.

Old and recent memories of Ned came flooding back to me, jumbled up, all of them happy, but now, in light of this shattering news, so desperately sad and poignant. I wiped my eyes with the back of my hand. 'He will be greatly missed,' I sniffed. 'He was a good man.'

'Yeah,' Mark mumbled. 'The best.' He paused again, then asked, 'So will you come down for the funeral then?'

'Oh Mark, of course I will.'

'Thanks. It would mean a lot. He . . . died in his sleep. Reckon it was prob'ly quite peaceful. Best way to go really, I s'pose.' I heard him take a deep breath. 'And he was a very old man. Good innings and all that.'

'Yeah,' I sobbed. 'That's what he'd have said. H-how's your mum bearing up?'

'Not so good.'

'I'll come down tomorrow and stay until Wednesday,' I said. 'It's reading week next week anyway.'

'OK. Cool. Sorry to upset you Caz. I know you've prob'ly got other things on your mind . . .'

'No, I'm really glad you called . . .' I stopped myself from saying 'I miss you', which was not strictly true anyway as I had been fortunate enough to have other things on my mind of late, and instead I whispered, 'I am so sorry.' Because that is the thing to say to a grieving friend when you can't think of anything else. Because I really *was* sorry.

'Yeah,' he said, 'Yeah. Me too. See you tomorrow then, mate.'

'See ya.' I felt weak and giddy as I put down the phone, and after going back to my room and sitting on my bed to stare at the wall in silence for a few moments, I let the tears pour down my face.

So I finally got the chance to view the interior of Rivington Hill funeral parlour, that eerie, quaint little place I had puzzled over as a child. Less than twenty-four hours after Mark's phone call I met Bev there and we were led through a set of heavy red velour curtains into a tiny, dim room at the back by a stooping, saggy-eyed man who looked simultaneously sympathetic and suicidal. We stood at opposite sides of Ned's coffin bawling our eyes out, surrounded by abundant bunches of lilies and irises, Ned's favourite flowers.

The service was held at St Luke's, and Father McKinley, who had always considered Ned a close friend and 'a fine gentleman with a good heart and an eye for the best bargains', gave a passionate and moving speech. An assortment of Ned's drinking buddies from the Barley Mow assembled themselves on the back pew, Tom Thurston being the most vociferous and conspicuous of the mourners, blowing his nose with stentorian force at regular intervals and hacking sporadically into a handkerchief.

Such was Father McKinley's respect and affection for Ned, he organised a select gathering of close friends and family at his own home when the service was over, which at least took some of the strain off Bev. Over a smorgasbord of egg-and-cress sandwiches, pickled onions, cold quiche and potato salad, prepared and presented by a corpulent and rosy Mrs McKinley, I mingled with Rivington Hill's distinguished elders. Bev was, naturally, utterly devastated. For the entire day she could only bring herself to exchange the briefest and most perfunctory of pleasantries with the many attendees, and I observed a steady decline in her demeanour, as she became inconsolable by the end of the evening. Having stuffed myself on buffet sundries and exhausted my capacity to give and receive commiserations, I was about to slope off home when I suddenly heard a shrill female voice behind me.

'Hello, remember me?'

I spun round and Bev's sister, Mark's Aunty Val, flung herself at me, kissing me on both cheeks and muttering about how terribly sad it all was.

'Poor old Dad, you always think your parents are immortal, don't you? Invincible. It's knocked me for six, this has, really it has.' She expectorated noisily into a bedraggled tissue and regarded me contemplatively. There was an uneasy pause. 'It's Claire, isn't it?'

'Caroline.'

'Oh yes, of course, Caroline, I do apologise. Well, it's a shame we have to meet again under such . . . unfortunate circumstances, but . . .' She trailed off, snatching a glass of wine from the tray as Father McKinley passed by with his drinks selection.

'Your dad was a lovely man, I'm gonna really miss him,' I said. I glanced over at Bev, who was slouched on an armchair in the corner staring blankly into space, her eyes red and swollen from crying. 'Bev has taken it badly. I just wish there was something I could do.'

'Well, they were very close,' Val sighed. 'Bev always was a Daddy's girl.'

This emotive phrase choked me up, and I took a sip of my wine to wash down the sudden surge of sadness.

'You're at university now, are you?'

'Yes.'

'Enjoying it?'

'Yes.'

'I took a deep breath, primed for more prattle about darling daughter Emma and financial-director husband Tony. Sure enough, it came.

'My Emma's in her third year now. She really wanted to come today but what with being in the middle of her course – it's *very* intensive you know – and she's only just started a new job, just part-time of course, but you know what it's like. She felt a bit, well, *awkward* about asking for time off so soon . . .'

I didn't know what it was like. 'Ned was her *grandfather*,' I bristled.

'Yes, of course, and naturally she's *very* upset . . .'

I swallowed my vitriol with another slug of wine and scanned the room over Val's shoulder.

She sensibly swerved the topic back round. 'So what are you studying then?'

'Politics and History.'

'Is that . . . interesting?'

'Yeah, it's OK.'

'Tony studied Economics and Politics at Southampton, long time ago now of course. Best years of his life he says. Well they all say that, don't they?' Her expression shifted and she began tapping her fingernails against her glass. 'The best years of your life . . .' She forced a smile. 'Well,' she chirped, 'it's good to hear you're keeping well, anyway.'

'Keeping well' was not quite the truth – alcohol poisoning and perpetual lethargy had become my trademark ailments of late.

'And that you're making something of yourself,' she went on, not detecting the pain that lurked behind my forced smile. 'I never went to university and that's something I will regret for the rest of my life. So just you make sure you make the most of your opportunities, won't you dear? We only get one stab at life so we just have to take our chances when we can. Emma's such a bright girl, she's going to be a doctor, you know – my daughter, a doctor! But really, I am so glad she is using her talents. So many people these days, they just don't use the brains they're born with, do they?'

She studied me a moment, rotating the glass in her hand. 'So what do you want to be then, Claire?'

A loaded question indeed. I ignored the misnomer. 'I'm not really sure yet. Maybe a teacher, eventually. I'd like to travel first.'

I knew as soon as I'd uttered the word 'travel' that I would be inundated with tales of darling Emma's intrepid gap-year expeditions. Sure enough, five minutes later, Val was winding down and I was well and truly wound up.

'Well, like I said,' she said, 'be sure to make the most of your opportunities. Hard work always pays off in the end.'

How many times had I heard that old chestnut? 'Yes, well, I certainly hope so,' I said. And, with that, I excused myself and sidled away, blissfully unaware of what a mixed bag of 'opportunities' the future held for me.

This is how it goes: you get born, you get educated, you get uneducated, you get a job, you get fucked over, you retire, you go senile, you die.

The first is relatively easy of course, and assuming you're lucky enough to be born into a civilised society in a developed part of the world, so is the second. It's all right to be stupid if your genes have made you that way, but there's no excuse for ignorance. Just look around you! There's new knowledge to be learned all over the place, freely available, just waiting to be picked up, absorbed, inserted into the brain, stuffed deep into those vacant cerebral crevices. Unlearning stuff is also quite easy – that's what university is for. You conveniently forget that all you are is just one more person in a vast and seething ocean of hopeful jobseekers at the end of it. Deluded into believing your 'graduate' status will set you apart from the rest of the potential workforce, it is easy to overlook the fact that while you were screwing and spewing your way towards a degree in something or other, thousands of your contemporaries were doing this weird thing called *work*. I suffered from this delusion after university. I assumed every self-respecting and discerning employer would be beating a direct route to my door, sniffing out my talent with bloodhound determination and offering me bumper cash incentives to join their workforce. After three years of sweeping my brain clear of everything worthwhile I had learned in my GCSEs and A-levels and refilling it with pissed-up musings and regurgitated garbage about modern world history and politics, I truly and firmly believed that I was fully equipped for gainful employment. I was *Caroline Shaw BA (Hons)*, and I was going to get the job of my dreams and pay my student debts off and – eventually – buy my own house and lovingly equip it with all the latest state-of-the-art fixtures and fittings, perhaps even a couple of cats.

Oh yes.

Oh no.

It was only after university, after the illusion of a carefree youth was irretrievably shattered and the grim truth was staring me full in the face, that I finally realised: I now have no excuses. I am on my own and there is nowhere to hide and nobody else to blame. I was in the real world now. A world that I could no longer view through the bottom of an empty wine glass.

The childhood that I had willed to pass so quickly when I was living it had now all but passed, too damn quickly. The future I had dreamed of as a girl – the adult Caroline with her good job, nice home, healthy bank account, fit and healthy physique, trustworthy network of close friends, perhaps even an attentive Adonis of a boyfriend – was now an adulthood so far removed from the dream that I really did not know where to begin in order to actualise it. I should start with a job, perhaps – always a good place to start. A good job. That's all I needed, and then maybe the other facets of my perfect adult life will follow. Yes, it would all fall into place with just that little bit of effort to get me started.

Part-time paper-girl for Sanjay's newsagency, burger-flipper at Merry Munchers, sales assistant at Woolies, waitress at Spud-U-Like, checkout girl at Tesco . . . no pathetic little jobs for me any more, this was the real world and I needed a real job. And I was going to get one.

As far as I was concerned, I could do anything. I had the world at my feet. I could be anyone I wanted to be, with my mounted certificate and my mortarboard snapshot and my clever old brain veritably bursting with knowledge and initiative. Barrister? Of course! Journalist? Naturally! Teacher? Yes, I could just about teach anything to anyone; that conviction had remained with me ever since I was a little girl. Editor for big glossy magazine? Goodness, yes, I was full of ideas and had a way with words that came as naturally as breathing. Advertising genius? It was what I was born for, surely! City high-flier? That was me, in a nutshell. I even had computer literacy now! I knew what Microsoft was all about; I knew all about the new technology thingies. I could find my way around a keyboard and navigate the Internet no problem. My typing speed was knocking on for fifty words a minute and if I got enough time in between job-hunting, I had every intention of learning at least two other European languages and reading up about management skills. I was going to make it big. There was no stopping me!

Except one thing.

Reality.

Weeks and then months after graduation, I was still flicking through the 'situations vacant' pages of local papers, still buying the *Guardian* every other day, scouring the graduate section for jobs that paid the 'upwards of £15,000' I had been assured I was now worth. Nothing tickled my fancy. Absolutely nothing appealed to me. And I didn't seem to be a suitable candidate for any of the better-paid jobs anyway, as most of them stipulated 'experience preferred and must have own car', or 'European languages and a secretarial qualification a bonus', or 'a bulging book of contacts [?!], a proven track record, NCTJ qualification or equivalent, and demonstrable subbing skills essential'.

Alas, not even the jobs that paid substantially *less* than fifteen grand (and therefore charitably stated 'no experience necessary as full training will be given') quite fitted the bill, as they would usually finish off with some audacious proviso. For example: 'Training will be given to the right candidate but he/she must have full clean driving licence, lots of enthusiasm and a willingness to "muck in", [oh and, by-the-by] a first-class Maths or Statistics degree and a second language, preferably Russian.'

Most advertised jobs required at least two years' experience (a somewhat nebulous expression as they rarely stated what the experience was supposed to be *in*), and how was I going to get that when I'd been at university for the past three? My overdraft was creaking away, exhausted to the last penny, my graduate loan was fast drying up, and I certainly couldn't hope to live for much longer off my family's dwindling benefits or Mark's mother's patience and generosity. I was becoming increasingly bored and impatient and disheartened, stuck in a shitty little town I had promised myself I would have abandoned long ago, with no means of escaping. In desperation, I looked through the 'situations vacant' section of the local paper. I wasn't even going to rule out shop work or waitressing, if that's what it came to. I was certainly in no position to be picky.

I started signing on. I went to the local job centre every day. I resorted to having to beg for the very worst kind of jobs rather than being selectively plucked for the best.

Was envelope-stuffing, box-packing, shelf-stacking, photo-copying, errand-running and data entry the kind of thing I was looking for, the gap-toothed lady behind the desk with the shocking pink lipstick wanted to know.

I referred her to my CV once again.

'No, as I was saying,' I explained patiently, 'I have nine GCSEs, I have four A-levels, all A and B grades. I have a degree in *modern world history* and *politics*, yeah? See this bit of my CV, the bit that says, "education"? I didn't go through all that just for fun, you know.'

This was partly true. Some of it hadn't been much fun at all. The lady sighed, as if I was wasting her time.

'Look, you have no job and you need money, right?' She raised a ragged eyebrow and regarded me analytically. Two of the middle buttons of her orange blouse strained as she pushed out her pneumatic chest, sitting back in her chair and glaring at me as if I had just crawled out from under a rock.

'Yes,' I conceded. I studied the badge pinned to her breast pocket: the name etched onto it was 'Pauline'. Beneath the badge was a ketchup stain. Two biros, both blue, were sticking out of the pocket. One of them had leaked slightly. 'Yes, I have no job and I do need money. Hence I am here.'

'Then why so picky? Eh? Do you think these jobs are *beneath* you?' Her lip curled derisively at the very thought that I could be so brazenly arrogant. 'Most of the people I see in here week after week would jump at the chance.'

I couldn't imagine anyone from the Rivington Hill dole queue jumping at the chance of giving up their seventy-pound fortnightly cheque in exchange for two quid an hour sticking junk mail fliers into peel-and-seal envelopes all day.

I said nothing.

Pauline had a weird accent, it was almost as if she was choking on something. It was the faint Mancunian lilt of someone whose tongue was too big for their mouth. I was beginning to hate her quite vehemently.

'I mean, this one . . . "data-entry clerk", that's a fine job to start off with,' she said. 'You'll be using all that computer knowledge an' all.'

There was a wedding picture on her desk. Somewhere out there was a man who had voluntarily joined with this woman in holy matrimony. This woman had been chosen – voluntarily *elected* by someone – as their one of twenty thousand, their perfect partner for life.

'With respect, Pauline, I was hoping for something a little more challenging,' I said.

'Ooh, challenging, eh?' she snorted and shook her head. 'I like that. *Challenging.*'

'Is it too much to ask?' I simpered, ignoring the condescension.

'Well, hold on a minute and I'll just see what I can do.' The curved, acid-orange painted talons on the end of her sausage-like fingers pecked out a number on her desk phone with vicious efficiency as she whistled through her teeth. After a couple of rings, a man's voice answered and Pauline unclipped her left earring, picked up the receiver and put on a ridiculous voice. 'Good day to you, Bernard [giggle], how's the daily grind going up your end?'

I wondered if this was some strange sexual code, but I decided to stay well out of it. I picked at a frayed bit on my cardigan sleeve and let my mind go blank.

'I have a young lady here,' I heard Pauline drawl after subjecting the poor man to a nauseating but mercifully brief flirtation, 'and she's possibly interested in that data-entry job you placed with us last week . . .'

Now, understand this – as I was yet to meet a proper, professionally trained City recruitment consultant, Pauline appeared to me to represent the very pinnacle of conniving vacuity and falseness. Surely no human being could stoop any lower? *Interested?* How did she get 'interested' from 'not really what I'm looking for at all'? Why hadn't she listened to a word I had said?

'Yes, she's just graduated from Leicester University . . .'

'Leeds,' I muttered, as if it would make any difference – it was becoming increasingly obvious that nobody gave a shit about my degree, let alone where I got it from.

' . . . oh yes, I'm sure she won't mind that. Better than being on the dole for ever!'

This woman did not know when to stop. I had only been signing on for a month. It wasn't like I was bleeding the economy dry or anything. I seethed silently and refused to look at her even though I knew she was looking straight at me.

'No, she's got no previous experience, no . . .'

What? I needed previous experience to tap a load of numbers into a keyboard? Jesus wept, surely they are not serious?

'She's about twenty.'

More than a cursory glimpse at my CV and she would have noticed I had turned twenty-one the previous month. Yes, I had the key to the door.

'No, she doesn't smoke.'

Good guess, Pauline. Is he going to ask about my height and weight next? Or my bedroom habits maybe?

'Just a minute, Bernie, I'll ask her . . .' She cupped her hand over the mouthpiece and leant forward. 'What is your telephone manner like?'

'What?'

She tutted and rolled her eyes as if I was being deliberately slow. 'What are you like on the *telephone*?' she enunciated, as if to an infant.

What did she want me to say? That I can talk dirty? *Hey big boy, so glad you called, I was just slipping out of my silk panties and thinking long and hard about your throbbing member*, that kind of thing? Or was she thinking more along the lines of 'Yes sir, no sir, three bags full sir'?

I assumed the latter. 'My telephone manner is very good and I have many valuable customer-relations skills from my previous retail jobs at Woolworths and Tesco,' I quipped smartly, pronouncing each word in my most refined accent. Hey, I could talk the talk. Slick as you like. Suck on that one, Pauline.

She put her lips back to the mouthpiece and breathed heavily. 'Uh-huh, yes, well, she's willing to learn,' she said, batting me a look that said, *touché, bitch.*

If I hadn't been down to my last penny I would have picked up that phone and beaten her head in with it. I sat on my hands and restrained myself.

'Yes, yes, alright, that should be fine. I'll just talk to her now and I'll confirm everything with you later. Sounds like just the kind of *challenge* she's looking for! Yes, you leave it with me. Bye bye. Haha! Yes, that's right! Ciao for now!'

Ciao for now?

Pauline slammed the receiver down, clipped the hideous earring back onto her fleshy lobe and smiled at me; the odious, sinister smile of someone who had just sucked a lemon. 'He's half Italian, Bernie is,' she said, as if this justified her heinous Anglo-Italian salutation. 'It's just our little way.'

'Really?'

'Anyway, when can you start?'

'Well, let me just consult my busy, action-packed social calendar,' I said, trying to ease the distinctly unamusing situation with feeble sardonic humour.

Pauline picked up her coffee from her desk. I noted her mug said 'You don't have to be mad to work here . . . but it helps!' She sipped ruminatively at her coffee, gazing at the blue screen on her computer and inputting a few more numbers. 'So you can start immediately . . .' she muttered, almost to herself. 'Good.'

'But I've already said, I would like to have a little bit of choice when it comes to which job I'll do. I mean, surely there must be loads of *interesting* positions out there for someone vibrant, intelligent, capable, well educated . . .'

'You start Monday,' Pauline said, scribbling something on a piece of paper and then sliding it across the desk towards me. 'No strict dress code, just don't turn up late.'

I looked at the piece of paper:

Bernard De Cristifiano, Accounts Manager

DCS Business Supplies
Ruskin Business Park
Rivington Hill
01245 772 811
Hours: 8 a.m. to 5.30 p.m. Monday to Friday
Salary: £9,500 p.a. (plus benefits tbc)

'You'll be reporting to Bernard,' she said. 'I think you'll find him a reasonable boss. Firm but fair. His wife used to be a colleague of mine, you know. Very nice lady. Sheila. Had to have a hip replacement last year. Been off work ever since.'

Pauline knew that she had the advantage over me, and that she was therefore at liberty to talk at me about anything she pleased, no matter how irrelevant and uninteresting. I was the poor unfortunate who needed a job, and she was the all-seeing eye with a host of unappealing local vacancies at her disposal.

'This is a joke, right?' I spluttered, having read and reread the information in disbelief, trying to keep the wavering edge of desperation out of my voice. 'I mean, what does this job actually *involve*?'

'I've already told you all you need to know. You'll get full on-the-job training. It's all quite straightforward: as you're so *clever* I'm sure you'll pick it up no problem. The wages are paid monthly in arrears, straight into yer bank account. Don't look so horrified, anyone would think I'm sending you to a labour camp!' She chortled drily and hoisted her bosom up inside what must have been a steel-reinforced bra. The wispy moustache on her upper lip bristled. 'Really, I thought you might be grateful. You don't have to stay there for ever!'

'What does the company *do*?' I demanded. 'You haven't told me anything about them!'

This lamentable scenario was not what I had envisaged on that proud, sunny day when I collected my degree certificate. This was not what I had anticipated at all.

Pauline produced a packet of digestive biscuits from her drawer and dunked one into her coffee. 'They do rubber stamps,' she said, cramming the entire soggy mass in her mouth all at once. Then, with her mouth full, she continued, 'and that posh paper with the, you know,' she made a vague gesticulation with her hands, 'business header to make it look right professional. General personalised stationery stuff for businesses. They're branching out. They'll be goin' global. The nineties has been a big decade for them so far, and it's just going to get bigger. They've got lots of clients. Some of them famous. It will be a good . . . *springboard* for your future career.'

Going global, my arse. Did she want to hit me with any more misleading statements and gross exaggerations? Rubber stamps indeed. Springboard? To what? Famous clients? Bollocks.

'The salary is awful,' I noted.

'Great prospects,' she retorted.

'The hours are too long.'

'They can be flexible.'

'It sounds boring,' I said.

'It is.'

'Huh?'

'But it's money, and that's not to be sniffed at, is it?'

Maybe she had a point there. I thought about the latest foreboding letter I had received from my bank, not to mention the fact I had a student loan that needed paying back at some point, and I decided to give in. 'What's my job description then . . . exactly?' I asked intrepidly.

'You'll have a . . . dual kind of role.'

'Meaning?'

'Multitasking. Kind of a stock control, shipping monitor, general office maintenance job. Not just data entry. Actually, if you just bear with me . . .' She fumbled through some documents on her desk then referred to her computer screen again, her bovine face illuminated sickly green by the monitor. 'Ah yes, what I've got written down here is *office administrator and account co-ordinator*. Hmm. So quite a bit of responsibility really. It will be great experience. A real feather in your cap.'

'Oh fantastic,' I intoned. 'I can hardly wait to get started.' I read the details on the piece of paper one final time, feeling my last fragments of hope and dignity drain away. As if they hadn't been forcibly squeezed from me already by the sadistic Pauline.

The business park was less than ten minutes' walk from where I lived. I sometimes took a short cut through there while I was at Mason Tyler. It was dismal; always teeming with fork-lift trucks, delivery vans, heavy articulated lorries and heavy inarticulate men in blue overalls.

A feather in my cap? A jackboot in my arse, more like it.

But still, as I had learned well enough, beggars can't be choosers.

That one lasted six weeks. There was only so much unprovoked telephone abuse, inane keyboard-tapping, tea-making, stocktaking, stationery-replenishing and interminable clockwatching I could take, so I handed in my notice. I might have been able to stand it for a little longer had I not discovered I was earning less than half of what Rebecca earned at her 'fantastic' new PA job at a solicitor's firm in Holborn. She suggested I sign up with some London agencies, and recommended a few names. 'You'll get loads of work, it'll be great' were her exact words.

I remained healthily sceptical but resolved to update my CV and buy a new suit before the year was out. Might as well make as much effort as possible, then I can at least say I *tried*.

At about the same time that I quit my job at DCS, Mark jacked in his bar job. He had been working at a pub in Shenfield called the Fuzzy Duck for nearly a year, and despite the perks (free beer and spirits, an agreeably drunk and easy-going boss, and more sexual opportunities than he could realistically cope with), he had become bored with it. He said the pub had gone downhill since new management had taken over, and he was growing wary of serving so many girls with whom he had once shared bodily fluid. So now we were both stony broke, out of work and pissed off, with yet another bloody Christmas just around the corner.

'I'm going to write up a new CV, and I'll do yours too if you like,' I offered one afternoon when we had grown tired of playing I Spy on the bench in the park for the fourth day in a row. There are a limited number of things you can realistically spy when your imagination is tired and you are surrounded by nothing but trees, foliage, squirrels and pigeons. I felt as if all my verve and creative energy was atrophying by the second, just going to waste. We had fed most of our cheese-and-pickle sandwiches to the ducks and now there was nothing left to do except sit and talk and daydream.

'What good would that do?' Mark scoffed. 'I've got nothing to put on mine. I'm thick, lazy and hopeless.'

This was true. Poor Bev had long since given up on Mark, and wearily resigned herself to feeding him and ironing his shirts for the rest of her life. Still, I tried consoling him as best I could.

'Mark babes, that's the whole point of having a CV. They are designed to mislead potential employers into thinking you are worth employing.'

Mark looked at me as if I was slightly unhinged. 'Yeah? Alright then, I'm game,' he said eventually. 'Back to mine and I'll cook us up something nice.'

'Microwave curry again?'

'You got it, sister.' He chucked the last crusts of the soggy sandwiches in the bin and we wove our way through the overgrown paths that we had once skidded, skipped and skateboarded through, just a few years before.

'You still with that girl?' I asked him as we turned into Bluestone Rise.

'Whatsername . . . Samantha? Sarah?'

'Sarah. Nah . . . single at the moment.'

'Yeah, me too.'

I had trouble keeping up with Mark's love life, although applying the word 'love' to Mark's frivolous entanglements is probably stretching it. His longest relationship had been a shallow but apparently satisfactory four-month dalliance with a girl called Kylie in 1992 (the Beautiful Girl), closely followed by a six-week liaison with an equally forthright candidate called Jenny or Penny. I sometimes got the impression that Mark *was* after something more meaningful, despite his seemingly inexhaustible propensity to carouse in habitual debauchery, but perhaps it was a case of not being able to see the wood for the trees. There was simply too much *choice* out there. And Mark was a natural, lethal charmer, and he knew it.

I suppose you have your 'trophy' boyfriends and 'trophy' girlfriends. While Mark wasn't exactly a 'trophy', he was certainly the kind of bloke that most girls would feel quite proud to step out with. Until he opened his mouth, that is. Conversely, I never saw myself as much of a catch. At the other end of the sexual attainment scale, you have consolation prizes. That's me. I am the 'Blankety Blank chequebook and pen' of partners. You have your star prizes, your plasma TVs, all-inclusive Caribbean holidays, sports cars and luxury yachts. I've always seen myself as a bit of an ornamental carriage clock. The cuddly toy, if you like.

'So you finally broke up with that shithead did ya . . . Stuart innit?'

'Oh God, I don't want to talk about it. He was such a tosser. I'm staying single. It's easier.'

Mark sighed and nodded. 'I think you've got the right idea there, Caz.'

Except it wasn't so much out of choice as necessity. I had enough to deal with already without adding a boyfriend to the equation. I hadn't had much luck in love, my latest boyfriend being the biggest loser in a select but steady succession of lamentable losers. I had met him while I was working on the till at Tesco at the beginning of my third year at university. Scanning barcodes for hours on end does tend to ignite an overpowering need within the moderately intelligent person to instigate random conversations about anything, with anyone. Towards the end of a fairly quiet evening shift, then, I had foolishly ventured an opinion about a male customer's purchases as they rumbled down the conveyer belt. That male customer was twenty-five, his name was Stuart Best, and he asked me out without much further ado once it had been established that we both had a penchant for Crunchy Nut Cornflakes and used the same brand of toothpaste.

You would be forgiven for assuming that these wondrous and profound commonalities would have rendered us perfectly suited, but alas it was simply not meant to be. Although it took me nine long months to realise it.

Even so, I still secretly pined for a partner who would actually *enhance* and *enrich* my life, rather than complicate it. There remained a part of me that romanticised the future; and looking across at Mark at that moment as we approached the front door of his house, I realised I was essentially torn between two slightly outlandish extremes. There were two incompatible, conflicting facets of my character – one was a determined, ambitious, high-flying, career-minded successful single businesswoman who lived in her own home and always called the shots. The other part of me was a rampant bohemian and incurable romantic; the part of me that yearned to live in some remote trailer park by the sea with no hope of riches or splendour whatsoever, eking out a sweet, modest but blissfully happy existence with Mark in a brightly coloured caravan on the coast with dozens of barefoot, grubby-faced children.

Silly dreams. Silly, persistent, irresistible dreams.

'Right, the idea is to divide it up into experience, education, interests and achievements, with bullet points and headings,' I declared, once we had arrived at Mark's and the microwave was busy ticking down from three minutes. 'We've got to get all the relevant points down, make it look snappy and concise.'

Mark cracked open some beer from the fridge and gave me his typical blank gaze.

'What?'

'Now, you've got five GCSEs, yes?' I said, picking up a chewed pen and a scrap of paper from the breakfast bar.

'Caz, leave it out. I have a C in woodwork and a D in English and that's just about as good as it gets.'

Having been presented with a choice – the first major choice of his life – between continuing with an education that bored and restricted him, or dropping out of school to earn some money, Mark had not needed much time to deliberate. His parents never expected either of their sons to achieve anything academic beyond a few scraped GCSEs and did not try to change his mind when he announced his unsurprising intention to leave school the summer after his seventeenth birthday. Since his promotion at the Post Office, Billy had been shacked up in a flat in Barking with his first serious girlfriend, and the pair of them lived a tranquil, simple and relatively honest existence, saving up for a wedding and a baby and a mortgage, in whatever order. Bev and Sean couldn't realistically ask for much more from their offspring, and at least one of them was starting to settle down now.

As for Mark, he had no aspirations other than to be a millionaire before he was thirty. You don't need A-levels and a degree to dream, do you? And you certainly don't need them to become a millionaire. 'Look at Richard thingy, that Virgin bloke, thick as a plank!' Mark once said to me during an impassioned argument about the attainability of wealth. 'But rolling in it! Fuckin' minted, he is! Bill Gates – yeah, he may *look* clever, but I bet he didn't earn his billions by scribbling stupid essays in some shitty old library, or being sent to his room to read dull fuckin' textbooks about history and whatever. It's all about grabbing your chances whenever you can get them, and not letting anyone get one over on you. That's the name of the game. Trust me Caz, you don't get anywhere in this life just by being a nice, decent little smartarse.'

'No, you're either born into it, get stupidly lucky or else you work your arse off and hope for the best,' was my reasonable counterargument. But to my exasperation, Mark never listened. I was an idealist, and worse, I was female – what did I know? Idealistic females were two-a-penny in Mark's chauvinistic, simplistic, materialistic world. He didn't want idealistic. He wanted ideal. Big bucks, fast cars, easy women, free lifestyle. The works. With no work.

I had long since given up trying to convince Mark that money wasn't everything – in fact, if anything, he had managed to convince me that it *was*. We both bought our weekly lottery tickets and kept our fingers crossed, to no avail. Money for nothing: the greatest temptation of them all. Especially to those who have never had any.

In truth, Mark had that one GCSE (woodwork), but I could not foresee this achievement as being entirely relevant to a fulfilling career, given that he had no interest in carpentry or indeed any kind of craft. Still, I scribbled it down on the piece of paper with just the minimum of embellishment: *Five GCSEs grade A–C, including Woodwork, English and Maths.*

Then I crossed out 'Maths' (nobody would ever believe it, he couldn't even work out how old he was on his last birthday) and put 'Physical Education' instead.

'I'm good with my hands, me,' Mark said, taking the curry out of the microwave and stirring it with a fork.

'And such a *fantastic* cook, too,' I drawled. 'Hmm, that smells almost good enough to eat.'

'Give over, it's lush, this stuff.'

'Yes, you'll make someone a lovely wife some day.'

'Kiss mine.' He plonked the plate of orange gunk and adhesive rice in front of me and offered me some water.

'Yes, make it ten litres.'

He poured me a small plastic beaker of filter water. One of the cats – I had long since given up trying to remember all their names – hopped up onto the table and sniffed the curry gingerly before leaping back to the floor and mewing pitifully at the back door.

'See, even the cat can't stomach these bloody curries,' I moaned. 'You must have a cast-iron stomach, Mark.'

'Shut up, and let's get on with this. What else do they need to know, other than that I fucked up my education?' He peered at the scrawls I had made so far and raised his eyebrows. 'Physical Education?' he intoned blandly. 'And I got a D for English, actually.'

'Yes, well they don't have to know that,' I persisted. 'And it still counts as a pass, anyway.'

'You sure about all this?'

'Trust me.'

'I know you too well to trust you.'

I extended my finger and suggested he might like to do his own CV without my assistance. He shrugged and stuck a curry-laden fork in his mouth, swallowing it without even chewing.

Almost immediately after leaving school, Mark had managed to land a three-month apprenticeship at the local garage, with a view to a potential long-term job offer at the end of it. Due to Mark's drug and social habits at the time, not to mention his pathological laziness and existential contempt, things didn't quite go according to plan. Even so, Mark had always seemed to demonstrate immense interest in and knowledge of the internal workings of all kinds of engine, and so I assumed he would make a natural mechanic. Plus he looked oddly sexy in the shapeless greased overalls, with grime on his cheeks and a spanner in his fist, buggering about with spark plugs and exhaust pipes. Such a manly vocation, I always thought. It suited him so well.

Sean had given Mark his old banger as an eighteenth-birthday present (really just to get rid of it once and for all), and Mark spent months diligently reconditioning the engine and revamping the bodywork, ripping out most of the inside to install a powerful stereo system and new seats. Even after all this careful and presumably expensive work, the car still always broke down, the petrol gauge was broken, the gearbox was dodgy, and it emitted a high-pitched squeaking sound whenever it went below forty m.p.h. This was rare, however, once Mark had nestled himself kamikaze-style in the battered driver's seat behind that punished steering wheel.

The possession of any kind of vehicle (even if it was nothing more than a defunct rust-bucket on bald tyres) always seems to have the effect of enhancing a young man's status and ego to an inordinate degree, and Mark was certainly no exception to this rule. The ability to drive – especially the ability to drive recklessly in a car with an obnoxiously loud stereo blaring out at full volume – tended to send the fickle young Essex girls into an inexplicable flurry of lust. The car itself didn't have to be flashy, it merely had to be manoeuvred in an overtly life-threatening way, at speeds that might make Damon Hill himself think about packing a spare pair of underpants. In fact, the less roadworthy the car, the more cretinous the driver, and the greater the likelihood of that driver meeting with a violent self-inflicted demise, the more the opposite sex lusted. There were indeed some cunning stunts performed in and around the area, with skidmarks at every bend and the sound of drum 'n' bass, techno, jungle or reggae music blasting distortedly over the sound of revving engines as far as the pained ear could hear. It was a veritable hive of hormonal activity.

I made a note of Mark's three-month apprenticeship, using nebulous but potentially impressive phrases such as 'practical and proven engineering skills', and 'completion of challenging independent mechanical project' (meaning that he had transformed Sean's car from scrap-heap challenge to undisputed 'fanny magnet' within just six weeks). I scribbled at the end 'References available (?)', and contemplated what else I could include on Mark's CV to make him appear anything more employable than the idle prat he objectively was. While we continued to ingest the almost palatable microwave curry and share a couple of cans of beer, I diplomatically manipulated various facts about Mark's education and career history so that unimpressive truths and half-truths became remarkable distortions of the truth and, in desperate circumstances, downright lies. As with my own CV, the sporadic dole-signing periods miraculously vanished, or rather, they were overlooked.

'Now, what about interests and hobbies?' I asked, keen to fill more than half a side of A4 with feebly unconvincing selling points about Mark's questionable employability.

'Oh yeah, I got that covered,' he said confidently, snatching the paper away from me and scribbling something at the bottom of the page. I let him get on with it, although my hopes that he was finally taking this venture seriously still weren't high. After sucking the end of the pen for a while, he scribbled something else then pushed the paper back towards me.

'OK,' I sighed. 'Interests and hobbies.' I peered down at what he had written, and sighed again. 'You have down here: *drinking, having a laugh, going to clubs, football (play and watch), skateboarding and skydiving.*' I glared at him.

He looked back at me with vacant nonchalance. 'Yeah. What's wrong with that?'

I was beginning to lose my patience. 'Mark. Would you employ someone who listed those things as their interests?'

'You bet I bloody would, that's my kind of bloke. I'd admire them for their honesty. I mean, who the fuck wants someone who just sticks down the same old boring noncey shit like reading and writing and poetry and . . . God, I don't know . . . embroidery, stamp-collecting, golf and masturbation? Or whatever the fuck you're supposed to put on these bloody things.'

I put my head in my hands, despair rapidly overtaking my previous good humour.

'Mark, even *that* would be closer to the truth at least. I mean, *skydiving*? When have you *ever* gone skydiving?'

'Last time me an' Tam an' Kermit went to Ibiza, they stuck me on a parachute thing on the back of a speedboat. It was great, I mean I was fucked off my tits of course, but I'd definitely do it again. And if you do something more than once, it's kind of a hobby, innit?'

The end of my tether was in sight. I sighed in exasperation. 'That's not skydiving, that's acting like a pissed-up prick on a lads' holiday. Skydiving is when you jump out of a plane and freefall for a bit and . . . well, bollocks, whatever, it doesn't even bloody matter, because it's *not* one of your hobbies. You've got to think of something that will make you appear interesting *and* sociable.'

He belched and shook his head. 'Sorry, you've lost me, love.'

I was wasting my time, and I knew it. Still, ever the masochist, I persevered.

'Something that makes you out to be physically fit and active and yet, at the same time, intellectually deep. A free thinker. A team player but an independent and unique individual.' Yes, during my time at university, I had developed the enviable craft of talking out of my arse and naturally I liked to show off this skill whenever I could. Indeed some may argue that this skill, acquired by the vast majority of students whatever their chosen course and regardless of whether or not they take an active interest in it, is the skill that will ultimately make them truly worthy competitors in the job market.

He shrugged, losing interest now. 'Croquet? Naked volleyball?' he suggested. 'I don't really give a toss, Caz, this is so pointless anyway.'

'Hey, I know!' I exclaimed, picking up the pen triumphantly. 'Chess!'

'Yeah, OK, whatever,' Mark said. Both of us knew that Mark had never so much as touched a single chess figure in all his twenty-two years. As far as he was concerned, a rook was a big black bird, a pawn was something you did with your brother's electric guitar when you needed money for drugs, and a bishop was a thing to be bashed. Still, I wrote it down anyway, feeling ridiculously proud of myself.

Running short of further inspiration and equally low on motivation, I opened the previous week's paper to 'situations vacant'. My heart sank as I was confronted with the usual dreary black-and-white array of unappealing and undignified dead-end jobs available in the local vicinity, from part-time telemarketing agent to campaign-leaflet distributor to the ineffably dreadful 'mobile sandwich-board wearer'. One quarter-page ad did catch my eye, however: *GENERAL ASS REQUIRED, full-time, immediate start.*

It wasn't a very informative ad, merely stating a name and a telephone number to call. I pointed it out to Mark.

'What the hell is a general ass?' he asked.

'Don't know love, but it sounds right up your street,' I replied, circling it in red pen.

'Hey, that new casino down in Harley Square is looking for a croupier, y'know,' Mark said. 'Fantastic job that, I reckon. Rakin' in other people's money all night. Watchin' the faces of the stupid rich cunts when they realise they've lost it all with one spin of the bloody roulette wheel. Reckon I should apply for that, sounds perfick fer me. Whaddaya reckon, eh? Would I make a good croupier or what?'

He hardened his tone and made some ferocious gesticulations, using the salt and pepper pots on the table as tenuous props. '*Oi, I said no more fuckin' bets sunshine, wot you deaf or summink? . . . Nah, you ain't won fuck-all mate, now you got nuffink left on the table so why don't you piss off home to your poor old missus and explain why she ain't gonna get no fuckin' new Mercedes this year? . . . Alright my son, seein' as it's you, I'll pretend I didn't see them fuckin' cards up your sleeve this time round, but if it 'appens again, I'll get the heavies over 'ere to take you round the back room and stick a pool cue up you, alright, so don't say I didn't fuckin' warn ya.*'

He beamed at me, relaxing back into his usual, marginally less offensive persona. 'I'm a natural, innit?' I studied him sceptically and decided to lie. 'Simply brilliant, darling. Such boundless charisma. Now . . . can we get on with the CV, please?'

He pouted, sighed, and took my plate away, stacking up the dirty crockery in the sink for his poor mother to deal with when she got home from work. 'Whatever. You still 'ungry, Caz?'

'What's on offer?'

'Chocolate ice cream.'

'I'm still hungry, babe.'

He winked and opened the freezer. 'You got it.'

He handed me a dessert spoon and we ate it straight from the tub, as I continued to poise my pen on the page, scheming up new ideas to transform Mark from no-hoper into potential professional. Sadly, this is what I came up with, even after a further ten minutes of painstaking effort, complete with Mark's own little embellishments:

CURRICULUM VITAE
Name: Mark Christopher Sean Crozier
Address: 28 Bluestone Rise, Rivington Hill, Essex IG12 7DX
Date of Birth: 29/12/73
Education: Mason Tyler Comprehensive, September 1986–June 1991. 5 GCSEs grade A–C including Woodwork, English and Art [Mark insisted on this addition, since he was adamant that he had once achieved an 'A' for an abstract clay sculpture of an erect penis.]
Criminal Record: Yes. Extensive.
Driver's Licence: revoked after two weeks. Only two speeding offences, one head-on collision with a minibus and one failed roadside breathalyser test since reinstated in September 1992.
IT Skills: None whatsoever.
Work experience: Various stuff. References available(?). Subject to successful bribery.

Hobbies and interests: Chess. Skydiving. Football. Cars. Skateboarding. Drag-racing. Wanking.
Outstanding achievement: shagged both the Kirby sisters in one weekend.

Stuck in that dreadful job-hunter's hell after graduation, I was at least granted time to reflect. Days on end, one after the other, as I applied to job after job, countless and mostly inappropriate vacancies, rewrote my CV time and time again, set my sights lower and lower, temping whenever I could for a pittance, just to get out of Rivington Hill. Every other day, with ever-depleting hope and patience, I would contact one, some or all of the five recruitment agencies I had signed up with.

I had assumed – not unreasonably, I thought – that registering with a number of recruitment agencies might mean the offers and opportunities would soon come in thick and fast. After all, that is what such agencies exist for, right? Adding extra fuel to my hopes, each agency had enthusiastically assured me that their consultants would do their utmost to place me in a stupendous job, relevant to my skills and specified preferences, and they made countless empty promises after rigorously testing my PC skills while stealthily dissecting my character. However, not one of them ever bothered contacting me after my initial interview, unless some poky little firm needed a brainless, subservient desperado to stand next to a photocopier or sit behind a switchboard for a day or so.

Such glittering assignments would come my way once, maybe twice or thrice a month. Then and only then would the agencies merrily pimp me out, creaming off their twenty per cent with a good deal more attentiveness than they had shown for my expressed requests of 'nothing too boring please'.

My time had been valued at around six pounds per hour, give or take fifty pence or so, although I didn't suppose I would ever find out who decided that this was what I was worth. What is the going rate, after all? Why is it that one person's time is worth more than another's? We all get old, don't we? At more or less the same rate? Do we all lose heart at the same rate, too?

I started to collect rejection letters and became horribly familiar with the standardised methods companies adopt in order to disappoint prospective candidates in the most gentle manner possible.

Unfortunately on this occasion you have been unsuccessful. Just on this occasion?

We have been inundated with applications and regret to inform you ... Spare me.

Thank you for your application to the position of [insert invariably menial role here], *and we have read your CV with interest.* I haven't even made it to first-round interview stage, right?

It would appear that your skills and experience are not quite relevant to the demands of this particular post ... Am I to interpret this as meaning I am a retarded chimp?

Worse were the companies who didn't even bother responding to my applications at all; obviously I was such a risibly inadequate applicant that I wasn't even worthy of a standard letter and a second-class stamp to tell me so. At first each rejection I received represented a personal attack on my intelligence and competence, but eventually I became immune to it, more or less.

Endless, fruitless job applications and daytime TV slowly sapped my will to live. All the ads that interspersed the invariably inane chat shows and topical tedium and DIY programmes were for 'no win no fee' insurance claims companies and any-purpose loans for those people who were already up to their eyeballs in debt. Generally, that was likely to be a sizeable proportion of the poor souls who were subjected to the dross on a daily basis.

My mother, already having enough negative vibes to deal with, became weary of my perpetual gloominess and despondency and ordered me to keep 'plugging away' and stop moaning. Or at least stop moaning in her presence. So I concealed myself in my room behind that chipboard barrier and read and reread a thousand books and old magazines, ate endless toasted-cheese sandwiches, drank vats of coffee, aimlessly played with myself and wrote an angry, self-pitying diary every day which I somewhat dramatically named 'Chronicles of a Suicidal Graduate'.

Even Mark managed to find a job before I did. And the pay was reasonable, too. Four weeks' annual holiday entitlement, possible future commission opportunities, even a company car after six months. Bev and Sean were beside themselves with joy. So delighted were they, in fact, that they took us out to celebrate – a hearty pub meal in Ilford just opposite the Estate and Lettings Agency where Mark had landed the prestigious role of 'trainee sales negotiator'. Secretly, I thought it must have been my cunning CV-tweaking skills that got him the job, but naturally I didn't say anything, and I was genuinely pleased for him. I really was.

Bev must have noticed that I was in something of a depressive state that night, even when the drinks were flowing and the food was piled high, and she leaned across the table to touch my arm, and assured me that my time of glory would come. Mark surprised me by gripping my hand underneath the table and telling me much the same: 'You got what it takes Cazzie, just don't give up,' were his exact words.

And I didn't give up.

The following month, after what felt like an eternity of rejections, dejection and sporadic, menial temporary work – filing, answering and transferring telephone calls, typing and enveloping letters, being obsequious to Important People, and acquainting myself with an archaic photocopier for hours on end – I finally achieved my Ultimate Goal. My first rung on the career ladder. I was invited to attend an interview and it went so well that they offered me the job on the spot, and I nearly died of shock and excitement, thanking my lucky stars above and wondering if this really might be the start of something brilliant at long last.

My job title? Junior administrative assistant.

My duties? In the main: filing, answering and transferring telephone calls, typing and enveloping letters, being obsequious to Important People and acquainting myself with an archaic photocopier for hours on end.

The company? A small but allegedly eminent PR consultancy firm called Franklin and Barrington, based in west London.

The usefulness of my degree to the role? Hmm, pretty much minimal, to be honest.

The salary? A bank-bulgingly abundant and bewilderingly precise £12,385 per annum.

The first day of the rest of my life? Monday 3 March 1997.

I have to concede that, in comparison to a number of the stopgap temping assignments I had recently endured, the company itself was not too bad and the work, although mostly mind-numbing and morale-killing to an almost criminal degree, was at least undemanding. I couldn't complain. A job's a job, and I was more than willing to give it all I had. Sure enough, I soon became a dab hand with a stapler, and my immediate boss – a piggy, sonorous, florid little man called Martin Bradley ('You can call me sir,' he had joked on my first day) – claimed I made the best cup of tea this side of Westminster Bridge. To be damned with faint praise! As bosses go, he fluctuated between being faintly absurd and utterly unbearable. Fortunately the former was more often the case, and on a good day he provided unintentional amusement on an almost continual basis. Most of my colleagues were female however, and the vast majority were over thirty and/or obsessed with celebrity magazines, media parties, effluent gossip and affluent fashion.

The routine set in before the first week was out.

And no sooner had one arduous search ended than another one began – and no less challenging than my quest for a job had been. My mission was this: find affordable digs in London (at least zone four), where 'affordable' means having enough money left over at the end of the month (allowing for rent, bills, food and travel expenses) to enjoy the occasional night out or purchase any necessary sundries (such as underwear, contact lenses, etc.). Every day I spent in Rivington Hill seemed to knock another year off my life expectancy, such was its draining, dispiriting influence. I simply had to get the hell out of there. Strike out on my own, get a life of sorts.

Loot was therefore scoured on a daily basis, and Mark even searched the Internet for me during his quieter moments at work (alas, Internet access was one of many privileges denied me at Franklin and Barrington). At length, a bedsit in Leytonstone was found – even the suspiciously succinct description provided in the ad cast immediate aspersions over its inhabitability. Still, it was cheap(ish), and when Mark accompanied me to check it out, we could both see why. Nevertheless, I signed on the dotted line and ignored my distaste of the landlord, whose own brand of repulsiveness was of a quite breathtaking standard. Mark warned me against it, and my own common sense was screaming at me, but I went ahead and paid the deposit anyway – all of my first week's wages, plus a chunk of my reinstated overdraft.

Bev became very worried about me, despite my assurances that things were starting to look up. As far as I was concerned, anywhere away from Rivington Hill was a positive step forward. I could see the light at the end of the tunnel.

'But it's not just where you're living,' she said to me, looking around at my new rented space and trying not to appear quite as disgusted as I knew she probably felt. 'Although I can't think why you would want to live in a place like this on your own. And the amount you're having to pay for it, too.' She turned to me, her face awash with concern as she perched gingerly on the edge of a battered wicker chair. 'It's just criminal,' she said, putting her hand over her nose. 'So poky and damp and smelly.'

It was a very humid afternoon and admittedly the smell from the drains outside was particularly pungent and unpleasant that day. I had made some brave but fruitless attempts to beautify the room – a poster or two to cover a damp patch or ten, a few scattered cushions and voile drapes to detract from the shabby décor, an embroidered quilt on the bed, an ornate mirror, some novelty lighting angled in the dreariest corners. But certainly there was little that could be done about the stench, which was bad enough even on mild days. And there was little I could do about the general atmosphere, which was perceptibly gloomy on a perpetual basis.

'Give me another couple of weeks to jazz it up a bit more,' I chirped. 'I'll make it nice in no time.'

Bev shook her head. 'This on its own is bad enough,' she sighed. 'But it's everything else, too. I can't help worrying. I can't believe you're really happy in that job, Carrie. I'm sorry, I don't mean to interfere, but . . . it's just not what I had envisaged for you. You're so . . . *bright.* You can do better, surely? I don't know, it seems like a waste, that's all.'

I did feel inclined to agree with her to a certain extent, but was determined to stick with my mindless optimism plan. After all, if things can't get much worse, it's always worth assuming that they will probably get better. Right? I sat down heavily on my steel-framed bed, and it creaked and squeaked painfully beneath my weight. This wasn't so much to do with the rusted, antiquated condition of the bed itself as with the fact that I had put on over half a stone since leaving university. Put it this way – if someone told me I was worth my weight in gold, it would be one hell of a compliment.

'Most people have to start at the bottom and work their way up,' I explained cheerfully, feeling my buttocks sink into the thin, sagging mattress. 'That's just the way it is. As a first step, it's not that bad.'

She gave me a dubious look.

'Honestly,' I said. 'And it's not far from where Becca works, so we get to meet up for lunch once a week or so.'

'Is this Becca who is on nearly twenty grand already and gets a bonus and good prospects thrown in? Becca who is being funded through a postgraduate course by her rich parents next year?' Bev seemed uncharacteristically fractious, and when she met my astounded stare she smiled sheepishly and quickly said, 'I'm sorry . . . It's just I want to see you make something of yourself, that's all. You deserve it. More than anyone. It doesn't seem right to me.'

It had been three years since her father's death, and Bev was still struggling to come to terms with it. Every now and then I would notice a very distinct and extreme change in her mood and demeanour, but she kept insisting that she was fine and would soon be back to her usual self. For some reason, Bev had become even more protective of me recently, checking up on me more often and always asking about my dietary and sleeping and lifestyle habits.

'Shall I make some tea . . . or coffee?' I offered, pushing myself with some difficulty from the bed and pacing the shabby beige carpet towards the kitchenette. My bedsit wasn't big on luxury, that was for sure, but it did have its own designated kitchen area – a sink, a kettle, a cupboard, a small fridge with a frosted-up icebox, and a very old microwave.

Bev followed, standing behind me as I filled the kettle with yellowish water, which sputtered angrily from the tap. 'Did you ever get to see the boiler certificate for this place?' she asked.

'What?'

'I mean, is this really safe? And what if there's a fire? You're right at the top of a four-storey building, and the stairs are wooden and rickety. Is there a fire escape?'

She peered out of the window onto the rear courtyard below – a steel, spiral staircase was blocked off at the bottom by a junk-filled skip and a scattered assortment of overspilling refuse sacks, and a couple of vagabonds were rummaging through the putrid treasures.

Bev regarded the dismal scene and shook her head. 'I'm *really* not happy about you living here,' she reiterated. 'Not at all.'

She tried to open the window but it wouldn't budge. She turned the hot water tap and nothing came out. She continued turning it and finally a sudden torrent erupted with a violent sputter, spraying her clothes. She shrieked in surprise and turned it off immediately, spinning it several times before the stream finally reverted back to its steady sporadic drip. I silently handed her some paper towels, smiling apologetically.

'It has a habit of doing that,' I said. 'There's no hot water anyway. The cold tap is slightly less temperamental.'

'Oh, Caro . . . ' she sighed, dabbing ineffectually at the wet patch on the front of her dress, 'why don't you come and live at my place? Billy's room is free, and Mark's rarely there anyway, as you well know. Sean won't mind. I can't stand the thought of you here . . . all alone . . .'

I searched the cupboard for two clean cups, but I only owned three and they were all in the sink, requiring an urgent and thorough wash. Undeterred, I gave a cursory rinse to the two less stained receptacles and, after another rummage in the cupboard, realised I was out of tea bags.

'Er . . . no tea left, is coffee OK?'

'Fine, fine, whatever.' She looked at me intently. 'Caro? What do you say?'

I sighed, realising I was also out of biscuits and sugar. 'I really appreciate it, Bev,' I said distractedly. 'But I have to do this. I have to break out on my own. It won't always be this awful. Everybody's got to start somewhere.'

I watched a spider emerge from a crack in the crumbling plaster above the cupboard, and scuttle toward the back of the fridge. I didn't mind spiders, it was the rats that bothered me slightly. I had my suspicions that the whole place was infested with them, but until I actually witnessed irrefutable evidence with my own eyes, I tried to draw a veil across the very possibility.

Bev knew better than to beg. 'Well, the offer is there,' she said. 'Our door is always open to you.'

I smiled at her. 'Thanks. That's good to know.'

The kettle came to the boil with a rumble and a hiss, and I poured the water into the cups, stirring in the instant granules.

It was only then that I realised I was also out of milk.

Mark got himself a girlfriend and a mobile phone. The girlfriend was called Claire and he kept her quiet for a while before introducing her to his nearest and dearest. This fact alone demonstrated that he must have been quite serious about her. The mobile phone was initially used as a device for keeping track of Claire, or rather vice versa. It was apparent that the relationship was a pretty intense one, and had been right from the start. Mark didn't talk about her very much at first, merely mentioning to me quite casually that he had recently pulled someone 'really fit and nice', but I noticed a change in his character around the time he met her. He would often come around to visit me on the flimsy premise that he was 'just passing', and ended up browsing through my copies of *Marie Claire* and *New Woman*, often kipping over on the floor after we had stayed up half the night drinking wine.

As he got increasingly drunk, Mark asked me earnest questions, such as the ominous: 'What do you think is the most important thing you look for in a boyfriend?' and 'Can a relationship work even if the geezer is a lot less rich than the bird?'

Naturally, this was all entirely of character for Mark. I had my suspicions that he had finally been hit with the 'L' thing, and I supposed it was about time.

Mark arranged to meet me in a pub on a Sunday afternoon, and brought her along with him. He said she had 'freaked out' a bit when he told her one of his best mates was a girl, and had at once demanded to meet me. This set alarm bells ringing even before I met the poor girl. Unfortunately, my first impressions when I did meet her did little to stop them ringing. She was an old St Jude's girl – at least, she had taken her A-levels there, but she would have been four years above me so I didn't recognise her. She was extremely attractive, well-spoken, unreservedly feminine and genteel and – as far as I could see – not even remotely suited to someone like Mark. Call me biased, but I took an instant dislike to her, even though there was nothing obviously unlikeable about her.

But who was I to voice my misgivings about their compatibility? I was a crap judge of character anyway. Anyone neutral would have said she was far too good for him. I was not neutral, I couldn't even pretend neutrality. But it still seemed a fairly bizarre mismatch to me.

Still, they appeared happy enough, and did have a noticeable rapport going on. The chemistry was unmistakable: I could almost feel the torrid sexual energy pass between them every time they touched or kissed, which was more often than my stomach would have preferred. They couldn't keep their hands off each other. Mark wasn't usually keen on public displays of affection, but seemed more than willing to make allowances in this instance. I managed to keep down my one lager shandy and then hastily made my excuses, leaving Claire with the perfunctory and perhaps not entirely sincere, 'It was lovely to meet you,' and Mark with the standard, 'Laters mate.'

It was obvious that Mark was beginning to find peace within himself now, at last. Or some semblance of harmony and contentment. His job was tolerable rather than enjoyable – that is to say, he didn't exactly relish it, but the wages kept him going. But he always did remind me that work is not something that you are *supposed* to enjoy. Work to live, don't live to work. That had become his motto. And Mark certainly knew how to live.

And I knew how to work. For all the good it did me. By midsummer, I was stuck in a rut. In your early twenties, this is not a desirable situation to find yourself in. But stuck I was.

Already disillusioned, I became even more so every time I endured the dismal daily commute or chatted with friends about how great their life was, or even if I merely read a paper or turned on my rented television set in my nasty rented room. The news was consistently saturated with Spice Girls, celebrity sex scandals, new scientific theories trashing the old ones, murders and disappearances and abductions, Government proposals, international crises, drugs epidemics, disaster heaped haphazardly onto disaster.

In no time, I created my own small-scale version of Rivington Hill in that little bedsit. Every time I turned the TV on, or made myself a Pot Noodle and actually salivated at the smell of it, or tuned my radio to yet another relentless commercial station to endure yet another hastily cobbled-together pre-packaged bland pop band of corporate fuck-puppets trilling out a cover version of some dismal tune that had been bad enough the first time round, or when I merely switched off the light at bedtime, that same suffocating oppression bore down on me, crushed my soul.

Cynicism took over. I was sick of being one of the docile masses, of having my intelligence systematically insulted and undermined by the incessant bombardment of advertisements and subliminal suggestions that invaded my every waking hour. Ads where inanimate objects came to life to tell you how your existence could be improved beyond your wildest dreams if only you purchased BRAND X. Even out on the streets, at night, illuminated placards displayed rolling advertisements for pension plans and holidays and lipsticks and luxurious toilet tissue and cars and Internet providers, all of them screaming: *We want your money! You want to give us your money!*

And always, everywhere, there were just so many things to want, to need, to covet, to crave.

I was sick of being brainwashed, of feeling brain-dead. Of feeling mediocre, standardised, stereotyped, just another statistic. Every day, the gruelling journey on the Central Line, back and forth, the grinding nine-to-five routine, the incessant ringing of phones, the tapping of keyboards, the mechanical rattling of the photocopier as it churned out page after page of non-stop black-and-white boredom. I was sick of dedicating the majority of my waking hours to something that was neither vocational nor educational, simply a means to an end, and for such precious little reward. I was sick of pandering to all the elevated people from the 'Me Generation' who could only think of prestige and profit when all I could think about was 'freedom' – not riches, not recognition, just some *respite*, for heaven's sake. And I was sick of feeling so deeply aggrieved and negative and miserable about everything. Yes, it was one hell of a rut I was stuck in.

And no, I think it's fair to say I was not a happy bunny.

Things got worse before they got better. I had been unwittingly sharing a residence with rats, slugs and a number of East London's most notorious drug barons, pimps and escaped convicts. Summer had brought uncomfortable, stifling heat and sickening stenches, and as winter approached, the lack of heating and the unreliable electrics had stretched my patience and tolerance too far. So now I found myself, once again, back in Rivington Hill. Straight from the frying pan into the fire, you could say. But my mum's abode was, for the time being at least, a palatial haven of tranquillity in comparison to that dodgy block of converted flats and bedsits. Rivington Hill was like a black hole; no matter how hard I tried to claw my way out of it I never seemed to get very far – it would always suck me right back in again.

I had been working at Franklin and Barrington for a year now, and it felt like nigh-on eternity. Even after I was granted Internet access on my desk PC and subsequently began regularly receiving 'amusing' and generally obscene emails from Mark, nothing sufficiently eased my stupefaction and dissatisfaction. I started taking days off sick, skiving in effect, just so I could languish at home until I really did feel sick. I became a malingerer. Meanwhile, Bev really did get sick, and was admitted to hospital just before Easter 1998, and diagnosed with a rare condition that nobody could pronounce, let alone spell. She was put on a course of medication and had to give up both her part-time jobs.

Mark moved into a flat in Redbridge with Tamworth and another guy who he had met at work, a cheeky Welsh chappy who went by the name of Jonesey, presumably because his first name was Rupert. So Mark had his bachelor pad at last, and the trophy girlfriend, although he had recently confided in me that, after sixteen months of relative bliss, relations were not so good between him and Claire. Things apparently reached boiling point shortly after they returned from their first holiday away together, a romantic week in Malaga in April 1998. This was Mark's first holiday alone with a girl – myself excluded of course, because I don't count, and because we'd never been any further than Cornwall or Dublin. More precisely and importantly, it was his first holiday alone with a *girlfriend*. It was therefore a fairly significant event.

But Claire had her own demands. Apparently the poor deluded soul had been anticipating that Mark would suggest that she and he move in together, not that he would opt to live with two hopeless wastrels. She got the strop, and rather than talk it through with her, Mark had found solace in the arms and legs of a random, pleasingly undemanding and very accommodating girl while drunk at a mate's party.

Meanwhile, Rebecca broke up with her boyfriend of four years, and placed the usual demands of the woeful heartbroken friend upon my shoulders. *Of course* I cared, I really did, but I was selfish and wanted *her* to sympathise with *me* as well. She wasn't the only one with problems.

'I'm quitting my job,' she told me, emphatically, after she had finished crying into her wine glass.

'You're what?'

We were at a pub near Holborn station, and it was the first time I had seen Becca for a few months. Lately, whenever we met or even just communicated via phone or email, she always seemed to be going through some traumatic life-changing transition, or at least a minor upset of some kind. Physically, she hadn't really changed at all since St Jude's – still the lustrous cascades of blonde hair, perfect skin, pleading doe-eyes, trim little body, etc, etc, ad nauseam. I suppose it was a little bizarre that I had remained friendly with Rebecca beyond St Jude's, but she was now probably my closest female friend, particularly since she effectively lost touch with CJ, who had gone away to study at a university in America and never came back.

I think the reason our friendship endured is because we each saw something in the other that we felt intensely drawn to. I only say this because, on the face of it, we had absolutely nothing in common. But I liked Becca because although she could have been a snob and a bitch, the wisdom of experience had mellowed her and most importantly made her aware of her shortcomings – vanity, selfishness, pettiness. And she made sure I was aware of mine, for which I was grateful. So, at least while we were together, she played down her vanity, selfishness and pettiness, and I did my best to come across as a sassy, successful, emotionally secure and self-satisfied woman.

'I'm handing in my notice. I'm gonna do it next week,' she said, refilling her glass.

I was dumbfounded. 'But . . . why? You love it there, don't you? What about your promotion?'

She put the bottle back on the table after topping up my glass, even though it was already practically full. 'Promotion?' she intoned. 'Wow, they might actually give me something *interesting* to do. Oh joy. I don't think so, Caroline. Yeah it was OK at first, but I've been there for nearly two years now, you know. I need to spread my wings.'

I was thinking that a broken heart had either made her delirious, or else possibly supremely sensible. I asked her what she meant exactly.

'I'm getting out of the country. I have to . . . explore. You know? I need an adventure. London is great and everything, but . . .'

'Weren't you going to study to become a barrister?' I interrupted. 'Isn't that what you always wanted?'

Becca frowned. 'No, it's what my father wanted. God, Caroline, if you could only meet some of the cretins where I work, if I ever ended up like that I would have to ask you to put me out of my misery. They're so . . . false. So shallow and greedy. So *annoying*.'

I smiled, remembering what Becca had been like just a few years ago, especially in cahoots with CJ. Being a good friend, I didn't remind her. I simply said, 'Where were you thinking of going?'

Becca smiled and reached into her handbag. 'Not thinking, *doing*,' she said, taking out a brochure and sliding it across the table towards me. 'I *am* going. Next year. On my birthday, my twenty-fifth birthday. South-east Asia, Thailand, Japan . . . then Australia, New Zealand . . . I want to spend at least six months in Oz, I might even stay for longer, find work and stuff, see how it goes . . . look here . . .' She turned to a page flagged with a post-it note and pointed excitedly. 'That's my itinerary. Starting out in Kathmandu. I'm booking it next week. I've saved up loads. I was going to use it for a deposit for a house, but now that Adam has dumped me, and I can't afford to buy on my own, I thought, fuck it, why not?'

Why not indeed? I studied the map in front of me and felt an effervescent thrill well up inside me. England was tiny, so appallingly tiny, and I only really knew one small dreary corner of it. Horizons needed broadening. And minds. And *lives*, dammit.

'There's a whole lotta world out there,' Becca said, tuning into my thoughts. 'Go see it while you have the chance.'

I swallowed some wine, still focusing intently on the map. 'What do your parents say?' I asked, glancing up at her. 'Are they OK about it?'

'They don't know. I haven't told them yet.'

'Why next September? That's over a year away, Becks. Why wait?'

She downed her second glass of wine and sat back, crossing her legs. She may not have been aware of it, or maybe she was, but a group of suited men at the adjacent table were ogling her quite conspicuously. Oh, the agonies of having a beautiful friend. The power of invisibility strikes again.

'Believe me, I'd go tomorrow if I could,' she said. 'But I need to get more money together first. I've already got three grand, and Adam owes me five hundred. Trust me, I'm not going anywhere until I get that back off him, every last penny.' She refilled again and added, 'Bastard,' before knocking back the third glass in one go.

I tried to imagine the luxury of being in a position to lend a loved one five hundred pounds. Mark and I would sometimes loan each other the odd fiver or tenner, but that's as good as it got. There was rarely more than a few quid in my account even at the best of times.

I ventured another obvious question. 'Why are you quitting your job if you need more money?'

'Better money in temping,' she explained. 'Especially now I've got experience and all. Need some variety. The agency I'm with reckons I might be able to get about twenty quid an hour in some companies.'

I did a quick calculation. Three times what I was earning. Becks noticed the involuntary shift in my expression, and leaned across the table with a smile. 'You can do it too, you know,' she said. 'Don't sell yourself short.'

At first I thought she meant that I could also earn twenty quid an hour, which was blatantly untrue as far as I was concerned, but then I realised she meant something entirely different when she added, 'Come with me. You have a year to save. I'll lend you some. Or just do Oz with me, and get yourself a work permit if you have to. It will be brilliant.'

I gawked at her, stuck for words. She was apparently quite serious.

'It's the kind of thing you'll never regret doing,' she went on. 'We're still young, we've got nothing tying us down, no commitments or any shit like that.' She waved her hand at a passing member of staff and ordered another bottle of wine and a bowl of olives.

I found my voice, but it came out as a stuttering squeak. 'B-but . . . I can't . . .'

'Why not?' she demanded simply, and I have to admit at that moment I couldn't think of one substantial answer. 'What's holding you back?'

I did another quick calculation: bugger all. Fear, maybe? I began nervously picking at the label on the wine bottle, peeling it off in strips. Mark used to say that this was a sign of sexual frustration, which would explain why I did it all the time.

Then I started thinking: *why not?* What *is* holding me back?

'Hey, you'll never guess what,' Becca chirruped, lighting up a

Marlboro. 'Remember Tanya Bletchley from school? The one with the really high-pitched voice and funny teeth?'

I nodded slowly. 'You and CJ called her Bugs.'

Becca grinned and blushed. 'Hmm, yeah, that's right. Well, anyway, she quit uni and went to live in Melbourne.'

'Really?'

'Yeah, CJ kept in touch with her for a bit, and Tanya emailed me totally out of the blue a couple of weeks ago. She's in Sydney now, working as a lapdancer in a lesbian strip joint.'

'You're kidding.'

'No, I'm totally serious. She said I can go and stay with her for a bit, she's staying at some kind of free-for-all student house by the sounds of it.'

'Sounds cool.'

'Yeah, dunno about the whole gay scene thing though . . .'

A fresh bottle of wine arrived, with a small bowl of black and green olives and a few cocktail sticks. Becca smiled up provocatively at the waiter as he splashed the wine in our glasses, and he smiled back, leaving the bill on the table under the ashtray before he turned and minced away. Becca had a way of making the opposite sex fall helplessly to their knees with one glance of her big brown eyes, and even though this waiter was quite obviously not of the heterosexual persuasion, she charmed him enough that we received notably assiduous service throughout the evening.

'You managed to catch up with CJ at all recently?' I asked, stabbing an olive with a cocktail stick.

'Nah, not since last year. I'm lucky if I hear from her direct at all. I did hear recently on the grapevine that she's getting married.'

I wasn't surprised at this. 'Let me guess,' I said, 'he's rich, good-looking, well connected, and his daddy is a billionaire oil tycoon with a thousand acres of land and an estate the size of the entire solar system.'

Becca chuckled. 'Not far off.'

'That's our CJ,' I muttered, not without a modicum of perverse affection. 'Good luck to her.'

'CJ's not the type to need luck,' Becca said. 'She never has been.'

'True.'

'So, what do you say?' Becca put the brochure back in her bag and gazed at me expectantly. 'Two old St Judettes doing the old explorer thing? Yes or no?'

I tipped my glass at her and she clinked hers against it, both of us tacitly accepting that my answer was, in theory at least, a resounding 'yes'.

9

Let She Who is Without Sin Shed the First Stone

'A man doesn't have to be good-looking to get a woman, or to get ahead in life. But men value women for their looks. And it's a man's world.'

Cindy Jackson, cosmetic surgery adviser

Football fever, summer 1998. Argentina beat England, then, as if the English patriots hadn't suffered enough, France went on to win the World Cup. Still tending a broken heart after his split from Claire, Mark's spirits sank ever lower.

Meanwhile, I continued slogging away at my job, now spurred on by those stupendously outlandish ideas that Rebecca had planted in my otherwise listless and stultified mind. Dreams of breaking free. In August, to my immeasurable joy, I finally found a suitable and just about affordable flat-share in Woodford Green, and the day after my twenty-third birthday, the last shred of my sanity still just about salvageable, I moved out of Rivington Hill for the last time, and moved in to a small but smart third-floor flat with a girl called Suzie. So began an unlikely but generally easy and amicable friendship, and a new chapter in my life. Feeling that I needed to establish some realistic goals to strive towards, I compiled a list with a view to ultimately boosting my *joie de vivre.*

1. Lose a stone, preferably twenty pounds.
2. Find a hobby – yoga? judo? new man?
3. Join a gym, and find energy and motivation to go at least once a week, preferably twice or even thrice (can it be done?)
4. Learn another language fluently – not German. Maybe Dutch? Chinese?
5. Save up to go travelling.
6. Stop watching so much shit on TV.
7. Stop eating so much junk.
8. Quit work.

9. Forget Mark (not literally).
10. Get on a plane and get the hell out of here.

1–4 should have been, theoretically, quite straightforward, and hopefully those in turn would have given me something good to concentrate on and therefore made 6 and 7 a little easier. The others may have taken a little more effort and/or luck.

Suzie, my new flatmate and quite possibly the thinnest and most neurotic woman I had ever met, was a health and fitness fanatic and her boundless energy alone was enough to motivate me. In addition to her gym habits (every Monday and Thursday, no excuses), she swam and jogged and had salsa-dancing classes twice a week. This was despite having a high-pressure full-time career as an IT Research Analyst. Or perhaps, after more careful consideration, because of it.

'You don't need to lose a whole stone, babes!' Suzie trilled out to me one Saturday morning. I was sleepy and irritable, and Suzie had been up since six, as she was every Saturday (earlier on weekdays). She was now standing on her head in the middle of the lounge, performing some breathing exercises with a tape of meditative whale music ululating eerily in the background. I was measuring out Slim Fast in the adjoining kitchen while swearing at Capital Radio. This was about as active as I got in the morning, at least until my first coffee.

'No, I need to lose *two* stone,' I retorted. 'My arse has started to take on a life of its own!'

'Nonsense, at least you have some *shape*. Look at me, I'm a bloody twig!'

'*Shape?* Don't make me laugh. Since when was there a shape called "flabby great splat"? And anyway, you're not exactly a *twig*. You're fit and . . . disgustingly slim.'

'Bless your heart for saying so, little buddha,' she said equably. She closed her eyes and breathed deeply and rapidly, like an over-zealous woman at an antenatal class.

'Now, hush for a bit please,' she murmured. 'I'm entering nirvana or something now.'

'Whatever, Suze.' I mixed up my Slim Fast breakfast, peeled a banana and sat down glumly on the sofa, thinking of bacon, fried eggs, grilled tomatoes and big beef sausages in a sea of baked beans, with lavishly buttered toast on the side.

'Hey, have you considered going to a slimmers' class?' Suzie said, suddenly spinning out of nirvana, her eyes flicking open again to stare at me from her upside-down perspective. 'They're supposed to be good. More like a support group really. There's a local one, right near here. My salsa partner's sister goes, I think. And I'll drag you to the gym with me, if you like. Once you get started, you feel so damn good and you just can't stop.'

I wasn't entirely convinced. 'Maybe,' I muttered.

I had only been living with Suzie for six weeks, and already I felt exhausted merely by spending so much time with her. She was a hive of energy, even when she claimed to be 'meditating', and had a personality that some might describe as 'off the wall'. I found her company refreshing, but often felt the need to go and hide in my room, away from her incessant vivacity. It was enough to make even a moderately active person feel like a loafer.

The next day, I went to Lakeside on my own to buy some new clothes before popping in to see Bev. Untypically of the vast majority of my sex, shopping was a chore for me. I preferred food shopping to clothes shopping, even during the sales. *Especially* during the sales. After all, what is twenty per cent off something that was overpriced by practically a hundred per cent in the first place? In particular if the item only really appears attractive purely by virtue of the misleading reduction tag. No, I was not a dedicated follower of fashion. I was somewhere between frump and flump. Perhaps every so often I might experience a glimmer of gratification or enjoyment from my infrequent wardrobe-replenishing missions, but generally speaking I found clothes shopping tiresome and even degrading at times.

Unable to squeeze myself into a pair of size-sixteen jeans in Oasis, and then being told by a shockingly tactless Irish woman in the lingerie department at Debenhams that my bra was two cup sizes too small ('Oh my dear girl, oh no, you'll be wanting a *36DD* so you will! You'll be much comfier in something like this "minimal bounce" jobbie, with the firm support cups and wider straps!'), I felt extremely desolate. I consoled myself with a muffin and an espresso in Starbucks, and was absorbed in a copy of *Time Out* when I heard a female voice call my name.

'It *is* you, isn't it?' The girl approached my table, accompanied by an older woman, probably her mother. They both had the same elegant, angular features, although the older woman didn't look as if she smiled very much. I recognised the girl almost immediately.

'Hello Claire, how are you?' I indicated a vacant chair next to me, and Claire sat down, depositing a variety of bulging carrier bags under the table by her feet.

'I'm fine, thanks,' she said. She turned to her mother and asked her to get her a cheese-and-salad sandwich on wholemeal, a bottle of carbonated water and a 'very little' slice of lemon cake. I looked at the crumbs on the plate in front of me – the only evidence left after my rapid demolition of the double chocolate muffin – and instantly felt a surge of guilt over my shameless gluttony.

'This is Caroline, by the way,' Claire said. 'Caroline, this is my mum, Lesley.'

I smiled politely. 'Pleased to meet you.'

The woman smiled back – a tight-lipped, constipated rictus of a smile, the smile of a woman who was blatantly terrified of crow's feet and laughter lines, but nevertheless a smile of sorts. 'Likewise,' she said. 'Old school friend, darling?'

'Oh no,' Claire giggled. 'Caroline is Mark's best friend.'

'Oh.' I watched the pained smile falter and collapse. 'I see.'

'I did go to St Jude's as well, though,' I said, hoping this might redeem me. I remembered Mark had mentioned being 'scared totally fucking shitless' by Claire's mum, and I was beginning to see why. She was wearing a fitted trouser suit in royal blue, with an expensive-looking brooch on one lapel, and her make-up and hair were immaculate. She looked like one of those unconscionably patronising and overpaid talk-show hostesses on early-morning TV. There was something of the nouveau riche about her, a shimmering, simmering sense of superiority and importance that I picked up on as soon as our eyes met.

'Would you like anything, Caroline?' Lesley asked, extracting her purse from a shiny leather handbag. 'Another coffee . . . ?' She regarded my empty plate in a manner that I felt verged on reproachful. 'Another cake, maybe?'

'Oh, that's very kind of you, but no thank you.'

'All right then. I won't be a moment.'

As soon as her mother had disappeared to join the queue, Claire pounced with a fusillade of questions about a certain someone, the one and only thing connecting her to me.

'How is Mark?'

'Fine, as far as I know.'

'When did you last see him?'

'Er . . . the day before yesterday . . . I'm going round to see his mum later.'

'Is she better?'

'So-so.'

'Does he talk about me?'

'Er . . . sometimes.'

'Does he miss me?'

'I . . . don't know. I think so.'

'Does he want me back?'

I sighed and told her she would have to ask him herself. 'It's not like Mark is the type to share his feelings, anyway,' I explained. 'He's a bit of an emotional enigma.'

I was shocked to see tears well up in Claire's eyes.

'Has he . . . has he got another girlfriend?' she asked tremulously.

Well, it depends what you mean by 'girlfriend', I thought to myself. I decided to be kind. 'No, I think he's sticking with the single life for now,' I said. Then, seeing that Claire was not entirely placated by this, I added, 'I don't think he's over you yet.'

She perked up a little at this and, to my immense relief, changed the subject. 'Have you bought anything nice?' she enquired, glancing at my Debenhams bag.

I shook my head. 'Just a bra and a shirt for work.'

'Ooh, can I see?'

'Er . . . it's really not that interesting, Claire. What did you get? Looks like you've been on the rampage.' I eyed the plethora of polythene by Claire's feet. I had always been very wary of spending more than a maximum of a hundred pounds during even the most extravagant shopping sprees, and could only even afford to allow myself that relatively moderate and modest degree of retail therapy two or three times a year. But it looked like Claire had blown thousands in one morning.

'Oh, just a few bits and bobs,' Claire understated. 'It's my cousin's bar mitzvah next week, so I had to get a new dress . . . and I'm going to Florida with my best friend soon, so I needed a new swimsuit, and some nice new undies, and some other . . . stuff. You know, just various things.'

'Lucky you.'

'So . . .' Claire began, tapping on the table with her long, curved fingernails, 'how's everything going? I haven't seen you since . . . since . . .'

'Flynn's New Year's Eve party,' I said. 'I'm sorry, I think I was very drunk that night.'

Claire flinched. 'Mark was worse. He passed out in the back of my car, wet himself too. I could have killed him.'

I suppressed a laugh. 'Well, that was nine months ago,' I said. 'What have you been up to since then?'

'Oh, nothing much,' she trilled lightly. 'Same job, still living at home, dying of a broken heart . . .' She blushed, immediately and rightly embarrassed about this last admission. 'I mean . . . obviously I still miss him. I still love him, you know, despite everything. I don't know why I do, but then you can't help who you fall in love with, can you?'

I shifted uncomfortably in my seat. 'Why don't you just call him?' I asked, anxious to leave now.

Claire looked sheepish and simultaneously irreproachable. 'I did try his mobile,' she said. 'Several times. But I couldn't get through.'

'Oh, he got a new one!' I exclaimed, suddenly remembering. 'He's always losing mobile phones. He's hopeless. The last one ended up down a manhole, promptly followed by Mark himself, who I believe was attached to it at the time.' I allowed myself to enjoy the fleeting expression of horror that passed over Claire's delicate, pretty features. 'Drunk again, silly sod,' I elucidated pointlessly.

Claire pouted and continued to drum her fingers on the table. I reached into my shoulder bag and rummaged for my own mobile; a relatively recent accessory that I had initially despised and only acquired out of what felt like social obligation, but was now learning to appreciate. Mobiles were fast becoming a necessary impediment in pockets and bags and briefcases all over the country. The novelty ring-tones and double-beep text alerts sounded out all over the place; the persistent mating calls of the technologically sussed competing against each other; private lives spilling out obtrusively in the public domain; trains, shopping centres, parks, playgrounds, restaurants. The side effect of this breed of technological advancement, I had noticed, was that people no longer talked to each other any more, not really, not properly. They talked against each other, past each other, around each other, *through* each other. And it isn't even true communication most of the time, it's communication's lowest common denominator – *talk* – simple, straightforward talk, largely bereft of true meaning, nearly always bereft of feeling. Just words. Commercial communication. Blah, blah, blah, blah.

I accessed Mark's new number and read it out to Claire, who gratefully programmed it into her mobile, the latest model, complete with funky fascia.

'I know I should probably have some pride,' Claire warbled, 'but . . . I just can't stop thinking about him. I don't know why.'

I tried to smile, but found I couldn't quite manage it. 'I'm sure he'll be pleased to hear from you,' I said, unsure of whether this was true. In any event, I planned to give Mark a call as soon as possible to warn him that his ex was back on the scene, with unsmiling mother in tow, just in case it wasn't.

'One thing's for sure, I'm never inviting that cunt Kermit back to my parents' house ever again. Ever,' Flynn said, gesturing wildly as he related the shambolic events of the previous Saturday night to Mark, Tamworth and me as we sat respectively playing, commentating on and yawning at Gran Turismo on the Playstation.

Mark didn't shift his eyes from the screen, twiddling furiously with the control pad as he attempted to get on to the next level. Playstation games had become the defining factor of his weekends recently, and his addiction to them had long since overtaken all his other predilections, even sex. Apart from, I gathered, the solo variety.

'Did he get too pissed again?' Tamworth asked.

'P-pissed?!' Flynn squeaked. 'Totally f-fucking trolleyed, mate. I've never seen him so bad. I suppose I should have learned my lesson after the fucking shambles that was my New Year's Eve party, but stupidly I thought I'd give him another chance.' He sat on the floor behind Mark and pushed his hair out of his face, twitching with agitation.

Flynn used to have quite a severe stutter, and when he got wound up it tended subtly to creep back into his speech. 'Get this. F-first off, he headbutted the hall mirror cos he said he didn't like the look of the shady geezer with the m-mad bulgy eyes.'

Tamworth grinned. 'His own reflection?'

'Of course. The prick. He raided the fridge, vomited in the k-kitchen sink, tried to have sex with my d-dog, pissed in the aquarium . . . '

'No shit!' Mark exclaimed, pausing the game to light a cigarette. 'What about your dad's precious bloody tropical fish?' He offered a cigarette to Flynn, which was readily accepted and lit.

'All of them fuckin' d-dead in minutes,' Flynn said, puffing away on the fag as if his life depended on it. 'Floatin' on the top of the water with a look of "why me?" on their poor bastard faces. Th-three hundred quid's worth. Thanks to that stupid fucker and his t-toxic piss.'

'Fuck, your old man must have gone apeshit.'

'You b-bet he did.'

'Was he OK?' I asked.

Flynn glared at me. 'Was who OK?'

'Kermit.'

'Who cares? Shit Caz, the wanker brings it all on himself. Every single bloody time, he just doesn't learn. I've had it with him.'

Kermit's love of narcotics had, over the years, had a progressively detrimental effect on his personality and behaviour. It was now impossible to go out with him on a casual social basis without ending up being his carer and cleaning up after all the mess he was bound to create. Our last venture into the great unknown with the perennially spaced-out Kermit had been a drum 'n' bass night in Romford, when Mark had ended up going home in a car with five strangers at around midnight, after I had helped him stuff a boisterous, puke-spattered Kermit into a cab. Kermit had taken a dodgy pill before they had even left the house, and so the night started badly and rapidly got worse. The memory of that night served as a sharp reminder to both Mark and me of why we must, at all costs, avoid going out with him ever again. Anywhere.

We had only been at the club for about half an hour or so when Kermit started getting lairy and aggressive and then, all too rapidly, very ill. We had seen him rush out of the toilets, and followed him past the mob at the bar. Kermit only just made it out of the club in the nick of time, pushing aside an unnecessarily bolshie bouncer before finding himself outside, staring down at the pavement as he bent over with his hands on his knees. He threw up once, twice, and then retched unproductively for a few moments. Mark watched him from the club entrance, smoking nervously. I stood just behind him, feeling anxious and enervated. The smaller of the two bouncers guarding the door glowered at Mark, his bald head shining alternately red and purple in the fluorescence of the overhead striplights and spinning mirrorballs.

'What's up with 'im then?' he asked with mild bemusement, exaggerating his sarf-London accent to an almost incomprehensible garble.

Mark shrugged, flicked his cigarette, yawned. 'He ain't feelin' too clever,' he replied casually.

This astute prognosis seemed to impress both bouncers and they nodded gravely and descended into moody silence while Kermit noisily evacuated the remainder of his gut. He continued to groan and stagger, leaning against the bonnet of a nearby parked car before collapsing to the ground. Mark had also taken a pill and was grinding his teeth and chewing the inside of his mouth. A couple of vodka redbulls got him a little fired up right from the outset, and a brief tussle with a touchy-feely curly-haired girl on the dance floor also served to boost his spirits a little.

It's what Saturday nights were all about. Mark had only recently split from Claire at the time but was readily reverting back to his old ways, and making up for lost time. Every conceivable kind of physical excess. Take this drug, then take this one, try that, cop a load of this, it's really got some thump, smoke that, experience this high and that low, because you haven't even lived until you do, drink that, try that combination, how about another cocktail, whack it back in one my son, go on, show us you're a man.

Earlier that night, however, Mark and I had found the opportunity for a rare little heart-to-heart session and he told me that he couldn't stop thinking about Claire and eulogised at great length about how wonderful she was and how much he missed her. He was neither drunk nor play-acting, and when he mentioned the 'L' word, I began to feel a little perturbed. It had never been a component of his vocabulary before, never mind his emotional make-up. But I reasoned that Cupid's arrow had to strike him some time and it was just that Claire had the dubious honour of being the object of his affections.

So Mark was in love. He had even admitted it – firstly to her, albeit just after a particularly energetic fracas when the adrenalin was presumably still pumping and the endorphins were disseminating, but later, perhaps too late, to himself.

And now, oh happy day, to me.

For the first and last time in my life, I purchased, in earnest, a leotard, a tracksuit and a pair of proper running shoes, total cost £104.98. In the same week, I purchased a month's trial-period membership to Suzie's 'exclusive' health club at a cost of fifty-five pounds (it was so 'exclusive' that this joining fee applied to anyone and everyone who could afford it, and even – in my case – those who couldn't). I also took Suzie's advice and joined the local Slimmers' Club, which held sessions every Thursday evening in the church hall down the road, with affiliated aerobics classes on Mondays for those who felt committed enough.

Every meeting lasted one hour – not a minute longer – and cost ten pounds. The aerobics sessions cost five pounds a time, but I only attended one and although it stiffened muscles I never even knew I had, this wasn't enough to persuade me to do it again. November 1998 proved to be one of the most expensive months of my life, but I reasoned that my extravagances would prove worthwhile in the long run. And it seemed like it was going to be one hell of a long run.

The first Slimmers' Club meeting was not quite what I had expected. Certainly I had been losing the pounds sterling at a fast rate, that was *too* easy, it always had been too bloody easy, but shifting the pounds in weight was proving to be more problematic.

The chattering clusters of women at work all seemed generally obsessed with the same things: their own bodies, celebrities' bodies, and the bodies of their contemporaries. Every now and then, from outside in the corridor or while enclosed in a lift or toilet cubicle, I would catch floating, inconsequential tail-ends of female conversation and wondered if I was missing something. And in the office I might overhear feverish discussions about things so inane and gratuitous that I had hitherto assumed they could not possibly invoke any real opinion in anyone with an evolved brain.

For the first few months of my employment, I reached the conclusion that there must be few more persuasive arguments against the existence of God than being forced to spend every working hour in a claustrophobic office surrounded by jabbering, jumped up media types and a facetious boss with BO. But as I had always had to do throughout my life, as we all do, I adapted. It became routine, of course, but not insufferably so. I became numbed to it, almost learned to enjoy it in a way. Or at least I managed to convince myself that it wasn't *that* bad. It gave some order and tenuous purpose to my life.

I sat opposite a brash, elaborately coiffured lady called Mags who had an adenoidal voice and an avid fascination with *Hello!* and other celebrity magazines, almost to the extent that she cared more about the lives of the rich and famous than she did about her own family. Despite my extreme cynicism, I had also been taken in by the glossy lure of women's magazines, and allowed myself to be exposed to and inveigled by their monthly columns of disingenuous prattle and frivolity: *Change your life. Change your body shape. Change your man. Get one first! And make sure he's a good'un. Be thin, be spectacular, be you. You're so perfect. But look at this. Isn't SHE more perfect? Oh yes. Go on, do something with your hair. Do something with your face. Look good. Feel good. Do it this way. Take notes. Be your own person. Change your mind. Don't be sad, be happy. Don't let people get you down, don't let them tell you what to do. Be satisfied, but don't believe in yourself until you look incredible. You can be everything you want to be. Just buy this first. And this. And this. Do what's right. This is what's right. White is black until next season. Look like this, because this is beautiful. Be good, be bad. New black, old black, in and out, hot and not, on and on. Glamour and style, chop and change, stay the same, make up your mind. Change it again. Be different. Eat this, it has fewer calories than that. Keep up, stay pretty, know your friends. Be nice to them, outshine them, do better, be the best, keep it real. Wear this. And make sure you look* this *good in it. Read the right things. Have fun, be sensible, be you, be her, get a life. Obey the right authorities. Pout and gossip, bicker and purchase, sparkle and saunter. Desire fame and scrutinise the famous. Sleep well, eat well, enjoy your freedom but don't be stupid and gullible. Diet diet diet, exercise! Be happy. Read this before you decide anything.*

The 'health and fitness adviser' at my Slimmers' Club was a feisty little lady called Debbie, and she presided over each meeting, encouraging and guiding her select band of hopeful tubbies through the emotional turmoil of breaking their way out of Fat Hell. At the beginning of the first session she wrote 'Self-CON' three times on the whiteboard with her squeaky black marker pen, and explained that 'Self-CONsciousness must ultimately lead to self-CONfidence and self-CONtentment. When that day comes, you know you've achieved your goal.' At that first meeting, I knew almost straight away that losing weight was almost certainly not the answer to my problem. Or rather, it would probably only make me *incidentally* happier. It was a symptom, not a cause.

Every attendee was required to check in at the scales and their weight and height was recorded, along with their specified target weight and the length of time in which they hoped to achieve that weight. I gave myself three months to get down to a small size fourteen or preferably a twelve (so that I might fit into my favourite jeans once again, for the first time since I was nineteen), and to achieve a weight well below one hundred and thirty pounds. So began another miserable diet of rice cakes and carrot sticks, and of donning the new leotard and running shoes for a session of abject humiliation down at the gym with Suzie twice a week. But it was all supposed to galvanise my soul and give me a new lease of life, so I resolved to do my best to see it through to the bitter end.

In February 1999, after almost three years' service at Franklin and Barrington, during which time I estimated I had spent over five thousand hours either photocopying or filing, or otherwise arranging bundles of paper in some kind of logical fashion, I was the lucky recipient of a promotion, of sorts. That is to say, my boss called me into his office to ask me how I would feel about becoming his PA, to wit, 'his right-hand girl'. He announced it with all the gravitas of a marriage proposal, as if he expected me to lay myself at his feet and weep for joy and gratitude. Instead I just blinked at him and waited silently for further elucidation.

This promotion would naturally entail a good deal more responsibility, I was assured, with such momentous tasks as minute-taking, letter-typing, 'more involved' archiving (ooh, yes please!), meeting arrangement, diary management and the old favourite, tea making, all firmly on the agenda. The role would also mean a pay rise, 'of course', although when I asked how much, Martin was vague and evasive.

'It will be . . . substantial,' he said. 'I realise you have not had a raise for some time, so . . .' He made a pretence of looking up something in a file on his desk, then glanced up at me and beamed, showing off his yellow teeth. 'I'll let you know.'

I looked at my hands. 'OK,' I muttered. 'When do I start?'

'Well, no time like the present.' He continued to grin, leaning back in his leather chair with his hands behind his head, displaying his impressive sweat patches. 'Now, I'm expecting a visitor at half past ten, his name is Arnold Hemingford and he's the chief exec at a new London-based media group called Arcade.' He lowered his voice almost to a whisper and said, 'What you'd call a VIP. Know what I mean?'

Again I blinked at him, my blank expression belying my innermost thoughts.

'When he arrives down in reception, could you please show him up to my office and make sure he's fed and watered appropriately.'

'Yes, of course,' I intoned robotically, wanting to say something substantially less subservient but once again, as ever, compelled by the rules of convention and etiquette. I assumed my role so diligently, to the letter, obedient and eager to please. Inside I wanted to scream. I wanted to ram my fist straight into that self-satisfied smile and tell him to kiss my arse. I wanted to get fired in style, with all guns blazing, I wanted to make a scene that every employee at that godforsaken firm would remember for ever. (*And you can tell Arnold fucking Hemingford he can kiss my arse too!* I would scream hysterically through my laughter as security hastily bundled me out of the entrance, P45 floating in my wake.)

Instead, of course, I said nothing. I studied the over-familiar face of the man who sat so confidently and importantly opposite me, on the right side of the manager's desk, beyond a door, with his name and position inscribed on a plaque. He was in his mid-forties, perhaps younger, and had receding hair and bad skin. The armpits of his shirts were constantly drenched with sweat, whatever the weather. The office was always too hot in winter because the heating was cranked up too high, and it was too cold in summer because the air conditioning was a little too powerful and positioned directly above my head. Even so, Martin's armpits were guaranteed to steam and stain, whatever the season. They had become part of the whole distinctive office aroma, the defining musk underlying the Franklin and Barrington working ambience. This persistent sweat problem hadn't prevented someone from marrying the man. Yes, somewhere out there was a woman who had decided that Martin Bradley was their one of twenty thousand.

'Oh, and make me a cuppa as well, would you, Caroline?' Martin asked, visibly uncomfortable with being stared at for longer than two seconds. 'Just how I like it, milky and sweet, there's a dear.' He dismissed me with a wave of his hand, turning back to his computer screen and grabbing his mouse to recommence his next important business strategy, or possibly another game of Minesweeper.

I nodded, got up and shut the door quietly behind me.

Being Martin Bradley's PA was not a job for everyone. The pay rise turned out to be less than I hoped for, but it was just about enough incentive for me to put off handing in my notice for a little longer. Just about.

Rebecca had been keeping in touch with me more consistently lately, sending regular emails relating to her impending travel plans, adding further fuel to my dream of escaping the insipid humdrum that had become my life.

To: caroline.shaw@franklinbarrington.co.uk
From: rebeccadelaney@hotmail.com
Subject: OZ – AGAIN!!
Date: Tuesday March 16 1999 14:07PM

Hi Caz, just a quickie – only six months to go before I'm off! So excited. I have attached some info for you about getting work over in Aus, it's really easy and the hardest part is just making the decision to go for it! Ask at STA Travel (the ones I told you about) about a work permit. You only really need to save up for the flight, and a little extra to tide you over when you arrive maybe. Anyway, if my itinerary goes according to plan, I will be in Sydney from mid-January until late February, and then I am moving on to Queensland. I have also attached a copy of my itinerary so if you fancy coming with me on any of my jaunts, let me know. Might even hire out a little camper van and drive all round for a bit, although my mum would go ballistic if I did that on my own. Have you got your licence yet? Drinks in the usual place, 7 pm this Friday – don't forget. Just started a really crappy temp job on the other side of London (near Kennington). Only two weeks so guess I'll stick it out. Leave that awful dead-end job of yours, a better life awaits you. Get away from it all, you know you want to. Gotta go, boss is giving me evils. RSVP ASAP, love Becks x PS How is the fitness regime going?

After a ridiculously protracted ten months apart, Mark and Claire were officially reunited following a series of tentative post-split meetings and 'trial dates'. Claire agreed not to bring up the 'cohabitation issue' on the strict conditions that Mark didn't get drunk every weekend and rationed his stints on the Playstation, for which Claire had a burning hatred. He was to cut back from six hours per day to one hour every other day. He was also required to learn how to iron and clean, and forbidden from waiting more than forty-eight hours between shaves (Claire also had a burning hatred for stubble and indeed facial hair of any kind).

When I heard of these conditions, relayed to me by Mark over the telephone, I laughed out loud.

'I never thought I'd see the day when Mark Crozier would succumb to the will of a woman,' I cackled. 'I do believe the phrase is "pussy-whipped", babes.'

Mark retaliated vehemently. 'Don't be so fucking stupid, Caz, I think she might have a point, actually.'

My laughter ceased at once. 'Pardon me?' I spluttered incredulously. 'What was that you said?'

Mark was silent, a sure sign that he was thinking hard or sulking. 'I dunno,' he said, 'I just think it's time I stopped acting like such an arsehole.'

I nearly dropped my mobile. 'But . . . but that's what you *are*, Mark. I can't see you being anything else. Don't let anyone change you. I just couldn't deal with the shock if you suddenly reinvented yourself and became a decent human being.'

'Give it up mate, I am actually serious. I . . . I'm serious about making a go of it with her this time, y'know. No girl has ever been this into me before. I think I must have freaked at first, but now . . . I reckon it's kinda cool.'

Mark rarely spoke like this, as even his deepest and most heartfelt human feelings could usually be summed up concisely and quite precisely in a few basic platitudinous four-letter words.

'And you're still into her too? Even after all that time you two were apart?'

'Well, yeah, pretty much. Course I am. Just . . . I s'pose I'm scared of letting her down. I feel like I've got fuck-all to offer her.'

Mark really did seem serious about ditching the arsehole act. I was lost for words.

'Caz? You still there?'

'Er, yeah, I'm still here, I just don't know what to say.'

'Do you . . . do you think I'm an arsehole? Really?'

'Mark, what does it matter what I think? I'm one of your best mates, and I've stuck with you for this long, haven't I?'

Now Mark was silent again. I listened to his heavy breathing and felt an inexplicable rush of sadness. 'Well, haven't I?'

'S'pose.'

'All I'm saying,' I sighed, 'is that you shouldn't have to change. She loves you, doesn't she?'

'But . . . but that's what birds do when they love someone, innit? Isn't that what love is all about to them? Changing the geezer so he's more like . . . OK, so he's just less of a wanker?'

I thought about this. 'I think you're simplifying the matter a bit,' I said.

'Oh well, anyway,' Mark breathed out hard and yawned. I assumed from the dozy gruffness of his voice that he had only just woken up, even though it was a work day and gone eleven o'clock. 'I'm bored of this subject already. We're back together and . . . this time I'm gonna make a real go of it. Get me act together at last.'

'Well, I'm glad. Really I am. Wanna hear my news?'

'Sure.'

'I've lost eight pounds since I started at Slimmers. That means I'm halfway to my target already. And . . . I've made a big decision about my future.'

'Oh yeah? What's that?'

'Can you meet me for drinks after work?'

'What? Today?'

'Yeah. It's been a while. Lots to catch up on. Tell you what, how about meeting at the Barley Mow for half-six? I need to pop in and see your mum anyway.'

'Er . . . yeah, OK. Why not?'

Perhaps he was just being uncharacteristically polite or characteristically sarcastic, but when Mark saw me walk through the door of the Barley Mow later on that day, he stood up and let out a low whistle. 'Is it just me, or have you lost some weight?'

I kissed him on the cheek and sat down with a sigh. 'You wouldn't even have noticed if I hadn't told you,' I said. 'Now, get me a pint please. My feet are killing me and I've been gasping for a beer all bloody day.'

Mark was about to protest, but as he had skived work and almost certainly spent most of the day engaged in listless masturbation interspersed with strange, erotic dreams in the moist recess of his bed, he was somewhat amenable to my bossiness on this occasion.

He was just about at the bar when I called after him: 'And a packet of Worcester-sauce crisps!'

He responded with a two-fingered gesture, but returned two minutes later equipped with two pints and a packet of my favourite. 'So,' he said, taking a gulp of his Carlsberg, 'what's this all about then?'

I ate the crisps ravenously, and downed half my pint before I responded.

'Oh, heaven! My first beer and my first packet of crisps for . . . shit, for ages! Over a month!' I exclaimed, relishing the taste. 'And God it feels good.' I took a couple more gulps and tipped the last crumbs from the crisp packet into my hand. 'I can't tell you what it's like to have to deprive yourself of all the things in life that you love. Calorie-counting sucks, you know.'

'Hmm, yeah, so why are you doing it?'

'Why do you think? I'm sick of being so damn big.'

'You're not big, you're little.'

I eyed him cynically. 'I'm short, yeah, but I'm hefty. Bad combination.'

Mark shrugged. 'Whatever, Caz.' His eyes rested on me for a while. 'You know, you really do look great, no bullshit, mate.'

I felt my cheeks flush and I looked away, muttering something dismissive and coy. He gave me the wonky smile that used to have an inflammatory effect, but this time just made me feel immensely self-conscious.

'Is your mum alright?' I enquired, deftly changing the subject.

'You probably saw her more recently than I did. I just gave her a call, told her we were both comin' over. She's got something she wants to talk to us about, apparently. Oh, and she's cooking that vegetarian shit . . . the one with the rice and the lentils. I told her I'd get something from Macky-D's.'

I shook my head. 'You are really horrible, your mum is a great cook.'

Mark decided to drop the subject of his mum's culinary skills, a subject he and I had always disagreed on. 'I was thinking today,' he began, placing a certain amount of dread and caution in my mind at once, 'it might be nice if you and me and the boys and maybe a couple of your mates went away together . . . Spain, or Greece maybe? Some time this summer? Before we get too old for all that shit, I mean?'

I was mildly and pleasantly surprised by this suggestion, although not unduly circumspect. 'What inspired that idea?' I asked.

'Well, I was watching this holiday programme last night, and there was this cool report about package holidays in places like Ibiza and Benidorm . . . and I just think it would be a good laugh. Well, I've done Ibiza already a couple of times but I'd definitely go again. A few lads, a few birds, a lot of pubs and clubs, gorgeous foreign chicks who only know the English word "yes" and give head like it's a national sport or something . . . y'know. That kind of thing.'

'Oh Jesus, you're not talking about Club 18–30 are you?'

Mark hesitated for a second too long. 'No . . .'

'Oh, you *are*! Oh no *way* Mark! You've *got* to be joking. Haven't you and the lads had enough of that scene? Wouldn't you rather go for something more sedate and civilised?'

Mark pouted and supped ruminatively on his beer. 'I dunno.'

'What about Claire? Is she invited?'

Mark looked at me like I was insane. 'Of course not! Fuck that! She's going to Poland to visit some mad old relative of hers in July, so I thought I could maybe . . . organise something around that time.'

I looked horrified. 'Is this what you call "being serious about someone"?'

'Oh, you know Claire. She just ain't into that. She doesn't even drink. She'll only try to act like my fuckin' mother the whole time. I'll take her away to Paris or something when I get my bonus in the new year. She'll go for that.'

Mark was the type of boy who genuinely believed that a half-arsed gesture – a bunch of flowers, a weekend in a budget hotel in Paris, a slap-up repast in a fancy restaurant – would entirely compensate for a catalogue of heinous deceits, an infidelity, or even worse misdemeanours. Such gestures effectively wiped clean the slate of his conscience every time.

'Oh very noble of you, Mark,' I quipped. 'And what do you think she'll say if you told her you were going away on a lads' holiday? Reckon she'd take kindly to that?'

Mark leaned forward and raised a devious eyebrow. 'Don't need to tell her, do I? And anyway, she'd be OK if she knew you was coming along with me. She trusts you. She reckons you keep me in line.'

I snorted with laughter. 'The poor girl, she really has no idea does she?'

Mark held up his pint glass and smiled back at me, igniting the flame once again when our eyes briefly met. 'What can I say? She loves me. Love is blind, innit.'

And deaf and dumb. I finished my beer and said, 'Fetch the men in white coats, the woman needs specialist treatment.'

An hour later, over at Bev's, the meal was served up, and a bottle of chilled wine was opened and distributed. Bev was looking much perkier than she had been for a while, but Sean looked absolutely shattered. I told him so and asked him how he was feeling.

'Work,' he replied simply, his head in his hands. 'Nearly twenty years I've been at that same bloody place, and it's just killing me right now. Overtime. Sadistic boss. Crap pay. Boring, so damn bloody boring. Reckon I've just had enough.'

I nodded compassionately. 'I know how you feel.'

'With all respect, darlin', you've only been working for three years. You got a long time to go yet before you can get to the level of total fuckin' disillusionment and tedium that I've reached at this late stage.'

'Christ, will you lot stop moaning?' Mark grumbled. 'We waste enough time at work when we're there without bloody talking about how much we hate it when we're *not* there.'

Bev interjected, obviously feeling a little riled because she hadn't worked for many months now due to her health, and she was missing it. 'Does anybody actually *enjoy* their job?' she said. 'Honestly you lot, you're so bloody miserable! Work isn't that bad, you just have to stick with it and hope that you eventually get somewhere. Stay positive or you'll just go mad. Anyway . . .' She sat next to her son and changed the topic of conversation, albeit to one that I liked even less than work. 'You're back with Claire now, are you?'

Mark spooned a few grains of rice into his mouth. Under my duress, he had agreed to try a small morsel of his mother's vegetarian dinner but, like a petulant toddler, he made a show of not particularly savouring it.

'Yeah, we decided to try again. She can't live without me, what can I say.' He chuckled humourlessly, reaching across the table for the salt.

Bev and I exchanged looks.

'Hmm, I'm sure,' Bev said. 'And how are Tamworth and ... Jonesey? Are you boys all still getting on alright?'

'Yeah, yeah, fine.'

'Good.' Bev cleared her throat, picked up her fork, then put it down again. 'OK you two, there's something I'd like to discuss with you, now I've got you both here. I've already spoken to Billy about it, but I think it's a matter I should perhaps have brought up some time ago.'

At once I felt a little alarmed. 'It's not bad, is it?' I said. 'Please tell me it's nothing serious.'

Bev picked up her wine glass and smiled at me fondly. 'No, it's nothing bad sweetheart,' she assured me. She took a couple of sips before elaborating. 'When my dad died, he left some money in his will, mainly from the sale of the house he had with Mum. Half of it went to Val, of course ... I think she's used most of it towards a new conservatory and Emma's tuition fees, and a couple of holidays. Well, I don't need to remind you where my sister's priorities lie ...'

'Get to the point, Mum,' Mark snapped impatiently. I shot him an admonitory glare.

'Well, I know this will sound ridiculous to you, but I didn't know what to do with my share. After having virtually no money at all for so long, and then suddenly receiving a windfall of nearly ten thousand pounds ...'

There was a guttural noise as Mark choked on a mouthful of mashed chickpeas. 'Ten grand?' he spluttered, dropping his cutlery with a clatter. 'You had *ten grand* and you never even *told* us?'

I kicked Mark under the table. 'Shut up and let her finish,' I hissed at him, although I was probably just as shocked as he was. Mark ignored me and stared at his father.

'Did you know about this?'

'Of course I knew,' Sean sighed.

'But ... but ... he died *five* years ago! Five years! You had all that cash and you never ... you never ...'

'We never *what*, Mark?' Sean demanded. 'We never bought you a new car, or treated you to a fortnight in the Carribbean, or gave you a nice big cheque just for being our bloody son? What do you expect?'

Mark's expression softened and he lowered his voice. 'No,' he said, looking slightly humbled. 'I meant ... why didn't you guys just take a holiday, or whatever? Why didn't you *do* something with the money?'

'I put it in savings,' Bev said. 'As you know, after my dad died I was not . . . myself for a long time. I didn't really think about the money, I just wanted my dad back.' She paused and looked down at her hands, clenched on the table in front of her. She twisted her wedding ring and sighed heavily, waiting for her voice to steady before continuing.

'Anyway, it's about time I *did* do something with the money, you're right Mark, I mean that's what it's there for after all. Isn't it? So, I've just told Billy he can have three thousand to put down as a deposit on a house with Anna. And Mark, as much as it pains me, because I have my doubts that it will be spent wisely, I am going to write you out a cheque for the same amount.'

She looked squarely at her youngest son, waiting for a reaction. It was just as she must have expected. He was euphoric. He clambered down from his chair and flung his arms around his mother and thanked her profusely and assured her it *would* be spent wisely. Sean caught my eye from the other side of the table and we smiled at each other weakly. *Typical Mark*, we were both thinking.

'My God,' Mark jabbered, 'I just can't believe you kept it quiet for so long, Mum . . . I mean, that's like . . . two months' wages! Tax free! Wallop! Straight in there! Fantastic!' He composed himself a little and sat back in his chair, now taking a renewed interest in his mother's cooking, finding it quite edible all of a sudden, even ambrosial. He averted his eyes as he chewed a hearty mouthful of rice, and mumbled reverentially, 'Thanks, Pops. You're the best.'

His reaction made me feel a little angry and frustrated, but not surprised. I also felt awkward, as this was very much a private family affair, and I felt I shouldn't really have been there. Nevertheless, my presence had been specifically called for, so I continued to sit, quietly kicking my legs back and forth like I used to when I was a little girl. I had only eaten half of the meal on my plate, but already felt full. Perhaps my stomach was shrinking already – Suzie had promised me that it would.

'And Caroline . . .' Bev murmured, sensing my discomfort, 'I know you wouldn't expect anything because you never do . . .'

I swallowed hard. 'No Bev, really, this is a family thing . . .' I glanced across at Mark and to my surprise he reached under the table and squeezed my hand, insinuating solidarity, implicitly assuring me that he wanted me to be there. I fell quiet, unable to say any more. My legs stopped kicking. I gulped my wine, a whole glass in one, too quickly.

Bev sighed deeply. 'Sean and I have talked about this, and although I am probably going to regret this because I love you like my own daughter and if I had my way I'd want you to be around for ever . . .' She paused, and I felt my breath catch in my throat. Mark was still holding my hand under the table, but his eyes were fixed intently on his mother as she spoke.

'I would like to pay for your ticket to Australia,' Bev said. 'And help you out with anything else you might need while you're settling out there. I know it's what you really want, and I can't think of anyone more deserving.'

All was silent. She beamed at me. Sean beamed at me. My mouth dropped open.

So did Mark's. He turned to me incredulously. 'You're going to *Australia*?'

Bev chipped in. 'She's been thinking about it. Her friend Rebecca is going travelling in September, and it's something Caroline's always wanted to do herself. So . . . why not?'

Mark's eyes were firmly focused on me, but I didn't return his gaze. 'When? How long are you going for?' he demanded, letting go of my hand.

I ignored him and spoke to Bev, my voice wavering with emotion. 'I can't expect that from you . . .' I felt myself well up, and immediately looked away, blinking back tears. 'I . . . I just can't expect you to do that for me . . .'

I had shared my Australia plans with only three people: Rebecca, who had of course been the primary instigator, and Bev and Sean. They had only ever been 'plans', though; heartfelt plans, yes, but still very much at a distant, nebulous stage in their actualisation.

'Consider the subject closed,' Sean said assertively, lifting his glass as if to propose a toast. 'Now, quiet everyone, if you don't mind. Here's to me old father-in-law, God bless 'im. And here's to me eldest getting a nice place of his own. And me youngest sorting himself out once and for all. Touch wood.' He gripped the edge of the table and gave Mark a loaded stare.

'And you . . .' He raised an eyebrow at me – he had the exact same eyebrow-raising mannerism as Mark – '. . . *You* are destined for great things, young lady. Go find them. We're behind you all the way.'

Bev lifted her glass and, after looking around in bewilderment, Mark finally lifted his, and then all three pairs of eyes were on me, as I sat in mute astonishment. I had never felt so loved, and had never, in all the eighteen years I had known the Croziers, felt so entirely at one with them. I raised my glass and brushed away my tears.

'What about you two?' I asked, addressing Bev and Sean. 'What are you going to do?'

They looked at each other, smiling the inimitable smiles of two people who know each other far too well.

'We'll probably go to Clacton and live in our caravan, now that the boys have gone,' Bev said. 'Take all our pets and whatever few possessions we can't live without, and relive the old days together, as much as we can. At least for a little while.'

She blushed a little, and Sean added, 'Call it a second honeymoon, with a difference.'

I thought this was a mad, silly, glorious, extraordinarily romantic idea, the stuff of classic love stories, but I could tell that Mark was having trouble taking everything in, so I decided then that I should add my contribution to what was becoming a rather ceremonious family meal. 'Here's to everyone,' I stammered, for want of something more eloquent and meaningful. 'Especially Ned. And . . . thank you so much. You have helped me make the biggest decision of my life.'

Following this wonderful development, I warmed to Mark's holiday idea and somehow managed to persuade both Suzie and Becks to join me and five hormone-pumped Neanderthals for a week of fun and sun in Benidorm that July. It did take some effort, however. Suzie's first reaction had admittedly been 'I would rather have my toenails pulled out,' but when she learned that one of the Neanderthals was the somewhat Beckhamesque Flynn, she changed her mind. Becks was dubious because the holiday was so near to her round-the-world adventure, and although she liked Mark well enough, she was dubious about a couple of his mates, in particular 'the lobatomised one called Kermit'.

Even so, it came to pass that on the evening of Friday 16 July 1999, eight excited twenty somethings got on a plane at Gatwick, five of them getting drunk on duty-free spirits before landing in Benidorm some three hours later, leaving us three girls to chaperone, pick up the taxi fare and locate the villas.

The holiday was immensely significant for me – it was my first time abroad with friends, and quite possibly the last of its kind. And when I returned, I was going to quit my job, revamp my CV again, check the progress of my work-permit application, book my flights and find accommodation. Becca had recommended I start off in Queensland or Sydney. I didn't care where. The other side of the world sounded good enough for me.

By this time, I was only three pounds away from my target weight, but I had long since ditched the celery sticks and Ryvita. I was determined to drink the boys under the table, or at least Tamworth, who was known to be a bit of a lightweight and would regularly be ridiculed by his friends for failing to hold down even 'poof's measures'. I was also resolved to try every Spanish speciality dish, and drown myself in sangria every evening. My bikini was a size fourteen, shaped to flatter, and when I had tried it on in the shop, even under the pitiless glare of the changing room lights, I had felt heartened by my reflection. For the first time in years. At least, I had felt no disgust – and that was one hell of a step forward as far as I was concerned.

'Hmm, your mate is a bit of alright, actually,' Jonesey remarked to me, surreptitiously appreciating the vision of Becks in a neon-pink bikini through the blue tint of his sunglasses. 'I mean, I *definitely* would. Do you guys reckon I'm in with a chance?'

Mark and Tamworth were similarly captivated, their attention momentarily diverted from an article in *Maxim* called 'Breast of British' by Suzie and Becks playing frisbee a tantalisingly short distance away. Just a little further out, another group of young women were sunbathing topless, although sadly too far away to establish adequate eye-to-nipple contact. Fortunately Jonesey had come prepared and had a pair of foldaway miniature binoculars with him, and was sufficiently lacking in shame to use them quite openly.

I slapped on some suncream and decided to stay well out of this conversation. Mark pondered his friend's question, and opted for the brutally honest approach.

'Stick to your own league, mate,' he said. 'She'd never fancy you in a million years.'

Jonesey sighed and looked decidedly crestfallen.

'Why not?' he asked, bravely anticipating another brutally honest answer.

'Well,' Mark said, pausing a while as he considered incorporating a degree of tact and diplomacy into his answer, but then trying his typically straightforward, lay-it-on-the-line, no-holds-barred approach. 'You're short, you're going bald, your dick has inverted due to years of drug abuse, you're skint, you buy your clothes from Madhouse, your mum calls you "petal", and sorry mate, but you fuckin' stink, too.'

'And you're Welsh,' Tamworth added, lying back on his towel with his arms stretched above his head.

'Oh you two, you're so cruel,' I scolded, but perhaps my failure to offer an alternative opinion was equally cruel.

Jonesey was silent for a while, still mesmerised by the sight of Becca's chest swaying up and down, up and down inside her cheeky pink lycra cups, the motion doubtless mentally slowed down for him via an in-built Baywatch-fixation mechanism inside his brain.

'Alright,' he said eventually, 'but apart from all that, am I in with a chance?'

Mark heartily slapped his friend's back, which had already turned red in the sun. 'Go for it, son,' he said.

'Hey you guys,' I piped up. 'Looks like you could both do with some suncream. You're burning up.'

'Suncream's for poofs,' Mark stated emphatically. 'Anyway, I'm going for a swim in a sec. Anyone coming with?'

'Nah, go for your life, I'm workin' on me sunburn,' Jonesey said. 'The ladies go wild for that pasty, red-raw look, don't you know?'

Mark flicked sand at him playfully. 'Well, you'll come with me won't you, Caz?'

'Yeah, I'm game,' I chirruped, even though I had only just applied my Factor 20 and knew from bitter experience that Mark's idea of a 'swim' was ducking me under the water repeatedly until I squealed for mercy, then doggy-paddling out a little for a surreptitious pee when he had tired of trying to drown me. 'Becks and Suzie are always up for a bit of a dip, too . . . so if you change your mind, Mr Jones . . .' I stood up and removed my sarong, experiencing self-consciousness and self-confidence in more or less equal proportions. Again, still one hell of a step forward.

Jonesey squinted at me suspiciously. 'Alright mate, gimme a minute and I'll be right with you.'

'Watch it you guys, Flynn and Kermit are over there and it looks like they've both got lucky already,' Tamworth warned, nodding towards four figures in the distance.

'Oh, Jesus,' Mark sighed, as Flynn and Kermit approached, each with a dark-haired girl attached. 'We've barely arrived at the sodding place and already those two are up to their usual. Come on Jonesey, come with us, last one to the sea is a wanker. I need a piss anyway.'

'That'll be me, then,' Jonesey confessed, not moving. 'I'm just gonna pretend to be asleep so I don't have to talk to those two.'

'Good idea, mate,' Tamworth said. 'Right, shut it lads, they've spotted us and they're comin' this way.'

Jonesey and Tamworth fell silent and without too much deliberation, Mark got to his feet and grabbed my hand and we ran across the scorched sand towards the sea, grabbing Becks and Suzie on the way.

The holiday took an unexpected, almost supernatural, turn on the penultimate evening.

Unable and unwilling to subject myself to another night of alcoholic oblivion, I ignored the collective protests of the boys, and even of Becks and Suzie, who despite their vulnerable gender had been successfully roped in to the en masse slaughter. We had all crammed ourselves into another dark and overpacked club at nine o'clock, and successive jugs of cocktails were being bought and imbibed at a dizzying rate. But instead of sticking around, by half past ten and after just a couple of drinks and dances I decided to leave the bustle of the tourist hotspots and go for a moonlit wander on the beach, on my own. Mark tried to make me stay because there were so many 'dodgy foreigners about' (he of course being neither dodgy nor a foreigner), but I insisted I just needed some fresh air and exercise, and furthermore that I wasn't premenstrual or 'in a strop'.

After walking a mile or so, carrying my sandals and hitching up my sarong as I padded the wet sand, I found a secluded spot and sat down, staring out to sea and thinking of nothing. I had always felt there was something about the sea, especially at night, that instilled a beautiful feeling of total calm and tranquillity. This section of the beach was almost totally deserted, give or take the occasional shoreline wanderer and the copulating couple on the sun lounger a hundred feet or so to my right. I snatched up handfuls of cool sand and let the grains run through my fingers, feeling alone but totally at ease with that feeling of solitude. I leaned back on my elbows and tilted my face to the sky, closing my eyes and enjoying the warm breeze that occasionally lifted loose strands of my hair. *Moon-bathing,* I mused, smiling to myself. *I am much more beautiful in this light.* I stretched out my legs and pulled back the light fabric of my sarong to reveal my bare thighs. Yes, even those stumpy old legs looked *so* much better in this light. I put my hand on my stomach and sucked it in. At that moment, I believed in myself totally and unequivocally. *The up-side of being myopic,* I smiled to myself, studying my body with an unusual portion of appreciation. I was happily drunk, just a little tipsy, and the tokes I had taken earlier of Kermit's joint had mellowed me out. I knew that by now the others would be well on the way to total and complete intoxication; that same old skirmish on the dance floor, looking to pull and pop pills, living like mad until sleep or sickness got the better of them. I was glad I was away from it all, and not in the midst of the sweat and the noise for a change.

I listened to the lulling resonance of wave after wave on the shore, then gazed out at the lights sparkling and fragmenting on the sea's vitreous rippled surface, feeling utterly at peace.

It was like this for an hour, maybe more, when I suddenly became aware of another presence nearby. When I turned my head, I was dumbfounded to see Mark standing a few feet away from me, his hands thrust in the pockets of his shorts, looking young and slightly silly with his baseball cap positioned askew.

He regarded me shiftily. 'Alright,' he said.

'What the hell are you doing here?' I demanded. 'How long have you been standing there like that, Mark? Christ, you freaked me out!'

'Felt a bit shite, and Kermit started acting the wanker again so I came down here to skim some stones for a bit,' he explained. 'You OK?'

I nodded. 'Yeah, just . . . wanted to be on my own for a bit.'

He walked towards me, fumbling for his cigarettes. 'Am I disturbing you?'

'No more than usual.'

'Good.' He lit up a fag and offered me one.

'You know I don't smoke.'

'Go on. It will help you relax.'

'I *am* relaxed. At least I was until you came along.'

'Soz.' He smiled and sat down beside me. The smell of his aftershave and smoky clothes made me feel strangely homesick for some reason. He smoked silently and I watched him a moment, pulling my sarong around me and sinking my bare feet into the sand, feeling it rush between my toes. The street lights behind threw muted light onto the sea, which reflected back a pale glacial glitter onto Mark's brooding expression. Neither of us spoke for a long time, wrapped up in our own private thoughts.

Mark suddenly said, 'The sea looks best at night.' It was a fairly commonplace and banal remark, but the sound of his voice sent a shiver down my spine. When I looked at him and he looked back at me, and smiled the smile I had become so accustomed to over the years – not a real smile, but not a false one, either – it was like a wave breaking against my heart. It was one of those magic moments – like the moment of enlightenment I experienced at St Luke's in September 1982 when Mark first sent me into a tailspin of relentless infatuation. The sensation momentarily took my breath away – the unexpectedness of it as much as the extremity and immediacy.

'Don't you think?' he said. I was aware that his eyes had not shifted from my face, but I turned my face away and felt unable to look back at him. I shivered and pulled my knees up against my chest.

'I suppose,' I murmured, non-committally. Stone-cold sobriety was returning to me quite rapidly, and with it I could feel my common sense and self-consciousness coming back, bit by bit.

'Y'know,' Mark said, after another agreeable silence, 'I think it's great that you're going to Australia.'

'Do you?'

'Sure. I think you're very fucking brave.'

I started to feel cold, and rubbed the tops of my arms. Mark finished his cigarette then extinguished it in the sand. 'Thing is, Caz,' he went on, 'you're my closest mate, out of the lot of them I prob'ly trust you most of all, 'cos, well, you've always, like, been there . . . look, I'm not just saying this 'cos I'm drunk or nothin' . . .'

I glanced at him dubiously.

'Honest,' he said. 'I'm . . . gonna really miss you when you go.'

I couldn't help laughing at this. 'OK Mark, whatever,' I said.

'That's your problem, Caz. You never fuckin' take me seriously.'

'Oh. Really.' I stopped smiling and our eyes locked for a moment. Finally I said, 'Heard the Aesop fable about the boy who cried wolf, Mark?'

'Oh bloody hell, don't go off on one. Not now.'

'Alright. I'll spare you this time.'

'Will you miss me?'

'Oh for heaven's sake, what do you think?'

'Dunno, that's why I'm askin'.'

'Don't be soft, you know I will.'

'You cold?'

'What? No, not really. Well, a little bit, maybe.'

'Yeah, it's gettin' a bit parky now innit. 'Ere.' Mark, the least chivalrous of all the men I had ever known – and this was no mean feat – then proceeded to take off his shirt and, taking care to minimise unnecessary bodily contact, placed it around my shoulders. The material was thin but warm from his body, and aromatic with the consilient spice of his sweat and aftershave. Taking a few seconds to recover from the shock, and then a few more seconds to work out how to react, I said, 'Er . . . thanks. But aren't you going to freeze now?'

Mark grinned and lay back on the sand, his arms crossed behind his head. 'Nah, I've got me lucky pulling T-shirt on, see. That'll keep me hot as fuck, don't you worry.'

I regarded him, slipping my arms cautiously through the sleeves of his shirt. 'It just looks like a plain old white T-shirt to me,' I remarked. 'In fact . . . it makes you look a bit gay, if truth be told.'

Mark raised his head, his face creased up in disgust. 'You fucking *what*?'

'Well, it's one of those tight, sleeveless jobbies, isn't it. Shows off your . . . muscle.' I knew that this sounded absurdly flirtatious and immediately regretted the compliment, but Mark seemed to disregard it, still preoccupied with getting to the bottom of the unforgivable 'gay' comment.

'Well, yeah, that's prob'ly why I always get lucky when I wear it. But not, I fuckin' repeat *not*, with geezers. Christ Caz, don't say things like that.'

I held up my hands in defeat, vaguely perplexed and certainly bemused by Mark's vehement reaction. 'OK, forget I said anything. You look like the most heterosexual being on the planet. Is that better? Anyway,' I went on, 'you don't need a pulling T-shirt do you?'

He looked at me quizzically.

'Because you've got Claire,' I explained. 'And, correct me if I'm wrong, but haven't you actually managed to remain faithful to her for the last six days?' I nudged him playfully and cried out, 'Praise be! It's a miracle!'

'Give it a rest.'

He reclined back on the sand and closed his eyes, and I remained sitting, staring out at the sea until my eyes glazed over. Breaking another long silence, Mark suddenly announced, 'I do love her, you know.'

I sighed. 'I know you do. And I'm glad you've found someone who will . . .' I was going to say 'keep you in line', but I thought that sounded wrong, so I opted for the trusty cliche, '. . . make you happy.' Then I sighed again, hoping I had made my opinion on the matter perfectly clear, without being rude or hurtful.

I was about to say something else, in fact I felt inclined to inflict a bit of a rambling monologue on him before the final effects of the alcohol and pot dwindled out of my system completely. But then I felt a hand touch my back, and the words, and my breath, caught in my throat. Mark was touching me, and something wasn't right about it. It wasn't the gesture of a friend. It wasn't the touch of the Mark I knew. Mark didn't touch me at all, as a rule. Certainly not like this.

I didn't turn around to look at him. I shut my eyes and tried to breathe steadily. I felt his fingers through the fabric of the shirt, and it was like a caress, tender and sensual. I thought I could be imagining it, that I *must* be imagining it, and so I tried to think of something, anything, to swerve the mood back to its previous, easy-going state. That good old natural platonic rapport. With some effort, I almost managed it.

'I'm going to quit my job as soon as I get back,' I said, forcing jollity and casualness into my voice.

The hand didn't move. 'Good for you,' Mark replied. His tone hadn't changed, still the laid-back, lazy drawl. 'I always said you could do better.'

'And . . . I'm hoping to get bar work to start off with. Out in Oz, I mean. Live like a student for a bit. Beers and barbies on the beach, that kinda thing. But eventually I want to train to be a teacher. There's this really great website . . .' I trailed off, partly because I forgot halfway through my sentence what I was going to say, and partly because I was more than a little distracted.

Slowly, the hand crept beneath the shirt to touch my bare skin, one finger at a time brushing my spine. Madly, desperately, I tried to rationalise what was happening – *it's just a little gesture, it means nothing, he's just being pissed and suave and you're the only girl around.* At the same time, my body became internally animated with a bizarre mixture of horror and disabling desire.

'Yeah, my mum said,' Mark murmured. 'You'd be brilliant. You'll do well. I know you will.'

I still couldn't look at him. His hand slid across my back, venturing up as far as my shoulder blades and then back down before resting on my hip. After a few deep breaths, I whispered, 'Mark . . . ?'

'Hmm?'

'How much have you had to drink tonight?'

The hand remained but the fingers stopped moving. 'Not that much. Why?'

'Oh, no reason,' I said.

The atmosphere was eased slightly, to my utmost relief, when a group of three teenage Asian girls jumped down from the wall just behind us and raced across the beach, stopping at a spot just a stone's throw from where we were sitting. One of them had a CD player and turned it on just loud enough for us to hear, while the other two performed a series of gentle but impressive gymnastics routines on the sand, chatting quietly amongst themselves. The girl with the radio sat cross-legged, facing away from us, smoking a joint. Every now and then, we caught a whiff of the smoke, wafted over by the sea breeze, which had now turned much cooler. After a few moments, the girl turned up the volume a fraction.

The CD was by Robbie Williams. The song, at that moment, was 'Angels'.

'Mm, I could do with a joint right now,' I said.

'Same here,' Mark whispered.

A thought occurred to me. 'Do you want to go for a walk? Just to the other end of the beach?'

Mark shook his head. 'Nah. I like it here. It's quiet.'

He had retracted his hand now, but still something inexplicably and overtly sexual crackled in the air, and I couldn't stand it. My heart was having palpitations and I felt giddy, almost a little nauseous. I shoved my hands into the sand and tried to think rationally.

'Well, maybe I should be getting back to the villa,' I said, although I could quite happily have stayed there all night.

'Maybe you should,' Mark responded, somewhat enigmatically. It was then that I dared to turn around and look at him. His pupils were big and black and at once I was hopelessly lost in them. Everything about what I was feeling at that moment was so wrong, and yet so right, so completely natural. He removed his cap and put his hand through his hair, trying to resurrect his gelled spikes but succeeding only in making himself look even more like a dishevelled British tourist. A very, very sexy dishevelled British tourist.

I opened my mouth to say something but no words came out. Wasn't this a situation I had dreamed about? Wasn't this what I had always wanted?

Mark spoke, his voice soft and mellifluous. 'Don't go to Australia.' He touched me again, this time on the arm.

His eyes scanned my face. I eked out one syllable. 'Why?'

Instinctively, I reached out for him and he grabbed my hand and, to my astonishment, brought it to his face and kissed it, then turned it over and kissed my wrist and my palm, slowly opening my hand out, his fingers interlacing with mine. No more words were spoken. When our eyes met again, this was closely followed by the meeting of our bodies as we connected physically in a kiss. My mind effectively closed down as I spun out into my own private galaxy of stars, each efflorescing one after another, bursting out of darkness and fading into each other, a kaleidoscope. I found myself on my back, half terrified, insensible with lust as Mark continued kissing me; a wonderful, passionate, indisputably non-platonic kiss that just went on and on. I thought I might go mad with the sensation of it, the feel of him, the taste and smell of him, the closeness of him.

A part of my brain was screaming *this is wrong, this is so wrong, this is ABSURD.*

Another part was drowning it out with a looping chant: *he wants me, he desires me, he is cheating on the woman he loves with ME, ME, ME.* Both parts were quashed by an all-consuming animalistic aspect that cried out for touch, for intimacy, an overdue interchange of passion.

I had speculated about Mark's sexual technique before; many times I had lain awake wondering what he was like, how he kissed, how he felt, what noises he might make, how big he was. He slipped my bikini straps down my shoulders and ran his hand over my breasts, across my ribcage, reaching underneath me and pulling me hard toward him. His breath was hot and hard in my ear as he continued exploring, and I explored him, too – ravenously, frenziedly. Those were *Mark's* hands on *my* body, *his* tongue in *my* mouth – it was real, but it didn't seem real. Then, still kissing, never stopping, the warm shirt was removed and discarded, sarong untied and whipped free, sent floating carelessly on the air; gusset rubbed, legs parted, fingers inserted, tongues and hands everywhere. His lips on my neck, my earlobe, my nipple, my stomach; my hands on his buttocks, thighs, back, feeling the hardness of him, the muscles tightening beneath my touch. The sound of a zip going, the snap of elastic, knickers pushed down to my ankles, shorts pushed down to his knees. I opened up to him and he was inside me all at once; at the same moment our eyes met and as alive as I felt in that instant, it was then that I consciously knew something precious had died and could never be brought back.

Seventeen years is a long time to want someone. Seventeen years of lust were purged in seventeen minutes. I know this because I caught a glimpse of Mark's rip-off Casio before we lunged at each other, and then again after he rolled off me, panting heavily. Seventeen minutes. A thousand seconds or so.

I fell asleep wrapped up in his arms, and we woke up together at dawn, just in time to watch the sun rise behind the sea, a vibrant scorch of vivid red on the horizon diluted to pale shimmering orange on the still water.

'Are you cold?' he asked me dozily, snuggling up against my back and kissing my hair. I thought about Claire and I was consumed by conflicting feelings of guilt, and – shockingly, shamefully – smugness.

The situation was so surreal that I was unable to analyse my immediate feelings any more closely than that.

'No. Are you?'

'Surprisingly I'm quite warm actually,' he said. He tilted my face towards his and kissed me full on the mouth.

We remained there for what could have been an hour or longer, side by side, Mark's right hand resting on my stomach, which I was too tired and relaxed to hold in. Then, suddenly, he pulled away, searched for his lighter and lit up a cigarette. His mood changed, almost as if the nicotine aggravated rather than relaxed him. He stood up and looked down at me, half of his face in shadow. His expression was hard to read.

'I'd better go,' he said.

I felt a pang of shame then. It felt like we had broken some terrible taboo. The rational voice inside me wanted to scream out loud, *What have we done? Oh my God Mark, what the hell have we done?*

But instead I simply looked away and mumbled, 'OK.'

'Will you be alright? I mean . . .'

'I'm fine, I just want to stay here for a bit longer.' More than anything, I wanted to be left alone.

'Right. Well.' He sighed and stuck his baseball cap on, back to front, patting his back pockets and scanning the ground, presumably to check he hadn't dropped anything. He glanced at me one last time and said, 'See you round.'

For seventeen minutes I had been Mark's girlfriend; now I didn't even feel like I could call myself his friend. I felt cheap. Cheap, and yet still exhilarated. I turned my back, pulling his shirt tight around me. 'See ya.'

'You can keep the shirt if you like.'

'Cheers.'

There was a long silence, and I assumed he had gone, but then I heard his voice again, even closer than before. 'Caz?'

'Hmm?' I moved my head to face him but neither of us could directly look the other in the eye.

'Er . . . you are . . . on the Pill, aren't you?'

I quickly turned back round. 'For fuck's sake . . .'

'I'm sorry, I'm sorry, I just . . . forget it. I'm sorry.'

'Go away, Mark.'

He hesitated a while, but I didn't move and kept my back to him. Finally he walked away and I was left there with my own tangled thoughts.

After so many years as friends, to have crossed that boundary, overstepped that line, torn down that barrier . . . how could things ever be the same again? I knew the answer already. Things would never be the same again. The repercussions would stay with both of us, and the implications of those repercussions would stain our friendship for ever. I curled up on the sand, sniffing the collar of Mark's shirt and holding back tears. I tried to get back to sleep but was too fraught and now, despite the rapid ascension of the sun that shone bright through my eyelids, too cold.

Much later that day, the last full day of the holiday, we found ourselves alone together, sitting at opposite ends of a table in an otherwise deserted bar, staring at our cocktails in awkward silence.

Mark cleared his throat and mumbled, 'Er, Caz . . .'

I was so on edge I was tempted to ask him for a cigarette. Instead I managed to blurt out, 'Please, please don't, Mark.' I stared at him imploringly. 'Just don't say those three dreadful words, I couldn't bear it.'

Mark's expression turned to one of confusion, tinged with mild panic.

I clarified. 'About last night.'

Still his brow remained furrowed, but the panic left his face. 'I wasn't going to say that, actually.'

'No? Then what?'

He fingered the stem of his glass nervously. 'I don't know. I really don't know. I'm sorry.' Mark had possibly apologised to me more in the past twelve hours than he had done for the entire time I'd known him. He waited for me to say something else, and when I didn't, he got up, knocked back the last of his cocktail, and mumbled, 'I'm outta here. I can't cope with this.'

And with that, he was gone.

Becks found me in the same spot some time later, still on my own and still with the same half-empty glass, and I broke down and told her everything. She didn't seem surprised. 'It was always on the cards,' she said. 'It was a matter of when, not if.'

She took me back to our villa and we packed in preparation for our early morning flight home and then chatted until Suzie rolled in with an idiotically grinning Jonesey at dawn and, to our surprise and repulsion, locked herself in the bathroom with him.

So that was how the holiday of my life ended. At the airport, whereas before the eight of us had been a relatively harmonious conglomerate, we split up into insular pairs and there was a palpably frosty atmosphere that only Flynn and Kermit seemed unaware of. Becks and I swapped books for the return journey: I gave her my copy of Alain de Botton's *Essays in Love* and she gave me her copy of the *Rough Guide to Australia.* I pretended to be too involved in it to notice that Mark was staring at me quite openly from across the aisle throughout most of the flight, but engrossed as I indeed was, I did notice. I just wasn't prepared to give him the satisfaction of showing how deeply and irrevocably the experience had affected me. But I suppose that event, that abandoned moment of weakness and madness I shared with my best friend on that tranquil Costa Blanca beach in the final week of July 1999, was what made my decision to emigrate seem not only rational but inevitable. Before we touched down I had read Becca's book from cover to cover and mentally planned out my itinerary, without granting Mark a single glance.

With cheerful aplomb, I resigned and worked out my notice to the end of September. As a parting gift, Martin and the rest of my colleagues bought me a cuddly toy koala and a 'comedy' wide-brimmed hat replete with dangling corks, which Martin claimed to have crafted 'with his own fair hand'. I told him I didn't doubt it for a second, and wore it for the entire evening, thereby running the risk of looking a complete fool in all the obligatory photographs. I felt closer to the Franklin and Barrington team during one leaving party piss-up on a Friday after work than I ever had done during the three and a half years I had worked there.

Mark sent me a card on my birthday with the somewhat cryptic message 'Have a great day and I hope you find what you're looking for out in Oz next year.' He had started to write something underneath but scribbled it out and signed off in the usual way, a big 'M' underlined twice. There was one random lost weekend with Mark and Tamworth in Dagenham in late August, to celebrate Tamworth's surprise whirlwind engagement to a lovely Ukrainian girl called Mila who he had met during the Benidorm holiday. But apart from that, I barely saw Mark until the day he drove Bev and me down to Newquay to enjoy the last of the British summer on the coast, where I spent one last night in that lovely Cornish cottage, and said a final farewell to his grandparents.

Although it was never directly brought up in conversation (well, can you imagine it? *Oh Caz, remember that time in Benidorm when we both went a bit mental and ended up shagging each other?*), all I could think of was that prohibited liaison and how it had eradicated my illusions about the very nature of our relationship. And the natural fragile affinity that had been so carefully built up between us, which I had come to take for granted as the defining factor of our friendship, had now so easily, so quickly and absolutely, been replaced by something awkward and intractable.

As for Mark and Claire, their own relationship appeared to be going from strength to strength, and although Mark diplomatically refrained from referring to her in my presence, I was polite enough to ask after her pointedly. On Mark's twenty-sixth birthday, Claire treated him to a day at the dog races in Walthamstow and Mark, buoyed up after winning over a hundred quid, pledged to her that he was now ready for them to move in together. And so it came to pass that Mark braced himself for commitment at last. There was much rejoicing in the Crozier household: even Bev, who had always agreed with me that Mark and Claire were a 'slightly odd' couple, was delighted by her son's latest revelation. I in turn made similarly surprised but encouraging noises, although I chose to say precious little on the subject to Mark himself.

I called round with a birthday present for him the morning after his birthday and we managed a brief, relatively civilised conversation, concluding with a hug and a tongue-tied exchange of sentiments. It became a little too mawkish for comfort when we both realised that it would probably be the last time we'd see each other for a very long time, and so I left before either of us had the chance to say what I believed almost certainly needed to be left unspoken.

Then I went back home and made a start on my packing, and selected something sparkly and kitsch to wear to an eighties-themed New Year's Eve party the following night.

In a basement room at a relatively tranquil house party in Hammersmith in the late evening of the last day of 1999, I wondered what I'd miss most about my old life. I exchanged a volley of text messages with Mark, but he stopped replying after eight o'clock and instead I used my mobile to call my mum in Liverpool, where she and Teri were staying with my grandmother, true to the Shaw family tradition. At five to ten, anticipating imminent drunkenness on a grand scale, I then called Bev while I still had my wits about me, and reiterated my promise to pop in and see her one more time before leaving for the airport on Tuesday morning. She and Sean were both drunk already and boisterously wished me a Happy New Year and promised to visit me in Sydney once I had settled. I told them I'd fly back and stay with them in their caravan in Clacton when I got bored of the outback and the beaches and the bronzed Ozzie surfer dudes. We laughed, I hung up, I burst into tears.

Then I thought about my family again, my real family. I knew deep in my heart that I would miss them, all of them, much more than I ever thought I would. Even my recidivistic brother. And my mum, my dear determined mother, who had taught me nothing if not how to survive on nothing and galvanise myself against adversity. I had a lot to thank her for. Jolene was staying with her boyfriend's family and Shaz was shacked up in a commune of like-minded disaffected dissidents, celebrating the new millennium by causing as much mayhem as possible in central London. Kev was still in prison, his fourth stint in as many years, but was due for parole in mid-February, subject to good behaviour. Which seemed unlikely I supposed, given his record: 'Kevin Shaw' and 'good behaviour' didn't really go together. Still, I wasn't too worried about him; he was a survivor. We all were in our own ways. We'd always had to be.

I returned home fairly early from the party, arm in arm with a crapulent Suzie, who immediately passed out on the kitchen floor after offering to make a 'nice cuppa tay'. Now I just had to finish my packing and sort out a sack of stuff to drop in at the charity shop. I had to be ruthlessly selective about what I wanted to keep and what I wanted to take with me, what I might have been able to sell, and what I had to get rid of. It was a tough and disheartening process, but as I felt for my flight tickets and passport in the front pocket of my bag, ready and waiting by the door, my overriding emotion was one of euphoria. In my rented room, the little bit of space that had cost me nearly five times the price of my air ticket for little over a year's tenancy, I arranged the last of my favourite clothes into piles, some of which I knew I would have to adjust or possibly grow into. I put on a CD that reminded me of old times, one sentimental song after another, but this time I didn't cry.

Epilogue

'We kicked and talked. The thick salt kept us up. I see us floating there yet, inseparable – two cork dolls. What keyhole have we slipped through, what door has been shut? The shadows of the grasses inched round like hands of a clock, and from our opposite continents we wave and call. Everything has happened.'

Sylvia Plath, *The Babysitters*

From One Millennium to the Next

Mark, in bed with a girl at the end of the world, 31 December 1999 – 1 January 2000

Street parties in their seething masses erupt to an orgasmic crescendo as the last seconds of an old era are chimed out, the resonance pierced by the shrill ascent of impatient fireworks. Linking arms and wailing the traditional song, almost in unison, almost in tune, swaying and meandering in disoriented groups down the street or collapsing across bars and beds all over the country.

Mark celebrates fifteen miles away from his best friend on the other side of the same city, a distance that will be increased five hundreds of times over in just a few days. He is at a party with the usual crowd, although Jonesey overestimated his drinking prowess once again and passed out at quarter to eleven after demolishing a bucket of lethal punch and a quick succession of shorts. He is now snoozing in a puddle of dribble with his arm wrapped around the leg of a table, and his friends have taken the opportunity to decorate him for an amusing photo shoot (green food dye in hair, pink feather boa, one shaved eyebrow, '666' in permanent marker across forehead and a ropey carrot sticking out of left ear). Flynn's new girlfriend ('new' meaning that a few hours ago she was just 'some bird') is down to her underwear already, and threatening to run out into the road if she is plied with any more drink. Another glass of suspicious liquid is hurriedly obtained from the kitchen. Tamworth, already the grateful recipient of a hurried hand-job and half-cut on cheap champagne and even cheaper coke, spins the bottle for a third time. Mark rediscovers Claire beneath a pile of coats in an upstairs room, and they coalesce to the romantic sound of retching as someone reaches the bathroom a second too late.

After midnight, the world is still in one piece, the population is still alive and thriving, the moon is still up and glowing, and most of the pubs are still open. Some of the parties are only just beginning. Mark tries to call his mother and can't get through so he hurls his mobile across the room and replaces his cold hands on Claire's warm thighs.

'You and me,' he murmurs to her, easing himself back between her legs and holding her face in his hands, reiterating the promise he had made two days before, 'we will move in together this year Claire. Soon. I promise.'

These are the words she has wanted to hear for as long as she can remember, one monumental step up from the relatively flimsy 'I love you', which had after all been played to death and was only now beginning to be *demonstrated* at long last. Actions speak louder. Still, she says those three words to him in the absence of anything more original and appropriate.

Back at his place, in his bed, one hour later, Mark pulls Claire close to him and they entwine beneath the insulating weight of the quilt, dozy and drunk and drifting on a cloud of beatific intoxication. This transcendental state is due more to their effects on each other than the effects of the copious celebratory drinks, effects that are almost as strong now as they were when they first met, three years ago. But they are still too mentally charged to sleep.

Claire's lips touch Mark's ear. 'Are you happy, Mark?' she whispers. 'Are you feeling as happy as I am right now?'

The answer is of course 'yes', but Mark doesn't reply immediately. He savours the moment, kissing the top of her head and inhaling the spicy smell of her shampoo, tracing his hand across the hot skin of her shoulder, down her spine, over the sensuous curve of her hip beneath the quilt.

It is so cosy and comforting, curtains pulled tight against the cold night outside, where people are still celebrating in their vociferous droves, where fireworks still sporadically splinter the sky with sonic screeches. The warmth of the bed, the post-coital glow radiating from their bodies, the dreamy flicker of tealights around the room, a gentle chill-out tune floating from the radio, such a calm and romantic ambience. It is enough to make Mark truly believe in himself, at least at that moment, when he tells her, 'I've never been happier.'

Claire tilts her face up toward him and kisses him full on the mouth. Mark strokes back her hair and tells her she's beautiful. She rests her head on his shoulder and closes her eyes, as content and sleepy as a cat on a hearth rug. She mentally makes plans and turns the fantasy around. She loves him more than she has ever loved anyone, ever. She wonders if she would care at all if the world really did end right here, right now.

Beside her, the man who has inspired such limitless adoration and bliss within her is still wide-eyed as his hand continues to glide across her body, absently now more than affectionately. She naturally mistakes this for genuine tenderness and arches herself into him, as close as she can possibly get, feeling every sinew and contour of his body against hers, relishing the intimacy. She marvels at how well they fit together. During sex, and after sex, it is just so right. It feels like it was meant to be. They mesh so perfectly.

Mark is thinking of nothing, or at least nothing he can put into words, so instead he utters more sentimental verbiage, reiterating his heartfelt promise, because it seems so appropriate. 'By Valentine's Day, babe,' he begins, his eyes still fixed on the ceiling, 'you and me, right, we'll be living together, I promise. Six weeks or so, that's all. I mean it.'

'Hmm . . .' Claire deposits a number of kisses on his chest, runs a fingernail down his chest to his navel. 'A place of our own. I don't really care where just so long as we're together.'

This isn't really true; Claire is extremely picky and particular, but Mark is quite touched by the sentiment. 'Yeah,' he sighs, pulling her up towards him to kiss her on the lips again, as if to seal his fate. 'Just you and me. That's all that's important.'

'More quality moments like this,' Claire murmurs, curling up luxuriously in his arms. 'Every day. For ever.'

He thinks: *This is the woman of my dreams. I am so lucky. I am so in love.* He feels cocooned in this irresistible belief, protected by it, no longer scared of it.

But then as her grip around him tightens the calmative cloud lifts for a second and he thinks of less gratifying thoughts; tiny doubts creep in, one by one. He remembers with surprising clarity what Caroline said to him, after he had introduced her to Claire for the first time. He can recall her exact words, even though they had made so little real impact on him the first time: *Well, they say opposites attract, don't they? I do like her, really I do. Not a lot, but just so long as you're happy, right.*

He hadn't expected Caroline to hit it off with Claire anyway. He supposed there was a little bit of jealousy working in there somewhere, and this hypothesis didn't please him as much as it would have done in his younger days. It actually perturbed him slightly. Claire's words after she had met Caroline for the first time, also recalled with some clarity: 'She seems nice . . . I'm glad I met her because it's put my mind at rest.' He asked her what she had meant by that, but he knew the underlying meaning was, *thank God she's not beautiful.* Claire's remorseless paranoia and fearsome pride made a rod for her own back, and therefore, quite naturally, also served as a millstone around the neck of her boyfriend. She had simply replied: 'Well, she's not your type, is she?' Typical Claire. She could get away with it though, because she absolutely was. Beautiful. His type.

But they really were a great couple. They were. They are. He doesn't need anybody's approval; what counts are *his* feelings, *her* feelings, that moment. Just *knowing* that it's right, a gut instinct. That's what matters.

Claire is now half-asleep. He touches her cheek, caresses her gently, studies her face, exploring the soft contours with his fingers – her eyelashes, hair, forehead, lips. From this angle, in this light, she looks like someone else. He wonders what the hell she sees in him. He leans across and blows out the candle by the bed, lies back across the pillows and tries to relax.

His mind is racing.

Securely ensconced in that darkened bedroom, he remains wide awake for some time, long after Claire has surrendered to sleep. In spite of the sticky heat of her body, the warmth of the quilt, the heavy curtains pulled tight against the double glazing, and the steady, comforting clank of the hot radiator, he feels strangely cold and he wonders why.

Drawing Claire against his chest, he shuts his eyes and waits for sleep.

New Millennium

Caroline, starting again, 2 January 2000

All my life I had dreamed of disappearing. Of being swallowed up by glorious swathes of candy-fluffed cloud to be whisked away to a better somewhere, to a magical, mystical place like in a fairy tale. But not an ephemeral fantasy land, not an ethereal vision; somewhere real, *real.* Somewhere I could be *me.* Me, without the guilt and disgust and disappointment. My girl's dream, and my woman's dream. I never stopped dreaming. For a while, I had wanted literally to disappear. All I saw every time I looked in the mirror was a nobody, and worse than that, a nobody that took up far too much space. The worst kind of nobody.

But now, finally, I was disappearing.

It was the first time I had been to an airport on my own. They are very vast, very scary places when you have nobody else there with you.

Heathrow was busy, but not as frantic as I thought it would be at that time of year: the usual droves of business suits and white robes, immaculate stewardesses with painted smiles, couples in casuals, tense families, exhausted or excitable groups. But after I checked in my suitcase (my entire everything, accumulated over my whole life, totalled little more than ten kilos), I was able to find a fairly quiet spot to sit and read my *Lonely Planet* and scoff my wine gums and watch the world and their assorted backpacks go by. I was travelling alone to a faraway destination I knew little about and every nerve of my body was alight. I was so afraid I felt sick. Fervid excitement welled up inside me, spilling over into terror. Fear of the unknown. Anticipation that the unknown, whatever it was, would be beyond my wildest dreams.

The best place in the world to disappear into. Anywhere, *anywhere* but here.

In my hand luggage: hairbrush, two aerosols, a silly paperback from W. H. Smith (impulse purchase, already halfway through before even boarding the plane), one of the lesser nasal-scourging perfumes selected from duty free's heady collection, my passport (double check that again), strawberry lip balm, purse with dollars and travellers' cheques and emergency credit card, sun cream, spray-on aftersun, cocoa-butter body lotion, Walkman with Robbie Williams tape (still couldn't listen to 'Angels' without crying), pink-rimmed sunglasses with negligible UV protection, diary, address book, three biros, scrawled note from Mark's mum, chewing gum, new bikini and sarong, old bikini and sarong (memories), Mars bar, camera and film, aspirin.

I suppose there was a very tiny part of me that secretly half expected (or possibly half wanted) an emotional send-off. Maybe Suzie could have turned up and wished me well, never mind her terminal hangover. Maybe the boys might have jumped into Tamworth's old banger and sped on down to say goodbye and demand postcards and belt out boisterous innuendoes as I waved to them, blowing ironic kisses from the asphalt flight path, a final soft-focus scene in a movie that ends on a perfect plateau, a resolution. Something tacky. Something to make me laugh, make me wonder: am I doing the right thing? Am I mad for wanting to leave? Am I cowardly? Am I in denial? And Mark; why did I expect more from him than a hurried five-minute phone call an hour before my taxi turned up? More than a typically flippant and cool *take it easy Caz, yeah sure thing I'll miss you, but it's what you wanna do innit.* Had I really expected more, or was I just *hoping* for more?

I pushed him out of my mind; it was too late now anyway. This was going to be one thing I wouldn't regret. (Always better to regret something you have done than something you haven't, isn't that what they say?)

My flight was delayed. One hour, then two. On and on the waiting stretched out.

I finished the awful paperback, which ended predictably; a clinch between nubile heroine and dashing hero, a sunset and a gushing acknowledgements page. I paced up and down outside Tie Rack, took another aspirin, skimmed through an abandoned newspaper supplement, bought yet another bloody sarong just because I liked the colour.

The airline apologetically offered fractious victims of a 'faulty fuel tank' some free snacks to compensate for the delay while they set about fixing it. I temporarily mislaid my boarding pass and had a mild panic attack.

Found it within five minutes between pages 218 and 219 of crappy book. Put boarding pass in pocket of jacket, and book in bin. Got myself a hot chocolate and a croissant, though wasn't really hungry. Stuffed them within a couple of minutes, consciously and smugly rebelling against the number one rule of every tedious diet I had ever naively followed. Looked across at cluster of payphones and considered (again) calling Mark or his mum, or even my mum. Just for a final farewell. Decided not to – instead resolved to give them all a casual and laconic phone call from Bangkok just to say *Yeah, having an awesome time, missing England soo-oo much, gotta go, wish you were here, see ya when I see ya, adios.* After all, I was a spunky, spirited little adventure traveller now. I was doing it solo. I didn't need anyone, and I certainly didn't need emotional valedictions at a victorious time like this.

A middle-aged Australian bloke in stonewash jeans and a dirty baseball cap sat down next to me and started up some idle chitchat. He offered me a Silk Cut and looked absolutely shocked when I declined.

'Jeez, this is my third packet since gettin' here,' he grunted, shoving the filter in the corner of his mouth. He looked irritably at his watch. '*Four and a half bloody hours ago*,' he huffed. 'If those incompetent shitheads are gonna keep us waitin' round till kingdom fuckin' come, there's nothin' else to do but smoke yourself stupid.' We had a short verbal exchange and established that we were both waiting for the same flight, while numerous public announcements overhead heralded seemingly every other flight to every other destination on earth.

'So, what's your plan then? You got rellies down under when you get to Oz next month? Place to stay?' Australian bloke touched the peak of his cap and eyed me darkly. 'Or you one of them trekky types?'

'Pardon?'

'Them backpacker sorts. Vagabond. Hobo. You know.'

'Er . . . not really. This is my first time outside Europe, to be honest. I'm just . . . travelling around for a while. A year, maybe more.'

'Yeah? Well, good for you. You could do worse. Oz is the place to be, take it from me.' He stretched his legs out and considered his scuffed trainers for a moment. 'Not meeting up with anyone?'

I shook my head. 'Not until later. I do have a friend or two out there, but . . .' I shrugged, feigning insouciance to belie a resurgence of trepidation that sparked inside me as I said the words. 'Quit my job, sold my stuff, bought the air tickets before I could change my mind. After Bangkok, I'm in Singapore for a week before going on to Oz. I s'pose I'll stay there for a few months, then I don't know . . . New Zealand maybe. I've got a work permit sorted and all that, so . . .' I was aware that I might have been rambling a little, so I cut myself short and quickly finished with, 'Well . . . I guess I'll have to see how it goes.'

'Hacked off with England?'

I smiled at the understatement. 'You could say that.'

'New start for the new millennium?'

I cringed to hear this hackneyed phrase but tactfully concealed my distaste with another non-committal shrug. Bloody new millennium. How is it that one word had turned itself into a universal cliché in such a short period of time? How is it that so many people *still* couldn't spell it properly, even after all the hype?

'I would like to think so,' I said.

'All on your lonesome too,' he remarked. 'Brave.'

'Well. Not really.'

There was a silence while he finished his cigarette. I stared ahead blankly as a small child bungled towards me, toddler reins trailing on the ground, his awkward, unsteady steps hampered by the restrictive bulk of his nappy. He had grubby, mottled cheeks and a tuft-covered, potato-shaped head that seemed far too big for his ungainly little body, and as he approached me he held out a half-chewed biscuit, shiny with spittle, his inquisitive expression full of hope that this proffered gift might earn him a friend.

'Cute,' muttered the Australian bloke humourlessly, dropping his fag butt into my empty polystyrene cup. The child whimpered at me, indignant that I appeared unmoved by his generous gesture. He eventually crammed the damp biscuit fragment into his mouth, along with his chubby pink fist, and sucked on it purposefully, gazing at me all the while with wide, unblinking eyes.

'Ugh, gross,' I said, under my breath. 'I hate kids.'

'You an' me both,' the Australian sighed, digging his hands deep into his pockets and staring straight ahead.

It wasn't true; I didn't hate kids, not really. I just didn't have a single maternal bone in my body. Just as well really. My life could have turned out very differently.

'Or*lan*do!' A piercing shriek shrilled out behind us from a flustered-looking woman with highly animated vermilion lips and wild hennaed hair, who blazed briskly into my line of vision and hurried forward to snatch up the child. She produced a tissue from her sleeve and spat on it, rubbing at his smeared, outraged face and tutting to herself. He began to cry. I almost felt like crying with him. 'Orlando darling, don't go running off like that,' she scolded him, her voice still wavering a pitch too high. 'Mummy has enough things to worry about without you making a nuisance of yourself.'

She tilted her head at me, raised her pencil-sculpted eyebrows and gave me a faint smile, exasperated more than friendly. 'Terrible twos,' she murmured, by way of explanation. She leaned down slightly towards me as she said it, because as women we are all apparently supposed to be involved in some tacit consensual understanding about the trials of motherhood.

'Or*lan*do?' Australian bloke repeated incredulously, once the woman had turned away and disappeared in a resonant clicking of high heels and potent swish of perfume, with the child (now screaming and writhing) wedged under her arm. 'Fuck me. Poor kid.'

I agreed with a silent nod.

'I'm Bill, by the way,' he said after a few seconds, presenting me with a huge hand that crushed my much smaller one in a vigorous handshake. 'Not short for anything. Just Bill.'

'Caroline,' I said, keeping my guard up, not overstepping the boundaries of politeness. 'Short for Orlando,' I mumbled as an afterthought, also not wanting to appear aloof.

'Heh, heh. Good one.' He grinned and lit up another cigarette but stubbed it out almost immediately when our flight was finally announced, more than three hours late, over the tannoy. 'About friggin' time,' he grumbled, getting to his feet and putting the cigarettes into his back pocket. 'Was beginning to reckon we'd be stuck here 'til the next bloody millennium. I tell you, my connecting flight had better be on time tomorrow or I'll . . .' The rest of his irascible tirade faded into the general drone of the background noise, as by this time I was already heading off impatiently towards the departure gate, my new hiking boots squeaking rapidly on the shiny floor.

Within half an hour, I was boarding the plane, drifting dreamily through the tussle of tourists before taking my humble place in economy class and nevertheless feeling unusually wealthy and worthy, despite the lack of leg room and personal space.

By the time the plane took off, the roar of the engine and the chaotic blur of the view outside the oval window filled me with such overwhelming exhilaration that all my fear just dissolved away. It was replaced by relief. I was leaving. I was disappearing. I was *really* leaving. At last. At last.

I was seated next to a barking mad Buddhist from Berlin. My ears had only just finished popping when she began amiably babbling at me about reincarnation, her holy lama, a bowel operation recently inflicted on the father of her two 'brilliant' grown-up daughters, and the thirteen miniature goats she kept in her back garden, with names such as Bilbo and Hank. She talked rapidly and excitedly in slightly stilted English, her accent full of strange inflections and misplaced question marks.

'I'm clairvoyant as well,' she informed me, cramming her mouth with sugared almonds as she made several failed attempts to fold up a copy of the *Independent.* 'It's true.' She paused, casting me a sideways glance over her half-moon spectacles, arching her thin eyebrows. 'Some people may say it is an affliction, a curse? No. Darling, I assure you, it is a gift.'

Catching sight of my expression, she turned in her seat and seized my hand. 'I read palms too,' she said, pushing her glasses up onto the top of her head with an air of authority while I just looked at her with a bemused and cautious smile. She smelt of a powdery floral scent and had watery blue eyes that stared intently back at me, almost through me.

'You are doubtful,' she said, the rising intonation making it sound like a question, when I had a feeling it was meant as a statement.

'No, I think I keep an open mind about most th–'

'Your life line is a strong one,' she interrupted, raising a finger as if to silence me. 'As is your head line. You will live to be an old woman, I think. No worries about that. And you are very strong-willed, no? Very . . . passionate.' She traced a long, lacquered fingernail over my sticky palm while I tried to decide whether or not this was all just a pointless wind-up from a bored eccentric.

'But your life has not been a very happy one so far,' she whispered, shaking her head.

'What–?'

'I can read it in your eyes as well. The eyes always give things away.' She did not let go of my hand, clutching it tighter as her gaze fixed on me again. 'You have a lot of spirit, and that is important of course. But . . . I sense a troubled past. You have not had much reason to be joyful in your short life so far. And . . . if I may be bold, my darling . . . a boy who is not good for you?'

I chuckled bitterly, less than enthralled by this line of enquiry. 'Ha!

Don't even get me started on that one,' I trilled. 'I attract bastards like you wouldn't believe.'

Her staid seriousness made my smile falter. 'Try me,' she said.

I began to feel my bravado crumble away. She was one of those kindly, understanding strangers that I could almost feel tempted to open up to. Her face was a vision of human compassion, the pale evening light from the window behind shining through her reddish bouffant of fuzzy hair, glistening around her head like an aureole.

I pulled my hand away. 'It doesn't matter,' I muttered, retreating back into my favoured cynical and secretive persona. I turned back to face the front, unfastening my seatbelt and pretending to be interested in the utterly banal contents of the in-flight magazine while she remained turned towards me, continually staring with the same unnerving earnestness. She was very difficult to ignore.

'You are so young and yet you have been through so much,' she whispered reverentially. 'But things will get better for you from now on. Trust me. You'll see.'

Then her tone promptly changed, became almost jaunty. 'Do you know,' she began, 'this will be my first holiday outside Europe since I was sixteen.'

'Really?' I said dozily, glancing at her with a small appeasing smile. 'It's my first time ever.'

'I know.'

Of course you know, you're psychic, aren't you, I thought derisively. *Well, if you can read minds, read this: it's all a load of bollocks and I don't believe a word of it.*

'It's long overdue, really,' she continued, apparently failing to tune into my negative thoughts. 'My eldest daughter Lauren has been living in Cairns with her husband for nearly two years now, and I haven't seen her in all that time. It's a shame really, but I just haven't had the opportunity to go before now.'

'Hmm,' I murmured absently, leaning my head back and closing my eyes with a sigh.

'And it's long overdue for you, too,' she went on, raising her voice slightly. 'How many years have you dreamed about escaping?'

My eyes flickered open again. 'What?'

'You just kept putting it off, didn't you? Making up all those excuses, agonising over all those other dismal choices? We are permitted precious few attractive choices in our lives as it is, wouldn't you agree. You nearly lost your nerve for a while. I think . . .' She paused, scanning my face anxiously before continuing. She leant in closer to me and whispered, 'I think you were waiting for something that never happened.'

I tried to think of something clever to say. 'You tell me.'

Her eyes brightened at this challenge. 'I am correct though, yes? Yes. People can be cruel. Life can be unbearable. I know it. Unrequited love is a horrible thing under any circumstances, my dear girl. It doesn't go away. It cannot fade. Not the kind of love I am feeling from you. So strong and powerful. And yet so . . . misguided. Your heart has opened up like a flower and the love just keeps pouring out, with nowhere to go. You cannot help yourself, my dear. You are passionate, impulsive. And yes, you are romantic, but you pretend not to be. Passion. Oh, such passion! I can see it now in your aura, all pinks and fiery yellows. Yes. This love, it takes over your life, no? Terrible. I'll never forget, when I was nineteen . . .'

I had barely said a word to this woman and she already had me sussed out, albeit not necessarily in words I would have used myself.

'OK, whatever,' I interrupted, 'That's enough now, if you don't mind.' I was aware that I sounded shirty and haughty, which was not the impression I wanted to give. But I was now feeling slightly on edge, far too mentally drained to cope with the pie-in-the-sky ramblings of a persistent and percipient goat rearer from Deutschland.

'I'm sorry,' I said, softening my tone, 'I just . . . want to relax right now. I'm tired. Stressed. And anyway, I don't even know you. Sorry.'

She nodded, but the wry little smile remained. After a short silence, she reached into her bag and pulled out a magazine. 'Here, have a read of this. It's in German, I'm afraid, but you can always just look at the pictures if you like. These silly old magazines are nearly all full of pictures anyway.'

My impulse was to refuse, but she thrust it into my lap. 'Take it,' she said. 'And don't you be so uncomfortable and irritated. I am a friend, no? I am not meaning to upset you.'

I gave in with a weary sigh. 'Oh . . . OK. All right. Thanks.' I opened the magazine randomly, restlessly flicking the polished pages with undisguised boredom. One gorgeous gaunt model after another grinned and pouted out from each lurid page, accompanying captions in German presumably telling the naturally awed reader how to achieve the approximate look without resorting to drastic plastic surgery. The magazine was predominated by outlandishly baroque advertisements for frivolous fragrances and minimising knickers and maximising bras and clump-free mascara; chock-full of airbrushed images cunningly designed to both encourage and dishearten, with the same overriding message as tacitly transmitted the world over by women's magazines in general, whatever the language. Words were not really necessary. I remembered very little German from my GCSE days, but was still able roughly to translate one heading as 'Lose the Weight and Keep your Man!' The prosaic pictures that went with it (a woman-shaped woman looking miserable and single on one side, and an ecstatic-looking boy-shaped woman with disproportionately full breasts and a surrendered Adonis lying at her feet on the other side) confirmed this was probably the approximate theme.

I snorted disdainfully. 'God al*mighty*,' I muttered aloud to myself. 'Get real!'

My companion's hand reached out to touch my arm. It was a surprisingly smooth and elegant hand for someone who must have been at least fifty years old. I glimpsed her shrewd grin out of the corner of her eye.

'You know what that means? It is sad, no?' she said. 'Here, look at this . . .' She took the magazine from me and turned to an article near the end. 'Here. See? Do you know what this one means?' She stabbed an accusing finger at a double-page spread which depicted a pair of lissom, lush-skinned women lolling on a beach in skimpy swimsuits, all sparkly teeth and flaxen hair, beneath dark-blue lettering: 'Dich Liebe Egal was dein' Form.'

'Er . . . no,' I confessed. 'But I don't think I want to know.'

She paused momentarily for effect. 'It says, "Love yourself whatever your shape." Yes. This article, you see, it is about how women should not feel needful to look as pretty as a picture and dainty as a daisy all the time. How the person inside is what is important, no matter what the outer parts look like. You know? Listen . . .' She slid her specs onto the end of her nose and squinted at the page through the narrow semicircular lenses. After a couple of heavy sighs, she read out a little illustrative extract, stumbling hesitantly over the trickier German-to-English translations: 'The beauty industry has for years been . . . enforcing the belief that women should be . . . er, decorative? . . . erm, yes, and consequently a preoccupation with aesthetic matters has been a predominating factor in our day to day lives. But despite all this . . . blah, blah, boring, boring . . . ah yes, we must *surely begin to discover our true worth is reflected in much more valuable and enduring traits* . . . ' We exchanged cynical looks at this juncture. '. . . and it is upon these we should primarily focus our attentions in order to become truly lovable and virtuous people. After generations of submitting to a superficial society's narrow and inaccurate definitions of what the very idea of beauty is, it is high time we used our collective ... *ha*!' She let out a delicate peal of scornful laughter and excused herself before continuing, now with acidic cynicism, '... our *collective feminine powers* and worked together to create a more harmonious and accepting society, one in which we are judged not by how we look, our faces and figures, blah-de-blah, but by what degree of goodness and caring we display to our fellow beings. We may enhance but we cannot realistically *change* our physical appearance and the very idea of physical perfection will always frustrate and elude us, but in the meantime we *do* have control over how we behave towards others, and the important life choices we make. This, surely, is what defines us as humans, and is the very *essence of humanity*. Women ... oh, I like this bit ... women are *creatures of beauty whatever they look like*, but in order to become *truly beautiful* we should look inside of ourselves, way beyond whatever image the mirror reflects back at us.' She folded the magazine shut between her knees and looked up at me, her smile twisting into a grimace that I felt inclined to reciprocate. 'Interesting, isn't it? Wouldn't you agree that this is all a little ... what is the word? Hippocritical?'

'Most definitely,' I agreed, believing wholeheartedly that the emetic little snippet of the article I had been subjected to was unspeakably crass, never mind hypocritical.

After a short pause, I said, 'I stopped buying these kinds of magazines last year. They're all the same. They depress me.'

Her eyes looked me up and down appraisingly. 'Very wise, my darling. I must explain, I only bought this one at Berlin airport yesterday for the free millennium diary, you see?' She held up a small, flimsy, silvery booklet, with the magazine's title emblazoned in hot pink capitals across the front. I thought it looked like another reason not to buy the magazine, rather than an incentive, but I didn't say anything. She stuffed the magazine back in a bag under her seat then settled back against the headrest with her hands clasped across her chest. There was a long silence, and I assumed she had fallen asleep. Before too long, a stewardess came around with the drinks trolley and I asked her for a glass of water.

'And your friend?' she asked sweetly, offering me the standard mechanical smile along with the Perrier. 'Would she like anything?'

'Erm ... yeah, better make it two I suppose. Unless ... actually, I don't suppose you've got anything a bit stronger?'

'Um ...' Her immaculately manicured hand hovered over a

selection of glass bottles and aluminium cans and stacked plastic tumblers. 'There's whisky . . . gin and tonic . . . er . . .'

'OK, great. Whisky on the rocks for me, gin and tonic for, er, my friend please.'

Whisky on the rocks indeed! Who did I think I was, some kind of Sloaney jet-setter? What next? *Moët à frapper*?

Nevertheless, the drinks were dutifully poured – tiny weeny measures of course, but they were complimentary so I couldn't complain. I downed the whisky, rattled the ice about ruminatively for a bit and then guzzled the gin and tonic after a nanosecond's hesitation. Momentarily lost in my own little world, I was jolted back to the real one when the Buddhist's dreamy voice suddenly came drifting over to me.

'I died in a plane crash, you know.' The tone was hushed, solemn rather than whimsical, despite the apparent inanity of the statement. I choked on the last bitter mouthful of my drink. She said nothing else for a while, and I thought perhaps she had finally lost the last shred of her sanity. Or perhaps she was just talking nonsense in her sleep. I looked over at her. She still had her eyes closed, but a ghost of a smile lingered on her thin lips.

'In my last life,' she explained, half opening one eye to peer at me serenely. 'I was an Argentinian man called Paolo. Tragic end. Most sad. So young. I was killed when my flight took a nosedive into the Atlantic and burst into flames.' She sat forward, now animated, and illustrated the catastrophe with a wild series of hand movements, signifying the explosion with an elaborate gesticulation and a possibly unrealistic *Bang! Boom! Poof!*

My mouth involuntarily dropped open in astonishment, and she patted my arm and murmured, 'Don't worry. It is not very likely to happen again. I still have much left to do in this incarnation.'

'Well. That's reassuring.' I wanted to throw up. The prospect of a long-haul flight had initially not really bothered me, but now I was painfully aware of my vulnerability as a passenger at an altitude of thirty thousand feet, helplessly left to the mercy of aeronautics and the unknown vicissitudes of fate.

'Look at me as your personal saviour,' she quipped. 'You'll be fine so long as you stick with me.' She gave me a gentle nudge in the ribs and a dry little chuckle.

'Righty-ho. Whatever you say.'

She cocked her head and sighed sadly, obviously dismayed at my attitude. 'Come on. You must try to not be feeling so negative. Now . . . may I ask your name?'

I was tempted to say *don't you know?* but strangely, although my reservations remained, I was beginning to warm to this odd little German lady. Sure she was mad, but good mad. Nice mad. Inoffensively foaming.

'Caroline,' I said. 'And yours?'

She neglected to answer. Instead she said, 'You are a lovely soul, Caroline. Why do you not love yourself?'

My head whipped around in astonishment. 'Excuse me?'

Her face lit up as she gripped my arm firmly in her long, slender fingers and held me in a beguilingly rapt gaze. 'Let me tell you something. You know what I taught my daughters? The one thing that I think has made them the wonderful young women they are today?'

I blinked at her dumbly, stunned by her forthrightness and not knowing quite how to react. She took a deep breath, as if she was about to launch into a rhetorical sermon. And then she did. 'I told them, darlings, I said, *love yourself.* Always. No matter what. Never forget how special you are, as an individual. As a one-off, a unique and wonderful thing. Now . . .' She leaned even closer so her lips were practically touching my ear. 'Now listen to me, Caroline. By loving yourself, in this instancy, I do not mean ego. Oh no. Please hear what I am saying now, it is so important. Ego is not the same as esteem, as positive self-love. Ego is bad, because it is selfish and greedy and jealous. It saps away from the true spirit, it grabs and kills with avarice and arrogance. You understand what I mean by love, by *real* self-love?'

I shrugged, murmured something vaguely affirmative despite my growing confusion and she pressed on, satisfied that I was following and absorbing her humorous homily. 'Love yourself before, but *not above*, all others. And if you cannot love yourself, at least . . . how you say? *Dig yourself?* Is that right, no? Respect and *like* the person you are, at least. Do not deny or undermine or compromise your true self. You understand? That is so important. So very important. Otherwise how can you ever be a loving person towards others? How can anyone else love you?'

She appeared to require a definitive answer to this, blinking at me expectantly. There was only one response I felt disposed to give. 'I'm sorry, I don't mean to be rude, but are you on drugs?'

The brilliant whites of her eyes sparkled as her pale, oval face broke into a broad smile. 'I am high on life,' she said, without a trace of irony.

'So . . . you agree with that crappy magazine?' I asked, trying to keep the sardonic edge out of my voice. 'That you should, er, love yourself whatever your . . . shape?'

'My darling, I think you miss the point.' She placed her right hand over her heart, and her left hand over her right, in an overtly sententious manner. 'What you are is what's in here. *This*' – she indicated her body with a sweeping gesture; a slight figure in a formal pearl-buttoned blouse and ankle-length floral skirt. 'What, after all, is this? It is not the person, it is just the body. Just a shell. This is what rots away when you die.' I mused over a number of alternative responses to this, none of which seemed entirely appropriate. 'Well. I see,' I said eventually. 'That's nice. I'll bear that in mind next time I look in the mirror.'

'Oh, my dear. You think I am a silly old hippy person?'

I shrugged. 'Look, I know you mean well, but I really –'

'It is all right, Caroline. This stupid old woman will shut up now. I just want you to know that . . .' She looked around, seemingly to make sure nobody was eavesdropping. The soft cadence of her voice and the benign sagacity of her manner made her words seem so compelling that, in spite of my misgivings and incredulity, I sat upright in my seat and shifted nearer. But she put a finger to her lips, as if to stop herself from saying any more, then lowered her gaze and turned her head away.

'Want me to know what?' I urged, surprised at my own curiosity. It was weird, but there was something about her that reminded me of Bev – the same honest, open warmness, a special, captivating presence of ardent spirituality that had all the ostensible appearance of unabashed eccentricity. I knew I would probably remain closer to Bev than anybody else in my life, after so many years of tirelessly standing in as my mentor, my advisor, my oracle, my counsellor, my sympathiser, my comfort food supplier, my phone a friend, my sounding-board. She and this nirvana-seeking German woman both had the vivacious and untrammelled *joie de vivre* of those few special people who, despite being mere mortals like the rest of us, are somehow able to embrace the world, warts and all, with a rare and uninhibited delight. I admired and envied this. I was twenty-five and already jaded.

The German woman spoke to the window, not turning back to face me. 'You'll be fine from now,' she said, matter-of-factly. 'Two days ago it was an old millennium. That episode of your life is over now. History past. Water under the burning bridges. Whatever they say. It has made you stronger, but it is gone, no? Look at it this way. Your life is different from today. In every way. The new millennium will be your chance to start again, the mark from which your real life starts. And it will be everything you wanted. You are doing the right thing, I promise you.'

She permitted herself one last glance at me, a brief squeeze of my hand, and then she slipped off her shoes and curled up in her seat, pulling a tartan blanket around her. 'I will leave you alone now, Caroline,' she mumbled, rolling her head back with a sigh, those bright eyes closing once again. 'Please wake me up when the food comes round.'

A yawn, and then silence.

Despite my bewilderment and scepticism, a strange feeling of euphoria coursed through me. Somehow I didn't mind hearing the 'M' word this time, nor did I object to the mildly patronising suggestion that I was looking to 'start again'. It was true, after all. And for what it was worth, I felt encouraged to know I had good karma on my side at last. It was about time a bit of good karma caught up with me.

I felt instantly emboldened, invincible, electrified. I wasn't running away, I was running *towards* something; leaving behind the things that had been holding me back for years, shackling me to a second-rate life that I had been deluded into accepting as the only one I deserved; my fate, a fixed reality, my dismal destiny.

But despite this head rush, my fizzing euphoria, I was so tired, still so very tired. I could feel my eyelids getting heavy as I squinted dozily towards the scratched, misted little window through to the clouds outside, veiled pink in the corona of dusky light . . . wispy pink and white, like marshmallow pillows, cotton-wool shreds, nebulous feathery quilts . . . the plane was sucked further and further into the vast, billowing expanses, taking me away to a happy ending, a new beginning . . . Way below, a patchwork planet became obscured beneath the gauze, all broccoli tree tops and matchbox houses with mosaic fields of browns and greens and yellows edged with hedges or intersected by coiling roads and lanes. My tiny, remote corner of the world, getting tinier and remoter by the second.

Exhaustion washed over me, and I submitted to the dream that was at last becoming a reality, lulled into sleep by the persistent low hum of the aeroplane's engine and a fuel tank that was (hopefully) not faulty, strangely comforted now by the presence of the woman beside me who I had now decided was (probably) not crazy. It was happening, it was *really* happening.

I was disappearing and for the first time in my life I no longer felt invisible.